Praise for Louisa

'A hugely promising debut. Overturns every assumption you have at the beginning in a startling and clever twist'
Cara Hunter, bestselling author of *Close to Home*

'I absolutely raced through it and couldn't put it down! It was so unsettling and had me holding my breath the whole time. And then that ending ... it had me questioning every-thing! So clever and twisted and disturbing'
Elle Croft, bestselling author of *The Guilty Wife*

'In a crowded thriller market, it's hard to stand out, but *The Dream Wife* by debut author Louisa de Lange pulls it off with a could-never-have-predicted-that ending'
Good Housekeeping

'A clever tale where things aren't what they seem ... The real cleverness lies in the way the plot and those dreams weave together. Thriller-writing at its best' *Daily Mail*

'There's double trouble for DS Kate Munro in her intriguing first case ... a tangled web of secrets and lies'
Peterborough Telegraph

Louisa de Lange studied Psychology at the University of Southampton and has lived in and around the city ever since. She works as a freelance copywriter and editor, and when she's not writing, she can be found pounding the streets in running shoes or swimming in muddy lakes.

Nowhere To Be Found is her third novel, and the second in the series featuring DS Kate Munro.

To find out more, you can follow her on Twitter @paperclipgirl

Nowhere to be Found

Louisa de Lange

ORION

First published in Great Britain in 2020 by Orion Fiction,
an imprint of The Orion Publishing Group Ltd.,
Carmelite House, 50 Victoria Embankment
London EC4Y 0DZ

An Hachette UK Company

1 3 5 7 9 10 8 6 4 2

Copyright © Louisa de Lange 2020

A CIP catalogue record for this book is
available from the British Library.

ISBN (Paperback) 978 1 4091 9515 3
ISBN (eBook) 978 1 4091 9516 0

Typeset at The Spartan Press Ltd,
Lymington, Hants

Printed and bound in Great Britain by Clays Ltd,
Elcograf S.p.A

Nowhere
to be
Found

Prologue

She put her face in the water. Nothing but green. Murky silt, small particles floating in front of her eyes. The cold was startling; she breathed out slowly through her nose, bubbles dispersing around her face. She stood up again and looked around, acclimatising to the chill.

The sun was rising behind the trees, throwing a red and yellow tinge across the lake. The water was calm, only a few swimmers and a lifeguard on a paddleboard disturbing the surface. Surrounded by trees, she could hear nothing except the early-morning birdsong.

She loved it here. After a stressful week, there was nothing better than waking up before the day began and driving on empty roads, coffee in the thermos flask next to her. At the lake she'd throw off her clothes, tug her body into the graceless rubber of her wetsuit and slowly lower herself into the cloudy water.

She felt the cold trickle in through the zip at the back, and took a sharp breath. She felt rocks under her toes and a cool wind on her skin.

Then she pushed away and took her first strokes across the lake.

Swimming outdoors was different. Seeing the haze through her goggles after the clear blue of a swimming pool was a shock to the system, but slowly her mind learnt the new normal and her breathing became calm and even.

The methodical swoosh of each stroke of her front crawl soothed her nerves. She left her usual worries behind at the water's edge. She had nothing to focus on here, bar the movement of her arms and legs in rhythm, breathing out through her nose, then in through her mouth. Every third stroke, in and out. In and out.

She came to the first buoy, marking the route across the lake, then set off to the furthest point. It had been a distance that once seemed impossible, but each week she'd swum further and further, and now the route all the way round was her standard.

She felt the pull in her muscles; a reassuring tiredness in her legs and arms. She knew she would enjoy her breakfast when she got home and looked forward to the drive back – skin cool, hair matted and wet, smile on her face.

She felt something brush against her leg and kicked it away. She looked down into the water: green. Sometimes there was a glimpse of a fish, sometimes a piece of pondweed or the rope from a nearby buoy, but now, as usual, nothing.

Or was there? What was that? She calmed her breathing and forced herself to take another stroke, telling her mind to stop conjuring up images in the murk. But then she saw it again. A dark outline. Something shadowy below her in the water.

She stopped swimming and bobbed for a moment, catching her breath.

'You okay?' One of the lifeguards paddled towards her on his board. She squinted up at him, the sun silhouetting him into shadow.

She nodded. 'I thought I saw something down there.'

'Watch out for those catfish,' he joked, and she smiled.

She readied herself to swim again, kicking away with her

legs. But her bare foot came into contact with something. Something spongy, that gave way. Her body jumped at the unfamiliar feeling and a reflex breath forced her to inhale. She lifted her head again, choking.

She waved her hand away at the guy on the board.

'I'm fine,' she said, coughing and spitting out water. 'I'm fine.'

But he wasn't looking at her any more. His mouth was open, his paddle paused in his hand, staring at a spot just behind her.

She trod water and followed his gaze. Floating on the surface was a shirt. A patch of navy-blue check. It looked strange, out of place in the lake. But it wasn't just a shirt. There was something coming out of the collar.

She frantically splashed away from the mass next to her, her foot coming into contact with it once more. It felt soft and malleable, and a piece broke away as she kicked. She screamed, the noise waking the lifeguard from his shock. He hastily paddled backwards, grabbing the neck of her wetsuit as he moved, tugging her onto his rocking board. She pulled her body out of the water as quickly as she could, then sat with her knees tucked up to her chest. The lifeguard steadied them both, and she pulled her goggles away from her face so she could see better.

She regretted it.

The body in the water was bloated and deformed. It had rotated and was now floating face up, looking towards the sky with glassy, opaque eyes. Short hair stuck to a white face. A man, but deformed and surreal. His skin looked like it was coated in egg white – rubbery and translucent – flakes peeling away in the water.

She put her hand over her mouth and looked away. Next

to her the lifeguard was shouting into his walkie-talkie, asking for the police, repeating himself over and over again.

'No, a dead body,' he was saying to the people back on shore. 'It's definitely dead. Not one of our swimmers, no. A dead body.'

Crackling on the end of the line confirmed the police had been called. A foghorn blasted across the calm, calling the other swimmers out of the lake. Faces popped up above the water, wondering what the problem was, annoyed at being disturbed from their swim.

The guy looked down at her. 'I'm sorry, I need to stay here. Mark the location. You stick with me? You've had quite a shock. I don't want you getting into trouble on the way back.'

She wrapped her arms tighter round her knees. She wasn't arguing; there was no way she was getting back in that water.

'Are you okay?' the lifeguard asked.

She nodded, then looked down at the body.

But no, she wasn't okay. Not okay at all.

Part 1

Monday

I

The house was quiet. Strangely so. Scott called out as he closed the front door and placed the bunch of flowers on the hallway table. He took off his coat, hanging it up next to Lucy's, and walked through to the kitchen, taking the bright red roses with him.

They were large, fat, posh ones, reserved for special occasions. He left them on the kitchen table, cellophane crackling, and moved through the house. It was getting late, the night closing in, and Scott assumed Lucy must be out in the garden. He knew she was here – he'd parked his car next to hers on the driveway – but the house was still.

He looked around the room. The kitchen was tidy: the work surfaces clean and everything put away. In the living room, the cushions were all perfectly plumped and in line on the sofa. There was no trace of his wife having been there. He went back into the hallway and climbed the stairs to the bedrooms.

'Lucy?' he called. No reply.

He stood at one of the top windows and looked out to the garden. The lawn was a perfect square of green, behind it the vegetable patch, triangles of canes holding up runner beans, lines of cabbages and unruly rows of carrots and potatoes. The garden was Lucy's project, and he was surprised at

7

how well his wife had taken to the plot of land. Meticulously weeding and planting, reading up on the best time to plant cucumbers, the ideal seeds for their type of soil. But as far as he could see, the garden was empty.

Beyond the vegetable patch was what Lucy generously referred to as the wildflower orchard – in reality an ignored patch of scrubland, overgrown and vicious, full of nettles and thorns. From here Scott could just see the informal path, leading through the long grass, worn where Lucy had walked that way over and over again.

He went into the bedroom, and hummed under his breath as he changed out of his suit. He picked up his jeans and jumper, discarded the night before on the chair, and put them on, hanging the suit up in the wardrobe and throwing his shirt in the laundry basket.

He called out again as he checked the other bedrooms. Empty. She must have gone out for a run before dinner, although it was getting dark. Scott looked out at the grey sky. There weren't many street lights around here, so running at night-time was almost impossible along the tricky country lanes. She would be back soon. While he waited, he'd get dinner on.

He went downstairs, back into the kitchen and opened the fridge. The usual food looked back at him: milk, bread, eggs, cheese. But nothing obvious planned for dinner. He tapped his fingers on the work surface, thinking, and glanced at the clock: 7.17 p.m. It was unlike Lucy to be out this late.

He walked into the hallway and gathered up the pile of post, thumbing through the usual boring bills. Lucy managed the admin in the house, so he left the envelopes on the side. As he did so, his attention was caught by the sight of Lucy's trainers, neatly poking out of the shoe cupboard by the door.

So if she wasn't out for a run, where on earth was she? Her car was here, her keys were here.

He picked up his phone and dialled her number, waiting for it to connect. He heard the tone, then paused. He could clearly hear her mobile, going off somewhere in the house. He dialled again, letting his hand drop to his side with his phone as he listened. There it was again. He followed it.

Up the stairs, into their bedroom. Dialling the number again and again. He stopped by the bed, closer now, then heard it coming from the wardrobe. He opened the door and riffled through her clothes, looking for the source of the noise.

Scott pulled out her handbag. It was small and brown, one of those you could sling round your body, and he picked it up, digging in the main pocket to find her phone.

He took it out and looked at his own name and photo on the screen. Five missed calls. He held it in his hand and stared at it. Where was she? Where could she have gone without her handbag or phone or keys? He frowned. This was getting silly. Perhaps she was in the garden after all, and he'd wander down there, worried, and she would laugh at him, having lost track of time, wiping her brow in the darkness with a dirty hand.

He opened the back door and stepped out into the dusk, pulling trainers onto his feet. The cold wind whipped through his clothes; summer was definitely over. The garden was Lucy's domain; Scott wasn't a fan of the great outdoors. Nowadays he preferred to relax in the evening in the comfort of the living room, glass of something alcoholic in his hand, some drama on the television. Increasingly, he'd been doing that alone. Lucy said she couldn't stand the violence on TV. So he'd be inside, and she would be in the garden, or out for a run, or reading whatever was up for that week's book club.

He called out into the grey. He could only just see the lawn now, the black starting to envelop the many acres behind. He wrapped his arms around his chest and walked quickly to the vegetable garden.

'Lucy?' he shouted. He stepped over the neatly tended beds and followed the green border of grass, reaching the start of the wilderness. He tracked along the line of compressed meadow in the middle, swearing as a bramble attached itself to his leg and a determined nettle found bare skin.

He was losing patience now. 'For fuck's sake, Lucy,' he muttered.

The makeshift path through the long grass ran to the end of the garden where Scott knew the old well and concrete air-raid shelter still stood. She wouldn't be down here, would she? Surely not. He hadn't been near it in months. It looked sinister in the dim glow. Two pieces of concrete side by side marked the entrance to the shelter, blanketed with soil and overgrown shrubbery. The curve of the old well stood to his left, metal grate covering the top, drilled into the brickwork.

He could hear rustling in the undergrowth next to him, and a slow drizzle of rain started to fall, resting in his hair and on his jumper.

He peered across to their neighbours' house, towering behind the large hedge to his right, but dismissed the thought of Lucy having gone there. She always described the couple next door as '*those* people' – she wouldn't have popped over for a cosy coffee.

He swore again and turned, heading back to the house. She'd probably be home by now, he told himself. But in the back of his mind something was niggling. This was unlike her. She wasn't the sort of person to do anything out of the ordinary, although after the events of the weekend, he wasn't so sure ...

He pushed open the back door and went into the kitchen again, walking round the house fruitlessly. At work Scott prided himself on being decisive and sensible. In any given situation he had a clear head and was quick to figure out the solution. But this was new. He hadn't had a wife disappear before. Employees – yes. He'd had a few people not turn up for work and he'd get HR to call them, leave messages asking where they'd got to. One had overslept, and another, unfortunately, had had a car accident.

But that wasn't the case today. He repeated it like a mantra: her car was here. Her keys were here. Her mobile. He sat down at the kitchen table and put the two phones in front of him – one hers, one his. He pressed the home button on the front of Lucy's and the screen leapt into life: a photo of the two of them taken during the summer. A selfie: both grinning towards the camera. *Try again*, the phone said, asking for Lucy's fingerprint. It switched to the passcode screen and he glared at it. She had told him the code probably half a dozen times, but for the life of him he couldn't remember what it was now. He tried a few obvious number combinations but it just vibrated at him. *Try again*, it said. *Try again*.

It was now 8.23 p.m. And there was no sign of his wife.

'Where the hell are you?' he muttered under his breath. 'Where have you gone, Lucy?'

2

By anyone's standards, the date was not going well. For a start, it was a Monday night, and as a consequence the restaurant had the atmosphere of a black hole. Kate looked at the man in front of her and tried to remain objective. He was hot, yes, with nice eyes, and a good head of hair hanging on despite the approach of his mid-thirties. He was clever and passionate, and was animatedly talking to her about something called value proposition. She had no idea what that was. She wasn't sure she cared enough to ask, either.

In front of her, her mobile started to buzz. The man paused.

'Take it, if you must,' he said.

'Sorry, I . . . it's just . . .' Kate grimaced apologetically then stood up, rushing away to the far side of the restaurant.

'This better be good, Jamie,' she hissed.

'Sorry, boss, am I disturbing your free time?' the voice at the other end asked innocently.

'Briggs . . .' she warned. He knew full well where she was.

'Okay, okay, it's our dead body. We've got an ID.'

'What? How?'

Three days ago, a body had been found in a lake. For seventy-two hours the two of them had searched missing persons, waited for DNA results – anything for an identification of their man. And now, here it was.

'One-oh-one got a call about a car accumulating parking tickets in Portswood. Belonged to a local called Douglas

Brewer. Sixty-four years old, white, five foot nine inches tall. It's definitely our guy.'

'Fucking brilliant,' Kate said with glee, earning a look from a passing waiter. 'What do we know about him? Has he got a record?'

DC Briggs paused at the other end of the line. He cleared his throat. 'I have plans tonight too, Sarge,' he grumbled.

'Okay, fine,' Kate muttered. 'Just apply for the warrant to get into his place. Please?'

Briggs agreed reluctantly and Kate hung up, feeling guilty. If she could, she would have gone back to the station and done it herself, but there was no way she was getting away tonight.

She went back to the table. As usual she had taken the seat facing the door. Standard operating practice. Wanting to know who was nearby, constantly ready for what might kick off. Although, even she had to accept, it was overkill in a restaurant where only eight people were in the room and two of them were staff.

Opposite her, the man had his phone in his hand, eyes down, thumb scrolling. A waiter materialised next to them, pad in hand.

'Sam?' Kate said, and he glanced up.

'Oh, sorry, yes.' He put the phone face down on the table and ordered his meal, Kate doing the same.

She tried to relax. They'd gone to the new Italian and it seemed authentic enough – no pineapple on the pizza, waiters with the correct accents – but Kate couldn't help feeling a little bit of sham hidden behind the arty black-and-white pictures of the Tower of Pisa. Much like her, Kate thought grimly.

Put her in an interview room with a six-foot-four body-builder arrested for GBH, and she, Detective Sergeant Kate

Munro, would feel right at home. Show her bloody crime scene photos of mutilated bodies and she didn't bat an eyelid. But here, with the low lighting, the candlelit dinner and the small lonely glass of white, trying to be happy and fluffy and bloody-fucking-romantic? She couldn't feel less at ease.

Any other person and she would have made her excuses and walked away. But tonight, that was impossible. Because she had to make an effort. Because she had to save her marriage. Because the man in front of her was her husband.

It was six months now since they'd moved back in together. Six months since they'd scraped their relationship from the brink of divorce, and Kate was relieved. But that year of being apart hung over her, threatening to rear its ugly head the moment she put a foot wrong.

Before the separation, she'd pushed their relationship to the edge, constantly testing Sam's loyalty, fuelled by too much alcohol, eventually accusing him of having an affair with a co-worker. And now here she was. Sitting in a restaurant, soggy pizza in front of her, trying to concentrate on what he was saying while her latest case whirred around in her head.

She was desperate to start their investigation properly. Find out about this man, what his life was like, start digging into possible suspects. Then there was the forensics, the post-mortem results—

Kate realised Sam had paused and was looking at her.

'You good?' he asked. He leaned over the table and took her hand.

For the first time that evening, she felt a smile creep onto her face.

'Yes,' she nodded. 'Everything's fine.'

It was, she told herself, it really was. And, if she repeated it enough times, maybe she'd start to believe it.

3

Scott stared at his laptop screen. The familiar Facebook logo flickered in front of him, finally accessed after half an hour of resetting his password. Social media wasn't something that interested him, and he could barely remember the last time he'd bothered to log on.

Sure enough, his profile photograph was woefully old, a shot taken when he and Lucy had last been skiing, and there was nothing else on the page except for a few happy birthday messages he'd not seen from last year.

But he knew Lucy was a regular on all the main sites – Facebook, Twitter and some photograph one he didn't know the name of. He clicked onto her profile, taking in the pictures, the posts on her wall. She seemed to be always on there, her phone omnipresent in her hand, but for the last six months it looked like she hadn't posted anything at all. And before that? A few political petitions, some photographs from an environmental march he knew she'd gone on. It seemed she'd got into an online argument with someone complaining about traffic restrictions, with Lucy arguing fiercely for the removal of cars from city centres. He'd wondered why she'd chosen that topic to get so passionate about. But it wasn't providing any answers for where she was today.

Since he'd got home from work hours ago his stomach had been churning in a gnawing way. Hungry but unable to eat. Scott hated uncertainty; at work he did his utmost to control everything around him. It made him a nightmare to work for, but at least nothing got forgotten. At least, nothing important.

What wasn't important, he didn't think about. Closed it off in his mind. He knew other people weren't like him, that they worried and fretted, and he knew Lucy was one of those people.

But this. This was new. He couldn't work out where Lucy had gone. Her family definitely wasn't an option, they hadn't spoken in years. And friends?

He picked up his phone and looked for a particular number. He'd been putting off calling her but it was the obvious next move, as uncomfortable as it made him.

The number rang, then went to voicemail. Scott cancelled the call, then typed a quick text, sending it to her number.

Almost instantly three little dots appeared on the left-hand side, then a ping in response.

What do you mean, Lucy is missing?

Scott typed a reply. *I came home from work and she wasn't here. Have you heard from her?*

There was a pause, then his phone rang.

'What have you done, Scott?' Jen said the moment he answered.

'Is she with you?'

'No, I haven't spoken to her since last week,' Jen replied.

Scott could feel his body tighten. He hadn't contacted Jennifer for months, but he knew she and Lucy were close, meeting up as often as they could.

'All her stuff is still here — her phone, her car, her bag. She didn't call you this weekend? You haven't heard from her today?'

'No, why would she call me?'

Scott paused, not wanting to say the truth out loud.

He heard Jen sigh. 'Oh, you didn't . . . You arsehole. When?'

'She already knew. Sunday.'

'You idiot,' she muttered under her breath, followed by a string of profanities. 'So where is she? Have you called the police?'

'No, not yet.'

'Why not?'

Scott hesitated. Why hadn't he called the police? This whole thing still seemed ridiculous. Any moment Lucy would walk in the door and start talking, laughing at his worry. *I went for a walk and got lost. I got picked up by a friend and we lost track of time. I can't believe I was so daft to forget my bag.*

There'd be a reasonable explanation as to where she'd been, and he'd feel stupid for wasting police time. But perhaps that's what he needed to do – tempt fate. Call, and then as soon as he spoke to them she'd turn up.

'Don't you have to wait twenty-four hours or something?' he muttered, annoyed at having to explain himself to Jen of all people.

'I don't think so, no. Phone them now. Then message me and let me know what's happening.' There was a space; Jen could detect the reluctance in his voice. 'Message me, Scott, or I'll get in the car and come over there.'

'Fine,' he barked, and hung up the phone. 'Bloody woman,' he muttered under his breath, and dialled 999.

4

PC Max Cooper looked at the man in front of him. Scott Barker was casually dressed but looked tidy and expensive. Off-duty prep school. Max had been greeted with a firm handshake at the front door, the husband obviously having been looking out for the police car, opening the door as soon as Max pulled up on the drive. He glanced at the clock. It was 10.02 p.m.

'And when did you last see your wife?' Max asked. He'd already been through the preamble, used to spelling things out for confused relatives when their loved ones went missing. He'd refused the offer of tea or coffee, and was now sat at the kitchen table facing Scott Barker.

'This morning. She was in bed when I left for work.'

The man answered all of Max's questions evenly. He didn't seem upset or angry or anxious, reactions Max was used to seeing from relatives in these situations.

'Does Lucy work?'

'She used to, but she got made redundant about six months ago and hasn't been able to find anything since.'

'Do you have any children?'

He shook his head. 'Although we're trying for a baby,' he added.

Max paused. 'And has that been stressful?'

'No, no, it hasn't. It's only been few months, no one expects these things to happen immediately.'

'Could you talk me through what you've done since you came home and found her missing?'

Max watched him speak. Scott Barker had gathered up all her personal belongings, now on the table. He'd phoned hospitals, he'd contacted her best friend. He crossed and uncrossed his arms, picking up then putting down his wife's passport in front of him. It was expired, the date inside having run out months ago.

'And what's your wife's normal routine?'

He screwed up his face, thinking. 'She rattles around the house, spends a lot of time in the garden and she runs and goes to the gym. Apart from that, I'm not too sure.' He frowned. 'I'm sorry, that sounds terrible, but Lucy doesn't have a lot of friends, she's not sociable. Although she has a book club she goes to every Tuesday.'

'Do you know where?'

'She mentions the name Alex. I don't know where she lives, sorry.'

Max frowned. 'And she's never disappeared like this before?'

'No, never.'

'And does she have any mental health problems?'

The husband paused. 'Nothing, no,' he said.

'Mr Barker?' Max warned. 'If we're going to find your wife, you need to be truthful with us.'

But Scott shook his head. 'No, nothing, no problems.'

'And you haven't found a note?'

'No.'

'Have you noticed anything strange lately? Unusual cars, people you don't recognise, that sort of thing?' Max asked.

'No,' Scott replied again, then thought for a second. 'You don't think she's been abducted?'

'We have to explore all possibilities,' Max said. 'Do you mind if I take a look around?'

'Please do.'

Max stood up and started his check round the house. It was a big place, minimally decorated in greys and whites. He methodically moved from cavernous room to room, the husband following silently behind him.

In the hallway, Max pointed to the alarm. 'Do you use that?' he asked.

Scott nodded. 'It was off when I came home, but that's not unusual. Lucy often forgets to set it.'

'And the hallway looked like this?' Max looked round. It was tidy: shoes arranged neatly in the cupboard by the door, coats lined up above. 'Are all Lucy's coats and shoes here?'

The husband studied the garments, running his finger across, as if mentally ticking them off in his mind. 'Yes, I think so.'

Max continued his search, checking each bedroom, looking in wardrobes, under beds. He poked his head briefly into the loft – nothing interesting as far as he could see.

He was used to getting called out for missing persons – mispers were one of the most common requests. Husbands that disappeared to the pub after arguments, rebellious teenagers, mental health patients absconding from hospitals. Attention-seekers. But most were home within a few hours. He had been taught to treat every job as the first one he had ever been called to, but it was hard not to develop apathy towards cases like this, when often the police shouldn't have been called in the first place.

He finished his check of the house, the husband trailing him like a shadow, then pointed out into the garden.

'What's out there?' he asked.

'Few acres. Vegetable patch, shed, that sort of thing.'

Max sighed inwardly. Ah, yes. Huge house, huge garden. Bugger. The husband opened the back door and Max peered into the night, taking the torch out of his pocket and clicking it on. Better get walking, then.

This time the husband stayed behind, sensibly choosing to keep out of the wind and the rain. As Max walked through the garden, grass rustling round his legs, he thought through the facts of the case.

It was a strange one, that was for sure. She had none of the usual risk factors: no mental health problems, no previous history of running away, no drugs, no alcohol.

He'd been surprised when he'd got the call – they didn't often come out this way. The houses in this area were all big and remote, surrounded by acres of well-tended garden. They were more likely to be owned by retirees, so the usual deployment was in support of ambulances or sudden deaths. These weren't the sort of people to go missing. Burglaries, accidents, maybe even a touch of domestic violence, but no mispers.

Although perhaps this wasn't what it looked like. He glanced back to the house, where the husband was watching him from the window. Perhaps Scott Barker knew exactly where his wife was, and was reporting her to allay suspicion.

The more Max thought about it, the more he wanted to be out here, to do a thorough check, but the garden at the bottom was rambling and out of control. He paused next to an old well and pulled hard at the metal grid covering the top. It seemed secure but looking down he could see nothing but black. There was no way he could do any search justice tonight in the dark and the rain.

He walked back to the bright lights of the house, where Scott Barker waited in the doorway.

'Right,' Max began. 'After I leave here, I'll file the usual reports so everyone will be on high alert. Likelihood is she'll be back safe at home soon, but let's cover all bases. We'll double-check the hospitals and use the information you've given us to start contacting people who might know where she is. If it's okay with you, I'll take her laptop, passport and phone with me today, and if you could email me a few photos as soon as possible, that would be great.' Max paused. 'I'll go and see if your neighbours are awake now, and first thing tomorrow, we'd like to search your house and grounds.'

Scott looked up. 'Again?'

'It's standard procedure. We need to make sure there's nothing we're missing in the light of day before we take the search further afield. That's if you agree,' Max finished, and Scott nodded.

Max handed him the forms and the husband signed them all, giving Max consent to access her medical and bank records as well as permission to search the property.

'In the meantime,' Max continued, 'try and get some rest.'

He wrote down his name and contact details on a page of his notepad and passed it to Scott. 'Give me a call if you remember anything else, however small,' he said.

Scott looked at the paper. While they'd been talking he'd seemed restrained and businesslike, but now, all conversation finished, the husband had shrunk into himself. Curled up with tiredness and withdrawal.

'And of course, let us know if Lucy turns up.' Max stood, ready to go back into the rain. Scott nodded and Max left, rushing back to his patrol car and starting the engine.

Max looked back to the house. He saw Scott Barker move

out of the kitchen and the lights turn on in what Max assumed was the bedroom. He'd added that last sentence out of habit, but watching the husband, seeing the house and the details of the case, he had a funny feeling about this one.

Lucy Barker had none of the warning signs. All her personal belongings had been left behind. She wasn't a rebellious teenager or a whacked-out meth head. And despite his questions, this didn't feel like an abduction. House locked up tight, no suggestion of a struggle.

Coppers have a hunch; you get a feel for these things after a while. Something about Scott Barker wasn't sitting right with him, but he couldn't put his finger on why. It was rare nice, well-to-do wives with big houses disappeared without a trace.

This wasn't going to be one of those mispers where the person walks in completely fine after twenty-four hours. Something inside him knew this wasn't one of those at all.

5

Max pulled out of the Barkers' driveway and took the turning into next door. The neighbours' house was grand and modern; Max guessed an old residence had been knocked down to make way for a new build. He climbed out of the car and looked up at the windows shrouded in darkness. Who needed this many bedrooms? he wondered.

He could see a lone light on, so rang the bell. After a while, locks turned and the door opened.

A man stood in front of him in a dressing gown and slippers. He looked annoyed at the intrusion.

'Sorry to bother you,' Max started. 'But I'm investigating the disappearance of Lucy Barker, and wondered if you'd seen anything today?'

The man scowled. 'Who?'

'Lucy Barker? Your neighbour?' Max repeated.

'Oh, the little hippy eco chick. No, not seen her. My wife hasn't either,' he added dismissively.

'Was your wife around all day? Could I speak to her?' Max hovered on the step, waiting for an invitation. It wasn't forthcoming.

'She's in bed, asleep. May I suggest you come back to-morrow?'

Max paused, hoping his silence would convey his dis-approval. The man stared back for a moment, then sighed and went back into the house, trudging up the stairs without a word. Max took the open door as encouragement and followed him inside, shutting it behind him.

He could hear murmurs from upstairs, an annoyed exclamation, then a door closing. The neighbour appeared in the upstairs hallway.

'We'll be down in a minute. Go through to the lounge,' he grumbled. 'And take your shoes off, please.'

Max raised his eyebrows. Money doesn't equal nice neighbours, he thought to himself, obediently taking his boots off and perching on the edge of the sofa.

If Max had been feeling generous, he would have described the decor in the lounge as retro. As it was nearly midnight, he called it dated: the worn velour sofas clashing with the green flower-patterned carpet.

The pair came in and sat on the sofa opposite him. The wife was ball-shaped, a bobbly dressing gown tied round where anyone else's waist would be. She glared at him, her eyes tiny buttons in her podgy face.

'I haven't seen her,' she said.

Max nodded, swallowing his irritation. 'And when was the last time you saw Lucy?'

She frowned. 'She went out Sunday afternoon. Almost ran into me on the road out, she was driving that fast. Don't know when she came back.'

'And what can you tell me about Lucy and Scott Barker?'

'What do you mean?'

Max steeled himself. He wasn't sure whether they were being deliberately annoying, but it was certainly working. 'You live next door to them. What have you noticed about their marriage? What are they like?'

'We don't talk,' the wife said, and stopped. Max waited and after a moment she rolled her eyes. 'They seem quiet.

They don't disturb us much. We don't like to be disturbed.'

No shit, Max thought.

'Except for when they had those things put on the roof,' the husband interrupted.

'Yes, the solar panels. That made a huge racket,' the wife continued. 'She seems a bit pitiful, if I'm going to be honest.'

'Pitiful?' Max asked. 'Why?'

'It's just her and her husband in that big house. No kiddies. Don't see many friends. No family. She's always out in the garden. A bit lonely, if you ask me. And now she's gone missing?' The wife seemed to have perked up a bit, enjoying sharing her opinion of Lucy Barker. 'Probably gone off with a fancy man.'

'Have you seen anyone with Lucy?' Max asked.

The wife shook her head. 'No, but it's always the quiet ones, isn't it? And then there was that argument.'

'Argument?' Max asked. Could have mentioned this sooner, love.

'Yesterday, early Sunday afternoon. I was out in the garden and heard shouting. I couldn't place it at first, but then realised it was her, screaming her head off.'

'You didn't tell me,' the husband said accusingly.

'You wanted your lunch, I forgot,' she replied. 'Couldn't make out what she was saying, though. And it didn't last for long.'

Max pushed her, but she couldn't tell him anything else, except for sharing her opinion on the morality of infidelity. The husband showed him to the front door, but before he could close it Max noticed the camera above his head.

'Do you use this?' he asked.

The husband looked at it as if it was the first time he'd seen it. He paused, then: 'Yes.'

26

'Does it cover the road?'

The husband sighed. 'I'll email you a copy of the tape,' he muttered.

Max smiled. It felt like more of a grimace. 'Thank you, much appreciated,' he said, and passed him his contact details.

The door closed with a bang.

'Fuck me,' Max muttered, climbing into his car.

Back at the station, Max pulled up a chair at one of the many computers in the report writing room. Next to him DC Jamie Briggs was typing laboriously, one finger at a time striking the keys.

'You're here late,' Max commented, and Briggs looked up guiltily.

'Boss wanted this done tonight but I sneaked out for dinner first,' he said, and Max looked over at his screen. He was applying for a warrant to search a residence. 'Finally found out who our body is. And Munro wants in as soon as possible.'

Max and Briggs had started out together – two probies in Portswood nick – but over the years Briggs had transferred to being a detective in the CID while Max was still in uniform on Response and Patrol. Not that he begrudged his friend his success. Max knew Briggs had put in the effort to get the move, while he'd just coasted. But over the last few months Max had started getting fidgety, thinking about the exam and getting the additional training started. Something seemed much more interesting on the other side of the fence.

'What's the case?' he asked.

'Did you hear about that dead body in the lake near Ringwood on Saturday? At Ellingham?' Briggs said. Max

27

nodded and Briggs pointed at the face on the screen. 'This is our man. Douglas Brewer.'

'Murder, or accidental death?' Max asked.

'Still with the pathologist. Backed up, apparently, although he needs to get to it soon. That's the problem with water and dead bodies – if they're in there too long there's not much to make sense of later.' He pushed the file over to Max and he braced himself before opening it. Underneath a page of paperwork were photos of the body at the crime scene – bloated, grey. Barely recognisable as a human being.

'Not a pretty sight,' Briggs muttered, before turning his attention to Max's screen. 'What have you got, Coop?'

'Misper. But not your usual sort.'

'How so?' Briggs looked interested.

'Female, big house, lots of money, no drug or alcohol problems, no reason to go anywhere. All belongings left at the house.'

'Husband?' Briggs raised an eyebrow.

'Yes.'

'Well, there you go then.' He pointed a finger at Max then took his own case file back, adding it to his pile of paperwork. 'He'll have something to do with it. Any domestic violence?'

'Not that I can see so far, but I'll start digging.'

'Bet you it's the husband.' Briggs looked behind him at the clock on the wall. It was past one. 'Oh, sod this, I'll finish it tomorrow.' He quickly squirrelled the photos back into the folder and logged off the computer.

Max waved as Briggs left for the night, and looked at the notes he'd taken from the interview with the husband. He'd have expected someone like Lucy Barker to have turned up by now.

He'd get her on the system, make sure her photo was national in case she popped up in another county. Then there was the search to organise, medical records to check, people to phone.

He looked at the box on the computer screen. *Misper RA*, it said, asking for a risk assessment category. Max thought for a moment, knowing that whatever he put in that box would dictate the priority level of the resources dedicated to finding Lucy Barker. Briggs's words echoed in his head, saying out loud what he'd been thinking from the beginning. *Bet you it's the husband.*

He typed a figure 1 in the box. *High Risk.*

Tuesday

6

Kate's first thought when she walked into the ops room that morning was that Briggs's expensive face cream wasn't working. He looked knackered, black rings under his eyes. The second was whether he'd completed the application for the warrant.

'Before you ask, yes,' he said, when he saw her expression. 'But we don't need one. Landlord's going to let us in.'

Kate passed him one of the coffees she was holding. He pushed his empty mug aside and took it gratefully.

She walked to the whiteboard in front of their desks. Briggs had pinned a photo of the victim at the top – one of him alive, thankfully; nobody wanted to look at a dead body all day, especially *that* one – and written his name above it. Douglas Brewer. Poor sod. She picked up a pen and wrote *Post-mortem results?* on the board. Knowing whether it was determined as an accidental death or a murder might change the course of their investigation. *Search house, Drs records*, she added. *Speak to family. House to house enquiries.*

Briggs watched her.

'It's a lot,' he said. 'Added to our caseload.' Kate nodded. 'When are we going to be assigned someone to replace Yates?'

Kate sighed. DC Rachel Yates had been off for a month

on maternity leave with no sign of a replacement. 'I raised it with the chief, but nothing yet. In the meantime, we'll just have to cope,' Kate said, knowing it wouldn't make Briggs any happier. Sure enough, he scowled and went back to his coffee.

'Did you find anything of interest on the RMS?'

Briggs pulled up the screen for the Record Management System on his computer. 'A warning for possession of cannabis in 2016, penalty notice for drunk and disorderly, and then a voluntary interview but no charge for criminal damage.' Briggs looked up at Kate. 'That one was six months ago.'

'Interesting,' Kate said.

'Apart from that, nothing. Except for an application for a firearms certificate a month ago that was rejected.'

'Not surprising.'

'No,' Briggs agreed. He spun round on his chair again, then tapped the monitor. 'And I've just got a reply from the PCSO at Portswood who says she can give us a bit of background. She's going to meet us there after we've done a search of the house.'

'Brilliant,' Kate nodded to Briggs. 'We might even go home at a decent time today.'

'We can only hope,' Briggs muttered, turning back to his computer.

7

Scott stood in the kitchen and watched the officers methodically working their way around his house. When he had agreed to the search the night before, he hadn't realised how quickly they would descend. Like locusts they had taken over every part of his house and garden, stripping it of the things they needed as they went. DNA samples: her toothbrush, her hairbrush. The glass from the side of her bed with her fingerprints on. For elimination purposes, they said.

Last night he'd tried to sleep, staring at the ceiling for hours. The bed seemed huge and cold without her there. Every little creak left his body jumping, desperate to see Lucy walk through the door. The house felt odd. She had book club, and the occasional night out with Jen, but apart from that she'd always be here. He felt the absence of her keenly: even if they weren't in the same room, he'd hear her moving around, doors opening and closing, the squeak of floorboards. Noises he'd never thought about until he was confronted with the absence of them now.

Last night, after the police officer had left, he'd made a note of everywhere she could possibly be. Places she went, landmarks they'd visited together. He'd jotted down friends and family, and the list wasn't long.

He phoned the hospitals again, even though the policeman said they'd do it. He messaged anyone on Facebook who might know where she was. But no. Nothing.

At this point, the only thing he could think of was that she'd had an accident, and that was why she hadn't called. But then why was her stuff here? He kept on coming back to that. Where would she have gone, leaving her bag and keys and phone?

He looked out of the window into the garden. It was lovely and sunny; the sort of day Lucy would have enjoyed. He could imagine her, green coat on, welly boots, a trowel in her hand. She would be pushing her hair out of her eyes as she stood up, getting mud on her face, her cheeks pink in the cold.

They had dogs out there now. Sniffing around. What were they looking for?

A man cleared his throat behind him and Scott turned. The policeman from last night stood in the doorway, his black uniform sombre and intimidating.

'Mr Barker? How are you doing?' he asked.

'Please, call me Scott.'

'Scott.' The policeman waited.

'I'm fine,' Scott said, quietly. 'Well, not fine, but ...' His shoulders slumped. 'You know. I just want Lucy found.'

The policeman nodded. 'We're doing all we can. The hospitals have drawn a blank, but there's a UK-wide alert posted. I'm going to see Jen Lewis later today.'

Scott turned away so the policeman couldn't see his face. He knew that was to be expected, but Jen worried him. She was unpredictable. Who knew what she might say?

'What are the dogs looking for?' he asked, watching a German shepherd sniff its way across the garden.

The policeman paused, and Scott looked at him. Cooper. PC Cooper. That's what his name was, Scott remembered now. Since Lucy had disappeared he felt like he'd been in a daze. His mind would drift and even simple questions seemed confusing.

'They're looking for a dead body, aren't they?' Scott said.

PC Cooper nodded. 'Among other things. The spaniel there,' he pointed to a black and white springer, 'is trained to sniff out drugs.'

Scott shook his head. How had his life come to this? Yesterday on the drive home from work he'd been restless and worried, keen to see his wife. He'd known he might be facing harsh words, more questions, but not this. He hadn't been expecting this.

PC Cooper bent down and pulled Lucy's laptop out of his rucksack. It was in a see-through plastic bag, a red seal on the top. The policeman undid it and placed it on the table.

'I was wondering if you would help us here.' He opened the computer and the login screen flashed into view. 'If you could answer Lucy's security questions, we might be able to sidestep the password.'

'Sure, I'll do what I can.'

Scott sat next to the policeman, who clicked on the button. *Having trouble?* it said. You have no idea, Scott thought.

PC Cooper clicked another few buttons and a question popped up on the screen.

First pet? it said.

Scott frowned. 'Lucy didn't have any pets growing up,' he muttered. 'Try Isaac.'

It worked. The policeman looked at him quizzically. 'It's her brother,' Scott smiled. 'He was born when Lucy was thirteen. She said she used to take him for walks on the toddler reins like he was a dog.'

The policeman nodded. Another question had come into view. *Primary School.*

Scott frowned. 'She was homeschooled up to the age of thirteen. Why would she pick this question?'

'Who homeschooled her?'

'Her mother,' Scott suggested. 'Try *mum.*'

The computer refused to budge; PC Cooper looked at Scott again.

'Try her name, Martha.'

It worked this time, and the screen asked for a new password to be created. The policeman thought for a moment, then typed in a combination of letters.

'That's a bit different,' Cooper asked. 'To be home-schooled?'

'Her family are very religious. They were keen to educate their children their way,' Scott said, trying to keep the hostility out of his voice. 'But Lucy left all that behind years ago.'

'She's not religious now?'

'No,' Scott confirmed. He watched PC Cooper write the new password on the front of the evidence bag, until his curiosity got the better of him. 'Can we look?' he asked, but the policeman shook his head.

'I'll get the tech guys to do it in the lab. Better for evidence that way.'

Evidence of what? Scott wondered, but he kept quiet.

'Mr Barker, I spoke to your neighbours yesterday, and they mentioned an argument between you and Lucy on Sunday.' PC Cooper looked at him and Scott felt his stomach drop.

'It was nothing,' Scott said, forcing a smile on his face. 'Just the usual marital disagreement. You know?'

'I don't,' the policeman replied, and Scott glanced down to his left hand. No wedding ring. 'What was it about?'

'Domestic stuff. Chores. She was angry at me for not doing my share.' Scott smiled again. It made his cheeks hurt. 'Useless man stuff. I didn't mention it because I'd forgotten.'

'And she went out Sunday afternoon?'

'Yes, but not for long. About an hour or so. She calmed down, came home, we made up. There wasn't a problem.'

PC Cooper nodded, putting the laptop away in the bag.

'What's going to happen from here?' Scott asked. He hated how he felt – this dependence, this helplessness in the face of activity all around him.

'We'll finish the search here, and my colleagues are already out doing house-to-house enquiries and looking for CCTV footage. We'll assign you a family liaison officer to keep you updated,' he finished, but Scott shook his head.

'No, I don't want another stranger in my house. Can't you do it?' Scott wasn't sure why, but he liked PC Cooper. He seemed open and honest, not hiding behind the layer of bureaucracy and bullshit he had experienced from the police in the past.

Cooper hesitated, then nodded. 'Sure.'

A uniform hovered in the doorway, interrupting them. He tilted his head towards the garden. Scott could hear dogs barking and took a quick breath in.

'Coop,' the uniform whispered. 'There's something you need to see.'

8

Max could feel his body buzzing. There was something there. But he had to stay calm.

Scott Barker stood up from the table, his face stern. 'What have you found?' he asked.

'You need to wait here,' he said, leaving his colleague to ensure he didn't go anywhere. He couldn't have the husband marching up after him, contaminating a potential crime scene.

He pulled blue overshoes on his feet, plastic gloves on his hands and started the walk down the garden. One of the uniforms beckoned him over, through the vegetable patch, then down a trodden path. People had started to gather at the end of the garden.

'What have you got?' Max asked as he got near.

He looked at the circular walls of the old well he had noticed the night before. The metal mesh covering the top had been removed and now rested on the grass. Max peered down into the darkness.

'What's in there?' he asked, but the uniform next to him shook his head.

'We ran a camera down and had the dogs take a sniff. Nothing but dry leaves. It's empty. Not even any water.' He pointed to the rough brickwork structure next to them. 'It's this we're interested in,' he said. 'Left on the latch.'

The small building seemed to have once been an air-raid

shelter. It was made out of breeze blocks, hidden by ivy. A low entranceway, covered with mud and overgrowth, showed neglect, but coming closer Max could see a solid wooden door, now propped open, a new Yale lock shining in the sun. Stone steps led downwards.

Next to the door, a spaniel craned its neck on its lead, held back by a scruffy dog handler in dirty uniform.

Max hesitated. He was never sure in these situations what he wanted to see. Dead bodies were never pleasant, but at the very least offered closure to the family. Empty rooms were disappointing.

But as Max approached the doorway, he saw this air-raid shelter was neither of those things.

A bright electric light bulb had been rigged up in one corner of the room, casting a dazzling glow across the dark. Every wall of the small brick box was lined with shelves. Functional metal slats, drilled into the wall. And each one was filled with bottles and jars and tins, every shape and size you could imagine.

Max walked into the room, scuffing his feet across the floor. It was concrete and bare, with a sprinkling of old dry leaves. The room couldn't have been more than six foot square, but he could stand up straight in it, with room above him.

He picked up one of the tins. He recognised the familiar green of Heinz Baked Beans, but the label was faded. Across the back wall were blue bottles of mineral water, stacked up on each other.

There was one space on the shelves. A large square void in the dust where something had once stood.

He turned back to the officers waiting in the doorway.

'What did the dog detect?' he asked, expecting them to say drugs – coke or skunk or something run-of-the-mill.

'Firearms.'

'Pardon?' Max gaped at his colleague.

'Brodie detects firearms.' The dog handler pointed to the tall grey metal safe at the far end of the wall, almost buried behind a box of tins.

Max walked across to it. The heavy door was ajar, and he opened it slowly with a gloved finger. It was empty.

9

Kate stood in front of the shabby charity shop, staring up at the windows of the flat above. She scowled, then turned to Briggs.

'Are you sure we've got the right place?' she asked, and he nodded. There was a door in front of them, the glass and frame painted a uniform dark matt grey, a buzzer positioned to the left with *217A* stuck next to it.

Buses roared past on the road. A woman pulling a shopping trolley bashed it against Kate's ankles. Sometimes it would be nice to be in uniform, Kate thought, at least people give you a wide berth.

She took a step back to better see the flat above. The windows were all shut and Kate could see a line of chintzy net curtains. She pressed the buzzer.

Douglas Brewer's residence was far from salubrious. The landlord stood back from the door as a warm fug greeted them. Kate winced at the smell: a mixture of old socks and stale bong water. Sure enough, a large collection of glass pipes lined one of the bookshelves as they went inside.

There were three rooms: the front door opened into a living area, including the kitchen, with two doors off to the side, leading to what Kate assumed was the bedroom and bathroom. The room was dark, the curtains pulled shut, and Briggs flicked on a light in the kitchen. The bare bulb hardly lit the room, so Kate walked to the window and pulled the curtains open, releasing a haze of dust. They were both wearing gloves, but Kate wished she'd put a face mask on, too. Who knew what crap she was inhaling?

Briggs was standing in the kitchen, a disgusted expression on his face, peering at the dirty dishes in the sink. Beer bottles filled the teetering bin, more empties discarded around it. He had his hands out to his sides, desperately trying to avoid touching anything. Kate smiled, watching him. She knew Briggs took great pride in his appearance – she'd never seen him look anything other than pristine and primped; his suit probably cost more than the monthly rent on this place, despite his paltry detective's salary.

'Is this what your flat's like, Jamie?' Kate joked and he looked at her, a withering expression on his face.

'Are you kidding? I have a cleaning lady twice a week.' He picked up the post from the floor and flicked through it. 'All of this is postmarked this week, so he can't have been in the water for long.'

'He had quite a drug habit,' Kate said. She poked the ashtray on the coffee table with a gloved finger, overflowing with a mixture of fag ends and roaches from joints. 'Where do you think he keeps his stash?'

Briggs started looking along the bookshelves, reading out the titles on the spines as he went. Kate recognised the usual biographies – alpha males in the SAS, survival stories and daring deeds. Kate checked on the shelf below the coffee table. She moved a pile of porn magazines and picked up a tin, opening the lid.

'Here it is,' she said. 'Obviously a man who didn't like to be too far away from his next joint.'

Or wank, she thought grimly.

The tin contained the usual suspects: a few packets of Rizlas, the covers ripped, a pouch of Golden Virginia tobacco and two small plastic bags of what looked like cheap weed. Nothing that incriminating. She bagged it up before noticing the landlord hovering in the doorway.

She went over to talk to him.

'What have you found?' he asked, poking his head into the room.

Kate ignored the question. 'What was Mr Brewer like?' she asked.

The landlord pulled a face. 'Not the best tenant, not the worst. Paid his rent on time, but didn't keep the place in the best of shape, as you can see.'

'Did he have any regular visitors? Any friends?'

'Not many. He had a few buddies he went out to the pub with on a Saturday night. We go to the same place – the Gordon Arms? And a younger guy. His dealer, I think. I'd know when he'd been here because the next day when I opened the shop the whole hallway would smell of pot.' He looked at Kate guiltily. 'I just know what it smells like, I've never smoked any.'

Kate smiled indulgently. 'Do you know any of their names, these buddies?'

'No, and when I think about it now, I haven't seen him in the pub in months.' He looked inside again, where Briggs was still digging around. 'Do you know when I can have the flat back? He's dead, right?'

'I don't know, I'm sorry,' Kate said. 'Do you have details of next of kin?'

The landlord nodded and went back down the stairs to the shop. Kate shouted round the door to Briggs.

'Anything else?' she asked.

'This.' Briggs held up a laptop with two fingers. 'But not much else I can get to without catching something.'

Kate nodded. 'We'll get SOCO in here, see what they can uncover.'

The landlord emerged and passed her a scrap of paper. 'This was the only name he gave me. I think it's his sister, although he said not to contact her unless it was life or death.' He frowned. 'I guess this is.'

Kate went back into the apartment. A man's life all in one place, and what did he have to show for it? Some bad habits and even worse hygiene. Kate went into the bathroom: cheap white toilet, bath, sink. All covered with a thick brown grime. Her feet stuck to the lino, and she winced. Kate bagged up the toothbrush, then left quickly.

'Don't go in there,' she said to Briggs, then prepared herself for the bedroom.

It was much the same. The curtains were shut, but Kate could make out a duvet and pillow, both askew. Dirty sheets. A pair of boxer shorts on the floor. She tentatively opened the bedside drawer: more porn magazines, deodorant, a used-up bottle of aftershave and a phone charger. She pushed aside the porn with a cautious finger: at the bottom were two magazines about steam trains. She looked up at the shelves, where two die-cast models sat. Those discarded magazines and dusty relics made Kate feel unexpectedly sad. A forgotten hobby, a leftover from a more innocent life. Perhaps one where he wouldn't have ended up dead, she thought.

She shut the drawer and went back into the living room.

Briggs had packaged up the evidence and stood next to her in the doorway. She showed him the piece of paper with his sister's number on.

'We have a call to make,' she said.

'Poor sod,' Briggs said as he carried the stuff out the door.

Kate nodded and followed him. She knew bad things happened to people every day. Random, unpredictable things. But Kate had a feeling this wasn't one of those. You don't go from squalid flat to floating face down in a lake twenty-five miles away by accident. How had he got there, when his car was parked up just outside? And how had he died?

There were just too many unanswered questions.

'What do you mean, Lucy owned firearms?' Scott sat in front of Max at his kitchen table, astonished.

Max checked the computer screen in front of him. 'According to our records,' he said, 'Lucy had a licence to own two: a handgun and a rifle, approved three months ago.' He looked at Scott. The man opened and closed his mouth a few times. 'And you knew nothing about this? I mean, she would have had to join a gun club and been shooting regularly to be approved for the firearms certificate. She would have had someone round to inspect the gun safe.'

'Gun safe?' Scott Barker repeated.

'And you say you didn't know it was there?'

'What? No.' He shook his head emphatically. 'I told you, I don't go down there. I thought the old shelter was unusable.'

Max frowned. He believed him. Scott Barker genuinely seemed shaken and confused. Bugger, he thought to himself, staring at the screen. When he'd first got the deployment to investigate Lucy Barker as a misper, he'd asked Control to do the PNC check, look on the system for any red flags, and they'd said it had come up clean. They must have missed something, and he muttered a profanity under his breath, feeling like an idiot. But Scott Barker? He didn't seem to know his wife at all.

Perhaps the best friend knew more, he hoped, packing up his computer. He'd leave the teams here to finish their search. It was time to interview Jen Lewis.

'Scott? You don't think he's got anything to do with it, do you?'

Max had been sat in front of Jen Lewis for about half an hour and had barely got a word in edgeways. Her face was flushed, she was leaning forward towards him as if he was giving her the gossip from the latest episode of *Love Island*, rather than interviewing her about the worrying disappearance of her best friend.

'We're exploring all avenues,' Max said. 'And when did you speak to her last?'

'Tuesday. I remember because she was on hands-free in the car, and I always hate it when I talk to people on hands-free. You always have to shout, don't you? She was going to her book club.'

'You don't go with her?'

'Christ, no!' She laughed loudly. 'Boring stuff. And I don't know where it is, either. It's not with anyone I know.'

Max had already established that Jen Lewis knew Scott and Lucy from university. She'd been on the same course as Scott and lived in halls with Lucy. 'I was probably the reason they met,' she'd laughed. She now lived in a mid-terrace new build near the centre of town. Max had watched the estate go up and was interested to see inside the 'luxury developments' they had been going on about. To him, they seemed pretty generic. White walls, tiny rooms, square patch of grass masquerading as a garden. Jen had agreed to meet him on her lunch break, a small yappy dog glaring at him from her lap.

'And she seemed okay? Nothing out of the ordinary?' he continued, ignoring the dog as it started to growl softly.

'No, she was fine,' Jen stroked the dog's head and it licked her hand. 'She was talking about some documentary she'd watched and I tuned out, to be honest. Since she got fired she's been going off on these weird crusades, I lose track of what from week to week.'

Max flicked through his notes from the night before, then looked back at Jen. 'Sorry, you say she got fired?'

'Yes, a few months ago.'

'Do you know what for?'

'She was furious. She said she'd had a heated discussion with one of the directors about an environmental policy she wanted to change, and they said it was gross misconduct. Christ knows what she said to him, she wouldn't tell me. Personally I think they got fed up with her going on about all her green planet shit. She was their Corporate Social Responsibility person, or whatever it's called.'

'Right.'

Max paused and checked his notes again. The husband had definitely said she was made redundant, so why the discrepancy? Then he sighed. Why was he surprised Scott Barker had got that wrong, too?

'Was Lucy upset she'd been fired?'

'No, not really.' Jen shrugged. 'She's not as career-minded as I am. I could only just get away this lunchtime, normally I work through. I'm secretary to Dr Hutton at Southampton General. He's one of the UK's leading consultant neurologists,' she finished, puffing her chest out slightly.

'Hmm,' Max replied. He got the feeling he was supposed to be impressed but couldn't quite summon the enthusiasm. 'And how well do you know Scott, nowadays?' he continued.

Jen paused. 'What do you mean?'

'You said you were close while you were at university, but

what about now? Do you go out together, the three of you, or is it usually you and Lucy?'

'No, no, just me and Lucy. I don't see Scott now,' she answered, stroking the dog that little bit quicker.

Max noticed her hands were shaking slightly. 'And why is that?'

'No reason. We prefer it to be us two. Girl chat, you know.'

'Right,' Max said again. 'And do you have any suggestions as to where Lucy might be?'

Jen shook her head, her black curls bobbing to and fro. 'Not a clue. Lucy's pretty dull, all things considered. She's got some strong opinions, but apart from that she doesn't go anywhere. Always glued to her computer or weeding her vegetables.'

'And you say you and Lucy are best friends?' he repeated.

'Absolutely.'

'Hmm.' Max rather hoped his best mates wouldn't say something like that about him if he disappeared. 'And any friends you suggest we speak to? Scott said her family weren't close.'

Jen laughed. 'That's an understatement. She hasn't spoken to her parents in years. They're the God-bothering sort, you know. Church every Sunday, hate the gays, those ones. They had a falling-out when she married Scott, and she hasn't seen them since.' She lowered her voice, as if there was someone else in the room. 'Unforgivable.' She chuckled. 'Only rebellious thing Lucy has ever done in her life.'

'So disappearing is out of the ordinary for Lucy?'

'Completely.' Jen nodded. 'It's rare that Lucy even leaves the house nowadays.'

I'm not completely sure she has this time, Max thought. Outside her front door, Max shook his head in disbelief.

Wow, and this was her best friend? What were her enemies like? He looked at the hastily scribbled note of other acquaintances Jen Lewis had given him – there were three people on the list. This was not going to take long.

His phone buzzed a text message and he pulled it out of his pocket. His colleagues had finished at the house. Apart from the empty safe, they'd come up with nothing. No drugs, no sign of foul play. No dead bodies.

This was a good thing, wasn't it? So why did Max still feel something was wrong?

II

Kate and Briggs pulled into the car park at Portswood police station and saw PCSO Mina Shah waiting for them, bouncing on the balls of her feet. She had two takeaway cups of coffee in her hand and passed them across. Kate liked her immediately.

PCSOs, or Police Community Support Officers, did the neighbourhood engagement stuff: the house-to-house enquiries, everything that kept the local area running. More importantly for Kate and Briggs today, they had a level of knowledge about the people in their town that often proved invaluable in cases like this.

PCSO Mina Shah had sleek black hair, tied back tightly in a high ponytail with a scrunchie, a style more suited to a teenager than to a big-cheeked lady in her mid-forties. She ushered Kate and Briggs through to the kitchen and they all sat down around the table. Kate took a sip of her coffee – strong, black, two sugars. She looked up in surprise.

'I asked around about you,' Mina said. 'I wanted to get your coffee right.'

'It's perfect, thank you,' Kate replied. Then, after a pause, Kate added: 'And what else did you hear?'

'Only good things,' the PCSO replied, her cheeks reddening.

Kate didn't push further. She knew she'd made mistakes last winter, both professional and personal, and she'd heard edges of the rumours that followed her around. Cops like a bit of gossip, but they also like prosecutions, and that was one thing Kate was good at. So she'd held onto a modicum of respect, something she was more than thankful for now.

'So what can you tell us about our dead man?' Kate asked.

'Dougie Brewer? What you'd expect.' Mina looked down at her notebook, where Kate could see a few lines of scribbled writing. A printout from the RMS poked out the side. Mina pushed it over to her. Kate looked at it, then handed it to Briggs.

'Local man, grown up around the area, always in trouble for one thing or another. Most recently drunk and disorderly. We'd go and see him a lot for harassing students down by The Hobbit,' she said, referring to one of the local university pubs at the other end of the town. 'He didn't mean anything by it, but we'd have to take the calls. He was one of those noisy but harmless types, you know?'

Kate nodded. 'And what about this one?' she asked, pointing to a line on the printout for criminal damage six months ago. 'This doesn't seem harmless.'

'That was a weird one. We hadn't seen him for ages before that. I hoped he'd cleaned himself up and got a job or something, but then he turns up with that group from down Ringwood way.' Mina frowned. 'Border-something? I forget, it's an odd name. Arrested five of them for breaking into the pharmacy on Highfield Lane, but released without charge in the end. No definitive evidence.'

Briggs looked up. 'I heard about that one. Wasn't there something weird about it?'

Mina nodded. 'Yeah. You'd expect them to be going after oxy or methadone – but they'd taken a whole range of stuff.'

'Like what?'

'They did take some painkillers, but antibiotics mainly. Lots of different types. Also nutritional supplements, and some topical local anaesthetics. Plus a few things I hadn't heard of. I could get you the full list. It was a real random mix.'

'Please. And you think he'd got in with this local group?' Kate asked.

'That would be my best guess. They came to collect him after the interview and I didn't see or hear from him then until you got in touch. Have you been to his place?' she asked, and Kate nodded. 'What did you find?'

'Nothing of great interest. Some weed, empty bottles, the place was a state but the landlord said he paid his rent on time. Do you know how he made his money?'

Mina frowned. 'He did a stint at the local Sainsbury's but I know he was fired pretty quickly. I suspect he did a lot of cash-in-hand stuff. Building work, handyman errands. Although I wouldn't have let him in my house.'

'Why's that?'

'He was nearly always half-cut, and his personal hygiene wasn't great. Not the sort of man you wanted to be around for too long. Quite sad.' She fiddled with her notepad. 'And now he's dead?'

Kate nodded slowly.

'Very sad, then,' Mina said.

Kate and Briggs let Mina get back to work, thanking her effusively for the coffees. Kate rested back in her seat and stretched.

'Have you heard of them?' Kate asked Briggs. 'This group she was talking about?'

He shrugged. 'No, but let's ask around, I'm sure someone will know.'

Kate saw a man in uniform go to walk into the kitchen, then turn around, as if changing his mind.

Briggs shouted out into the corridor. 'Coop! Come here.'

Kate cringed. She knew who it was who had done the double take, and precisely the reason he had reconsidered.

PC Max Cooper appeared back in the doorway. 'What?' he said. He looked over at Kate and smiled. 'DS Munro.'

'PC Cooper,' Kate replied. She looked away, suddenly very interested in the file in front of her on the table. She could feel her back grow sweaty, her face hot. She didn't want to give him the satisfaction, and willed her body to calm the hell down while Briggs questioned him.

'I don't know much,' Max said. He leaned forward and took control of Briggs's laptop, opening up a Google search and typing something in. He was standing close to Kate, and she could smell his aftershave. She chanced a look at him as he stared at the laptop. He had messy sandy-blond hair that needed a cut, his short-sleeved black shirt showing just the right amount of toned bicep. She looked away again quickly.

'There you go,' he said, turning the screen round to face them.

It was an amateur website, white writing on a black background, big lettering across the top. *Borderland*, it said. *We Welcome Everyone.*

'Sounds like a theme park,' Kate commented, pulling the laptop away from Briggs.

'Anything but,' Max replied. 'You're welcome,' he added sarcastically, then started a conversation with Briggs, making himself a coffee and discussing some misper he hadn't managed to track down.

Kate started reading the text on the screen. It was vague, talking about inclusivity, collaboration and future-proofing, but never actually clarifying what they were all about. There were a few photographs of grinning toddlers and their families, then a section that asked for login information and a password.

'We should go and see these guys,' Kate said to Briggs.

'You might want to check with the DCI first,' Max said, and Kate looked up at him, face flushing again as she met his brown eyes with hers. 'They don't get on well with the police. We've been told to be discreet.'

'I'm always discreet,' Kate said.

'I know you are,' Max replied slowly. He raised his mug to her in a mock salute, then left.

Briggs looked at her and raised an eyebrow.

Kate waved him away. 'Let's go. We have a dead body to investigate.'

She picked up her file and pushed the laptop back in the bag, swinging it over her shoulder. They started walking down the narrow corridors of the police station towards the door, and as they went, Kate cast her eye across the whiteboard on the wall in the sergeant's office.

It was an old habit from her uniform days, when anything they needed to know before heading out was written up there. Outstanding warrants, urgent call-outs, current mispers.

She turned away from the board, then stopped. A name had caught her eye. Three rows down: *Lucy Barker. Grade 1. High Risk. PC Cooper.*

'Max!' she shouted back down the corridor and Cooper emerged out of one of the side rooms. Kate pointed at the board.

'Your misper,' Kate asked. 'What does she look like?'

He thought for a moment. 'Blonde, petite, pretty.'

'Kind of posh?'

'I don't know,' he frowned. 'Here.' He reached through the doorway of his sergeant's office and picked up a photo left on the desk. 'She looks like that.'

Kate held the photo between two fingers and looked at it. Briggs glanced over her shoulder.

'Isn't that ...' he started, and Kate nodded.

Kate looked at Max. 'Your misper. We've met her.'

'How? When?' Max asked, all his attention on Kate.

'On Saturday, when we fished that dead bloke out of the lake.' Kate looked at the name on the whiteboard. 'Lucy Barker was the person who found the body.'

12

DCI Alexa Delaney had the sort of elegance Kate had only seen in ballet dancers. She had a long neck, elegant limbs and the posture of a swan. When their last DCI had been moved on, euphemistically to work on a 'special project' and never seen again, the whole team had been worried about who they would be faced with next. Surely no one could be worse? So when Alexa Delaney walked in on her first day, the entire station had a crush.

Kate was no exception. She revered her with an adoration usually reserved for movie stars. Every meeting she'd had with DCI Delaney so far had been respectful, empowering: she'd listened, nodded, then let Kate make her own decisions. It was a big change.

But Kate had never been summoned up to her office before. The moment they arrived back at the dirty beige lego brick, otherwise known as the Central Southampton station, she received the message. Now she hovered outside, fidgeting with the file in her hand, unsure about what she was being called to discuss. She'd heard their new DCI had superhuman ways of finding out what was going on: she was always on top of the latest news, whether it was a break in a case or the gossip around the station. Kate hoped she was being asked to talk about the former, although when she saw PC Cooper walking down the corridor towards her, she was suddenly much more worried.

Max stopped, waiting on the opposite side of the doorway. Kate swore under her breath.

'What are you doing here?' she said.

'I could ask you the same,' he replied. 'I was called to a meeting with the DCI.'

'From Portswood?'

He nodded.

'Now?'

'Now.'

They waited in an uneasy silence.

'Do you know what it's about?'

Max shook his head. 'Why? Are you worried?'

Kate smiled wryly. 'Why should I be worried?'

The door opened, making Kate jump, and the DCI ushered them inside. She gestured to the chairs in front of the desk and Kate and Max sat down. Kate looked at her, taking in how she was dressed, wondering how she managed to look so effortlessly good. The DCI's hair was up in a formal bun, but tendrils fell gorgeously round her almond-shaped face. She was wearing a simple grey shift dress, and Kate knew that on anyone else it would look boring, too basic, but not on Alexa Delaney.

The DCI took her seat slowly behind her desk and looked at them both.

'I hear you've made a connection between your two cases,' she said, and Kate inwardly relaxed. 'Tell me more.'

She looked expectantly at Kate.

'The high-risk misper that Max – PC Cooper,' she said, correcting herself, 'has been looking for, Lucy Barker, was the first person to come into contact with the body in Ellingham lake. She was swimming and discovered the corpse.'

Max involuntarily winced next to her.

'That must have been traumatic for the woman.'

'Yes,' Kate continued. 'But she had a good support network around her. We spoke to her a few times that weekend and she seemed to be okay.'

'But now she's disappeared?' the DCI asked, looking over at Max. 'How was the link missed before? And is there anything to indicate that it's related to the death?'

Kate noticed Max flush slightly. 'It wasn't flagged on the system. And not so far as we can see, guv, no. She seems to have had a quiet life up to this point, and, if I'm honest, signs seem to point towards the husband having something to do with it. Especially since he failed to tell us about her finding the body.'

'Oh? And do you have any evidence against him?' Alexa asked.

'Well, no, not yet. But we're looking.'

'Let's make sure,' the DCI said. 'I don't like the fact that she experienced a traumatic event, then disappeared. Send the balloon up. Let's get this woman found.' She paused and both Max and Kate got up to leave. 'But do it together.'

'Sorry, guv?' Kate hesitated.

Alexa looked up from her desk. 'I want you to merge your investigations. There's no point both of you looking at the same lines of enquiry, and Kate, you want someone to replace DC Yates, don't you? From now on, PC Cooper, you will report into DS Munro, and your misper investigation will fall under Kate's caseload.'

'But—' Max began, but DCI Delaney cut him off.

'You were thinking about a move, weren't you?'

'Yes, but—'

'So here's your opportunity to show us what you can do. As from today, you're seconded to the CID for the duration of this case. I've spoken to your sergeant, and he's in agreement.'

Kate and Max looked at each other, their mouths open.

'Is there a problem, PC Cooper?'

Max paused, then shook his head. 'No, no, guv. Thank you for the opportunity.'

'Keep me in the loop,' DCI Delaney added, smiling. 'And Kate? I don't want you going near the Borderland Family until you have good, solid evidence against them. They're sealed shut tighter than a clam, that lot, and poking them with a stick only makes them worse.'

'What are they?' Kate asked. 'Some sort of crime gang?'

Delaney shook her head. 'More like a cult. Getting ready for the end of the world, that kind of stuff. You'll need to be going after them with a sledgehammer when the time is right.'

Kate nodded, and the two of them walked out into the corridor, shutting the door behind them.

Max paused, then slowly nodded his head. 'So you're in charge now?'

'Looks that way.' Kate paused. 'Is there a problem, Max?'

He turned to her, smiling. 'Not unless we make one, Kate.'

Kate tried her hardest to ignore his cheeky grin. 'Go and get everything you have on Lucy Barker. I need you to bring Briggs and I up to speed as soon as possible.'

He nodded, then headed off down the corridor.

'And it's DS Munro,' she shouted after him.

He raised his hand in acknowledgement as he walked away.

Kate watched him go. This was going to be awkward, there was no doubt about it, but short of going back into the office and admitting to DCI Delaney what had happened in the past, this was where they were. She shook her head. What the hell had she got herself into this time?

13

The three of them sat around the table in the ops room, files open, having gone through the finer details of both investigations. It seemed that apart from Lucy's terrible discovery that past Saturday, there were no other similarities between the cases.

And already Max was enjoying himself. At last, something he could get his teeth into and see through to the end rather than just hand over to the next shift. He liked working with Briggs again, both of them bouncing ideas to and fro. And Munro? Well, he was trying not to think about that one at the moment.

'And her medical history?' Kate asked.

Max pulled the report up on the screen. 'Just have a summary at this stage, but by the looks of this, she's barely been in to see her GP, except for a prescription for Microgynon two weeks ago.'

Kate frowned. 'That's a contraceptive pill. I thought you said they were trying for kids?'

Max looked up at his new team. 'That's what Barker told me.' More information the husband didn't know, it seemed. 'More importantly, no reports of domestic violence.'

'Not all trips to A&E end up on someone's medical files,' Briggs said. 'She could have used a fake name. And just because there were no injuries doesn't mean there wasn't domestic abuse.'

'But we have no proof,' Kate said. 'So no motive.'

'And you've never met Scott Barker?' Max asked.

Kate and Briggs both shook their heads. 'We were busy with the investigation when he picked her up that day,' Briggs said.

Kate drummed her fingers on the table, then looked at Max. 'I think it's time I met this man,' she said.

'Who goes to work when your wife's missing?' Kate whispered to Max, as they stood in the massive lobby of the retail business where Scott worked.

They'd phoned Scott Barker, and he'd directed them to his workplace. It was a big nationwide company with an impressive reputation, and had the posh headquarters to match.

They'd got looks when they arrived. Max was in uniform, and it looked like he was going to have to stay that way for a while, despite the secondment. Still a PC, for the moment. He looked across at Kate, now talking to the receptionist and signing them both in. He wasn't sure how this was going to work.

There wasn't a problem as such, but they had history. Drunken, messy, Christmas party sort of history. History which should not be mentioned to colleagues; history that made eye contact awkward.

So working together every day? That was going to be interesting.

But even given the events of that particular night, he didn't know much about her. He had known her by reputation – for solving cases at any cost – and he'd since heard she was back with her husband, so assumed the Christmas party had fallen while she'd been separated. But apart from that, he was in the dark.

He'd asked Briggs for advice on his new boss, but he'd just shrugged.

'She's all right,' was his comment. 'Keep her well caffeinated, don't ask her about any personal stuff, and you'll be fine.' Briggs then looked up from his keyboard. 'And don't get her drunk. She does unpredictable stuff when she's drunk.'

Yes. Well. Max knew all about that. They'd both been drunk that night. He'd been up for a good time, and, truth be told, he'd had his eye on the little blonde one from Custody. But then Kate had wobbled over.

There was something about her he couldn't take his eyes off, even now. She projected a sincerity that made people listen to her. He liked that. He knew people didn't take him seriously, considering him the joker, the guy you could rely on to have a good time, and while it meant he had many friends, it wasn't getting him far at work. Maybe it would be a good thing to spend a bit more time with DS Munro. Maybe some of her gravitas would rub off on him.

Kate gestured from the reception desk and he moved forward to have his photograph taken. A blurry black-and-white image was printed out and pushed into a clear plastic tag, which he clipped onto his shirt.

The receptionist pointed towards a young woman wearing jeans and trainers.

'Gemma will take you up to meet Scott,' the receptionist said, pressing a button and opening the automatic gates.

There was a massive wooden staircase to the right of the foyer, and Kate and Max followed the woman up. Max looked longingly at the coffee shop as they passed, then took in the rest of their surroundings.

The headquarters had full-height windows, occupying one

wall for what seemed to be three storeys. A large orange box stuck out from one side, obviously designed to be a posh meeting room or other such pointless architectural gesture. The rest of the building was separated into lurid categories of green, blue and purple, a sign saying GREEN STREET on the wall of the aisle they had started to walk up. Max already had a headache.

The woman showed them through the open-plan area: rows of identical desks, employees lined up like battery hens. Max noticed people taking them in, his uniform marking them out as a prime source of gossip. Scott was waiting inside a see-through meeting room on the far side, standing up as they entered. He shut the glass door behind them.

'Detective Sergeant Munro,' Kate said, shaking his hand. 'My team have joined the search for Lucy.'

Scott nodded and slumped back into a hard orange plastic chair. Kate and Max sat down opposite him. The room itself was empty and featureless; it felt like a fish tank. Scott noticed Max looking around.

'Not my office. Everyone here is open-plan, but I thought we would need some privacy,' he explained. 'At least, as much as you can get around here,' he added, gesturing to the glass walls and the employees beyond.

'Why did you come to work today, Mr Barker?' Kate asked, getting straight to the point. 'Surely they could do without you?'

Scott looked at his hands, fingers interlocked on the table. 'I was going crazy stuck at home, just waiting. I've never been good at sitting around, so I thought I should come into the office. I'm regretting it now. No one knows what to say to me.' Scott looked across to Max. 'Did you find anything on Lucy's mobile phone?' he asked.

Max shook his head. 'No, it was very unhelpful.'

'What do you mean?'

'It was empty. It didn't have any apps or contacts or messages on it at all.' Max paused. 'Almost as if someone had wiped it.'

'Do you think Lucy did that?' Scott asked.

'It's a possibility.'

'Scott,' Kate interjected, 'can you tell us about the events at the weekend? When Lucy found the dead body?'

Scott turned quickly to Kate. 'Do you think that's related?'

'We're exploring the possibility. What can you tell us about Saturday?'

Scott took a deep breath in. 'Lucy left the house before I was awake. She liked to be at the lake as the sun rose. I got up about nine-ish, and was surprised to see Lucy wasn't back yet, but when I turned my phone on I had loads of messages from her. She was upset, rightfully so. You don't expect to find decomposed bodies when you go swimming.'

'Did she often go to Ellingham lake?' Max asked.

'Yes, most weeks at this time of year. She was a good swimmer and liked the peace outside. She said it was soothing.'

'And what happened after you called her?' Kate asked, encouraging him to continue.

'I met her at Southampton police station, where you guys were taking her statement. I brought her some food, change of clothes, you know. What I thought she might need. Then I took her home. It was a pain because her car was still at the lake and we had to go back that evening.'

Maybe more of a pain for your wife to find a dead body, Max thought, but anyway. 'And how was Lucy?' he asked.

'She was quiet. Said she kept seeing his face in the water.

She had a broken night's sleep but seemed okay on Sunday. Back to her normal self.'

'And why didn't you mention it to me?' Max asked. He was annoyed with Scott Barker. Max should have known about Lucy's history, like the bloody guns. This shouldn't have been for someone else to tell him about. He was starting to look completely incompetent.

'I... I don't know. I guess I forgot. With Lucy disappearing, I was distracted. The events of Saturday seem like an age ago.'

'Right.' Max tapped his fingers on the table. 'Mr Barker, when we spoke before, you said that Lucy was made redundant from her job.'

Scott nodded. 'She was.'

'So why does Jen Lewis say she was fired? Some conflict with one of the senior directors.'

Scott shook his head. 'No, that can't be right. Lucy wouldn't get into a disagreement with anyone. She wasn't that sort of person.' He looked at Max. He seemed nervous. 'Ask them, they'll set you straight. Why would Jen say such a thing? What else did she tell you?'

'Why would Jen say that if it wasn't true?' Max replied.

'I don't know. I don't...' He paused, his face colouring. 'She's closer friends with Lucy than with me.'

Max looked over at Kate, but she was silent. So many questions, Max thought. But like Kate, he knew there was a time and place to ask them. Maybe later, under caution, when his replies could be scrutinised properly.

Kate and Max walked out of the office in silence, handing their passes into reception on the way. Max looked across at Kate once they were back in the car, Max in the driving seat. She was deep in thought, her brow furrowed.

'What do you think?' he asked.

Kate looked up at the massive building in front of them. 'He's a strange one, that's for sure. Very compartmentalised.'

'Do you think he has anything to do with Lucy's disappearance?' Max asked.

Kate frowned. 'I don't know,' she said. 'But did you notice? How he talked about Lucy?'

Max shook his head, thinking back. 'What do you mean?'

'He talked about her in the past tense. Like she's dead already.'

14

From the office window, Scott watched them leave, the bright yellow and blue police vehicle swinging out of the car park.

He knew what people were saying about him around the office. He could only guess at what the police were thinking, and it wouldn't be good. Nobody's wife just disappeared without a trace. And he knew he hadn't been honest.

When he'd said that Lucy hadn't seemed different after discovering the body, he hadn't been lying. But the truth was she'd been behaving oddly for a long time before swimming into a decomposing corpse. She often couldn't sleep; he'd hear her roaming around the house in the early hours, fidgety and restless. When he'd asked her, she said she had a lot on her mind.

He remembered the last time she'd behaved strangely, at university, in their first year. He'd ignored it that time, too. And look what happened then.

As if echoing the hesitation in his mind, his phone vibrated on the table.

'Fuck off,' he muttered at the screen, and rejected the call. Moments later it beeped again, showing a new voicemail. 'Will you just fuck off!' he shouted, slamming the phone down.

Scott leaned forward, resting both hands on the desk, taking big gulps of air. How had his life come to this? He glanced out of the floor-to-ceiling windows, seeing multiple pairs of eyes watching him through the glass. He smiled weakly.

His thoughts kept on coming back to Lucy's deception. The police said Lucy had been fired. Why would Jen lie about that? Or, perhaps, why had Lucy lied to him? Was that such a strange thought, now he knew what she'd been hiding in their air-raid shelter? What on earth did she need guns for?

He couldn't stand being near the police. He knew they could sense his dishonesty. He hadn't seen Lucy that Monday morning, of course he hadn't. He'd got up from the huge bed, had a shower, eaten his breakfast and gone to work. He'd lied. He hadn't seen her since Sunday, when they'd gone to bed in separate rooms, Lucy silent and furious.

He felt his muscles tense and his jaw contract. Anger burned through his body. How could she do this to him? His wife! She'd lied to him, gone behind his back, and now his life looked like this. Fuck!

He took deep breaths, forcing himself to calm down. Perhaps it would be better if he worked from home.

He picked up his laptop and pushed it carelessly into his bag, shoving down papers at the same time.

Without speaking to his PA, he hurried out of the office, feeling eyes on his back as he left. He'd done nothing wrong, he told himself as he walked. This wasn't his fault.

If only he believed it.

15

Kate sat at her desk, staring at the photograph in the passport in front of her. She remembered Lucy Barker. She remembered seeing those big blue eyes full of fear. She'd looked different to this photo – her long blonde hair had been wet and tangled, her face make-up free, large red lines from her swimming goggles round her eyes. She'd been badly shaken up, but she was able to give a good account of what had happened, something many witnesses didn't manage.

Kate couldn't imagine how harrowing it must have been to run into a dead body in that way. And corpses in water were pretty disgusting – water wasn't kind to the skin of a person left bobbing about in it too long. Kate shuddered. She certainly wouldn't like to be swimming alongside one. Touching dead rubbery flesh. Water going in her mouth.

Kate felt slightly sick and picked up the mobile phone that Max had left. She clicked on a few buttons and, now unlocked, the screen flashed into life. He was right, it was no use at all. But who had wiped it? Kate wondered. They'd get the techies to find out.

This was a strange one. Twenty-four hours since her husband had reported her missing, and they had nothing. No leads, no sightings, nothing on CCTV. Just a whole load of lies. She picked up Lucy's passport again and ran her finger round the edge. The top corner of the back cover was cut off and Kate squinted at the sharp edges. Sure, the passport had expired, but didn't the passport office cut the corners off once a new one had been issued? She glanced at the clock. It was too late to call them now; someone would need to do it first thing in the morning.

In the meantime, Kate picked up the phone and called their PR department. It was time to appeal to the public – to get Lucy Barker's face out there. Someone must have seen something.

She looked at her watch. Shit. She needed to be getting home. Sam would be waiting. She would just make the call first.

Sam was in the kitchen when she got home, standing at the cooker. She came up behind him, putting her arms round his waist and kissing the back of his neck.

'You're late,' he said, by way of greeting. He gave her a perfunctory kiss on her cheek and turned back to the spag bol bubbling in front of him.

'I'm sorry, picked up another case,' Kate said, walking over to the fridge.

'Another one? Didn't you say you and Briggs were already overloaded?'

'Yes, but they've assigned us someone new.'

'That's good,' Sam replied.

She nodded, peering into the fridge. An unopened bottle of New Zealand Sauvignon Blanc looked at her, her favourite. 'Yes, but ...'

'But what?' Sam paused, wooden spoon in his hand. She turned back to him and for a moment saw his gaze flick to the bottle of wine she was holding. She saw his forehead furrow, felt his disapproval.

Kate put the bottle of wine back in the door and picked up a can of Diet Coke.

'I just don't know if he's any good,' she lied. You know he's good at some things, her brain had whispered, and she felt her face go red.

But Sam had moved on and had started talking about something marketing-related called SEO and a woman called Felicity.

Kate had heard Sam mention Felicity before, but normally he called her Fliss. Fliss! Kate thought to herself. What grown woman calls herself Fliss? Kate imagined blonde curly hair, and one of those sing-song voices that made men stupid and women want to punch them. She probably went to the spa and had mani-pedis every fortnight.

Kate knew he had slept with people while they'd been separated. That was no crime – after all, she had done the same. As she would be reminded every day, working alongside Max. But neither she nor Sam had been truthful about it. So every name he mentioned, Kate imagined he'd been with her. Every time he went on a work trip, she wondered if he'd do it again. But don't ask, she told herself. Don't go near the house of cards.

Hours later, Kate lay in bed, staring at the ceiling. The house was silent, except for Sam's rhythmic breathing next to her. They'd spent the evening in front of the television – some awful film on Netflix – but she'd been distracted, flicking through the apps on her phone, reading social media. Scott Barker didn't have a Twitter or Instagram account, and his Facebook page was locked tight. Lucy's hadn't offered much insight either.

They'd gone to bed, cleaning their teeth, Sam muttering

about needing his sleep. It seemed that Netflix and chill was literally just that for yet another night.

So far, everything was quiet online regarding Lucy's disappearance. That would all change tomorrow with the press conference. In the darkness, Kate ran through in her head what needed to happen. First, she needed to be presentable. She would probably be the one in front of the cameras, so she would have to make a bit of an effort tomorrow morning. Did she have a shirt that was ironed? Ah, shit. She hated seeing herself on television. She needed to nag PR for the press release to be finished. They'd have to go and see the family first thing, and they needed to get Scott Barker prepped. She'd get Max to do that – he seemed to have a decent rapport with the man.

Sam stirred next to her in bed, and she looked over. She could make out the edge of his shoulder and the back of his head on the pillow. Kate leaned forward and kissed the curve of his neck. He rolled over sleepily.

'Are you awake?' Kate whispered, and Sam mumbled in response, pulling her into his chest. She rested her head on the dip below his collarbone and listened to her husband's breathing.

Kate remembered being apart from Sam last year. At that time she'd felt that if they could be back together, everything would be fine. She would be happy. But this – this twitchy restlessness – wasn't that at all.

But she couldn't risk losing Sam. She knew that if the slightest thing went wrong – if she told him the truth about how she was feeling – Sam would call an end to their marriage again.

And this time, for good.

Wednesday

16

From the outside, the house seemed innocuous enough. Mid-terrace, grey pebble-dash, brown front door.

Kate rang the bell.

The door was opened by a short, plump woman wearing a long grey pleated skirt and bulky woollen jumper.

'Yes?' she said, nervously.

'Mrs Wilcox?' Kate asked. 'DS Munro and DC Briggs from Hampshire Police.' The woman looked blank, so Kate continued. 'We're here to talk about the disappearance of your daughter, Lucy?'

'Let them in!' a voice boomed from inside. The woman glanced back, then reluctantly opened the door. A man appeared by her side. Tall with a heavily pregnant beer belly, he took up the majority of the doorway.

'Come in, come in! Would you like a cup of tea? Get them a cup of tea, Martha!' Kate went to protest but the woman had already gone. 'Isaac!' he bellowed next to Kate's ear and she jumped. 'Come downstairs now!'

The man held his hand out to Briggs and he shook it, wincing at the tightness of the grip. 'I'm Roger Wilcox. Detective Sergeant Munro, I assume.'

Kate sighed. For fuck's sake. 'No, I'm DS Munro,' she said loudly. 'I spoke to your wife on the phone.'

The man reluctantly offered his hand to Kate. He barely touched her before pulling away and ushering them both into the living room.

They walked in and perched on the sofa. Roger Wilcox sat opposite them, occasionally glaring out to the kitchen.

'I'll go and see what's keeping them,' he muttered, and left.

In the silence, Kate took in the room. The decor looked like it hadn't been touched since the eighties. The wallpaper was garishly patterned, starting to peel away at the edges. The sofa was brown velour, sagging into the centre; it was all Kate could do not to sink into Briggs's lap. There were no pictures or photos on the wall: the only decoration was a huge varnished wooden cross dominating the centre of the room. She looked at the rest of the furniture: large dark wooden cabinets, and in the middle of one of the shelves was another wooden cross – this one with a lifelike Jesus nailed to it, the agony clear on his face.

'Fuck me,' Briggs whispered, and Kate shushed him.

They could hear the dad coming back down the corridor and the jangle of tea cups, Mrs Wilcox his shadow. They both entered the room, a thin, pale boy following behind.

They sat down and looked at each other. Kate could feel Briggs shifting next to her, desperate for someone to speak.

Kate cleared her throat.

'We're here to talk to you about Lucy,' Kate began.

'Tea?' Mrs Wilcox said.

'No, thank you,' Kate replied. 'As I said before, she's missing and we're worried about her disappearance.'

'I'm sure she's at a friend's house,' Mrs Wilcox said with a laugh. 'Lucy was always like that, staying at friends' houses and not telling us where she was going. Sugar?' She offered a cup to Briggs and he took it, desperate for something to appease the woman.

'We don't think that's the case, Mrs Wilcox,' Kate persisted. 'She's been missing since Monday and there's no sign of where she might be.'

'Well, there's no use asking us,' Roger Wilcox cut in. 'We haven't seen her for at least ten years.' He took a cup of tea from his wife and stirred it, the spoon chinking loudly against the china. 'At least since she got together with that boyfriend.'

'Boyfriend?' Briggs asked, on alert.

'Scott something,' he said, and Briggs sat back, disappointed.

'He's her husband now,' Mrs Wilcox said softly. 'Officially, at least. We didn't go to the wedding, if you can call it that. Disgusting sacrilege.'

'Why do you say that?' Kate asked.

'A marriage isn't true unless it happens under the eyes of God, in the house of God.'

'They didn't get married in a church?' Kate said.

'No!' Roger Wilcox boomed. 'When we found out we told her what a disgrace she was to our family. We told her that she had to get married in front of the Lord, and when she refused . . .' He shook his head. 'And now she's disappeared. I told you, didn't I, Martha?' He looked to his wife and she nodded. 'I told you she would succumb to sin. Without the Lord as her guide, the Devil would infiltrate her mind and she would be cut down. Taken screaming to hell.'

He looked at Kate. '"Then, after desire has conceived",' he said, fixing his eyes on hers, '"it gives birth to sin; and sin, when it is full grown, gives birth to death". James, chapter one.'

'Do you think your daughter is dead?' Kate asked, firmly meeting his eye.

'Are you a child of God?' Roger Wilcox asked her. When Kate didn't reply, he turned to Briggs. 'Are you?' he asked.

'"Judge not, that ye be not judged",' Briggs said in response. 'Matthew, chapter seven.'

Roger Wilcox looked like he was ready to explode, and Kate interrupted them quickly.

'Do you know anything about your daughter's disappearance?' she asked.

'She's not my daughter any more. The day she indulged in sexual immorality with that man was the day she said goodbye to this family.'

Kate looked at the brother. He was standing in the doorway, watching the exchange. 'And have you heard from Lucy?' she said to him.

He looked at his parents, now staring at him. He shook his head. 'No, no I haven't, I'm sorry,' he almost whispered.

'Well, thank you for the tea,' Kate said, giving a long look to Briggs, who handed the untouched cup back to Martha. 'Please call us if you hear from Lucy. We'll be in touch.'

'Don't trouble yourselves,' Roger Wilcox replied.

The front door closed behind them and they hurried back to the car. They climbed in and shut the doors, Kate activating the central locking.

'Fuck me,' Briggs said again, his eyes wide. 'I'll never say a bad word about my parents ever again.'

'Can you imagine,' Kate said. 'Growing up in that house? And the boy still living there?'

The brother's face loomed next to Kate's, behind the glass, and she jumped. She opened the car window.

'I said you'd dropped your phone and I was giving it back to you,' he said, hurriedly. 'Drive to the end of the road. I'll meet you there in twenty minutes.'

He turned quickly and walked back into the house.

Kate looked at Briggs. 'Better do what the nice man said,' she replied.

Half an hour later the brother hadn't shown, and Kate was getting fidgety.

'Perhaps he was messing with us,' Briggs muttered, his hand hovering over the ignition.

'Wait.' Kate pointed, and sure enough the brother was loping down the pavement towards them. Kate went to get out but he gestured to the back of the car and Briggs opened the locks.

Kate turned in her seat to face him.

'This is very cloak-and-dagger,' she said.

'Yes, and I'm sorry. But my parents can't know I'm meeting you.'

'Why not?' Briggs asked.

'My parents are ...' He paused. 'Well, you met them. God is the most important thing in their lives. More so than their own children. They forbade me to meet with Lucy, but ...'

He went silent, and Kate exchanged a look with Briggs.

'Isaac,' she said, gently. 'Please tell us what you know. We're worried about Lucy.'

The boy frowned. 'We've always kept in touch. But we've been speaking more regularly recently.' He stared intently at his hands, unable to make eye contact with them. 'I needed her help.'

'You want to get away too,' Kate said.

'I do.' He looked like he was about to cry. 'I'm gay.'

'"Men shall not lie with a male as one lies with a female; it is an abomination",' Briggs said quietly.

Kate looked at him with surprise. 'Leviticus,' Briggs explained. 'Five years of Sunday school.'

'Exactly,' Isaac said, still fighting back tears. 'Lucy said she would help me the moment I turned eighteen. That's why I'm worried. She was supposed to call me on Monday night, we were going to make arrangements. I can't believe she would have forgotten me.'

'What do you think has happened?' Kate asked.

He shook his head. 'I don't know. She started saying some weird things when I spoke to her last, although she wouldn't say what she meant. She said, "They're lying, Isaac, they're lying to us".'

'*They*?' Kate asked. 'Not *him*? As in her husband, Scott?'

'Oh, I don't know. I thought she said *they* but saying that to you now, it makes no sense at all.' He rubbed his eyes again and looked at Kate. 'What am I going to do now, now she's gone?'

Kate went to answer, but Isaac pushed open the car door. The two of them watched him shuffle back down the road, his head bowed.

'Poor kid,' Briggs muttered. 'Do you think the parents have something to do with her disappearance?'

Kate watched him go, thinking about the conversation with the Wilcoxes, their house, the continued lack of evidence. 'I don't know, Jamie. I really don't.'

Briggs nodded, then pulled out his phone as it started to ring. He answered it and Kate watched him as he listened. After a moment he hung up and looked at her. 'That was Max,' Briggs said. 'He says the pathologist has finished the post-mortem of Douglas Brewer. But he'll only share the results with you.'

'Who's the pathologist?' Kate asked, but she already knew the answer.

'Dr Albie Adams,' Briggs replied.

17

'Katherine!' Dr Albie Adams greeted Kate wearing a mask, protective glasses and stained scrubs straining over his tubby belly. She took a step back from his open arms.

'I won't, if you don't mind,' she said, smiling.

'Fair enough. Especially as you have made an extra effort today. Is this for my benefit?' he asked, pulling off the mask and glasses, placing them next to the lump covered in a green sheet on the stainless steel table. He looked around the room and Kate pointed towards the top of his head, where his thick spectacles nestled in the mess of grey hair. He smiled at Kate and put them on.

She looked down at her smart suit, slightly embarrassed that he'd noticed. She'd even blow-dried her hair that morning. 'Press conference later,' Kate replied. 'Please don't get bodily fluids on me.' She tentatively leaned over to look at the cadaver. 'Is this Dougie Brewer?'

'The very same,' Albie said, removing part of the sheet with a flourish, revealing a bloated shoulder and arm. The flesh was a mottled white, a purple spiderweb of veins clearly visible under the opaque wrinkled skin.

Briggs made a funny noise behind her and Kate turned to look at him. His face was grey, his hand over his mouth. Even Kate had to admit, the smell in the lab wasn't great. A mixture of chemicals and metal, barely masking a dusty undertone of death. It reminded her of gone-off steak.

'What can you tell us about how he died?' Kate asked.

'A tricky one,' Albie said, prodding at the body with a gloved finger. 'Cold water immersion makes things difficult. Temperature, current, weather, your usual bugs, whether the body was submerged or floating on the top,' he said, ticking them off on his fingers. 'All makes a difference. Identifying a definitive cause of death is near impossible.'

'So what do you know?' Kate asked.

'We know he was found floating on the top of the lake, which would correspond nicely with the maggot infestation. Some loss of hair, some skin slippage,' Albie said, pulling the hand out from underneath the sheet and showing Kate where the skin had started to come away from the body.

Kate heard Briggs retching behind her, then the double doors slamming as he ran out of the room.

Kate and Albie watched him go without comment, then turned back to the body. They were used to the delicate sensibilities of others.

'Can you tell if he drowned?' Kate continued.

'There was substantial fluid and dirt in his nasal cavity and mouth, but that's common whether he drowned or not. But given the fact there was nothing in his lower respiratory tract, I would make the assertion he wasn't breathing when he went into the water.'

'So how did he die?'

Albie shrugged. 'Wouldn't like to say. No external injuries, no broken bones. Some damage to the backs of his feet, but that could have happened as the body moved around in the water.' He paused, looking at a piece of paper in the file. 'Blood tests show a blood alcohol level of 0.12 and the presence of THC, but nothing else of note.'

Kate nodded. Tetrahydrocannabinol, otherwise known as

the psychoactive component of cannabis. Not a surprise, given what they'd found in his flat. And a level of alcohol well over the legal limit.

'Was he a drug user?' Albie asked.

'Only cannabis, as you said.' Kate stopped, her interest piqued. 'Why?'

'Just that there was something odd. Two small holes, most likely injection sites. One on his thigh.' Albie adjusted his glasses and rearranged the green sheet, exposing part of the leg. He ran a gloved finger over the mottled skin towards a tiny hole, the sides puckered. 'Then one on the bicep, here.' He pointed towards the flabby upper arm.

Kate put a mask over her nose and mouth and leaned forward, as close to the body as she could bear. 'What would this indicate?' she asked.

'Hard to know for sure,' Albie said. 'Could be perfectly innocent. But your average drug user, as you know, would go for a vein – on the arm or foot.'

'So why would Dougie Brewer have two lone needle marks?' Kate asked, more to herself than to Albie. Odd places for them to be, and strange to be only two. She thought about the series of thefts in the area. 'Could you retest if we gave you the name of a specific drug?'

Albie nodded. 'Yes, if you can tell us what we're looking for. I have to say, unless you guys come up with something interesting, my best guess is we'll be looking at an open verdict.'

Kate sighed. That didn't help her much. 'Time of death?' she asked.

Albie pulled a face. 'No more than a week? Sorry, cold water slows down the usual decomposition, so I can't be more specific than that.'

Kate glanced at her watch. 'I'd better go,' she said. She needed to find whatever bin Briggs was vomiting in, she thought.

And it was nearly time for the dreaded press conference.

18

The room was big and bland. A large blue backdrop had been erected behind the generic wooden table running the width of the room. Max watched from the back as the scene played out, behind the press and the few members of the public who had turned up. Two monitors stood on either side of the room, showing a close-up of whoever was talking, a line of assorted microphones on the table picking up their speech.

DS Munro and DCI Delaney sat at the front behind the table, facing the room, to the right of Scott Barker. Kate looked hot and uncomfortable, body unnaturally straight. Max could tell she was trying hard to maintain a neutral expression – hiding her feelings was not one of her strong points. DCI Delaney was the opposite. Composed, calm and completely at home with the cameras, she was giving a quick summary.

'Thirty-one-year-old Lucy Barker was last seen on the morning of Monday the sixteenth of September by her husband. Since Monday evening, detectives have been searching her home and the surrounding areas, as well as her digital footprint for signs of where she might be.' She paused, taking a slow sip from the glass of water in front of her. 'We are exploring all possibilities, but would like to appeal to Lucy, and to members of the public who might know where she is, to get in touch via the hotline number.'

Max watched as the Freephone number flashed up on the screen, inwardly dreading the barrage of calls he knew they would have to field. It was the best way to get leads, but the sheer number of erroneous sightings was exhausting.

While DCI Delaney was speaking, Max looked over to Scott Barker. Scott was smart in a navy jacket, pale blue shirt and dark tie. His hair was neat, he was clean-shaven. He looked tired, but otherwise it could have been a normal day at work for the guy.

Max had done his best to prepare him for the press conference but Scott had been distracted, his gaze constantly shifting focus.

'Why do I have to do this?' he'd asked, and Max had been speechless. Normally, relatives were desperate to do anything to get their loved ones back home.

DCI Delaney handed over to Munro, who was summarising the facts of the case.

'There is a lot we don't know about Lucy Barker. We don't know what she was doing on the day of her disappearance, or even on the day before – Sunday the fifteenth of September. We don't know what she was wearing, but we do know she was not in her car, so she may have been picked up or taken public transport. Extensive police enquiries have been conducted by Hampshire Constabulary, but we are appealing to the public for any witnesses or dashcam footage, so if you were in the Romsey area that day, please think about whether you might have seen Lucy.'

Another large photo of Lucy flashed up on the screen. This was a photograph that Max hadn't seen before. She looked happy. Very different from the Lucy he had looked at on screen that morning.

The neighbours had come through with the CCTV

footage from their house, and Max had spent a dull morning before Scott arrived sifting through it. He was annoyed Briggs and Munro had gone to see the parents without him. This was *his* case; he'd been the one there at the beginning. It was sparse consolation that Briggs had returned from the morgue looking distinctly ill. Max had waved his sausage butty in his face.

'You're a wanker, Coop,' Briggs had muttered, before running off to be sick again.

'What have you found?' Kate had asked, smiling at Max. She looked nicer than usual today, obviously making an effort for the cameras. He was distracted for a second, before turning his attention back to the screen.

'Report from immigration,' he said. Max had followed up on Kate's hunch and she had indeed renewed her passport. But she hadn't gone anywhere. 'No one using Lucy's passport has gone through border control.'

Kate had frowned. 'And what's here?' she'd asked, pointing at the CCTV.

'Not much,' Max confessed. The neighbour's camera mainly covered their own driveway, but the gateway for the Barkers' house could be seen in the background. He scrolled through boring hours of nothing, before they finally saw Lucy's black Audi A1 move out through the gate. It was Sunday at 1.32 p.m. The car returned at 3.04 p.m., then nothing, until Scott Barker's blue A4 left on Monday at 7.45 a.m.

'Did anything happen after that?' Kate asked and Max shook his head. There had been no movement of Lucy's car all day Monday, and nobody entered or left the house until Scott Barker returned at 6.57 p.m.

'So we're confident it's not an abduction?' Kate asked, and Max agreed.

'I'd be surprised if someone had got her out with no evidence of foul play in the house, and without bringing a vehicle onto the property,' he confirmed.

Kate was still leaning over him, winding the CCTV footage on the screen backwards and forwards. Her hair was loose for a change, falling around her shoulders, and as she moved, he noticed her perfume. Surprisingly delicate and feminine.

The fragrance brought back memories of that night. *That* Christmas party. He'd known Kate from around the station, but hadn't spoken to her before. She'd appeared behind him at the bar, all tousled hair, dark eyes, laughing. Fun. She'd insisted he do shots with her, and who was he to say no? The night had blurred, he remembered them kissing, then her breathlessly saying no, we mustn't, not here. He'd backed away, but she had dragged him to a disused cupboard full of boxes and pulled him to her, kissing him again. Then ... Well. He hadn't been expecting the evening to end like that.

But end it had. The next day she'd ignored him. He'd wondered if she'd even remembered, but the glow in her cheeks and her slightly rude demeanour indicated she had. He would have liked something more. She had a ferocity about her that appealed to him. The way she attacked every situation head-on, sod the ramifications. It was a pity she got back with her husband, Max thought, he'd have liked to get to know her better.

And now he would. Max turned his attention back to Kate at the press conference. Now he was working with her. Working *for* her, to be exact. He had noticed her trying to keep her distance from him, taking Briggs to interviews, their conversation resolutely professional. Abruptly so.

Kate was getting to the end of her statement, and Max sat up and listened.

'It has been an agonising few days for Lucy's family,' she said, 'and we would like to hand over now to Scott Barker, Lucy's husband.'

Kate looked over at Scott and gave him a reassuring nod. Scott cleared his throat and looked up from his piece of paper, directly into the cameras.

'Lucy, please come home,' he started. His voice was clear, his tone steady. Max knew he was probably used to speaking to large groups of people at work, so was more equipped than most to manage a press conference, but he wished Scott didn't sound quite so calm. 'I miss you. I love you. If something has happened, then we can fix it, but please come home.'

Max scanned the crowd watching. He could see them fidgeting, whispering to each other, and he didn't have to hear to know what they were saying. Scott Barker was hardly the distraught husband the public and press were expecting. In the crowd, Max could see Jen Lewis, Lucy's best friend. Her gaze was transfixed on Scott, her mouth turned upwards in a slight smile. What was with this lot? he wondered. Why wasn't someone upset that Lucy Barker was missing?

'I would like to thank the Hampshire Police and our friends and family for their support at this difficult time,' Scott continued, and Max flinched at his standardised speech. 'Everyone out there – please keep posting on social media, please keep Lucy in everyone's minds, so that we can find her safe and well soon.'

Scott stopped and folded the piece of paper in front of

him in two. Kate looked back into the camera. 'Are there any questions?' she asked.

A few hands went up. Kate pointed towards one of the journalists at the front.

'Do you have any reason to believe this might be more than a missing persons investigation?'

Max knew what he was getting at. *Do you think Lucy is dead?*

'We are pursuing all lines of enquiry,' Kate said. 'But as yet, we have no reason to believe that Lucy isn't currently alive and well.'

Except the fact that we have no bloody idea where she is and her husband looks shifty as hell, Max thought.

'Mr Barker,' another member of the press asked. 'Can you tell us about your marriage?'

Scott looked up quickly. 'What do you want to know?' he replied, his voice hostile.

Max winced. Rein it in, mate.

'Were you happy? How long have you been married, that sort of thing?' the journalist replied.

'We've been married for seven years, together for twelve. And yes, we were happy. We had our disagreements, like any couple, but we were solid.' Scott paused and rubbed his eyes, showing the first bit of emotion Max had seen all day. 'I honestly believed we were a team, that we could deal with anything life threw at us.'

'And now?'

'What do you mean?'

'You said "believed". Like it's past tense,' the journalist said.

So they've picked up on that, too, Max thought, worried. Scott stopped for a moment, gathering himself. 'I still believe we can fix anything that might have happened. I just want Lucy to come home.'

Kate fielded a few more questions, all of them banal, Kate's answers unhelpful. They couldn't tell the press what they didn't know, and they didn't know much. DCI Delaney thanked the journalists and the public and drew the conference to an end.

Max looked over at Briggs, slumped next to him.

'They're going to crucify him,' Briggs muttered.

Max nodded, turning his attention back to the table. Scott Barker was motionless, his gaze fixed on the piece of paper in front of him. Briggs was right. The message about Lucy's disappearance was going to get out there and they might get some good leads, but in the eyes of the press there was one outcome, and one outcome alone.

Lucy Barker was dead, and Scott Barker was responsible.

19

Max waited with Briggs as the room emptied, the air abuzz with conversation among the press. Through the crowd, he saw Jen Lewis watching Scott, deep in thought.

His phone rang, and he answered it.

'Coop? It's Greg, from the digital lab. I've finished looking at that phone you sent me.'

Max's senses prickled. These guys were most at home in the dark, with only the glow from a monitor to keep them company. Something must be important for them to risk actual human contact.

'Did you find something?' Max asked. 'I thought it was wiped?'

The techie scoffed at the end of the line. 'Nothing's ever deleted, Coop. It's always in the memory somewhere, you just need to know how to find it. Sending you the report now,' he said. 'Web history, call log, all the usual. But I saw your press conference, then checked the system, and I thought you should know something.' He paused and Max could hear tapping on the keyboard.

'Your misper was reported on a 999 call at 21.36, right?'

'Right,' Max said slowly.

'Well, this phone was wiped at 21.32.'

Max stopped listening and turned to look at Scott Barker.

'Coop? You there?' Greg said. 'That doesn't make sense, does it?'

'No, no, it doesn't. Thanks, Greg,' Max said and ended the call.

'Who was that?' Briggs asked.

'Digital lab. Lucy's mobile was wiped just minutes before Scott Barker made the 999 call,' Max said, slowly.

'That cheeky fuck,' Briggs said. The two of them looked over to the table where Scott was now talking to Munro. 'What hasn't he lied about?'

'More to the point,' Max said, 'what's he trying to hide?'

'PC Cooper, isn't it?' A voice at his side broke into their conversation. It was Jen Lewis. 'Can we talk?' she asked. 'Quickly?'

Max introduced her to Briggs and the three of them moved away to a quieter corner. Jen Lewis seemed nervous, twirling one of her curls in her fingers.

'The thing is,' she began, 'I'm not sure I was entirely truthful the other day.'

'Go on,' Max said, warily. It was turning into one of those days.

'Well, I didn't lie as such. I assumed you probably knew already, and then I thought you might not, so I should tell you.'

Max waited. He could feel Briggs next to him, shifting his weight from foot to foot in exasperation.

'So, the last year we were at university there was a big fire, and the medical centre burned down. All their records, gone. They were paper-based, you see.' Jen frowned. 'So you probably don't know.'

'About what?' Max asked, starting to lose patience.

'Lucy and Scott had started going out. And she was happy. At least, she said she was. But then they slept together and Lucy was a mess. She kept crying, saying she didn't know what to believe, that she could never be forgiven for having sex before marriage. I said before that she'd grown up religious? Well, I think she just couldn't deal with what she'd done.'

Jen stopped, glancing towards the front of the room. Max followed her gaze and made eye contact with Scott Barker, who looked away quickly.

'Scott found her in the bath,' she said, her voice husky with emotion. 'Lucy tried to kill herself.'

20

The calls came in thick and fast. The team worked hard to keep up, painstakingly recording each one. Kate, Briggs and Max went through all of them, taking responses where they could and following up on the ones that looked promising.

They were all tired. Sugar and caffeine had been keeping them going for the majority of the day but dark had fallen and the artificial stimulants had worn off. Kate wanted to go home. She felt grubby, her eyes gritty.

'Fifteen minutes, then we go,' she said to the room. It was 7.45 p.m. It had been a long day.

Max and Briggs had filled her in on their discovery about Scott Barker wiping the mobile phone, as well as Jen Lewis's confession that Lucy tried to kill herself twelve years ago. This misper case was getting weirder and weirder. So they had doubts about the husband, but also about Lucy's mental stability. Had she killed herself and Scott covered it up? But if so, why? What would be the point?

Kate debated whether to bring Scott Barker in for questioning. But what did they have on him? No definitive proof, no motive. And, as yet, they weren't any clearer as to where Lucy was. They'd wait a bit longer. He wasn't going anywhere, after all.

Kate had spent some time online looking at the responses from the public. They weren't being kind. They'd shared the video of the conference on Facebook and Twitter along with the press release, and the general feeling was clear. Robotic. Cold. Murderer. And those were the kind ones. The judgement was that Scott had done her in, and it was just a matter of time until they found her body.

'I've got a good one,' Briggs called from across the room, holding up the phone receiver.

'Jamie,' Kate warned. 'I'm not in the mood.'

Briggs had been fielding the crazies all afternoon. The people who said Lucy had been abducted by aliens and they could prove it. The attention-seekers who claimed she'd been at their house on Monday, even though they lived in Cardiff and had never met her before. They'd even had a psychic who said Lucy had contacted her from the dead.

Through her years in the police force, Kate had learnt many things about the well-intentioned general public. She knew that the people who needed your help apologised for wasting your time, while those who wasted your time complained that no one was helping them. And the statement 'no such thing as a stupid question'? Blatantly not true.

'No, an actual good one,' he said, and Kate looked up, interested. 'She works in the Costa in Chandler's Ford and Lucy was in there on Sunday. She was with a man.' Briggs smiled.

Kate jumped up and snatched the phone out of Briggs's hand. Max looked over with interest.

'This is DS Munro. You saw Lucy on Sunday?'

'Yes, yes, I think I did.' The voice on the end of the line was young and softly spoken. 'She was with a bloke, except it wasn't that guy on the TV today.'

'What time was this?'

'It was about two p.m.' That would fit with the timings on the CCTV, Kate thought. 'They didn't stay for long, about half an hour or so, I think.' The girl paused. 'I remember them because the woman was crying, and also ...'

'Also, what?'

'The bloke was well fit.'

Kate smiled at the description. 'What did he look like?'

'Tall, big, longish hair. Muscles. Dark.' The girl hesitated. 'I couldn't work out why she was crying. I wouldn't have been crying if I'd been with that bloke.'

'You've been very helpful. Can you come into the station ...' Kate started, but the girl cut her off.

'I can show you if you like. We have cameras.'

Half an hour later, Kate and Max were in the coffee shop, crowding around the tiny CCTV screen. The girl was right: the man was certainly big – even from this perspective Kate could make out the size of his shoulders, the muscles underneath his clothes.

Lucy Barker looked tiny in comparison. They were at a table at the back of the coffee shop, mugs in front of them, alternating taking spoonfuls from a slice of cake. Sharing, Kate thought. You don't share cake with a man you've just met. You share with friends. With lovers.

Halfway through, Lucy leaned forward and started to cry. The man handed her a tissue and laid a large hand on her arm.

'And you don't know who he is?' Max asked the girl.

She shook her head and looked behind her to where her manager was hovering.

The manager squinted at the screen. 'No, I would have remembered. He's not the sort of guy you forget.'

'No,' Kate agreed. But something about him didn't sit right. Where Lucy was smart and well groomed, her blonde hair tidy and clean, this bloke seemed rough. Even on the tiny screen Kate could see he was wearing ripped jeans, large work boots and a dirty jacket.

'Do you know how they paid?' Kate asked, and the manager looked up the details on her till.

'You're out of luck, they must have paid in cash.'

Kate turned back to the screen and watched as Lucy Barker and the man gathered their things then moved out of shot.

'Do you have another camera?' Kate asked.

'Only this one, on the till,' the manager said, switching perspectives and picking a file in line with the right time-stamp.

On the screen, customers lined up, each one ordering their coffees, until at last the figure of Lucy Barker pushed by and left, followed closely by the man. The view was rubbish, but at the edge of the shot Kate could see them embrace outside the door, then go in opposite directions.

'No kiss,' Max remarked, articulating what Kate was thinking.

'First thing tomorrow, see if you can find any additional CCTV footage from the area,' Kate said to Max. 'Let's see if we can track where Lucy went from there.'

Max nodded, then a final movement on the video caught Kate's eye. 'Wait!' she said to the manager. 'Go back a bit.'

They watched Lucy and the man hug again, then seconds later the door to a truck opened, the man climbed in and the vehicle edged forward out of the parking space. Kate could make out some of the lettering on the side of the truck.

SHERWOOD TREE SU, it said.

Quickly, Kate typed it into Google on her phone.

A range of options came up, none of them helpful.

'Tree surgeon?' Max suggested, and Kate tried again. This time the search was more forthcoming.

Kate clicked on the link and a professional-looking website came into view. Shots of pretty green trees, with testimonials and quotes along the bottom. And videos. Kate clicked on one and watched, Max standing behind her.

On the screen, a well-built man in a helmet and with a chainsaw carefully took branches off a tree. Large pieces of wood fell in slow motion.

'That's our man,' Kate said, the shot paused on his face. 'Alex Sherwood.'

'Change of plan?' Max asked.

'Yep,' Kate said. 'Let's get this guy in for questioning.'

21

Up close, Alex Sherwood was no less impressive. The uniforms had collected him without a hitch and Kate and Max now sat opposite him in the interview room, his manner calm, tall frame almost poured into a chair comically too small for him.

You couldn't have found a man more opposite to Scott Barker. Where Scott was uptight and pinched, Alex was relaxed. Where Scott was wiry, Alex was huge.

'I didn't know Lucy was missing,' Alex Sherwood told Kate once she'd finished the standard warnings for his voluntary interview, waiving his right to legal counsel.

'You expect us to believe that you didn't know your friend had disappeared, although her face has been all over the news?'

He scowled. 'I don't have a television,' he replied. 'I don't read the papers.'

Kate read from the file in front of her.

'Voluntary interviews for criminal damage and trespassing, warnings for unlicensed use of a firearm. The list goes on, Mr Sherwood.' Kate looked up. 'What surprises me is you've never been arrested.'

He shrugged. The movement was languid and carefree, despite the fact that he was trapped in a police interview room. 'Just trying to live my life.'

'Which entails?'

'Being out in the woods, surviving off the land, foraging. Trying not to make an impact on the environment.'

'Well, it seems like the law doesn't agree,' Kate muttered. She pointed to his front. 'What's with the otters?'

Alex was wearing a large black sweatshirt that said *Ringwood Otter Sanctuary* across his chest, cut-off shorts to his knees and hiking socks. The absence of the large muddy boots, currently residing outside the interview room, as insisted on by him, lent him a slight air of vulnerability, at odds to the rest of his physicality. It was obvious to Kate what Lucy saw in him. In fact, if they weren't having an affair, Kate would be disappointed.

'I work there,' he said. 'Tuesdays and Wednesdays. Feeding, cleaning, doing talks, that sort of thing.'

'I thought you were a tree surgeon?' Kate said.

He nodded. 'I am. But I like the otters. They have a strong social hierarchy, fierce family bonds. They're good to hang out with, better than humans.'

Kate paused and looked to Max, who opened his eyes wide at the revelation. She took a breath and regained her focus. 'So how do you know Lucy Barker?'

'We met at the firing range.'

'And this was?'

'About a year ago.'

Kate waited, meeting Alex's stare with her own. He rolled his eyes, then tilted back in his chair.

'Lucy wanted to own a gun, and as you must know the only way you can do that in this country is to join a gun club.' He spoke in a monotone, clearly bored at having to explain these basics to Kate. 'You have to go at least twelve times, show your commitment for six months, then have all your usual police checks.' He sighed. 'Look at your records, you must have this on file.'

'We do,' Max said, speaking for the first time. 'We're just interested in hearing it from you.'

'So I'd see Lucy there every Tuesday. And I know she got her licence because she bought a few guns. A bolt-action two-two and a semi-automatic handgun.'

'Do you know why she wanted to own a gun?' Kate asked.

'Same reason most of us do, I guess.'

'And that is?'

He smiled. 'To shoot stuff.'

Kate was tiring of Alex's attitude. This guy was too used to speaking to the police and he was beginning to get on her nerves.

'Was there more between you than just gun club buddies?' she asked.

Alex shook his head. 'No. She's married.'

'Are you sure?' Kate pushed. 'Do you meet other friends from your gun club on a Sunday for a cosy coffee?'

Alex frowned. 'No, I don't.'

'So why did you meet Lucy?'

'She called, out of the blue. She said she needed someone to talk to. I didn't want to go, I don't like going into town, to places like Costa, but she sounded desperate, so I met her.'

'And what did you talk about?'

Alex paused, his mouth hardening, seemingly reluctant to share.

'Mr Sherwood,' Kate said, leaning towards him over the table. 'Lucy's been missing for three days now. I don't have to tell you this, but things aren't looking good. We need you to help us find her, one way or another.'

He frowned, pushing his fingers together into a steeple, then laying them flat on the table.

'Look at her husband,' he muttered.

'At Scott Barker?' Kate asked, sitting forward in her seat. 'Why?'

'She's told me about him, shown me photos. He's this *perfect* guy,' Alex said, showing some emotion for the first time. His eyes were narrowed, his jaw clenched. 'Proper career, nice suits, white shiny grin. More money than he knows what to do with. But he's not so bloody wonderful. I'd never seen Lucy so upset. It took a while to get it out of her.'

'And what did she say?' Max asked.

'Her wonderful husband, Scott Barker, has been having an affair.' Alex looked at them both, his gaze shifting from Kate to Max then back again. 'With her best friend.'

Thursday

22

Scott stood in the middle of his bedroom. The bed was made, corners and pillows smoothed down precisely. The one book on his bedside table was placed perfectly in line with the table's corners, his reading glasses resting on top. All clothes were put away in the tall floor-to-ceiling wardrobes, and he knew that if he opened the doors he would see everything grouped together, like with like, all the hangers facing the same way.

Order. Control. How he liked his life. But it couldn't help him now.

His wife was still missing. He wanted her home, back with him. If he could just undo the past, not have the argument, not have her discover the photos of Jen. If he could not have had the affair in the first place ... how different things might be now.

But Lucy had secrets, too. The air-raid shelter, filled to the brim with bizarre provisions. The guns. What else was she hiding?

Scott turned his attention to Lucy's bedside table and pulled the drawer open. There were all the things he expected: earplugs, a few pens, a pack of tissues, two books he remembered her reading a few months ago, and some old membership cards from Lucy's student days. He picked one up and looked at the photo. It was a bad passport-style picture, but he smiled at the bright red lipstick and her young features. She looked so carefree, so innocent, when Scott knew, just months before, she'd tried to kill herself.

It had been his fault. He knew her family was religious but he hadn't realised how internalised that brainwashing was. And she'd said yes to sleeping with him – they loved each other, so how wrong could it be?

Wrong enough to make her run a bath in their shared house. Wrong enough to climb into the water and put a razor to her wrist and push. She'd even done it the right way, taking the blade down the length of her arm. But she hadn't locked the door and he'd come back early, finding her within minutes in the bright red water.

Since that day he'd wondered what would have happened if his lecture hadn't been cancelled. What if she'd locked the door? Perhaps, subconsciously, she'd wanted someone to stop her. And he hadn't understood – wasn't suicide a mortal sin, too? But perhaps if you were going to hell, you might as well find out the bad news sooner rather than later.

The police at the time had been less than sympathetic towards him. His girlfriend had tried to kill herself and what did he get from them? Judgement. Blame. Was it any surprise he didn't trust them now?

Lucy had gone to counselling. She'd finished her degree and she'd put it all behind her. Or had she? When was the last time he'd seen her smile, Scott wondered? Even before she'd found the photos of Jen on his phone, she'd been stressed. What had she been so worried about?

He remembered her talking about something: ranting about the environment, or climate change, or ... what? Scott really couldn't remember, he just hadn't been listening. He'd been busy at work lately, he'd been distracted. But whatever excuse he tried to give himself, it didn't make him feel any better.

He put everything back in the drawer, then continued his search, pulling her wardrobe doors open and looking at her clothes. He pulled a jumper out and as he did so, he caught a waft of her smell. A mixture of her shampoo and her perfume, and it took him unawares, knocking him to his knees. A wave of loss hit him and he crumpled, balling the jumper up in his hands and pushing his face into it. He longed to hear her voice, to feel her back in his arms, and he started to cry, the tears coming in great racking sobs.

He couldn't go on feeling like this. This mess of guilt and worry and fear. He just wanted his wife back. He needed to go to the police and come clean about what he knew. But could he be that strong, when everything inside him just wanted to curl up tight on the floor?

As if answering his question, Scott heard a loud knock. He looked out of the window. Outside, two cars were parked on the driveway – an old white Ford Focus and a formal yellow and blue patrol car.

Scott heard the bang again. This was it.

He walked down to answer the front door.

23

Kate looked up at the windows of the house.

'Do you think he's in?' Max asked. 'His car's here.'

Kate nodded. 'He's in.' She banged on the door again, and more lights started to come on in the house – first in the bedroom above them, then in the hallway as Scott came towards the front door.

He opened it and Kate blinked at his appearance. His clothes were rumpled, his hair uncombed and he looked like he had been crying. For the first time, Scott Barker resembled a husband whose wife was missing.

'Scott, we need you to come with us.'

'Have you found Lucy?'

Kate shook her head. 'Sorry, no, but some new information has come to light. Scott Barker, I am arresting you on suspicion of the murder of Lucy Barker. You do not have to say anything, but it may harm your defence if you do not mention when questioned something you later rely on in court. Anything you do say may be given as evidence. Do you understand?'

Scott looked at them, his face miserable. He nodded silently.

Max followed Scott into the house while he put his shoes on, then escorted him to the uniformed officers waiting by their car. He went without a word, and the two of them watched the patrol car drive away.

'Let's have a look at this house, then,' Kate said, and Max showed her inside.

Kate knew that since Max had been there last the house and grounds had been thoroughly searched for blood and anything else that might point to the whereabouts of Lucy Barker. Max wordlessly showed Kate to the garden, to the unlocked air-raid shelter and the strange collected provisions, to the empty gun safe.

'Do we know where the firearms are now?'

Max shook his head. 'Jamie followed up with the gun club – apparently they're not stored there.'

'We'll need to get a statement.' Kate stopped in the garden and looked at Max. 'Did he shoot her and bury them all together?'

'If he did, they're not in this garden – they've been over it with metal detectors and dogs and they've found nothing.'

Max's phone rang and he pulled it out of his pocket, looking at the screen. 'Sorry, let me just answer this.' He turned away from Kate, then held the phone up to his ear. She started walking back to the house, catching the edge of his conversation.

'What is it, Charlie?' he asked abruptly. 'I'm working.'

Kate frowned, shutting the door behind her as she went back into the house. So Max did have a life outside of the police station. Why had she been so daft to think he didn't? Questions started to chatter in Kate's head. Charlie could be a girlfriend, or a son, or even a boyfriend. Kate wondered how long they'd been together. Had he cheated on them with Kate that Christmas? Was Max the sort of guy to be unfaithful? But why did it matter? And, more importantly, why did it matter to her?

She peered out of the window, watching Max wander

round the garden, talking on the phone. He was still in uniform and for that, she was glad. It helped her remember that he was a colleague, a direct report, not anything else.

Her phone rang. She looked away from Max and answered it.

'Boss? I've finished going through the CCTV.'

Kate had left Briggs with the undesirable task of tracing Lucy's steps back from the Costa on Sunday. 'And?' she asked, desperate for something else on Barker. She knew the evidence was weak to arrest him, but she had wanted to go ahead. It was the right time to get him in for a formal interview – to up the stakes and see how he responded.

'Nothing interesting,' Briggs said, and Kate sighed. 'Cameras show her leaving Fryern Arcade in Chandler's Ford in her black A1, then heading up Hursley Road and back towards Romsey. We pick her up again by the Potters Heron pub. And as you know, the car is at the house.'

'I'm looking at it now,' Kate said dejectedly, walking into the kitchen and staring out at the black Audi parked next to Scott's matching blue A4 in the driveway.

'But there's something else,' Briggs said. 'We've got the financials back.'

'Yes?' Kate asked. She continued to look out of the kitchen window. In the road a large tanker was reversing, rhythmic beeping disturbing the silence.

'There's the usual stuff on the joint account.' Briggs paused for a moment and Kate could hear the rustling of paper. 'But when you start to look more closely...'

Kate watched the tanker while Briggs explained what he'd found. The driver of the lorry was wrestling with various pipes and machinery, completely blocking their exit to the main road.

'Great work, Jamie,' Kate said, once Briggs had finished. 'We're heading back. Get everything ready to interview Scott Barker once he's booked in.'

Kate hung up the phone. Max came back inside and Kate pointed at the tanker.

'What's that all about?' she said.

He squinted towards the truck. 'Emptying the septic tank next door, I expect,' he replied, then looked at Kate with his mouth open.

She stopped and turned back to the driveway.

'Are you thinking what I'm thinking?' Max said slowly.

'This house doesn't have mains drainage. There's a septic tank under this property,' Kate whispered.

Then Max said it for her. 'And what better place to hide a dead body?'

24

Kate walked into the interview room and slowly closed the door behind her. Scott Barker looked up, his eyes red-rimmed, his body hunched.

Max was already waiting at the table opposite him. Kate sat down and he pushed the file across to her. She opened it and looked at the two pieces of paper inside: a list of numbers in two columns.

'Mr Barker,' she began, and he looked up.

'I didn't kill my wife,' Scott interrupted.

Kate said nothing. 'Mr Barker,' she repeated. 'We've discovered some new information and we want answers. Honest answers.' She paused. 'I believe PC Cooper has read you your rights?'

Scott nodded.

'And you've turned down free legal counsel?'

'Yes.' He met her eyes. 'What do you want to know?'

'What is your relationship with Jen Lewis?' Kate said.

Scott looked back to the table. 'We had an affair,' he mumbled.

Kate closed her eyes with relief. At last. The truth. 'And when was this?' she asked.

He put a well-manicured nail into his mouth and chewed on it for a second. 'About a year ago.'

'And how long were you and Jen Lewis having an affair?'

'About six months. But I ended it, it was a huge mistake. I don't even know why it started.'

'How did it start?' Kate asked. Her tone was soft, her voice measured. She didn't want to get his guard up at this stage.

Scott shook his head. 'Lucy was away for work, and Jen came over out of the blue. She said she had arranged to meet Lucy, but I don't know ...' Scott looked away and stared at the blank magnolia wall.

'You think she planned to get you alone?'

'Maybe, I ... I don't know. We were drinking.' He laughed, short and sharp. 'It always starts with alcohol, doesn't it?' He shook his head again. 'Whatever, we ended up sleeping together. I regretted it straight away.'

'So why did it carry on for six months?'

'I don't know ...' Kate stayed silent, waiting for him to speak. 'I do know.' Scott's mouth was turned down. He looked like a beaten man, someone so racked with guilt he would tell her everything just to get it off his chest. 'She was so different to Lucy. In bed. Lucy was very sweet, very innocent. She had a closeted upbringing. You've met her parents,' he said, his voice angry, and Kate nodded. 'She was taught that sex was a sin, that it was all bad, all awful, and I guess she never forgot that. So sex with her was ...' He stopped again, his cheeks colouring. 'Very vanilla.'

'What do you mean?' Max asked, and Kate threw him a look.

'Always with the lights off. Always missionary. Nothing God might frown on.' Scott said the last few words bitterly. 'Jen was different. She would have sex anywhere, any time, any position. I was enjoying myself. I was trying things I had only dreamt of. Constant fucking.' He said it all quickly in a rush of words, then stopped himself, his face flushed.

Kate raised her eyebrows at the detail but said nothing. She could make a fairly educated guess at what a red-blooded man might have been up to. After a pause, she prompted, 'So why did you end it?'

'Because I was married to Lucy!' Scott blurted out. 'And Jen was Lucy's best friend. Christ knows why Jen didn't care about that, but I couldn't stand it, so I ended it before Lucy found out. I loved her!'

Past tense again, Kate noted. 'So how did Lucy find out?' she asked, and Scott let out a long breath.

'She found some photos of Jen. Dodgy photos, you know? That Jen had sent me. They were on my phone. I thought I had deleted them, but obviously not.' Scott put his head in his hands. 'I tried to explain, I tried to tell her that it was over, but... I don't know.'

'And this was Sunday?'

'Yes. She slept in the spare room. The next morning I went to work. I didn't see her Monday morning.'

'So you lied,' Kate said. 'Again. So the last time anyone saw Lucy was Sunday night?'

'Yes,' Scott said, his body hunched, his gaze fixed on the tabletop.

'And you didn't think it worth mentioning that Lucy had tried to commit suicide in the past?'

'She hasn't killed herself,' Scott muttered. 'She wouldn't...'

'How do you know, Scott?' Kate pushed. 'How do you know?'

He shook his head, still staring downwards. Mute.

What was it with this guy? Kate thought. If he really was innocent, he was doing a shitty job of convincing them.

'And why did you wipe Lucy's phone?' she continued,

when Scott stayed silent. They didn't know this for sure, but Kate wanted to see how he'd react.

He looked up quickly, then back down at his hands. It seemed she was right. 'I was scared. I didn't know what was on there. I didn't want the police finding out about me and Jen. I didn't want—' He stopped and gestured around the interview room, 'this happening. Guess it doesn't matter now.'

Kate nodded. 'Thank you for being so honest, Mr Barker.'

'Did you manage to find Lucy's friend, Alex? The one from book club?' Scott asked, and Kate nodded. 'Who is she?'

'He,' Kate corrected. 'And not from book club. From the firing range. He met Lucy on the Sunday before she disappeared.'

'Oh. Of course.' Scott's face fell. 'Was she sleeping with him?'

'We don't know, Mr Barker,' Kate said. If Kate wasn't so pissed at Scott for being such a bastard, she might actually have felt sympathetic towards him.

She paused for a moment, then took the sheet of paper out of the folder and pushed it towards Scott. He looked up, surprised, then pulled it towards him, his eyes running over the list of numbers.

'What's this?' He ran his finger down the list. 'This is our joint bank account.' He stared at Kate.

'It is. You gave us permission to access it when Lucy first went missing,' Kate said. 'Have you reviewed it lately?'

Scott shook his head. 'Lucy deals with all our bank stuff.' He looked at the piece of paper again. 'What are these numbers here?' he asked, pointing to the transactions highlighted in yellow.

'We were hoping you could tell us that,' Kate said. She knew full well what they were. Briggs had painstakingly reviewed the bank footage to find the cameras from the ATMs, watching the video as Lucy took out two hundred pounds in cash every few days over the course of four months. Scott ran his finger down the list and Kate guessed he was adding up the amounts.

'Do you know why your wife was taking money out, Mr Barker?' she asked. 'Do you know what she planned to do with over six grand in cash?'

Scott looked up, startled. 'No, no, I don't. Six grand?'

'And you didn't notice the money going?'

'No, no, I said, Lucy deals with the money. I don't look at it at all. What does this mean?'

'You tell me, Mr Barker.' Kate sat back in her chair and looked at him.

He shook his head, an expression of bewilderment on his face.

'Well, here's what we do know,' Kate said. 'We know your marriage wasn't happy. We know you were cheating on your wife with her best friend. We know Lucy was taking out large amounts of cash and we know she renewed her passport a few months ago. We also know that Lucy went out of her way to get a licence to own a gun and had a history of mental instability. What does that tell you, Mr Barker?'

He didn't reply, closing his eyes and turning his face to the table.

'To me,' Kate carried on, staring at Scott Barker, 'that looks like a desperate woman. It looks like a wife about to leave her husband. Except where did she go? Her car is still in the driveway, her purse and credit cards and mobile phone – which you wiped – left at home. So, here's what we think happened.'

Scott shook his head again, starting to cry softly.

'You argued. She told you she was leaving and you weren't having it. You couldn't have someone ruin your perfect life, could you, Scott? You lost your temper. And, in a fit of rage, you killed her.'

Scott looked at Kate, his mouth open and closing wordlessly.

'Maybe you didn't mean to,' Kate carried on. 'Or maybe you did. Maybe you liked fucking your wife's best friend up the arse, and saw an opportunity to do it on a more regular basis without your wife divorcing you and taking your money like you knew she'd been doing already.' Kate was getting into her stride now, maybe going a bit over the top, but she was angry with this potentially wife-killing adulterer and wanted to get under his skin. 'Either way, you killed her and you needed to get rid of the body. So when that lorry at your house right now drains your septic tank, what do you think we'll find, Scott?'

She stopped and looked at Scott Barker. He was shaking his head, over and over again, sobbing into his hands, his head bent low over the table.

Kate took a deep breath, steadying herself. 'Think about it, Mr Barker. This is your one opportunity to talk to us. It will be easier for everyone if you come clean and tell us what happened.'

Scott shook his head again. 'No comment,' he whispered.

She paused, then stood up and gestured for Max to follow her out of the room. A uniform went in to wait with Scott and she closed the door behind them, to where Briggs stood waiting in the corridor. Kate motioned for them to move out of earshot.

'Wow,' Max muttered. 'You went down hard on the man.'

'Do you think it was a bit much?' Kate asked.

'I think the line about fucking her best friend up the arse went a bit far, but who am I to judge?'

Briggs turned wide-eyed. 'You said what?' he asked incredulously.

Kate looked sheepish. 'I was on a roll. Maybe I overdid it. But it will be interesting to see what he says now.'

Briggs shook his head in disbelief. 'Anyway, the chief wants to see you,' he said.

'Did she say what about?' Kate asked.

'Nope, but walls have ears, Sarge. Perhaps she didn't like the comment about the anal.'

25

'Chief?'

The door to the office was open so Kate poked her head round. Her DCI was sat behind the desk on the phone but waved Kate in with two fingers and gestured to the chair in front of her. Kate perched on the edge, nervously clenching and unclenching her hands.

Kate knew she had overdone it in the interview with Scott Barker. But she hated cheaters; she hated the duplicity of it, the lying to someone you supposedly loved. She hated it to the point that it was the reason she and Sam had broken up last time. Not an actual affair on his part, but her reaction when she thought there might be. Fuelled by too much drinking and paranoia, she hadn't believed Sam when he said nothing was going on between him and various work colleagues, searching his phone, checking his emails and breaking all trust between them.

She remembered their final argument. 'I can't prove that nothing's going on,' Sam had shouted. He'd held out his mobile to her. 'Do you want to call them? Every woman I've ever worked with? Do your detective thing you're so proud of and interrogate them one by one?'

Kate had shaken her head. He was right. She'd found nothing. And after moving out, their marriage was only saved a year later when she finally admitted she had been in the wrong. It had been one of the worst years of her life.

Miserable and rejected, she'd drunk too much, lost control and made mistakes. Her and Sam getting back together was the second chance she'd wanted with every fibre of her being.

In front of her, DCI Delaney ended the call.

'Sorry,' she said with a smile. 'Bureaucratic crap.' She stopped and fixed her gaze on Kate. Kate felt a bead of sweat run down her back.

'So. How's the new team going?'

'Good, thank you.'

'Max Cooper working out? Did you know him before?'

Kate squirmed inside. 'Only in passing.' Yeah, passing bodily fluids, her brain shouted. She felt her face colour. 'He seems a good copper. Has a good rapport with the husband.'

'And you've arrested Scott Barker for the murder, is that right?' DCI Delaney asked and Kate nodded, glad to talk about the case.

'He's confessed to the affair but nothing about the wife yet,' Kate said. 'Though I think given time and a bit more pushing he might tell us what happened.'

The DCI seemed pleased. 'Well, we have a new opportunity, so you may need to leave Cooper in charge of him for a bit. We've had a tip-off about your Borderland Family and time is of the essence.'

Kate sat up in her chair. 'A tip-off about what?'

'An anonymous caller phoned, with concerns about the firearms kept at the residence belonging to the Family. They listed a few weapons and we have no record of them. We traced the call and it came from within the house itself, so it seems legit. And, given your desperation to have a poke around, we thought it would be a good opening.'

'Absolutely, when?' Kate asked, keen to get going.

'We've set up a response team. The ARV is standing by for this afternoon.'

Kate looked up at the clock – it was eleven now. 'Go and get changed, and take Briggs with you. Get what you can.' The DCI looked at her sternly. 'And make it legal, DS Munro.'

Two hours later, Kate and Briggs waited in the van. They were surrounded by the armed response team: large burly uniformed guys, blessed with an abundance of muscles and hair gel, in black stab vests and helmets, clutching HK 417 semi-automatic rifles. Men used to the hit-and-hope attitude of a raid. They knew there would be firearms inside, but just how many and how prepared the Borderland Family were to use them, they couldn't know.

DCI Delaney had given the go-ahead but had been told to try a soft approach first. Knock, ask for entry, bring out the battering ram if the door was slammed in their faces. Even with that in mind, they had armed officers around the property, snipers waiting to kick off if anything happened.

The van drove slowly down the unmarked track, large overgrown hedges on either side, potholes marking the way. They stopped at the gates. Full height, solid, strong, metal. They had no way of knowing what was on the other side.

'Do you realise how close we are to the lake where Dougie Brewer was found?' Briggs whispered to Kate. She raised an eyebrow and he pointed to their right. 'Just over there.'

The police officer driving wound down the window. He looked at the buzzer in front of him, his finger poised.

'Let's hope this isn't another bloody Waco,' he muttered as he pressed it.

The entire van held their collective breath.

'Yes?' A metallic voice answered through the hiss of the intercom.

'Police. We have reason to believe you are holding unlicensed firearms, and we have a warrant to search this property under Section 46 of the Firearms Act 1968.'

There was a long pause, then a buzzer sounded. Kate jumped, then glanced around to see if anyone had noticed. The officer opposite gave her a sarcastic smile.

The gates opened and the van drove inside.

26

The van drove slowly into the compound. Kate took in the buildings – some old and falling down, others obviously well maintained. The driveway led to a large gravelled courtyard in front of a massive three-storey house. Unlike some of the outbuildings, this was newly painted and in good condition. The front door was open, and an elderly man stood on the steps, a scowling young man hovering behind him.

'Welcome!' the older of the two said, as if he was greeting a wedding party rather than a collection of suspicious police officers.

Kate climbed out of the van and straightened out her back. The officer in charge of the warrant walked to the older gentleman and handed him the piece of paper. The man looked at it for a moment before it was snatched out of his hands by the boy behind him.

To Kate, the older man seemed like someone you wouldn't give a second glance to in Waitrose. He was wearing a blue checked shirt and navy trousers, and had a slight bend at the waist. He held a walking stick in his left hand which he relied on to stay upright in the doorway.

'Graham Swift,' he said, holding out his other hand. 'And this is my son, Oliver.' Oliver continued to glare at the police officers. The officer in charge shook his hand. 'You don't need this warrant,' Graham carried on. 'You're welcome to look around.'

'Not exactly hostile,' Briggs whispered to Kate and she nodded. This wasn't what they were expecting at all. Briggs indicated towards the front door, where the armed unit were being directed by their senior officer. 'Go and join the search. I'll start out here,' she said and he rushed off, keen to be included.

Kate headed towards the outbuildings to her left. They looked to have once been stables, and Kate opened one of the wooden doors next to her.

It was dark inside and smelt of sawdust and animals. When her eyes adjusted to the light, Kate could make out brick walls dividing the large building into sections.

'You shouldn't be here,' a voice said, and Kate turned. The young man was standing behind her. Despite his grumpy expression he was impossibly pretty, the sort of youthful good looks that teenage girls swoon over. His eyes were dark, his hair curly, his skin tanned. The only imperfection was a scar that ran down from below his mouth to under his chin.

'Your father said we could look around,' Kate replied.

'My father's too trusting,' he said. 'If it's guns you're looking for, you won't find any out here.'

Kate's hackles were raised, but before she could take a closer look at the building, she saw Briggs wave to her from the front door of the main house. 'Boss!' he called, gesturing inside.

Oliver Swift looked at her closely. 'So you're in charge?' he said. 'Well. It's always the ones you least expect.'

Kate glowered at his remark. Bloody kid, she thought as she walked back to the house.

She headed up the stone steps and pushed through the front door. The hallway was huge, with an ornate wooden staircase rising up the middle. The wallpaper was colourful and patterned, fading at the edges. Dark wooden furniture lined the walls – cabinets, bookshelves, dressers – every shelf covered with ornaments or old books. It was all clean and laid out neatly; they looked like antiques, old and expensive.

And the house was crowded with people. The officer in charge had positioned the police officers throughout the property but at every turn she saw civilian men and women of all ages. A young woman with a baby on her knee sat on one of the sofas, watching them, her face solemn. An older man stood with his arm around a grey-haired woman. They all watched the police silently with an air of suspicion.

Kate followed Briggs into one of the large hallways, then stopped short.

Every wall was covered with wooden racks, and every rack held a gun.

'Woah,' Kate muttered under her breath. She had seen scenes like this, but only in films and only in America. There must have been over fifty guns lining the room, a mixture of rifles and pistols. She smelt gun oil, walnut and leather. The fact that they were in plain sight and not locked away made them illegal right from the off, but Kate also couldn't believe that all these guns were registered to this address, to these occupants.

The officer in charge was standing in the middle of the room, hands on his hips, staring at the arsenal with something like awe. He started pointing at each one in turn.

'Shotgun, Glock 17 pistol, AR15, 9mm Browning semi-auto, Magnum forty-four, Sig Sauer M17, HK MP5, another shotgun, Beretta 92F.' He leaned forward, looking at one closely. 'I mean, a lot of these aren't even legal in the UK. God knows how they got them.'

On the far side of the room, another officer was arguing

with Graham Swift and Oliver had gone over to join them. The officer was explaining how they would need to seize all the weapons, at least until they could identify and match each one to its registered owner. Kate, for one, would be happier knowing this lot were impounded in a police station.

'Can you believe this?' she muttered to Briggs, next to her, and he shook his head. 'What's through there?' she asked, pointing to the door on the opposite side.

Briggs went to have a look. Kate heard a loud exclamation, then a furious exchange of words. She looked curiously towards the voices.

Briggs came back in, his face grim. He shook his head, pointing angrily towards the door.

'What?' Kate asked.

'Go and see for yourself,' he growled. 'And I bet you'll have the same response I just did.'

Kate walked down a dark corridor and opened the door. In front of her was a basic kitchen – cooker, cupboards, fridge – and a large wooden table in the centre with people sat round it. She could sense their resentment and looked around, trying to work out what had made Briggs react so strongly.

She froze.

'What the hell?' Kate demanded.

Because across the room, behind the table, sat a young woman. A woman with blonde hair and blue eyes, whose picture had been splashed across every news outlet in the country. Whose face was burned into Kate's memory. Whose husband had just been arrested for her murder.

Kate cleared her throat, suppressing the anger bubbling up inside her. The woman stared at her.

'Lucy Barker,' Kate said. 'We've been looking for you.'

Part 2

27

The detectives sat down in front of Lucy at the kitchen table. Their faces were serious. Lucy was aware of other noises in the house – people moving to and fro, annoyed voices and exclamations of alarm – but not in here. This room was silent.

The woman detective cleared her throat.

'Why didn't you notify us that you weren't missing?' she asked. She'd identified herself as Detective Sergeant Kate Munro and showed Lucy her badge. Now she fidgeted in her chair, wincing as she adjusted her black vest, the dominant POLICE sign across the front.

'I wasn't aware anyone was looking for me,' Lucy said quietly. She didn't like the way these detectives were accusing her, making her feel guilty.

'There are appeals all over the news, in the papers,' the detective continued. 'Are you saying you didn't see any of them?'

'We don't watch TV here. And only Graham sees the newspapers.' She saw the two detectives exchange a look. 'I didn't want you to look for me. I left a note.'

DS Munro leaned forward in her seat. 'What note? We didn't find a note.'

'We left it on the hallway table, where I knew Scott would find it. In a blue envelope.' Lucy bit her lip, trying to hold back the tears. 'I said that I was coming here and that he shouldn't look for me.'

The male detective got up from the sofa and left the room quickly, his mobile clutched in his hand.

'And where is "here"?' the detective asked. 'Is this some sort of commune?'

'It's a refuge,' Lucy replied.

'Lucy, if Scott's been hurting you in any way, we can help,' the detective began, but Lucy interrupted her.

'No, not that sort of refuge. A refuge from the dissolution of modern life. Protection from what we know is coming.'

DS Munro blinked at her. Lucy had seen that look before. The long stare of disbelief. The silence where they thought of something to say. She'd seen it on Scott, when she'd tried to talk to him. She'd seen it on the faces of her employers, of her best friend. They thought she was crazy, or at best annoying. But then she'd spoken to Alex, and he had been different.

Alex had taken the time to listen to her worries and had added thoughts of his own. He'd agreed with her, then introduced her to Graham Swift. Graham knew why she couldn't sleep at night.

Munro looked up as the other detective came into the room. He whispered something to her, then sat down again.

'And what is coming, Lucy?' DS Munro asked.

'The deterioration of society. Violence. Chaos.' The male detective opened his mouth in response, then glanced at DS Munro and closed it again. Lucy took a long breath in, quelling her annoyance. 'You don't believe me, but look around for a moment. Look at the problems humanity is facing. Terrorism. Climate change. The threat of nuclear warfare.

You're telling me that the world can carry on how it is and everything will be fine?'

You wait, Lucy thought, you just wait, and we'll see who's right. Only time will tell.

'But how does living here help, Lucy?' DS Munro asked softly.

'We're safe here. We're ready.'

The door opened and Graham came into the room, followed by a large police officer in uniform. Graham was smiling, and he leaned against the door frame, looking at the detectives.

'Do you have all you need, DS Munro?' Graham asked.

Lucy saw the detective look sharply at him. 'And why didn't you let us know that Lucy was here?' she said.

Graham held his hands out in front of him, palms upwards, in a gesture of innocence. 'I simply wasn't aware. I'm sorry. You can't blame an old man for not putting two and two together.'

The detective pursed her lips, holding back a retort. Even Lucy could tell he was lying. She knew the Family didn't like the police. Not telling them she was here would have been a defiant gesture, a symbolic middle finger in their direction.

'And are you happy that Lucy is here on her own volition?' Graham continued. 'That we are not holding her captive in any way?'

The two detectives stood up slowly. Lucy could feel DS Munro looking at her closely, her brow furrowed.

She nodded. 'Yes, I think so. But we'll need to take a statement from you, Lucy. To close things off properly.'

'Of course. I'll be happy to come to the station.'

The detectives walked into the hallway and Lucy followed them. The house had a strange energy with the police there.

Where the residents had been bustling around, keeping the house running just ten minutes earlier, now everyone was motionless, watching and wary.

Lucy bit her lip again, then asked the question she'd been wanting to ask since she arrived at the house. The one thing she'd been trying not to think about.

'How's Scott?'

DS Munro turned. 'How do you think he is, Lucy?' Lucy felt hot tears blur her vision; something stick in her throat. 'Scott's distraught,' the detective continued. 'And I can't blame him. His wife has disappeared without a trace. We've been searching your house, the press have ripped his life apart. We arrested him for your murder.'

Lucy looked up quickly. 'I left a note. I didn't want that,' she said.

'Yes, this elusive note,' DS Munro added. 'But what did you think would happen?' Lucy could see the detective was angry now, her face flushed. 'People can't walk away from their lives without consequences, Lucy. However much they want to.' She gestured to the house. 'What's so different here? That you were prepared to destroy everything you had?'

Lucy angrily wiped the tears away with a corner of her jumper. 'I can breathe here. People understand me, and what I'm worried about. This is my family now.'

Graham pushed himself in between Lucy and the detectives, using his walking stick as a barrier.

'I think we're done,' he said, his voice hard. 'It's time you left Lucy alone.'

28

'Jamie, there's nothing we can do. We can't force her to leave.'

Kate and Briggs stood in the wide gravel courtyard. She knew what Briggs was feeling right now; she felt the same. A mixture of relief, overshadowed by stupidity, morphing to anger.

'Section 136?'

'Does she look like she needs care or control to you?' Kate asked, looking back at the house. 'Was she a danger to herself or others?'

'You could argue she's suffering from a mental disorder,' Briggs said. 'What was all that shit about the deterioration of society?'

Kate sighed. 'Who knows. But she's definitely not dead.' She gestured towards the mobile in Briggs's hands. 'What did Max say?'

'What do you think?' Briggs laughed harshly. 'He wasn't polite, that's for sure. He's releasing Barker now, and they'll go back to the house to look for the note. He'll call if he's got anything.' He paused. 'Wasting police time?'

Kate shook her head. 'I'm not arresting her, Jamie. We've spent enough resources on Lucy Barker already.' She looked over as the cop in charge of the gun raid walked towards them.

'We've got all the firearms logged and loaded, as well as their ammo.' He pointed to a series of large black boxes being hauled into the van. 'Who knows what they were going to do with all of this. It's going to take hours to unpick. Is there anything else you want to look at before we go?'

Kate nodded. 'Just give us ten, and we'll be with you.' She turned to Briggs. 'Let's give it a final check. Look for anything strange.' Briggs raised his eyebrows. 'More strange than normal. And anything that might link them to Dougie Brewer's murder.'

Briggs nodded and went off again towards the main house. Kate turned in the courtyard, taking in a three-sixty view.

The place was huge. Without knowing what they were looking for, a search could take them hours, and they could still come up with nothing. In front of her was the main house. Three floors, five windows across the front. To her left were the stables she had been in already, and on the right was a row of garages. She pointed towards the doors, all padlocked.

'Have we been in there yet?' she shouted towards the officer in charge and he shook his head, then said a few words to the uniform next to him. He left and returned a few minutes later with a bunch of keys.

Slowly Kate tried each one in the padlocks, opening them in turn. There were three garages in total.

Behind the first door was a large rusty tractor, pieces missing, next to an old red car, a quad bike and a Nissan truck, taking up all the available floor space. She scuffed her feet in the dust on the garage floor. Nothing else of interest.

On to the next. Another big truck stood in front of a range of tools. Crowbars, hammers, power tools, their cables trailing across the floor. A small cupboard was attached to the wall and Kate opened a few drawers – screws, nails.

She frowned. More interesting than the first, but they knew Dougie Brewer hadn't been killed with a blunt object, so none of this was relevant.

She moved on. But the stuff stored in the next garage was just plain weird. It appeared to be medical equipment. A high table with a metal top. A pole that Kate thought could be for an IV drip. Boxes and boxes of what looked like medical instruments.

'They're my dad's.'

A voice from the doorway made Kate jump. Oliver stood in shadow, leaning against the door frame. He was chewing gum and Kate could hear the slow movement of his jaw.

'What does your dad need with old medical equipment?' Kate asked.

'Veterinary.'

'Sorry?'

'It's not medical equipment. It's veterinary. Dad used to have his own practice.'

'He's a vet?'

'Was.' Oliver watched Kate as she poked around in the boxes. She felt his gaze on her back. 'What are you looking for?' he asked.

Kate stood up straight, brushing the dust off her hands and walking out of the garage. Oliver's glare followed her. It made her feel uneasy. In the courtyard she stopped and looked back at him.

'Do you know someone called Douglas Brewer?' Kate asked.

Oliver stopped chewing for a moment. 'Dougie.' He nodded. 'Yes. Why?'

'Did you know he was dead?'

Kate watched his face, looking for some sort of reaction, but his expression stayed blank.

'That's too bad. How?'

'How did you know him?' Kate asked, ignoring his question.

'He and Dad have been friends since they were young. He wanted to join the Family.'

'But Graham wouldn't let him?'

Oliver paused again, then looked back to the house. Kate followed his gaze. His dad was standing in the doorway, watching their conversation, arms folded across his chest.

'It's more complicated than that,' he said quickly, and walked back to his father. ·

Kate watched him go. His manner had changed when he'd seen Graham Swift. The arrogant facade had faded, replaced by what she could almost describe as a scared kid.

Briggs emerged from the house behind the Swifts and they moved to let him through. He shook his head at Kate in a wordless signal. Nothing.

She frowned. Whatever they were looking for, it would have to wait. She climbed into the van after the rest of the officers and shut the doors as they drove away.

Kate looked through the back window at the gates as they closed behind them. This wasn't the end of the story here. She knew that for sure.

29

After the bombardment of words in the interview room, Scott appreciated the silence. He sat next to PC Cooper in the unmarked police car as they drove away from the station towards home.

Home. He wasn't sure what that meant now. Anxious in the cold cell, all he'd wanted was to be back in his own bed, where he could sleep under a duvet rather than the scratchy blue blanket, where he was allowed a belt and shoelaces. And he wanted Lucy. He'd just wanted the nightmare to end.

But now? PC Cooper had come to the door of the cell and walked him out. But rather than taking him back to the interview room as he'd expected, he showed him into a different room, with sofas and a low table. He'd placed a mug of coffee in his hand, made using a kettle rather than a plastic cup from the machine.

'Scott,' PC Cooper had said. 'We have some news about Lucy.'

'Is she dead?' Scott had asked. That was what he was expecting. For someone to say they'd found her body. He'd gone through so many scenarios in his head – murder, abduction, car accident – but each time he settled on suicide. He wasn't sure how, but she'd killed herself and it had been his fault. The affair had driven her to it.

But no.

'She's alive and well, Scott. She's been staying with an

organisation outside Ringwood. The Borderland Family. Have you heard of them?'

Scott felt a wave of relief wash over him. She was alive! But he struggled to understand what this policeman was saying. She'd gone where? Somewhere deep in his memory he did remember Lucy mentioning a 'family', but of course he hadn't been listening. He hadn't been listening to Lucy for a while.

'I don't know anything about them,' he said. 'Did she say why she's there?'

'We were hoping you could tell us. Has Lucy said anything about this to you in the past?' the policeman asked.

'She was worried about the environment. She always talked about how the politicians were lying to us, but I never thought she would take things this far,' Scott muttered.

He desperately tried to remember what she'd said to him over the last few months. He knew she'd been online, reading websites, but he'd dismissed it when she'd tried to show him. He'd had a restructure at work, redundancies to do, and he'd been worried about that. Stressed and preoccupied.

Cooper watched him for a moment. Scott felt his cheeks flush. He knew what the guy was thinking: he was a shitty husband, no doubt about that.

'They picked Lucy up from the main road about ten o'clock on Monday morning,' Cooper said at last. 'She took a bag of clothes she'd been storing in the air-raid shelter, but nothing else.' He looked at Scott. 'She said she left a note.'

Scott could feel the man's eyes studying his face again, looking for a reaction. He'd shaken his head. 'No, there was no note. Where did she say she'd left it?'

'By the front door.' He paused, but Scott said nothing. The policeman had sighed. 'I'll take you home.'

*

They pulled up in the driveway outside Scott's house.

'I'll come in with you, if you don't mind,' PC Cooper said.

Scott slowly walked across to the front door and opened it. He stood at the entrance to the house. A pile of post lay next to the letter box, delivered since he'd been locked away in the police station.

'May I take a look?' The policeman said from behind him. He had put blue plastic gloves on his hands.

Scott moved out of his way. He felt tiredness overwhelm him, and sat hunched at the bottom of the stairs, watching PC Cooper as he picked up the post, sorting through it, then putting it on the hall table. He moved coats, looking in pockets, picking up shoes and checking underneath them. Then he got down on all fours and looked under the hall table. He sat back up, his hands empty.

'And you say you haven't seen any sort of note? She says she left it here,' the policeman asked, pointing.

Scott shook his head. 'No, nothing.'

PC Cooper stood up again and sighed. 'Okay, well, if you find something, you'll let us know straight away?'

'Of course,' Scott said. He could sense the policeman didn't believe him. He could hardly blame him. 'I will,' he added. 'I promise.'

He just wanted the copper to leave, but then suddenly he didn't. If PC Cooper left, that would be it. He would be alone in the house. No Lucy, no future. No nothing.

Scott took a deep breath in, trying to hold back the wave of desperate emotion. This couldn't be it, surely? He needed to speak to her, persuade her to come home.

He rubbed his hands over his face, pushing his fingers into his eye sockets. 'Can I see her?'

The policeman frowned. 'I don't know, mate, I really don't. She's going to come to the station though, to give a statement. We could ask her then.'

PC Cooper stood up to leave, then hesitated.

'Can I get you anything before I go?'

Scott shook his head, still staring at the floor.

He started to cry, his shoulders shaking in great heaving sobs. He didn't care any more. He was tired, his life had gone. He was alone.

He felt a hand on his shoulder for a moment, then soft footsteps and a click as the policeman closed the front door behind him.

The nightmare was over, but a new one had begun.

30

Kate pulled the laptop out of the evidence bag and turned it on. Now the case was closed the techies had sent it to Kate to be returned to Lucy Barker. But Kate was curious. The screen sprang into life and she inputted the password.

They had Dougie's laptop here, too. Returned with a report itemising the websites he'd been on; nothing else of interest found. They might just as well have written 'porn' and been done with it, Kate mused.

Next to her, her phone started ringing, Sam's face on the screen. She ignored it, then typed a quick text once it had finished. *Heading home soon xx.* It was a lie. Even though it was past six, Kate had no intention of stopping for the day. Her mind was buzzing with everything that had happened: with thoughts of Lucy Barker, the Borderland Family, Dougie Brewer.

Perhaps if she knew a bit more about Lucy, then she could understand her better. She clicked on the internet icon and looked at her Favourites. She recognised a few: Twitter, Instagram and Facebook, the *Guardian*, the website Max had showed them both earlier for the Borderland Family, then a few American sites: Fox News and CNN.

She clicked on Twitter, and a profile Kate didn't recognise loaded on the left-hand side: @readyforborderland. It certainly wasn't the one Scott Barker had told them about. Lucy seemed to follow mainly newspapers, people talking about climate change, social commentators with a penchant for doom: a litany of disaster and hate filled her newsfeed. It was making Kate depressed after the few moments she had been reading them; she couldn't imagine how Lucy would feel watching this stuff every day.

'You're still here?'

Kate glanced round, but even before she saw him she could feel her cheeks starting to redden. Get a grip, she told herself. She was his boss, she needed to get this under control.

Max sat down at the desk next to her and took his coat off.

'No note, nothing there,' he said, and Kate looked across sharply.

'Nothing?' she echoed. 'Why would Lucy lie about it?'

'To cover her back?' Max leaned back in the chair and stretched, his arms behind his head. 'Because she knew she'd caused a hell of a mess by leaving?'

'And you don't think Scott found it earlier and got rid of it?' Kate asked.

Max frowned. 'What would be the point? And I believe him, for what it's worth. Left him crying in his hallway, poor guy.' Kate looked at Max doubtfully. 'Honestly. He's not made life easy for himself through this investigation, but no one deserves their wife to disappear like that, out of nowhere.'

'Was it really out of the blue, though?' Kate asked. 'It's a pretty big thing, walking out of your home, your marriage, leaving everything behind. You're telling me her husband didn't suspect a thing?'

'Maybe he ignored it.'

'Or he wasn't paying attention,' Kate muttered, more to herself than to Max.

He leaned across and looked over her shoulder. 'Is that Lucy's laptop?'

She nodded. 'Could you fire up Dougie Brewer's and see what you can find? See if there's any crossover with Lucy's?' Then Kate stopped, feeling guilty. 'That's if you don't have to be getting home?'

Max shook his head. 'Nothing that can't wait.'

No plans tonight with the mysterious Charlie from the phone call, then. Kate smiled and turned back to Lucy's laptop.

They tapped away side by side in silence, staring at the laptop screens. Max sat with his head resting on his hand, elbow on the table, squinting. After a moment he got up and pulled a pair of glasses out of his bag and put them on.

'I didn't know you wore glasses,' Kate commented.

'I try not to.'

'They suit you,' Kate said, and Max smiled at her then went back to the laptop.

Kate felt her face flare again. For fuck's sake.

They worked companionably, every now and again cross-referring a website, comparing notes. Some were the same, some not. Douglas Brewer hadn't been a fan of social media beyond Facebook, and it seemed that his grasp of all things IT-based had been a bit rudimentary.

Kate looked over Max's shoulder as he loaded up Brewer's email.

'Can you check if he was in contact with Lucy?' Kate asked, and scooted her chair over to sit behind him.

She leaned over his shoulder to type Lucy's email address into the search bar, her arm touching his, then sat down again quickly. Max pressed search, but nothing came up.

'Doesn't look like they knew each other,' Max commented. 'Lucy's laptop the same?'

Kate nodded. 'Nothing relevant, as far as I can see.' She thought about her conversation with Oliver Swift. 'Could you have a look for anything between Dougie and Graham Swift?' she asked, and Max nodded.

Her own email pinged and she saw the address of PCSO Shah flash up on the screen. She clicked on it, to find three files.

List of items stolen from the pharmacy raid on Highfield Road as requested, Kate read. *I've also attached reports from two other thefts I thought you might find useful: an ambulance ransacked while the crew were tending to an RTA victim, and an operating theatre at a hospital broken into late at night, drugs fridge prised open. List of items stolen in both attached.*

Kate opened the files, looking at the unfamiliar words on the screen. Her mobile flashed again. Kate picked it up. Sam. More persistent this time. She sighed. 'I'm going to have to go.'

Max looked up. 'Kate, look at this first.' He pointed at an email. 'They definitely knew each other.'

Kate looked over his shoulder. There were a few messages, going back and forth over the course of a few months.

'Not all of it is friendly.' Max paused, his eyes scanning the lines of text. 'But you go. I'll tell you about it tomorrow.'

Kate nodded. 'And I've forwarded you an email. Can you pull out the list of pharmaceuticals and send it to Dr Adams?'

'No problem,' Max said, still staring at his computer. 'Have a good evening, Kate.'

Kate threw on her coat and picked up her bag. As she left the office, she muttered, 'DS Munro, not Kate,' under her breath. But the truth was, she liked it. She just didn't like to think about why.

31

Max didn't look up until he heard the slam, then he glanced at the closed door. She was a funny one. Married and going home to her husband, but throwing out all kinds of mixed messages. He could tell that he unnerved her, but he didn't know what that meant, if anything.

His thoughts went to Scott Barker, alone and crying on the stairs in his empty house. Max knew Scott had been far from blameless, but it was clear he loved his wife. Max wondered what it would be like to have that strength of feeling – to be left destroyed by someone's departure. He'd never felt that about anyone.

He sighed and turned back to his computer, looking for the email from Kate, then pulling out the names of the drugs from the three reports they'd been sent. It was a long list.

Penicillin, amoxicillin: antibiotics he recognised from having taken them himself. Morphine, oxycodone, fentanyl, ketamine: drugs he knew would fetch money on the street. But then there was a list of stuff he'd never heard of. Loperamide, rocuronium, suxamethonium, prednisolone, syntometrine, methylphenidate, diazepam, and that was only the start of it. What would anyone need all this stuff for?

He pulled it all together and sent it to Dr Adams, then turned back to Dougie Brewer's emails.

The more he read, the more he realised that Dougie and

Graham didn't just know each other, they seemed close. Early emails talked about meeting up, get-togethers at the pub, exchanging pleasantries about a woman Max assumed was Graham's wife. But then their conversations turned sour. It seemed Dougie wanted to come and live with the Swifts, in an early iteration of the Borderland Family, but Graham hadn't been keen. Time passed, and still he was refused, despite the many other 'waifs and strays' that Dougie was annoyed were there. Dougie mentioned 'favours' – Max assumed it was the drug theft he took part in. He offered money; Graham pushed for more.

There was no doubt their relationship turned nasty, but from the emails Max would have assumed that it would have been Doug trying to kill Graham, rather than the other way around. Perhaps that was what had happened, Max mused, and his death was the result of self-defence gone wrong. But Doug Brewer's body had been injury-free. It didn't add up.

So Dougie and Graham had started out as friends. But then why had Graham been so reluctant for Doug to join his Family, when it seemed that a perfect stranger like Lucy Barker had walked straight in? Was it just about the money?

Max clicked on the Borderland Family website and looked at the login screen. As yet they'd been unable to get access; Lucy Barker's laptop hadn't stored her password like they'd hoped it would. Max's cursor hovered above the button next to it. *Find Out More*, it said. Max clicked the button and another screen appeared.

It asked for name, contact details and included a few other questions. *The Borderland Family is a collaborative community. What skills or resources can you offer us?* Max glanced around the office. He was the only one there – nobody could see what he was doing. How could it hurt?

He clicked on the first question. *Max*, he typed in. He looked at the desk next to him, covered in paperwork completed earlier by Briggs. *James*, he added in the surname box, feeling a small thrill of excitement.

32

Since the detectives had left, Lucy had tried hard to keep busy. Being on kitchen duties was a blessing, occupied as she was, cooking and serving up dinner for the twenty or so people that lived as part of the Family.

But as she came to the end of each task, her brain started whirring again. Thoughts of Scott: the guilt, the worry. Missing her house, and the home comforts Graham told them all to eschew – television, central heating, a comfy sofa. The trappings of the modern world, he said. A glass of water to keep you comfortable while the house burned around your ears.

She heard the door open behind her and turned as Graham himself came into the room. He sat at the old table in the middle of the kitchen, placing the notebook he always carried next to him.

'I'm nearly done,' Lucy said.

'Leave it. Oliver can do it later. You're more important.' He tapped the chair next to him and smiled. Lucy felt the warmth of his attention. In this house with all these people, he had taken the time to single her out.

She joined him and he took her hands in his. His were wrinkly and old, with knobbly knuckles and veins showing through his skin. But they were clean, his nails short and neat. Since the moment she met him, Lucy had noticed that he took good care of himself.

'How are you?' he asked.

'I'm fine,' Lucy replied, her voice high and bright.

'Lucy.' He looked at her seriously, his eyes full of concern, and Lucy felt her resolution waver. Tears threatened behind her eyes.

'It's been a difficult day for all of us, but more so for you. Your past pushed into your new life. You're bound to feel conflicted.'

'I'm so sorry,' Lucy cried, staring at their entwined hands. 'I know you say we need to stay strong, but I can't help thinking about him.'

'About your husband?' Graham said, and Lucy nodded. 'Even after his betrayal?'

'I know, I know. And I know it's more evidence of crumbling morals, that even the people closest to me can't be trusted to maintain a high standard.' Lucy looked down, barely daring to let herself say it. 'But I miss him.'

'Of course you do,' Graham replied. 'These feelings don't disappear overnight. But please be reassured, my dear, with our help you will feel better again soon.'

Lucy nodded. For years she'd longed to be part of a real family again. Something more than just her and Scott – to be in the centre of a warm home, somewhere she could feel safe and secure. Graham's love felt like the father she'd always hoped for.

'When are you going to give your statement to the police?' he asked.

'Tomorrow,' Lucy sniffed.

Graham nodded. 'That's good. Get it over and done with. But don't go alone. You'll need all the support you can get.'

'I don't want to expose anyone else to the establishment,' Lucy replied.

'So go with Alex,' Graham said. 'He's an old pro at sniffing out the lies the police tell us. He'll help you stand your ground.' He patted Lucy's hand, then stood up slowly, using the back of the chair to push himself up. 'Don't despair. Everything will become clear,' he said, reciting the doctrine she'd heard him say many times in the house.

She followed him out of the kitchen. The rest of the house was dark, the majority of the Family already in bed. She wearily climbed the stairs to the bedroom she shared with three other women and got undressed in the darkness, climbing under the scratchy duvet in the small single bed.

Around her she could hear slow breaths from the other women. She didn't know them yet: she'd tried to start a few conversations, but nobody had been that friendly. She assumed that, like her, they were worn down by worry, or tired from their daily tasks preparing for the eventual dissolution.

Being here was safer, Lucy knew that in her bones. It made her feel better: she was protected, surrounded by like-minded people who knew the Truth. But the Truth was exhausting. The Truth was still uncertain.

Slowly Lucy drifted off to sleep, Graham's words resonating in her head. All will become clear, she told herself. All will become clear.

33

Sam had barely said a word to Kate since she'd arrived home from work. He was slumped on the sofa, television on, and looked up at her with a withering glance when she asked him a question.

'Pardon?' he sighed as he silenced the TV.

'I wondered if there was any dinner,' Kate asked.

She received a single finger in reply, pointed towards the kitchen, then the volume was turned back up again.

Kate rolled her eyes and went off to search. The dinner in question had been left in the saucepan on the stove and was now stone cold. A skin of congealed tomato covered the top. Sam Marshall, her husband: the king of passive-aggressive communication.

She poured the leftovers into a bowl and put them in the fridge, choosing to go for toast instead. While she waited for it to pop, she messaged Max at the office.

Sorry to leave you by yourself. Find anything?

She clicked send, then stared at the empty screen, absent-mindedly dipping her knife into the jar of peanut butter and eating a generous dollop. Three small dots appeared on the left-hand side, then a ping.

GS and DB not great friends, will show you tomorrow. DB sister available for iv, set up mtg at house?

Kate replied: *Yes, tom am if poss? Meet you there? Txt me address.*

Kate couldn't help smiling. Despite herself, she looked forward to seeing Max in the morning.

Technically, Kate knew, Max's involvement in her team was over: Lucy Barker had been found, and he should be going back to Response and Patrol. But they were still short-staffed, and nobody was complaining. They could all work Dougie's investigation together. Someone was dead, possibly murdered, she told herself. Surely that was more important.

Her toast popped and she layered on the peanut butter, carrying it into the living room and sitting down on the sofa opposite Sam. He still wasn't looking at her, all his attention focused on the screen.

Her phone beeped again.

Sorted. 9am.

Then another beep: a follow-up text with the address.

Opposite her, Sam made a noise somewhere in between a sigh and a grunt. Kate scowled.

'What's the matter?' she asked, slowly.

'Your bloody phone.' His eyes moved her way for a moment, then slid back to the TV.

'It's not just my phone. You've been like this since I got home.'

'Yeah, since you got home. Two hours late.'

Kate frowned. 'Two hours later than what? I didn't say when I would be back.'

Kate could see Sam's jaw flexing. 'What?' she barked. 'Just spit it out, Sam.'

'That's just it. You never say. You just leave me to wonder when I might see my wife in the evening. I'm always your last consideration – behind whatever poor sod happens to be dead that week, behind whatever traffic accident. Even Jamie-bloody-Briggs gets higher billing than me.'

Kate stared at him. 'You're a grown man, Sam. I assume you can look after yourself while I'm at work.'

His eyes were still trained on the television, his body slumped on the sofa.

'For fuck's sake, Sam. At least have the decency to turn off the TV if you're going to have a go at me.'

Sam glared at her. Then he reached for the remote and switched it off. He threw it onto the cushion next to him and stood up. 'Now you know how it feels,' he said bitterly. 'To be ignored.'

He walked away from her, then paused in the doorway. He turned and looked back.

'You know, Kate, it wouldn't hurt if you could try a little harder to make this marriage work.'

She watched him go, then heard the slam of their bedroom door.

'Fuck,' she muttered under her breath. She was screwing it up all over again.

Friday

34

Jean Brewer led Kate and Max into her living room, then perched on the sofa opposite, her face downcast.

'Our condolences on the death of your brother,' Kate started.

The woman shrugged. 'Doesn't make much difference to me. Like I told you on the phone, I haven't seen him for a while.'

'So you and Douglas weren't close?' Kate asked.

Jean shook her head. She had bright blonde hair tied back in a severe ponytail, and was one of those ageless women who could have been anywhere from forty-five to seventy, with a perma-tan, bright white teeth and a forehead that didn't move. 'Let's just say our lives went in different directions.'

Doug's sister was right: her house was poles apart from her brother's. The carpet was plush, the furniture shining and expensive-looking, the walls decorated with a chintzy pink-patterned paper. It wasn't Kate's taste but she couldn't deny it was clean and tidy, almost obsessively so.

'When was the last time you spoke to him?'

'Our father's funeral, about a year ago. I didn't think he'd show up, if I'm being honest, but there he was, in some baggy jacket probably bought from a charity shop.' She screwed up her nose. 'And he didn't smell good. It was the least he could have done, have a bloody shower. He was always Dad's favourite, although he was a disappointment to everyone else from the moment he was born.'

'How so?' Kate asked.

'He was just so lazy. Couldn't be bothered to apply himself, and expected everything to fall in his lap. He didn't finish his degree, he couldn't hold down a job ...' She tailed off, then reached down to the side of her chair, picking up a packet of cigarettes. 'Do you mind?' she asked, and Kate shook her head. She lit one and Kate noticed her hand was shaking. 'How did he die?' Jean asked, blowing out smoke. 'Was he murdered? The newspapers said he was found in a lake.'

'We're investigating the circumstances around his death, and I'm afraid we don't know at this stage. What can you tell me about his relationship with Graham Swift?'

Jean Brewer recoiled. 'You don't think Graham had something to do with it?'

'We're looking into all possibilities. Were they friends?'

She nodded, taking another drag. 'They went to university together years ago, but still met up to go to the pub: Dougie, Graham and this other bloke, Paul something. But then I think Graham moved on to bigger and better things, got married, had a kid, the normal stuff, and left Dougie behind. Story of his life,' she muttered.

'And did Doug have any other friends you knew about? Girlfriends? Workmates?'

'Dougie never held down a job long enough to get workmates. There were a few women flitting in and out, but none of them stuck around for long. I don't blame them. Have you seen his flat?' she asked, and Kate nodded. 'Shithole, isn't it?'

Before Kate could answer tactfully, her phone rang and she apologised to Jean Brewer while she went out of the room to answer it.

'Sarge?' It was Briggs. She spoke to him for a moment then hung up, pausing in the hallway.

Her first cup of coffee was starting to wear off and she desperately needed something to keep her awake. Kate hadn't slept well, the bed in the spare room hard and unfamiliar, Sam's words echoing in her head. What did he mean, try a little harder? It was all she had been doing. Forgoing the midweek bottle of wine, asking him questions about work, listening, laughing, smiling, when all she wanted to do was slump on the sofa and self-medicate her way to oblivion. It was all so exhausting, and it wasn't *enough*? But in the morning she'd apologised, resolving to do better. We'll spend the weekend together, she'd promised, just you and me, and he'd smiled and made her a coffee.

Kate sighed and went back into the living room where Jean Brewer was telling Max about her brother's predilection for drink and drugs.

'That was why he was always skint,' she said with a sneer. 'Spent it all on Strongbow. He didn't even have good taste when it came to alcohol.' She pointed the burning cigarette at Kate. 'Actually, now I come to think about it, him and Graham had a barney about that a while back. Dougie wanted to go and live in that hippy commune with him and Graham wasn't having it. Something to do with the drug habit. Dougie said he'd give up the pot to go, but, well ...' She stubbed the cigarette out in the ashtray. 'Never one to follow through on a promise, our Dougie.'

Kate nodded, then thanked Mrs Brewer for her time. 'I'm sorry, but we have to head back.'

Max looked disappointed as he was encouraged out of the door. 'She was just getting going on the real bitchy stuff,' he whispered.

'I know, but Lucy Barker's at the station for her statement. I want to hear what she has to say,' Kate said. There was something about the woman that had aroused her curiosity. 'And sorry to tell you, but Jamie's called shotgun on the interview. Alex Sherwood's come with her.'

Max rolled his eyes. 'Just because he fancies him,' he muttered, starting the engine.

'Yeah, well. An inappropriate crush never did anyone any harm,' Kate replied, then felt her face go hot. She could feel Max looking at her, his hand paused on the gearstick.

'Are we going or not?' she snapped, and he laughed and put the car into gear, heading back to the station.

35

Lucy and Alex were shown into a room with magnolia walls and scratchy sofas. She looked up at the poster Blu-Tacked to the wall: *See It, Say It, Sorted*, it declared, warning people to be on the lookout for terrorism. Lucy looked at it warily. Why bother looking for terrorism when much bigger dangers lay in wait from the very people supposed to protect you?

'You've got the comfy seats,' Alex whispered to her. 'This is the room for the nice people.'

Despite her nerves, Lucy laughed. 'Is this not where you usually are?' she asked, but before he could answer the detective came back into the room. Lucy recognised him from the raid at the house. He handed her a mug of tea.

'Sure you don't want anything?' he asked Alex and he shook his head.

They sat down: Alex and Lucy on one side of the coffee table, and the detective on the other, an empty chair next to him. She looked around – then pointed to the black dome on the ceiling in the corner of the room.

'Are you recording this interview?' she asked.

The detective glanced up. 'Yes,' he said. 'For our records. We'll give you a copy before you leave.'

He rattled through the paperwork and handed it to her. Lucy looked to Alex nervously. He nodded and she signed it.

She was glad Alex was there. He was on her side; he'd

keep a lookout for the police trying to trip her up, for any deliberate trickery with their language. As much as they claimed they were there to help her, they were the tools of the authoritarian regime, after all.

The door opened and the woman detective Lucy had met before came in.

'Thank you for coming in today, Lucy,' she said and sat down opposite her, her notebook poised in her lap.

'DS Munro,' Alex said with a nod.

'Mr Sherwood. What brings you here today?' she asked.

'Moral support for Lucy, nothing more.'

'Shall we get started then?'

Lucy had mentally planned what she was going to say, but in the face of the detectives' stares, the words came out in a mess. She stuttered over finding the photos of Jen Lewis on Scott's phone – naked photos. She said she knew then that there was nothing to stay for.

'So why the Borderland Family?' DS Munro asked.

'I'd always wanted to go there, but the timing never seemed right.'

'What about your husband?' the detective interrupted.

'I originally thought he'd come too. But he wasn't interested,' Lucy muttered. She'd tried to talk to him about it a few times, but he'd never paid any attention. So she'd done her research while he was at work, poring over her laptop as the evidence pointing towards the dissolution mounted up.

And then she knew why he hadn't listened: he'd had other things – Jen – on his mind. 'I hadn't wanted to leave him,' she continued. 'But finding those photos was proof of what Graham had always said to me, that one day I would know for sure, I just needed to look for a sign. And then there it was.'

'So you'd been in contact with Graham Swift before?'

'Yes,' Lucy agreed. 'Alex introduced us.'

'Really?' the detective said, her attention turning to Alex. Lucy flushed. She hadn't meant to get Alex into trouble, but he seemed unfazed.

'The Swifts are old family friends. I've known Graham for years. And when Lucy told me about her concerns, I thought Gray might be able to help.' Alex relaxed back in his chair, his arms crossed in front of him. He was completely at ease, but looked out of place in his big black work boots, his dirty trousers and baggy sweatshirt. Lucy had seen him working – out in the forest, around trees and mud and animals. That was his home. That was where he fitted in. She wondered where that place would be for her.

'But you don't live with the Borderland Family yourself?' the male detective asked.

'No.'

'And why is that?' DS Munro said.

Lucy listened with interest. She'd often wondered why he didn't want to join, given his close links with Graham and Oliver. She knew he lived alone; he didn't have any family.

Alex paused. 'They ask for a level of commitment I'm not prepared to give.' He stopped and let the silence fill the room. Lucy broke it.

'When you live with the Borderland Family, they offer you protection. But as with any family, you need to contribute to the functioning of the household.'

DS Munro looked closely at Lucy. 'You give them money.'

'Yes, but I know what you're thinking.' Lucy felt the familiar judgement. Outsiders didn't understand. 'I live there.

I eat and sleep there – that's not free. And my protection comes at a cost.'

'Protection against what?'

Lucy felt a flare of anger. They were just the same, these detectives. They were mocking her. 'You'll find out soon enough, Detective Sergeant Munro,' she said bitterly. 'The dissolution will arrive and you'll be vulnerable. With the Borderland Family we have everything we need – food, medical care. We have water for when supplies are polluted. We have generators for when the electricity fails. What price will you pay when the time comes, DS Munro? To survive?'

Alex placed his hand on her arm and she stopped, pressing her lips together.

'And that includes guns, does it?' Kate asked.

'Those firearms were legal, DS Munro, as you'll find out.'

'And what's going to cause this...' DS Munro paused.

'Dissolution,' the other detective said, filling in the blank.

'It could be anything,' Lucy said. 'Natural disasters caused by climate change leading to scarce resources. An electromagnetic pulse knocking out power grids. Nuclear warfare. Terrorism. A whole range of things could start it, but the outcome will be the same. Your government won't protect us.'

'And why is that?'

Lucy scoffed. 'The government not only lies but exploits these disasters for their own personal gain. In some cases they do this right in front of our eyes. Just look at Trump.'

'President Trump?'

'Yes. How else can you account for the fact that a reality television star is now the most powerful man in the world? You're telling me he was elected through a fair democratic process?'

DS Munro opened her mouth, then closed it again. The other detective raised an eyebrow. 'She's got a point there,' he muttered.

'So tell me,' DS Munro said. 'Why lie to your husband? Why tell Scott you were trying for a baby when you were on the pill?'

Lucy shook her head. 'Scott never understood. When I tried to talk to him about it he dismissed me. Some people find it easier to ignore the horrific things happening in front of them by burying their heads in the sand. Scott is one of those people.' Lucy looked at her hands, knitting her fingers together. 'I knew I couldn't bring an innocent child into this world. So I lied. And then I found that dead body in the lake.'

'Tell us about that, about finding Douglas Brewer,' the detective said softly. 'That must have been traumatic for you.'

Lucy remembered the feel of the man's flesh on her bare skin. The smell hovering on the surface of the water. His glassy eyes, looking at her. 'It was,' she whispered. She took a sip of tea from the mug in her hands. It was cold, but it didn't matter, she just wanted something else to focus on. 'But something inside me wasn't surprised. It confirmed what I already knew. The dissolution was coming. Everything would become clear.'

DS Munro opened her eyes wide but said nothing.

'Was that his name? The guy in the lake?' Lucy asked in the silence. The detective nodded. 'What happened to him?'

'We're still investigating,' Munro said. After a moment, she added: 'We couldn't find your note.'

'Did you check the hallway table?' Lucy gasped, surprised. 'Maybe it had fallen off, got caught up in the post.'

The detective shook her head. 'We couldn't find it, Lucy. Are you sure you left it?'

'I did!' she exclaimed. Lucy knew what the detective was thinking. But it had to be there. If it wasn't, then where had it gone?

DS Munro sighed.

'Okay, Mrs Barker, from what you've told me, I'm happy that you left your husband and your home of your own free will on Monday the sixteenth of September, and that you're not being held under duress at the residence of Graham Swift. Would you agree?'

Lucy pushed her lips together. 'I'm sorry for any trouble I may have caused, but as you can see, I'm fine.'

The detective gave her a look. 'I think we can agree to disagree on that last point, but there's nothing I can do to stop you.'

The four of them stood up and left the room. Alex shook the hand of the two detectives, then escorted Lucy out of the police station, his arm a steady presence on her shoulders.

They walked out, blinking in the sudden daylight.

'You okay?' Alex asked.

'I will be.'

'So, where to? Back to the house?'

Lucy shook her head. 'Do you mind if we take a quick detour?' she asked, and Alex looked at her curiously.

'I need to go and see my husband.'

36

'Do you believe any of that stuff?' Max could hear Briggs asking Kate as they came back into the office. He looked up from his computer.

Kate sat down next to Max and swivelled her chair round to face him. Briggs slumped opposite.

'I guess what's important is that she believes it,' Kate started, but Briggs interrupted.

'Yeah, and now she's living in that commune with all those weird people.'

'There's no law against that.'

Max pointed to Lucy's laptop screen, open on his desk. 'I've been doing some reading around on some of these sites,' he said. 'They do make it sound bloody convincing.'

'Oh, not you too,' Briggs laughed.

'No, really. They talk about climate change, and how all it would take would be for one out-of-the-ordinary hurricane to come along.' He pointed at the screen. 'Suddenly people are hoarding food and water, there are fights in supermarkets and the SHTF.'

'SHTF?' Kate asked.

'Shit hits the fan,' Max clarified. 'That's what they call it. You could argue we're already subject to media blackouts and censorship – there's so much fake news out there, we don't know what's true and what's not.'

Briggs knocked him on the arm. 'Next thing you're going

to tell me is you've been hiding cash around your house and you're growing your own veg.'

'No, but that's what Lucy was doing, wasn't it? Trying to be self-sufficient?' Max caught Briggs and Kate staring at him. 'All I'm saying is, for some people it's not such a big leap. You met Lucy's family. You grow up accepting organised religion and strict doctrine as your way of life, and this stuff...' he pointed to the survivalist website on the screen, 'isn't much of a stretch. It's just another way for fear to dictate their lives.'

Kate nodded slowly. 'Lucy Barker moved from drowning in one religion to living in the house of another. Even though God doesn't seem to be involved this time.' She sighed and put both hands flat on the table. 'So that's that. Case closed. Max – could you tie up any loose ends on the paperwork?' She stood up and looked at the whiteboard. 'Meanwhile,' she muttered, 'what about Dougie Brewer?'

Max turned back to his computer and went to shut down one of the windows on the screen. He'd had a response from the Borderland Family to his initial query. They – Max didn't know who, they never left a name – wanted to know more about him, what he believed in, and he'd drafted a response via the fake Gmail account he'd set up. But he hadn't sent it yet. He knew he needed to tell Kate what he'd done. Still, he hadn't made any progress, had he? No point in getting Munro's interest up if there wasn't anything to tell. Without thinking further, he clicked send on the email.

Kate turned round, hands on hips, and looked at them both. 'So where are we?' she asked. 'What do we know about Doug Brewer's untimely demise?'

Briggs pointed to the board. 'We know he was linked to Graham Swift and the Borderland Family. Nothing of note on his medical records. From what the landlord told us, he was basically a stoner with a few pub buddies, a dealer and a sister who thinks he was a total loser.'

'Do we know who these friends are yet? Are we assuming that Graham is one of them?' Kate asked. 'And where are we on his financial records?'

'On it,' Briggs muttered, turning back to his computer.

'And can you get on to the lab?' Kate added. 'Find out what they've got from his flat?'

The three of them went back to work.

Max started going through Lucy Barker's misper record on the system, logging the conversations, reports and outcomes of the investigation. He contacted the missing persons unit to close off the case. But something nagged in the back of his mind. Sure, she was alive rather than buried in the septic tank under Scott Barker's house, but she still seemed lost to him.

He could hear Briggs next to him on the phone to the lab, trying his hardest to be charming. The scene of crime officers had descended on Doug Brewer's house in their white suits, looking for fingerprints, blood, anything interesting that might indicate what happened to Dougie. Max just wished they had something to point one way or the other. To him it seemed unlikely that a dead body would end up in a lake without any external help.

Briggs put down the phone then started tapping nervously on the desk. Kate looked over. After a few more minutes of tapping, she said: 'Jamie? What?'

A ping answered her question. 'SOCO's found something, but the lab haven't finished running their tests. I've persuaded them to send me what they've got so far.'

Max watched him open the email, his face unhealthily close to the screen.

'And?' Kate said impatiently.

Briggs sat back in his chair, a smile on his face. He twirled his biro round in his fingers. 'Says here that SOCO found a woolly hat, wrapped up in a plastic Sainsbury's bag and hidden at the back of Doug Brewer's wardrobe.' He stopped again. Max could tell he was enjoying his little bit of power. 'It had blood on it.'

'Blood?' Kate echoed.

'And not just a little bit – it was soaked,' Briggs added with a grin. 'They ran the DNA through the system.'

'For crying out loud, Jamie,' Max said. 'Just spit it out.'

Briggs smiled again. 'It's come back to a misper, from six months ago. Male, aged sixty-five.' He paused for effect. 'Someone's father. And you're never going to guess whose it is.'

37

Even though it had been less than a week since Lucy had left home, it seemed longer. When she'd walked out of the back of her house to the main road on that Monday morning, she'd known she was doing the right thing. She'd felt the worry subside.

A rusty red Ford Fiesta had pulled into the lay-by and a young man had got out. He had one of those pretty, androgynous faces, offset by a physique and suntan fitting to hours spent working outside. He'd introduced himself as Oliver Swift, but then barely spoke as they drove the forty-five minutes to the Borderland Family house.

Lucy paused now, looking at her front door. Half of her wanted to see her husband. But the other half? She knew he was going to be angry. She knew he'd be upset. She didn't look forward to facing that.

'Do you want me to come with you?' Alex asked from the driving seat.

Lucy shook her head. 'No, best not.'

As she watched, the front door opened and Scott stood in the doorway. He was dressed in tracksuit bottoms and a T-shirt. He waited, watching them sit in Alex's truck.

She took a deep breath and climbed out of the car, walking towards him.

When she got to the doorway, she stopped, forcing her face into a semblance of a smile. 'Hi, Scott.'

'I wasn't sure if you were going to come in,' he said. He was unshaven and looked like he hadn't slept for a week. He moved out of the way of the door and she went past him into the hallway.

Without thinking she took her shoes off and hung her coat up on the rack as she'd always done. She turned round and saw Scott was watching her.

'Are you staying?' he asked.

'No. But I wanted to see you. To explain.'

Scott nodded wordlessly, then turned and went into the kitchen. He filled the kettle and put it on. She sat down at the table, her hands clenched tightly in front of her.

'I'm sorry, I didn't mean all that to happen.'

'For me to be arrested for your murder, you mean?' he said quietly, getting two mugs out of the cupboard and putting teabags in them. He was still facing away from her.

'Yes. I left a note.'

'But that doesn't make it right, Lucy!' Scott shouted, and Lucy jumped. 'One sodding note that nobody can find doesn't make it okay for you to walk out of our marriage. Didn't I deserve some sort of face-to-face discussion?'

Lucy shrank back in her seat. This was her fault. But she had tried to explain, so many times, and he'd never listened. Well, he was listening now.

Lucy swallowed. 'I explained in the ... in the note. I'm sorry, I don't know where it's gone. I need to be somewhere where I'm protected. That will look after me when the end comes.' She saw Scott shake his head. He still didn't understand.

Lucy saw him take a deep breath to calm himself. She knew Scott hated to shout, to lose control in that way, and seemingly today was no exception. He picked up the two mugs of tea and placed them on the table.

'Do you need to see someone, Lucy? Like you did before? There are professionals that can help you, you know.'

'What happened before has nothing to do with this. And I don't need some counsellor trying to convince me that what I believe is wrong.' She held onto her mug, trying to steady her resolve. 'There are people like me out there, Scott. That believe the same things I do.'

'And that's what? That the world is ending?' he said, anger edging back into his voice.

'Yes, put simply. It's not such a stretch to see what I'm talking about. You just need to look. To take the time to push away the fluff, the—' Lucy stopped, trying to find the right words. 'The insulation that the government and the press put around the truth. Societies are divided more than ever. Nations split. Climate change is real, and all it will take is one tiny match in a tinderbox and the whole world will go up.'

'Is that why you stockpiled all the food? Why you had guns? Of all things, Lucy? Why guns?'

'I thought I could build a fortress. I know you didn't believe me but when the dissolution came I thought we could survive with what I'd built for us here. But all the solar panels in the world aren't going to help, if you can't even stay faithful in peacetime.'

The statement hung between them. Lucy knew it was the one thing Scott couldn't deny: he'd cheated on her.

Lucy had been on Scott's phone trying to find a number for their electrician, when she'd found the photos. At first, her brain hadn't been able to compute what she was seeing. That was Jen, her best friend, naked on her husband's phone.

But why? Then it dawned on her. But after the initial shock and the argument, the reality of her husband sleeping with her best friend hadn't induced the reaction she expected. She'd felt a sense of inevitability. All would become clear. And it had.

'I'm sorry,' Scott mumbled, looking at his hands. 'Everything that happened with Jen, it was nothing. I know that now. Please come home, Lucy.'

He looked up at her. His eyes were bloodshot. She saw the man she married. The man she thought would keep her safe. But now she knew. Only Graham Swift could provide that protection for her.

'I'm sorry, I can't,' she said softly.

A knock on the door interrupted them and Scott got up to open it. Alex stood on the other side.

'I'm sorry, Lucy, but I need to go,' Alex said.

'Is this guy the reason why?' Scott asked Lucy bitterly.

'Don't be ridiculous,' Lucy said, putting on her shoes and coat and pushing past Scott.

'You're not taking her,' Scott shouted. 'She's not going with you.'

Lucy felt her anger build. Why, even now that she was an adult, did men constantly act like she was their property? Years of being told what to do, where to go, what to believe by her father – by God – an entity that didn't even exist! She thought Scott had been different, but when it came down to it, he was the same.

'I don't belong to you, Scott,' Lucy said. 'I wanted to see you, one last time. If you ever see the truth and realise what's coming, then please, get in touch, but until then I'll be with the Family.'

But Scott didn't seem to be listening. He pointed a finger at Alex's broad chest.

'Are you sleeping with this guy? Is he the reason you're leaving me?'

'Alex is a friend.' Lucy glanced up at Alex, embarrassed, but he didn't seem to have noticed the accusation. 'And the fact that you think that's why I left just shows how little you've been listening. Goodbye, Scott,' she said firmly, and walked away to the truck, Alex following behind.

She got in and slammed the truck door with more force than she planned. She felt tears roll down her cheeks and angrily wiped them away with her sleeve.

'I'm sorry, Alex, I didn't mean for you to get involved,' she said, but he was distracted. 'Are you okay?' she added.

He looked at her, then nodded slowly. 'Yeah, sorry. I need to go back to the police station.'

'Don't say they still have questions,' Lucy asked wearily.

'No, no, it's not that.' He started the engine of the truck. 'They need to talk to me. They've found evidence related to my father's disappearance.'

38

'Paul Sherwood was last seen on Friday the twelfth of January this year, before his son left on a work trip for the weekend.' Briggs sat back in his chair and read from the file in front of him. 'He was reported missing by Alex on Monday the fifteenth at Southampton Central nick.'

'So they lived together and worked together?' Max asked.

Briggs nodded.

'Cosy,' Max said. 'Room for disagreements?'

'Could be,' Kate said, sipping from her coffee. It was her fourth – no, sod it – her fifth of the day and the caffeine was starting to make her feel slightly out of sorts.

There was no doubt about it, all these links couldn't be coincidental. A bloodied hat found at the house of Doug Brewer. Doug Brewer himself friends with Graham Swift. And hadn't the sister mentioned someone else – could Paul Sherwood be the 'Paul something' they used to hang around with?

Tests continued on the hat and the plastic bag it had been found in, hoping for another contributor of DNA. And they were still waiting to find out more from the forensics sweep of Dougie's flat. They'd found one thing of interest. What else could be hiding beneath all that dirt?

'So what happened in the misper investigation?' Kate asked. She reached down and dug around in her desk drawer.

Nothing. 'Anyone got something I can eat?' she asked, and Max held up a KitKat. She nodded and he threw it to her.

'They took initial statements, but then border control flagged that his passport had been used on a ferry going to France.' Briggs twirled his biro between his fingers. 'Witnesses agreed a man fitting Paul Sherwood's description had been on that ferry carrying a rucksack, and the case was closed. He'd buggered off, left his life behind, end of story.'

'Apparently not,' Kate said through a mouthful of chocolate. Max reached across and took the last finger of wafer, then answered the phone on his desk.

'Alex Sherwood's here,' he said.

Alex Sherwood didn't look happy, and Kate couldn't blame him. There wasn't much they could tell him.

'So you've found suspicious evidence linking my father to Doug Brewer,' he repeated. 'Can you tell me what?'

They were back in the comfortable interview room with the sofas and nice coffee in mugs. Lucy Barker was waiting in reception outside.

'It was evidence of blood,' Kate said. She didn't want to share any more than that at this stage, not until they knew what they were dealing with.

'I see,' Alex said. 'And you think it means something's happened to Dad?'

'We don't know yet,' Kate replied. 'But we'd like to hear what you thought at the time he went missing.'

Alex Sherwood sighed and ran his hands down his face. He leaned back in the chair. 'As I told your detectives, I thought it was strange when Dad hadn't come home by Monday. He was many things, but he always showed up for work. He'd built the business, our business, up from scratch and he was proud of his reputation.'

'This is the tree surgery company,' Max clarified.

'Yes. You guys took my statement and came to look round the house, but after that, nothing. Until you said he'd been seen on a ferry to France, and that was it.' He shook his head. 'But I didn't believe Dad would do that – up and leave without saying goodbye. Something must have happened.'

'And how did your father know Graham Swift?' Kate asked.

'They were friends from university. Then pub mates. At one time all three of them lived in Portswood, so they were regulars at the Gordon Arms. That was probably, what, twenty years ago? If not more? Then they grew apart. Graham got married, moved to Ringwood, had Oliver. Dad started working harder, building up the business. And Dougie? Well, he didn't go anywhere, did he?'

'Did they keep in touch?' Max asked.

'They did, yes. Dad would mention them and they still went to the pub occasionally. I know they went on the Saturday night before he disappeared. And he did some work on the trees at Graham's estate.'

'And that's how you know Graham Swift and the Borderland Family,' Kate said, and Alex nodded.

'So what does this mean now? Will you reopen the investigation into Dad's disappearance?'

Kate looked at Alex. The man looked tired and worried. She nodded.

'We will, yes,' she said.

Something's up, she thought to herself. There were too many loose ends. And at that moment, it looked like all roads led to Graham Swift and the Borderland Family.

39

Scott realised he was sat in the dark. The mug of tea beside him was stone cold. He looked at the clock, surprised to see hours had passed since Lucy had left. Was this what shock felt like? He'd always expected it to feel jumpy, adrenaline-filled, but this was just numbness. A black hole where he was dropping through the void.

There was no hope now. Lucy had walked back in through the front door, like he wished she would, but then she'd turned round and walked straight out again. He didn't understand. All those words and thoughts and theories that came tumbling out of her mouth, none of it made sense. So she'd left because she thought the world was going to end, was that it? But deep down he knew the final destructive act had been his affair. Whatever else had been going on, that had been down to him and him alone.

He walked into the kitchen with his tea and poured it down the sink. Using the same mug, he took the vodka down from the shelf and poured a large measure. Scott looked at it, dirty swirls of brown floating around in the clear liquid, no more than he deserved. He downed it in one, wincing at the harsh taste. Then he did it again. And again. And again.

Lights coming on in his driveway. A car on gravel. A loud noise. The bell, over and over. The front door opening. The hallway light turning on. A voice.

'Scott?'

A woman's voice. It wasn't Lucy. He only wanted Lucy.

'Go away,' he slurred.

He was slumped on the kitchen floor, the cupboards holding him upright. He looked up and saw Jen standing over him, the emergency spare key from the outside lock box dangling from her fingers.

'Go away,' he repeated.

'For Christ's sake, Scott, what have you been doing?' she said, and leaned over to try and pull him off the floor. He mumbled a profanity at her.

'You can't stay there all night.' She stood over him, her hands on her hips.

'I can. I can bloody well do what I like,' he muttered.

'Get up, Scott. Self-pity doesn't suit you.'

Jen tried again, and this time Scott let her help him to his feet. He stood up on wobbly legs, feeling dizzy as the blood rushed to his head. She held him steady up the stairs to the bedroom then watched him collapse on his bed. He stayed where he fell, at an angle on top of the duvet, closing his eyes.

Saturday

40

Sam was up and out of bed before Kate had even opened her eyes. She heard the bedroom door close, then squinted at the clock: 8.43. She sighed. That wasn't a decent lie-in by anyone's standards, but if she was trying to make an effort she should shift her arse. Even so, by the time she'd made her way to the kitchen, the coffee machine was on and he had his porridge in front of him. He was wearing running gear.

She poured cereal into a bowl, smothered it with milk then sat down next to Sam at the table.

'I can't believe you eat that stuff,' he said. 'It's full of sugar.'

'That's why it's nice,' Kate replied through a mouthful. 'Are you going for a run?'

'I thought we could go together,' Sam said, and Kate gave him a look. 'Okay, but can we at least leave the house today?' Another pause. 'A walk, maybe?'

Personally, Kate fancied sitting on the sofa for a few hours catching up on Netflix, but the sun was shining and Sam had such an optimistic twinkle in his eyes that she couldn't bear to let him down again.

'Fine,' she said. 'Just let me finish my breakfast in peace.'

As she chewed, Sam told her about his week at the office. Some proposal he'd been working on had been approved and he was jubilant.

'Although it's going to be extra hours, and I'll probably be away Monday night,' he added.

'That's fine,' Kate replied, secretly glad. She could work late without any guilt. 'I'm sorry these cases have taken over,' she said, looking over at him. 'I thought things would get simpler now we've found Lucy Barker, but it's getting more complicated by the day.'

'Do you think that guy is dead?' Sam asked. Kate had told him the basics of what they had found out about Paul Sherwood when she got home last night.

'Probably.' Kate grimaced. 'When I spoke to Forensics they said that not only was the hat soaked in blood, but there was what they assumed to be grey matter inside. Bits of brain,' she clarified. 'And skull fragments. They'll have to refer it to the pathologist, but I'm guessing the bloke was hit so hard he left a good portion of his head behind.'

She looked at Sam. He was staring at his breakfast, his spoon poised in his hand. He pushed the porridge away slowly.

'Sometimes,' he said to Kate, 'I wish you had a normal job we could discuss over breakfast, and it wouldn't make me feel physically sick.'

'Sorry,' Kate muttered. 'But you did ask.'

Kate had to admit, the walk was pleasant. They had driven to the New Forest then set out at a march down the nearest footpath. It was a lovely sunny day – trees, horses, even the occasional donkey – this nature stuff wasn't so bad after all. She could see other people, families, kids, out with their dogs, doing normal weekend activities. Normal people. She was holding Sam's hand; she hoped there was a pub nearby.

But even so, her brain couldn't help ticking back to the case.

Everything reminded her of it. Alex Sherwood didn't live far from here, and she wondered what direction the lake was in. Kate remembered that she hadn't been down there yet to have a look at where Doug Brewer was found. Where poor old Lucy Barker had swum into his body.

She wondered how Scott was getting on, all alone in that big house.

'You're quiet,' Sam said, interrupting her musing.

'Sorry, I'm just—'

'You're thinking about the case,' he finished for her and she nodded.

'Have you ever thought about a possible apocalypse?' she asked, and he laughed.

'What? With zombies?'

'No! Not with zombies. With normal people, and nuclear war, and riots and...' She tapered off, seeing his face.

'No. Beyond watching *The Walking Dead*, it's never crossed my mind.'

'So what makes a normal person start to worry about this stuff?' Kate wondered. 'I mean, enough that they would go to the effort of getting a gun? Give up their entire life and go and live in some shitty commune?'

Sam stopped walking and pulled her round to face him. He took both of her hands in his. 'Do you need to go to work?' he asked. His cheeks were slightly pink from the walking, his hair ruffled in the breeze. Kate remembered how much she fancied him. 'Look, I don't mind. I'm sorry I snapped at you the other night. I know you have a difficult job. I need to be more understanding about it.'

'What? No!' Kate exclaimed. 'I'm fine. This is fine. This is better than fine. Let's finish our walk, and go and get some lunch at the pub.'

'And then you'll go into the station,' Sam said, a statement rather than a question.

'And then I'll go to work,' Kate admitted.

41

Scott felt a hand run gently down his back, rousing him from his dream. The room was silent, light streaming in through the open curtains. He felt someone next to him, then the hand moving round to his front, a warm body pushing up behind him.

He squeezed his eyes tight shut, trying to remember the night before. His head hurt. He thought he was going to puke.

'Morning, gorgeous,' a voice whispered.

A feeling of dread ran through his body and he tensed. *Jen.* She was here next to him in the bed. She'd been here last night. He'd been drunk. They had ... Had they? He didn't think so.

Jen's hand continued its journey, running down his bare chest. Scott realised her hand was in his boxers and she was ... Oh god. He had to stop this. He had to stop this now.

He leapt out of bed, grabbing clothes off the floor. He stood with them covering him, almost cowering, bent in two, anything to get away from her. Jen raised herself up in bed on one elbow, watching him.

'What's wrong?' she asked.

'What's wrong?' he shouted. 'What's *wrong*?' Scott scrabbled, putting his trousers on, almost falling over in the process. 'My wife's left me, and you're lying there like this is the most natural thing in the world.'

'Why shouldn't it be?' Jen said, smiling.

Scott stared at her. 'Because you're Lucy's best friend, aren't you? Don't you have any loyalty to her?'

'Isn't it a bit late to be asking me that? You know it was always about you, Scott. Even at university. Except Lucy got there first, with her blonde hair and blue eyes and oh-so-innocent expression.' Jen reached forward from the bed, trying to take his hand again. 'But now she's gone, we can be together. As we always should have been.'

Scott backed away. 'But . . . but I don't want you. I don't want this. I'm sorry.'

'Pardon?' Jen said, recoiling from his words. Her expression changed in an instant. 'You're *sorry*?' She sat up in bed, glaring at him. 'So what was I to you? Just a convenient fuck?'

Scott stuttered. He didn't know what to say.

Jen sat up in the bed, pulling the duvet over her naked chest. 'For six months we carry on behind Lucy's back and you don't care, as long as you're getting your end away. Then one day you get a flash of conscience and you finish it. I said nothing to Lucy. Nothing!' she shouted at him. 'I thought it was just a matter of time, that you were getting ready to leave her. But then *she* ups and leaves you without a word, and *this* happens? And all you can say is you're *sorry*?'

'Yes, I . . .' Scott stopped himself. Nothing was going to put this right. 'I need you to leave.'

Jen shook her head, her face contorted with disgust. She climbed out of bed, looking for her clothes. 'You sicken me, Scott, you know that?' She got dressed, then turned to face him again. 'You're a fucking coward.'

Scott stayed mute, watching her as she continued her tirade.

'I don't know why I thought you were something better,' she spat. She looked at him. Scott could see the hatred in her eyes. 'Why did I waste my time? You're nothing more than a pathetic excuse for a man.'

She went to say something else, then shook her head and stalked out of the room. Scott heard the front door slam and the gunning of an engine as Jen sped out of his driveway.

He let his breath out slowly. His hands were shaking: from the hangover, or relief that she had gone.

He'd always wondered about Lucy and Jen's friendship. They'd never had much in common apart from a shared past, and he'd often thought they spent time together for no other reason than a lack of options. He knew Lucy didn't have many other friends. But Jen? Had she stayed friends with Lucy just so she could be around him? He'd never realised how she felt, not to this extent.

At university they'd been close. After Lucy's suicide attempt they'd banded together, doing all they could to help Lucy, to get her back on her feet. And Jen had been someone he could talk to who understood. But he'd never thought of her as anything more, until that first drunken night. And after? Well, Jen had hit the nail on the head: he'd just been having too much fun.

Jen was right. He was pathetic.

Lucy had been right to leave him. What could he possibly offer her? He didn't understand her worries, but he'd never even made an effort to try and help her. Instead he'd cheated on her with her best friend, then carried on his crappy little life, moving from one day to the next without thinking about what she needed.

Scott wanted it all to go away. He wanted to stop feeling

like the shittiest person in the world. He climbed back into bed and pulled the duvet over him. In that moment he hoped Lucy's prophecy would come true: that the world would end and take him down to hell with it.

42

As Kate walked into the office, Max was cross-legged on the floor, surrounded by paper. A video was paused, mid flow, on the computer screen above him, showing grainy black-and-white footage. His trainers had been discarded under the desk and he had his takeaway coffee cup halfway to his mouth. He paused when he saw her.

'What are you doing here?' he asked bluntly. If he'd known he was going to see anyone today, let alone Kate, he would have made more of an effort. He would have brushed his hair, put on clean socks. Something.

'I could ask you the same question,' Kate replied, looking at the mess.

'Are you wearing hiking boots?' Max asked.

Kate sighed. 'Ridiculous attempt to have a normal life.' She slumped on the chair next to him and undid the laces, pulling them off her feet. 'And what are you wearing? Did you even get dressed this morning?' Max pulled his tracksuit trousers up a bit, aware he might have been showing the top of his bum. 'I'm not sure I've ever seen you in civvies,' Kate continued. 'Except ... well ...'

She stopped, her face turning red, and Max allowed himself a small smile. Except for the Christmas party, he thought. You definitely saw me out of uniform then.

'So what are you looking at?' Kate asked.

Max allowed her to change the subject.

'This pile here,' he said, pointing to his left, 'are all the statements relating to Paul Sherwood's disappearance. As you can see, there's not much. And this one here are the ones that cross over with Dougie Brewer.'

He held up the one piece of paper.

'That's it?' Kate said.

'Yeah, and it's vague at best. It's a statement from Doug himself, confirming that he was with Paul Sherwood at the pub on the evening of Saturday the thirteenth of January. The day after he was last seen by his son. And that there,' he pointed to the grainy image on the screen, 'is the CCTV footage from outside the pub that night.'

Kate leaned over and clicked play. Max pulled himself to his feet and stood next to her. 'There's Dougie,' he said, pointing to a man coming out of the pub. 'And there's Paul Sherwood.'

'That's Graham Swift,' Kate said, looking at the third man with them.

'That's what I thought,' Max said. 'But nobody interviewed him. There's nothing here mentioning him at all. And something happened that night.'

They both watched the screen as the three men stood outside the pub. Graham was waving his hands around wildly, seemingly directed at Paul Sherwood. Then Dougie put his arm around Graham.

'It looks like he's trying to calm him down,' Kate said.

'Keep watching,' Max replied.

A younger man appeared at the edge of the screen, coming from a different direction. He guided Graham away and walked him down the road, out of shot. After a moment, Paul and Dougie followed them.

'Who was that?' Max asked.

'That's Oliver Swift,' Kate confirmed, and Max nodded.

'That's what I assumed. So what happened there? It looks like they were arguing, but Dougie doesn't mention anything in his statement.'

Kate shrugged. 'I suppose the coppers at the time didn't think it was relevant because they had the sighting of Paul getting on the ferry at Portsmouth docks, so they let it all go.'

'I guess.' Max sighed. 'So what's your theory? Is he living a life of cheese and wine in France, or dead in a ditch somewhere?'

'I'm afraid my cynicism says the latter.' Kate peered more closely at the man on the screen. 'Same fate as Dougie Brewer. But if that's the case, where is he? And surely it's more than coincidence that two of the men on this video aren't around any more?'

'Exactly,' Max said. 'Although I have a theory about Dougie.'

Kate looked interested. Max sat down on the chair next to her, flipping his screen over to the email he'd received earlier. Kate scooted over, her body close to his. Max was relieved that he'd at least had a shower that morning.

'These are Dougie's financial records.' He scrolled down, noting Kate's sharp intake of breath.

'He's got more than fifty grand in there,' Kate muttered. She looked at Max. 'So why was he living in such a shithole?'

'Exactly. So I did some more digging and it turns out he received all the money about a year ago when his father died. But he hasn't touched it. He was only spending whatever crappy income he was receiving before – so basically benefits and a few jobs here and there. There's random amounts from different people, so I'm guessing handyman jobs.' Max leaned back in his chair. 'What if we're looking at his death from the wrong angle?'

'What do you mean?'

'His sister wasn't a fan, right? And then he gets all this money from their father. Who would get that in the event of his death?'

'She would,' Kate said, slowly.

'Exactly,' Max said, for the third time. He took a final swig of cold coffee and dumped the cup in the bin. 'Do you want to get something to eat?' he asked.

Kate smiled. 'Let's go one better. Fancy a road trip?'

43

The weather had been improving steadily as the day went on, so by the time Max and Kate arrived the sun was shining through the gaps in the trees, sparkling on the water. The lake was empty, a lone speedboat bobbing by the pontoon. The two of them stood at the water's edge.

'Hard to imagine a body floating here,' Max said, taking in the scene. Autumn was starting to touch the edges of the trees; a few discarded brown leaves littered the grass. 'Do people still swim in the lake?'

'I believe so,' Kate replied. 'I guess if you're the sort of person who likes swimming in freezing, dirty water, it would take more than a corpse to put you off.' She looked up at Max. 'After all, what are the chances of finding another?'

'True.' He looked back at the clubhouse. Toilets and changing rooms: a basic hut. 'No CCTV?' he asked, and Kate shook her head.

'No, and only one road in,' she said. She pointed to a jetty branching out from the far side of the lake. 'No road access to that either, footpath only.' Kate frowned. 'How did Dougie Brewer get here? Dr Adams said he wasn't breathing when he went into the water, so someone must have brought his body in some sort of vehicle. So how, and when?'

Max turned and stood with his back to the water. It would have been easy to get a car down to the edge – it was built for waterskiers and jet skis, after all – but the body had been found on the right-hand side, halfway across. It must have been a good kilometre away; the lake wasn't like a river, with a strong current. Could a dead body have floated there?

He looked over at Kate. She was still frowning, deep in thought. It felt good being with her today. And not just because he had a sounding board for the case. She didn't feel like his boss. Especially on a Saturday, out of uniform and away from the office. It was nice, although—

Max stopped himself. He had to get these thoughts out of his head. She *was* his boss. They were working. And she was married.

'The Borderland Family house is about half a mile over there,' Kate said, pointing past the trees into the distance.

'That close?' Max felt a flash of guilt. He'd heard back from them that morning. An email, talking about their way of life and what they believed in. Asking for still more information about him. He hadn't yet replied.

Max noticed that Kate had started wandering round the water. He followed her, quickly catching up as her progress was halted by thick undergrowth. They stared across to the other side. From here it looked the same; the lake was lined on all sides by reeds and overhanging trees. There didn't seem any way someone could walk around the edge.

'What about there?' Max asked, pointing to a break in the trees on the right. It was small, but it seemed like there was a definite opening to the water.

'Can you swim there and check it out?' Kate asked, and Max looked at her incredulously. 'I'm kidding,' she laughed. 'Come on, let's see if there's a way round.'

They pored over Max's iPhone, studying the satellite image of the lake. He zoomed in on the screen to where the opening seemed to be, and sure enough, a small gap in the trees showed a possible way through. The two of them went back to Kate's car, then drove slowly, Max guiding her in the right direction. A few times they had to turn round and go back, but eventually Max could make out a muddy track.

He looked at Kate. She had the same excited expression he knew he had on his face. Without talking, Kate opened the boot and passed him blue plastic overshoes. He put them on over his trainers. Even if this was nothing, they didn't want to be contaminating a possible crime scene. Kate did the same, then took a few other items out of the boot. They started walking down the track.

The road here was muddy and full of potholes. Any trace of tarmac or gravel soon disappeared, leaving behind little more than a river of mud.

'There's no way you'd get a normal car down here,' Max commented, and Kate nodded. She was picking her way round the edge of a particularly large brown puddle, hanging onto trees and branches for support. Max's trainers weren't faring well in this terrain, mud seeping into his socks.

After about a hundred metres the trees cleared, and Max could see the lake glistening in front of them. He looked at the gap – there was no room to turn a vehicle round. You'd have to reverse the whole way down; it wasn't an easy dump site.

'Someone would need to be familiar with this loca- tion,' Kate said, articulating what he was thinking. She was studying the ground, backing away from a layer of mud hardening in the sunshine. She pointed.

'Tyre tracks,' she said. 'Get SOCO down here.'

Max made the call, they did another quick review of the scene, then went back to the car to wait for the forensics team. Kate tapped impatiently on the steering wheel.

'You can go if you want,' Max said. 'I don't mind staying. I'm sure someone can give me a lift home later.'

'No chance. This is the first good lead we have,' she said. 'If SOCO can get some idea what vehicle was used to drop the body then we might be able to make some progress.' She looked over at him. 'Do you need to get back?' She paused. 'To Charlie?'

Max was confused. How did Kate know about Charlie? 'No, my brother can look after himself.'

Max watched a hint of a smile appear on Kate's face. 'Charlie's your brother?'

'Yeah. He's living with me at the moment while he gets his life back on track. His wife's kicked him out.' Max sighed, thinking about the discarded pizza boxes, the overflowing ashtray and empty beer cans he knew he'd have to face when he got home. 'He's a pain in the arse. The entire time when we were growing up, I saw him as the perfect older brother. Even my mum agreed Charlie could do no wrong.'

'And now?' Kate asked.

Max snorted. 'He's getting divorced, he has nowhere to live, he's been signed off sick from work and sits on my sofa all day, getting fat.' He stopped, feeling embarrassed from the oversharing. 'Do you have any brothers or sisters?' he asked quickly.

Kate shook her head. 'No. Although my aunt lived down the road, so my cousin Finn was always around. And I know what you mean. Finn's a doctor, PhD in weather systems or something impressive, I forget what. I'm always *just* a copper.'

'But you're not!' Max replied. 'I mean, you are, but you're a detective sergeant. You've made a lot more progress than me.'

Kate laughed. 'You have time. How old are you, anyway?' she asked. 'Twenty-five?'

'What? No!' Max grinned. 'I'm thirty-two.'

Kate smiled that small smile again, then paused. Max could tell she wanted to ask him something.

'What?' he prompted.

Kate turned to him. 'Delaney mentioned you haven't applied to take the NIE yet.'

Ah, shit. The National Investigator's Exam – one of the many obstacles you had to face to become a detective.

'Why, Max?' she continued. 'I thought you were serious about this transfer?'

Max turned his attention to the muddy path. He could feel Kate's eyes on him. 'I am,' he muttered. 'It's just ... I don't know.'

The car fell silent.

'We're back to our coincidences again, aren't we?' Kate said. Max was glad she'd sensed his reluctance and changed the conversation. 'This lake is less than half a mile from Graham Swift. Both Dougie Brewer and Paul Sherwood used to hang around with him. And then Lucy bloody Barker ends up staying in that house. You can't tell me this is all chance.'

Max nodded. His stomach started churning. He knew what he had to do.

'And that commune, or whatever we're supposed to call it, is just plain weird,' she carried on.

'Kate,' Max said, interrupting her. 'I've been in contact with them.'

She turned slowly in her seat. 'What do you mean?'

'A few days ago I sent them an enquiry via their website,' Max said quickly. 'I'm not sure why. Maybe I thought it would help the case to find out more, but they replied and I've been talking to them.'

'Who is "they"?' Kate asked. Max couldn't read her; he couldn't tell if she was angry or curious or something else.

'I'm not sure, they never sign off. But it seems to be just one person replying.'

'And you didn't think to mention this to me sooner?' Kate said. 'Who have you been saying you are? Not Max Cooper, for fuck's sake?'

'That's just it,' Max replied, gabbling now. 'I put a false name, and I set up a new email address and used that. I said I knew about mechanics and cars so they'd think I had some skill to offer. But they don't know who I am, they think I'm someone interested in their cause. But what if,' he turned awkwardly to face her, excited, 'what if I go in undercover?'

Kate opened her eyes wide. 'Oh, come on! We are so far off getting approval for that.'

'I've done all the training, I've been to Hendon, ask SO10. And none of them have met me. I haven't even met Lucy Barker.'

'You've met Alex Sherwood, and he's connected.' Kate sighed. 'But it's not just that, Max. Even putting those reservations aside, we don't have any actual evidence linking Graham Swift or the Borderland Family to Doug Brewer's death or Paul Sherwood's disappearance. We have no evidence at all. We'd never get sign-off.'

She stopped as they saw a white van roll up beside them, *Scientific Services Department* written on the side.

'Come on,' Kate said. 'Let's get these guys to work. And Max,' she added, 'just leave them be for the moment, right?'

Max nodded, but he'd already felt the flare of excitement take hold. He would get on the inside of that compound. Whatever it took.

44

When Lucy had asked Graham for permission to go and see her brother, she hadn't expected to be disappointed. But he'd shaken his head no, without hesitation.

'Going to the police station was fine, but I don't want you exposed to the establishment any more,' he'd said.

'But I want him to move in with us,' she'd pleaded. 'If it's about his fee, I can cover it, and more. The house is half mine when Scott sells it.'

After a moment, he'd nodded. 'Call him from the phone in the hallway. He can come here.'

But Isaac was late. Lucy waited on the stone steps to the house, looking out to the courtyard. She knew the house was a nightmare to get to if you didn't have a car, and what if he'd got lost? What if he'd had second thoughts?

At last the buzzer to the gate sounded and Lucy jumped to her feet. Isaac came in slowly; he seemed tentative and shy. Lucy remembered how it felt to arrive at the massive property, and rushed to give him a hug.

He saw her and smiled, wrapping his arms around her.

'I thought you were dead,' he muttered into her hair. 'They told me Scott had killed you.'

'All lies, Isaac,' Lucy said, looking into the innocent face of her brother. 'They'll tell you anything to distract you. To keep you away from the truth.' He looked at her quizzically and she laughed. 'It'll all become clear, don't worry.'

A bell sounded across the courtyard and Lucy grabbed Isaac's hand. 'Come on,' she said. 'The lecture's about to start.'

The dining room was full. The tables had been pushed back and chairs arranged in a semicircle around one chair in the centre of the room. Apart from squalling from the baby, everyone was silent.

Lucy and Isaac took a seat at the back of the room. Now everyone was there, she could see how many people lived at the house. She counted. Twenty-three, mostly faces she recognised from around the grounds.

Isaac gave her a puzzled look, but she just smiled and nodded as Oliver helped Graham into the room, sitting him in the chair at the front, resting his walking stick on the ground. Oliver moved off to the side, standing against the wall.

Graham put his hands together and rested his fingers against his mouth. He beamed at everyone in the circle.

'Today,' he said, 'I want to start from the beginning. Why are we here?' He paused, and Lucy looked nervously around. Nobody replied to him; it seemed to be a rhetorical question. 'We have had a few new people join us—' Lucy felt eyes on her, and she smiled. Expressionless faces stared back. 'So I thought it would be a good refresher. How might the dissolution happen? How might it begin?' He looked around. 'Tell me?'

'Inept government,' a man said to Lucy's left, and Graham pointed at him.

'Yes. What else?'

'Divided society.'

'Yes. Splits in the fabric of our societal make-up, due to differences in religion, in money, in social group.' He paused, smiling. 'Disagreements over whether Great Britain should stay or leave the EU. All hyped up by our government.'

Lucy watched him. Graham seemed more relaxed now, easing into his speech. He sat back in his chair, his hands loose in his lap.

'These rifts cause tension. Arguments on social media, exchanges on the underground, on public transport. Before coming here, we'd all seen it, hadn't we?' Nods from around the room. 'White thuggish man shouts abuse at poor brown lady in a headscarf. Immigrants told to go home, denied basic rights to stay somewhere they've lived their whole life. We're told we're not good enough, we're not thin enough, not butch enough. We're told not to cry, not to show weakness. But it's all carefully designed to break us down, so we don't see what's going on behind the scenes.'

People were murmuring in agreement, sitting up straight in their seats, their gaze fixed on Graham.

'And then what happens?' he asked. The room was silent. Waiting. 'Tornadoes. Floods. Hurricanes. Drought. A random climate change event.' Graham eased himself up slowly and pointed a finger around the group. 'A situation where we lose something we depend on. Water, electricity, anything.' He started to make tentative steps around the room, still talking. 'People stockpile. Supermarkets are stripped of bottled water, of tinned produce. Supplies are scarce. The media talk about it, the fear gets worse. There's looting in the streets, widespread panic, violence, fighting over silly things, like the last bottle of water in the corner shop.'

Graham paused. 'So what does the government do?'

'Media blackout,' the man next to Lucy said, and Graham smiled.

'Yes. The press is silenced. Particular topics are censored.

There's loss of free speech. People try to take cash out, the banks are closed, because, let's face it, they don't have enough money to cover the contents of everyone's bank accounts. The stock market crashes. Now for the really scary stuff.'

Graham's voice took on a deeper tone, slowing down his words for the benefit of his audience.

'First responders stop showing up for work. Doctors, paramedics, the police. They stay home, because they have their own families to care about. People start to die. More panic. Outbreaks of disease.' He paused again. 'Martial law. The country is controlled by the army, enforcing the will of the government. Full dissolution.'

Graham stopped his pacing and sat back down on his chair. He leaned forward, resting his elbows on his knees.

'Did you know it's been predicted that ninety per cent of people in the US would die within twelve to twenty-four months without electricity? And that's America. What do you think would happen on a tiny island like Great Britain? We'd starve. We'd contract a simple infection and die because we couldn't get the antibiotics to treat it. Well, let me tell you, my friends. Not here.'

He smiled, nodding slowly. 'We have water. We have a generator. We have pharmaceuticals and drugs to keep us going for months. We are a diverse mix of professions and knowledge.' He stood up in front of the group, opening his arms wide. 'We will be the ten per cent.'

Around Lucy, people had started cheering and smiling, and Lucy found herself doing the same. She looked over at Isaac. He was watching the group, his mouth slightly open, clapping slowly. She knew it. He couldn't deny what was happening out there in the world, not when he was faced with the truth. People were now standing up, going over to

Graham and hugging him, thanking him for letting them stay there.

Lucy led Isaac away to the kitchen, and sat down at the table opposite him.

His face looked stunned, but Lucy knew how he was feeling. This was the harsh reality, but he'd be safe here.

'Can I have some water?' he mumbled.

Lucy got up and filled a glass from the sink. 'I felt the same way as you,' she said, passing it to him. He looked up at her quickly. 'I was at this table the first time I met Graham, and I was overwhelmed by what he told me. But deep down I knew he was right. Our future lies in havens like this.' She reached over and took his hand. 'We're ready here, Isaac. You heard what he said. We're ready.'

Isaac took a long pull from the glass and swallowed. 'So you're telling me everything the government does—'

'Is designed to exploit events in the media for their own personal gain, designed to hide the truth from us.' Lucy nodded. 'Yes.'

'And that modern life will … What do you call it?'

'Dissolve. The dissolution is not only inevitable, but imminent, Isaac. Do you know why we're called the Borderland Family?' Isaac shook his head and Lucy sat up straight in her seat. 'Because we are the people on the edge of society, the border between modern civilisation and the future. And when it all collapses, we are the ones who will survive. A new land.'

Isaac nodded slowly, then looked at his watch. 'I have to go. Mum and Dad will be expecting me home.'

He stood up and Lucy walked him out of the house and back to the gate. He seemed deep in thought. 'It's a lot to take in, I know. But you'll come back, won't you?' she pleaded. 'Please?'

Isaac reached down and gave her a big hug. 'I will. I'll be back in touch. Do I phone on the number you called from before?'

'Yes. Any time.'

The huge gates opened, and Isaac started to walk through, then turned back for a second. 'Look after yourself, Lucy,' he said. 'I love you.'

Lucy watched as the gates closed behind Isaac. Graham was waiting for her on the stone steps as she turned back to the house.

'Come in, you have your chores to do,' he reminded her.

'How good would it be if Isaac could join us here?' she said to him, excited. 'We could be a family again.'

'Give him time,' Graham said. 'Not everyone is a believer. And in the meantime, the only family you need is here.'

Lucy felt his hand on her back, ushering her inside as the large wooden front door closed behind them.

45

The scene of crime officers got to work, donning white suits and masks, covering up every part of their bodies with protective clothing. They started their slow progression down the track, expertly negotiating their equipment over the mud, littering their path with yellow plastic triangles as they started to collect evidence.

Kate stood at the edge of the path watching Max talk to one of them – pointing towards the lake where they'd found the tyre tracks. She was pissed off with him for contacting the Borderland Family without telling her, but it wasn't only that. She felt like it was a betrayal – something personal. She started to walk away from the crime scene cordon, down a footpath into the woods, trying to get her emotions under control. This is ridiculous, she told herself as she walked, get a grip. Stop being so pathetic.

So he'd gone behind her back. As his supervising officer, that was annoying, sure, but not enough to get upset over. Perhaps she just needed a bit more sleep. Perhaps her worry over things with Sam was drifting into her work.

But she had trusted Max. She'd thought he trusted her. When she'd seen him in the office that afternoon, she'd been pleased, ridiculously so, to be able to spend some time with him. And the fact that Charlie was his brother? She'd felt a weird sense of relief that he was single. In the back of her mind she'd stupidly thought they had a relationship that was closer than just colleagues. It was different with Max to how it was with Briggs. But of course, it wasn't.

Kate heard footsteps coming up behind her. She cleared her throat before turning around to face him.

'Are you okay?' Max stopped a few feet away from her. Away from the sunshine, it was cold in the woods and he'd put a sweatshirt on, wrapping his arms round his body to keep warm. Mud coated his shoes and the bottom of his tracksuit trousers, and she noticed a smudge of it had somehow made its way to his chin.

'I'm fine, how are they getting on?' Kate asked, pointing back to the bustle on the track.

'They're going to be a while,' Max replied. 'Should we head off? I'm not sure there's much more we can do today.'

Kate nodded. She should go home to Sam. To her *husband*. She started walking to the car, picking her way carefully over the tree roots littering the path. She looked back to him. He seemed preoccupied, his gaze fixed on something in a clearing a few feet away from them.

'Are you coming?' she asked, then followed his line of sight, walking back and standing next to him. 'What?'

He continued to peer into the woods, then slowly pointed towards a patch of stinging nettles. In the gap in the trees they'd obviously flourished, taking advantage of the extra sunlight.

But it wasn't just that. The area of bright green weeds seemed isolated; where the rest of the clearing was still relatively bare, these had prospered.

'What does that say to you?' Max asked.

They both walked towards it, treading carefully around the brambles and undergrowth. Kate hardly dared to articulate it out loud. This was a plot of ground that had been fertilised.

That had received nutrients where there shouldn't be any. And it was an area roughly six feet long, two feet across – about the same size as a grave.

He looked at her, his mouth open.

'Max,' she said slowly. 'Call the cadaver dogs.'

Sunday

46

The sunshine had disappeared, and all Kate faced that morning was a depressing grey drizzle. It settled on her coat and hair, and a chill ran down her spine. The perfect atmosphere for viewing a corpse, she thought grimly.

It was just gone 6 a.m., but Kate knew the crime scene had been buzzing with activity all night. The dogs had arrived, quickly latching onto their quarry, barking enthusiastically. It had been a body, all right.

Large floodlights marked the scene from miles away, and the entrance to the track was blocked with white vans. She abandoned her car and walked to where she could see the tall figure of Max waiting. Like Kate, he was in a thick coat, boots on his feet rather than the light trainers he'd had on yesterday. He was wearing a baseball cap with a New York Yankees logo on the front. He scowled at her from underneath the peak.

'Where have we got to?' Kate asked. 'Did you call Briggs?'

'I left a message. Lucky sod's probably asleep. Pathologist's been here for about an hour.'

They started their walk down the track in silence, avoiding the SOCOs in their white suits carrying evidence back to their vans. The two SOCOs from yesterday had multiplied exponentially, and they now seemed to be everywhere. One tyre impression had turned into a full-scale murder investigation.

Kate had updated DCI Delaney the night before. 'This is yours, Kate,' her boss had said before ending the call. 'Follow it to the end.' Kate had every intention of doing so.

They put the blue plastic overshoes and gloves on, same as the day before. Pushing under the blue-and-white cordon into the crime scene, they followed the path of stepping plates laid out to avoid contamination. A basic tent had been erected in the woodland to their right, and Kate could see intermittent camera flashes coming from inside. She pushed the flap of the tent open and went in, Max following behind.

More floodlights lit up the inside, focusing down on the large hole in the middle. It wasn't deep, probably no more than a foot, and Kate could see orange-brown skin and fragments of clothing. A man was crouched over the body, a SOCO taking photographs next to him as the body was exhumed.

The man looked up at Kate. He lifted a gloved hand to acknowledge her, then stood up slowly. The white protective suit and glasses covered him from head to foot, but from his posture and obviously round tummy, Kate recognised Albie.

He climbed out of the hole, gesturing for Kate and Max to leave the tent, then followed behind. Outside, he pulled the hood down from his head, the mask off his mouth and squinted at them in the morning light, his grey hair in disarray.

'How lovely of you to join us on this fine morning,' Albie said with a grimace.

'Not what you were expecting on a Sunday?' Kate asked.

Albie chuckled. 'I was enjoying a particularly lovely dream about Natalie Wood when the phone rang.' Kate and Max both looked blank. '*West Side Story*? *Rebel Without a Cause*?' He shook his head. 'Never mind.' He pointed towards the tent. 'I think I've done all I can for today. I'll get the body transferred to the morgue and have a better look there.'

'Initial thoughts?' Kate asked.

'Dead a while, but probably less than a year judging by the state of decomp. Male, about fifty to sixty in age.'

'Any idea of cause of death?'

Albie smiled. 'You know better than to ask me questions like that before I've had a chance to do the post, Katherine.'

'I won't quote you on it.'

He looked back. 'Well, it's clear our friend sustained a nasty injury to his head. Skull is completely caved in at the back, absolute mess. But I wouldn't like to say whether that was pre- or post-mortem, or what caused it. I'll tell you more tomorrow,' Albie finished. 'Assuming they can get him out today, I'll do the PM first thing. Come and see me at lunchtime.'

'Do you think it's Paul Sherwood?' Max asked once Albie had retreated back into the tent.

'Keep your voice down,' Kate replied, ushering Max away from the crime scene. Already she could see a few curious reporters clustered at the edge of the cordon. She sighed.

'Because of those guys, I'll have to go and see Alex Sherwood today to warn him we've found a body. I don't want him to find out on the local news and think it's something to do with his father, even if we're not certain.' She looked at Max, then away to the crime scene. 'But yes, I'd guess at it being Paul Sherwood.'

'What are the chances of us finding a completely random dead body out here,' Max commented, 'so close to the dump site of Dougie Brewer?'

'And so close to the home of the Borderland Family,' Kate added. Those coincidences again, Kate thought to herself. They could be just that, in a horrific twist of fate. But Max was right to question it. What were the chances, indeed?

47

Lucy woke to the sound of the bell. Breakfast. Same time every morning: prepared by members of the Family and served at the dining table together. They were a civilised family, Graham had said, and as such, they would eat together.

The other occupants of the bedroom had already gone. Up and dressed before she was even awake.

She put some clothes on, then went downstairs to the dining room. A large table ran the length of the room, and already the majority of the chairs were taken. The atmosphere was still; there was none of the usual chatter Lucy would have expected from a room full of people.

Graham sat at the head of the table, Oliver to his right. Oliver was talking to him, Graham's head bent so that Oliver could whisper in his ear. She watched as Oliver held out a small container and tipped the contents into his father's hand. Graham swallowed whatever it was with a swig of orange juice.

Lucy took a seat next to the woman with the baby. She had the boy on her knee and was feeding him porridge from the bowl with a spoon. A considerable amount was smeared round the child's face and Lucy smiled at him.

'What's his name?' Lucy asked.

The woman looked at her. 'Nicolas,' she replied.

'How old is he?'

The woman glanced to the head of the table. Lucy

followed her gaze towards Graham. 'Nine months,' she said quickly without looking at Lucy, then went back to her porridge. Lucy finished her breakfast in silence.

The room emptied, and Lucy stayed behind to clear away the breakfast things. All Family members had a role to play in the group, and so far it seemed to Lucy that her role was doing the washing-up. Still, she was new, she told herself; perhaps things would change in time. And in a way, it was nice to have all your decisions made for you. Life was simple here.

As the other residents drifted away, Oliver stayed, carrying a stack of bowls into the kitchen. Lucy stood next to the sink and he joined her, picking up a tea towel.

'How are you settling in?' he asked.

'Good,' Lucy replied. 'But nobody seems that friendly. Is it because I'm new?'

Oliver took a glass out of her hand and dried it. 'We discourage friendships in the house. It's not good to be too close with the other residents.'

Lucy looked at him in surprise.

'Your only loyalty should be with the Family as a group,' he continued. 'With the people that provide your safety and shelter.'

'With you and Graham?' Lucy said, and Oliver nodded. 'But surely having friends is good for our happiness? For support, and ...' Lucy trailed off in the face of Oliver's stare.

'When the shit hits the fan, happiness won't get you anywhere,' he said. 'In a survival situation you need to be clear where your allegiances lie. With your friends? Or with the people that will keep you alive?'

Under the weight of his words, Lucy felt stupid. She

looked back at the washing-up as tears started to fall. She felt a hand on her arm.

'Hey, don't worry,' Oliver said. 'These things take time. It's all new to you.'

She nodded and wiped away her tears with the back of her hand.

They stood next to each other for a while, Lucy washing up and Oliver drying and putting the crockery away.

'What about you, Oliver?' Lucy asked. 'How old are you? Have you always been here?' Then she caught herself. 'I'm sorry, I'm just curious. I know I shouldn't be asking so many questions.'

Oliver laughed. 'It's fine, old habits die hard. I'm twenty-three, and no, I haven't always lived here.' He turned to put a glass away in the cabinet, then took the next one from Lucy. 'I grew up in this house, and once Dad retired about ten years ago he started up the Family. I went to university, but after a few years it became clear that he needed me here, so I quit and moved back.'

'That must have been tough for you,' Lucy said. 'I loved it at uni, it was my first taste of freedom. I never wanted to go home.'

'Not really. I believe in the cause. And university's not for everyone.'

His face was solemn. 'What do you mean?' Lucy asked.

Oliver didn't reply for a while. 'It was a lot of pressure. Constant deadlines, essays, so much to learn. In practicals they'd take the piss if you didn't know the answers – teaching by humiliation.' He paused, turning the tea towel round and round in his hand. 'Competition was fierce – we weren't told our marks, just how we'd performed in relation to everyone else. And everyone was always better than me. I couldn't stand that sense of failure. Some of the other students would hide library books or even remove chapters to get ahead.'

Lucy stared at him. 'But that's insane,' she said.

Oliver shrugged. 'That's the way it was. But it wasn't just the work. The endless enforced drinking games. Our course seemed isolated from the other students, and I think the alienation made matters worse.' He looked at Lucy. 'You wouldn't know to look at me now, but when I was born I was three weeks premature. I was tiny. So I guess I've always been trying to catch up. It was a relief to quit.'

'So you don't miss it?' Lucy asked.

'I miss certain things. I miss...' He shook his head. 'But no. I won't be going back.' He put the tea towel down on the side. 'Anyway, can you finish without me? I need to check on Dad.'

Lucy watched him go. Poor kid, she thought. He seemed vulnerable and unsure. He should have been having the time of his life, but he'd obviously had an awful experience at university. With that dark curly hair and physique, he was handsome, and he was obviously smart, but he seemed to have an inferiority complex he hadn't been able to shift. She knew how that felt.

Perhaps while he looked after his father, Oliver needed someone looking after him. To talk to him, check he was okay, to be his friend, as much as that was forbidden. Perhaps, Lucy thought as she put the last bowl away in the cupboard, she should be that someone.

48

She was back. Or at least, someone was back. And they were persistent.

Scott was lying on the sofa. He'd been there since yesterday; he even thought he might have slept there, but he wasn't sure, he'd been too drunk to notice. Now, sadly, the alcohol had worn off and he had run out of anything to replace it with. He hadn't eaten, he certainly hadn't showered, and whoever this person was, banging on his front door, was pissing him off.

'Go away,' he hollered. The banging stopped for a moment, then started again. 'Fuck off,' Scott screamed with all the force he could muster, making his throat ache.

'Scott?' Banging again. 'It's Isaac. Scott, please, open the door.'

'Isaac?' Scott said, sitting up on the sofa. His head spun. Lucy's brother? What was *he* doing here?

He stood up on wobbly legs and made his way to the hallway. Isaac started banging again.

'Okay, okay, I'm coming,' Scott shouted, his head throbbing.

He opened the front door and Isaac did a double take.

'What's happened to you?' he asked.

Scott walked back into the house. 'My wife left me,' he muttered. Isaac followed him.

'Yeah, but still ...' Isaac's voice trailed off and Scott could see him looking at the empty bottles strewn around the kitchen, the mess in the sink, the curtains drawn. The house was a state.

'Have you even washed?' Isaac asked, wrinkling his nose. Scott picked up a pack of paracetamol from where he'd left it earlier and swallowed a few tablets dry. He felt them move painfully down his throat.

Isaac handed him a glass of water and Scott took a big mouthful.

'Have you spoken to Lucy?' Isaac continued.

Scott shook his head and slumped back on the sofa.

'I have. I saw her yesterday.'

He had Scott's attention at last. 'And?' Scott replied.

'And we have to get her out.'

Scott sighed and picked up the remote control. 'Isaac, she doesn't want to come home. She made that perfectly clear.'

'Have you been there?' Isaac said, and Scott ignored him, switching on the television. 'Scott!' Isaac snatched the remote and turned it off again, standing in front of him. 'I'm serious. Have you been there?'

'No,' Scott replied, sulkily. 'I haven't.' He stared at the black television screen, willing Isaac to go. He didn't want him here. He didn't want anyone unless they could bring him alcohol. He wanted to sit and drink and feel sorry for himself.

But Isaac didn't seem to be leaving. Scott rolled his eyes and looked up at him. To his dismay he realised Isaac had started to cry quietly, tears rolling down his cheeks.

'Oh, Isaac,' Scott said, getting to his feet and putting his arms around the boy. They'd never been friends. Isaac had always seemed odd to Scott; he'd never been able to connect with him. And he hadn't realised Lucy was still in touch.

After a moment Isaac pulled away and perched on the edge of the sofa.

'I'm sorry, it's just…' he said.

'You've lost a sister,' Scott added, finishing his sentence for him.

Isaac wiped his eyes. 'Lucy wants me to go and live there.'

'With this "family"?'

'Yes. She invited me to visit, and I had a look around.'

Scott stared at him in disbelief. 'What was it like?'

Isaac chewed his lip. 'It was nice. I mean, on the surface. The man who runs it was welcoming, they showed me around, but…' He stopped again.

'Spit it out, Isaac.'

'It's weird. All these silent people doing their chores. Listening to lectures from this guy. Ranting about the end of the world, or whatever. It's like a cult.'

'They're preparing for the apocalypse, Isaac,' Scott said. In the breaks between his drinking, Scott had done a bit of research, his eyes widening as he read the propaganda on these sites. 'What did you think they were going to be doing? Singing about Jesus?'

Isaac glared at him. 'I'm used to the happy-clappy Jesus stuff, Scott,' he snapped. 'This was different. They're not allowed to leave the house. They're not allowed to speak to their families. When I tried to phone this morning, I couldn't get through.'

'And what did Lucy say?'

'She said she was happy. She said she was safe.'

'Well, there you go.' Scott sighed. 'You need to accept it, Isaac. Lucy has made her decision, she's living there now. I've realised that before she left, she was miserable. And when she came back last week, I hate to say it, but she seemed better.'

He looked at Isaac. 'If that's where she'll feel at home, then good on her.'

Isaac shook his head. 'Don't you remember, Scott? Don't you remember last time?' Scott looked at him. He knew what Isaac was talking about. 'She was the same then. She was miserable for ages, then a switch flipped and she was cheerful. Then two days later ...'

'She tried to kill herself,' Scott finished for him.

He remembered. As part of one of her therapy sessions he'd been invited along, and he'd asked her. Why did you try to kill yourself when it seemed like you were happy again? 'I'd made a decision,' Lucy had replied. 'I was stressed and worried about being sad for so long, but once I made the decision to kill myself it felt like a weight had been lifted. I had a plan. I knew what I was going to do.' Was that what was happening now?

Scott sat back on the sofa, thinking. But what were they supposed to do about it? If they weren't allowed to speak to her and she wasn't allowed out, what *could* they do?

'I've done some research, Scott,' Isaac continued. 'I've looked at cults and brainwashing and deprogramming.' He pulled some pieces of A4 paper out of his pocket and offered them to Scott. 'It's tricky, and it might take some time, but it's possible.'

Scott shook his head. 'I'm not going near there,' he said, his self-pity kicking back in. 'She doesn't want to know me. I did some awful things, Isaac.'

'But we have to try – we have to – otherwise ...'

'Otherwise what, Isaac?' Scott shouted. He didn't want this hassle. He wanted to stay here and nurse his broken heart and his misery and forget about her.

Isaac stared at him, hatred in his eyes. 'Fine, you stay here.

You wallow in your selfishness and forget all about her. I know about your affair, Scott.' Scott glanced at him quickly. 'Lucy told me. And it was a horrible thing to do. And you're a horrible person, yes. But Lucy loves you and she needs your help.' Scott stayed silent, his focus back on the blank television, frowning. 'Don't you want a chance to put it right?'

When Scott didn't reply, Isaac stood up. He angrily threw the pieces of paper at Scott and walked out of the room.

Scott watched them flutter to the floor. He reached down and picked one up. *Providing advice for the victims of cults*, it said across the top. Maybe Isaac was right. Maybe this was his opportunity. He didn't have to be that horrible person any more.

He stood up quickly and ran to the front door. 'Isaac!' he shouted at the figure striding away down the road. 'Isaac!' he bellowed again, pushing shoes on his feet and going after him.

Isaac turned and waited as Scott ran to catch up. Scott stood in front of Lucy's brother, getting his breath back. They looked so much alike. The same blond hair, the same naivety and innocence. Scott nodded.

'What do we need to do?' he asked.

49

Kate lay on the sofa, phone clutched in her hand. She had one eye on the crappy movie Sam had chosen, the other on her phone. It beeped, and she saw Sam glare at her.

How did it go with Sherwood? It was Max.

She replied: *As well as you can imagine.*

After she'd left Max at the lake, she'd driven down the road to Alex Sherwood's house. It had been peaceful, and the evening had been beautiful in the New Forest. Horses calmly grazing, the sun setting, touching the heathland with reds and yellows. She could see why Alex would live out there.

His house was in the middle of nowhere, ten minutes down a dirt track off the main road. It was little more than a shack: one storey, wooden walls, wooden roof. A rusted car rested on blocks on one side of the house, Alex's truck on the right.

The only sounds were the birdsong and wind blowing through the trees. Kate had climbed out of the car and walked closer, and as she did so Alex Sherwood opened the door. He had been wearing shorts cut off below the knee and a dirty T-shirt, stretched tight across his chest. He'd wiped his hands on an oily cloth. He seemed to have been waiting for her.

'DS Munro,' he'd said quietly.

'Mr Sherwood. Can I come in?'

He had opened the door wide. As Kate went past him she'd caught his smell: sawdust and sweat and diesel oil.

'Alex, please,' he'd said, gesturing towards the main part of the house. 'If you're here I'm guessing it's not good news, so we should at least be on first-name terms.'

The room was small, sparsely decorated with old, worn furniture, but it was clean and uncluttered. A kitchen area consisting of a cooker, sink and fridge and a few shelves was on the left with two old sofas on the other side of the room. A chainsaw was dismantled on what would normally have been the dining table. From where she was standing Kate could see into the bedroom – the bed was made and the room tidy.

Alex had gestured to the sofa opposite and they had both sat down.

'I'm sorry,' Kate had said. 'But we found a body buried in the woods near Ellingham last night.'

'And you believe it's my father,' Alex finished for her.

'It's a possibility,' Kate had said, 'and I wanted you to be prepared.'

She had watched him take a deep breath in and out, composing himself. 'It shouldn't be a surprise,' he'd replied. 'It's what I've expected all this time.' He looked at her. 'How did he – this person,' he corrected himself, 'die?'

'I'm afraid we don't know much at this stage. The postmortem will be completed tomorrow, and I'll be able to tell you more then. And we'll also be able to confirm whether it is definitely your father.'

'Can I see him?' Alex had asked.

Kate had paused, watching his face. 'If it's important to you, then we can make arrangements for you to visit. But you need to be aware, his body is badly decomposed. You might want to think about how you'd like to remember him.'

Alex had turned away from her and Kate had taken it as her cue to leave. But in the doorway, she'd looked back for a second. He was still facing away, but his shoulders were slumped, his hands over his face.

Remembering this now, Kate sighed. On the screen the vapid female lead was falling into the manly arms of the hero. Around them San Francisco crumbled. This film was such bullshit. Real disasters weren't huge and dramatic. They were the small details – a man, muscular and macho, turning his back so a police detective couldn't see him cry.

Another beep interrupted her thoughts: *Forensics team going to pass on results tomorrow. Won't give me anything tonight, not even their best guess.*

Forensics don't do guesswork, Kate typed back. *They like to keep their conclusions fact based and broad.*

Fucking great, Max replied, and Kate snorted at his sarcasm, appreciating the bit of light relief.

'Really, Kate?' Sam said. 'Can't you put the phone down? All I want is for us to watch one movie together. Is that so hard?'

Kate recognised the edgy tone in his voice and put her phone to one side. She shuffled up next to him on the sofa, trying to pay attention as the burly hero flew around in his helicopter.

She thought back to the body she'd seen in the ground. Nobody deserved to see their loved one like that. And nobody deserved to have their life ended that way. Seeing Alex that morning only hardened her resolve. She would find out what had happened to Paul Sherwood, and she would charge someone for his murder.

She fidgeted next to Sam. It's Sunday night, she told herself, there's nothing you can do now. Even Max had gone home. There were aspects of being a police officer she accepted as part of her life. As a PC she hadn't minded being the only sober person in a kebab shop, or the fact that her bank statements showed she shopped exclusively at coffee shops, McDonald's and the twenty-four-hour Tesco. Even now she didn't mind typing up case reports late at night as the motion-detector lights switched off around her. But she hated not making progress on a case when there was an injustice out there, a bully getting their own way. Kate wanted to win. She was impatient and impulsive – two traits that had got her in trouble more than once, but got cases solved. She didn't like sitting watching crappy films on a Sunday night when there was work to be done.

Sam stood up next to her and to her surprise, she saw the credits rolling on the film.

'I'm going to bed, are you coming?' he asked wearily.

Kate shook her head. 'I'll be there shortly,' she replied, knowing full well she was going to log on to her emails and see if anything had come through from Forensics, despite what Max had told her.

Sam walked away without another word. At the doorway, he turned and looked at her.

'Kate?'

'Hmm?'

'I think we should go to marriage counselling.'

She looked up at him quickly. Sam was serious, a frown on his face. He was staring at her, waiting for her response.

Kate nodded slowly. 'Okay.'

'I'll book an appointment and text you.'

He walked out and softly closed the door behind him.

Kate watched him go. She stayed in the silent room, motionless. She knew she should be upset, that his question should leave her mind reeling, but she felt nothing, silently resigned to Sam's request.

If that's what he wanted, that's what he would get.

Kate sat a moment longer, then got up from the sofa. She tidied the room, picking up the few discarded mugs and carrying them into the kitchen. She switched the dishwasher on and turned off the lights. She cleaned her teeth, pausing at the doorway to her bedroom and looking at her motionless husband, lying with his back turned to her side of the bed.

Then she quietly closed the door and went to sleep in the spare room.

Monday

50

Kate juggled the present in her hands, then rang the doorbell. She was new at this sort of thing; she hadn't known what to buy so she'd opted for a small bunny toy and a large bottle of champagne.

The door opened and Kate thrust them towards the woman in the doorway. DC Rachel Yates. Seasoned detective. Trusted member of Kate's team. And looking like shit.

Kate knew Yates had just had a baby, but even so, Kate was surprised. Her hair was lank, she was wearing tracksuit bottoms and what seemed to be her husband's T-shirt, and her eyes were so sunken into the black circles around them they were barely visible.

Rachel smiled, expertly balanced the tiny baby on one arm and took the champagne.

'I wasn't sure if alcohol was appropriate. On the websites they said you might be breastfeeding, and if so ...'

'I have three children under five,' Rachel replied. 'Alcohol is always appropriate.'

She showed Kate into her living room and pushed an armful of laundry off the chair so Kate could sit down.

'I'd offer you a coffee, but I can't be arsed,' Yates said, slumping onto the sofa, resting the sleeping baby on her chest.

'Do you want one?' Kate asked.

Yates smiled weakly. 'Please?' She gestured vaguely towards the kitchen.

Kate got up, scooting round the discarded toys and other detritus on the floor.

'Where are the boys?' she asked as she poked around in the kitchen, looking for clean mugs and coffee.

'Tony took them out. He thought the full experience might scare you,' Yates called.

'Mmm,' Kate muttered. He could have done the washing-up first, she thought. A crowd of used mugs had been left next to the dishwasher, and while the kettle was boiling, Kate pulled it open and loaded a few in.

The kettle clicked off and Kate poured the boiling water into the last two clean mugs. She didn't have to ask how Yates liked her coffee: after two years of working with her it was well ingrained in her mind.

When she went back into the living room, Kate did a double take, coming face to face with Yates's nipple as she sat down. She put the coffee on the table and tried to look the other way as Yates pushed the squalling baby onto her breast.

'Sorry,' Yates muttered. 'I don't even think of them as boobs any more. They're just udders, designed for feeding my children.'

'How's it going?' Kate asked, and Yates shrugged.

'Same old. Third time round you'd think I'd know what I was doing, but no. Apparently these buggers conferred, and they find new ways to baffle me each time.' She nodded to the baby now happily feeding. 'This one had a tongue tie, so breastfeeding was tricky. Never had that before. Oh well. All sorted now.' She sighed deeply and leaned back on her cushion. 'Tell me about you. Give me the gossip. What's going on?'

'Nothing interesting,' Kate muttered, and Yates laughed.

'I don't believe that for a second.' She raised an eyebrow. 'Jamie said Max Cooper has joined the team.'

'Yep,' Kate confirmed.

'And?'

'And what?'

'Didn't you and him have that thing at the Christmas party? I distinctly recall seeing the two of you doing shots and then disappearing.' Yates stared at Kate. 'You're telling me nothing happened?'

'Sober people shouldn't be allowed at Christmas parties, they ruin it for everyone,' Kate grumbled. 'Yes, there was a thing, but that was then. I'm back with Sam now.'

'And how's that going?'

Kate pulled a face before she knew what she was doing and Yates laughed.

'Kate! Come on! You were so pleased when you two got together again, what's changed?'

The baby pulled her face away from Yates's breast and she expertly swapped sides.

Kate's gaze shifted to the piles of washing, the discarded cars and railway tracks and superheroes littering the floor. She started sorting the laundry next to her as a distraction, folding tiny T-shirts and trousers into perfect quarters.

When she and Sam had been apart last year, Kate felt permanently torn in two, like a piece of her was missing, even when she'd been in the arms of another man. But it seemed that now she was back with him, the reality didn't quite match the image she'd built up in her mind.

Sam had got up early that morning to go on his work trip, but he didn't have to be there to relay his feelings – she could sense his disapproval by the cleanliness of the kitchen, the dishwasher emptied, washing-up put away. Of all the ways he could piss her off, he knew playing the martyr was the best way to do it.

But last time, she'd been single-handedly responsible for the break-up of her marriage. She desperately didn't want to be that person again.

At last she looked up at Yates.

'It's just...' she started. 'Is this it?'

'Is what it?'

'*This*,' Kate said. 'This monotony of life. We get up, we go to work, we come home, we get married, we have kids. Is this really it?'

Yates laughed, not taking Kate's blunt outburst personally. 'What did you expect?'

'I don't know.' Kate frowned. 'A bit more...' She paused. 'Something.' She smoothed a white Babygro over her knee. 'I always knew I wanted to be a copper, I just thought life would be a bit more...' Kate stopped again. 'Some days I feel like I'm living in black and white when I was expecting Technicolor.' Kate winced at her own words. 'If that isn't too cheesy.'

Yates gave her a weak smile. In front of her, the baby had fallen asleep, lulled into a milky stupor. 'Don't ask me,' she said. 'I've barely moved from this sofa in two weeks. A trip to the park is considered excitement nowadays.'

Rachel took the clothing from Kate and wordlessly handed her the baby.

Kate looked down at the warm bundle. Her arms felt stiff, she knew she was holding her awkwardly, yet the little girl slept soundly, tightly wrapped in a blue blanket. Only her face poked out the top: soft round cheeks, button nose and a fuzz of blonde hair. She snuffled slightly in her sleep and Kate could make out the gentle movements of her body.

Something about having that tiny person on her was soothing – she couldn't go anywhere, protecting that moment of
sleep was precious.

In the early days, Sam and Kate had discussed children but
in the same way they talked about space travel: as something
in their future that might happen but was too far away to
put a date on. It had probably been five years since they
last mentioned it, and certainly not since they had got back
together.

'But how did you know,' Kate asked Rachel. 'How did
you know this was what you wanted?'

Yates thought for a moment. 'It seemed like the right
thing to do. The kids drive me mad, Tony drives me mad,
but I couldn't imagine life without them. At the end of the
day, it's the small things that count. A sticky hug from the
boys, a kiss from Tony.'

'But how does that seem right?' Kate asked. 'That you'll
only kiss one man for the rest of your life?'

'You're married, Kate!' Yates exclaimed. 'Isn't it a bit late
to be asking these questions?'

'I know, I just never thought … The idea that you'll never
feel that rush again. You know, that excitement when you
kiss someone for the first time.'

'But Kate, that's replaced by other things. By security, by
love, by understanding. I remember that first rush, and as
well as the exhilaration, so much uncertainty. Don't you
remember the worry, the insecurities? I like that I can be
myself with Tony. That he can see me at my worst – and
believe me, this round of childbirth was definitely the worst
– and know that at the end of the day, he'll still love me.'

As if on cue, the front door opened and a barrage of
sound hit the hallway. Small voices shouting at each other,

balls and sticks being dropped on the wooden floor, a man repeating the same sentence over and over.

'Coats and boots off. Put them away. Put. Them. Away.'

The noise pushed its way into the living room.

'Mummy, can we have some chocolate buttons?'

'Mum, he pushed me over in the park!'

'No, you can't, we've just had breakfast,' Yates replied to her two sons. Mirror images of their father at differing heights, they threw themselves onto the sofa, fighting over the remote control and switching the television on. Instantly a cartoon of superhero dogs filled the screen at top volume and Yates gestured to them to turn it down.

Kate could see Yates's husband in the hallway, wearily hanging coats up and putting welly boots away, a thin layer of wet mud covering the floor.

The baby began to stir and Kate handed her back to Yates, who rocked her gently, looking tenderly at her face. 'I'm hoping this one will be less fond of sticks and mud, although I expect not.'

'I'd better be going,' Kate said, standing and picking up her bag.

Yates nodded, pulling herself up gingerly and handing the baby to her husband, who carried her away from the noise into the kitchen.

'Kate?' Yates said as they went into the hallway. 'Be careful of the charms of Max Cooper.' She paused. 'The grass isn't always greener, you know.'

'But one man,' Kate muttered. 'Kissing one man for the rest of your life?'

'If you don't like that idea, Kate,' Yates replied, as Kate walked out to the street, 'perhaps you're kissing the wrong man.'

51

Max replayed the segment of footage over and over on the screen. It showed the disembarkation gates of Portsmouth ferry, foot passengers slowly moving off the boat to Le Havre, loaded with hand luggage, coats and hats. Max knew who he was supposed to be looking at – the passport had been logged by border control at 2.35 p.m., so all he needed to do was study the corresponding timestamp on the video – but the man on the monitor with Paul Sherwood's passport was wearing a large grey coat and a peaked cap and was carrying a black rucksack. It could be anyone, Max thought.

Next to him Briggs was having as much luck. They'd located a traffic camera from one of the gantries above the M27, running the automatic number-plate recognition on the off-chance one of the vehicles registered to the Swifts had been used to transport Dougie's body to the lake, but he was getting nowhere. Briggs sat back in his seat with a sigh.

'This is a waste of time.' Briggs pulled at his tie, loosening it slightly. 'When's forensics back?'

'They said this morning, but you know.' Max shrugged. 'Could be today, could be tomorrow.' He reached forward and picked up his coffee. 'How was your weekend? Did you manage to actually have a life?'

Briggs smiled. 'Yeah, better than yours by the sound of it. Went out for a drink with someone Saturday night.'

'And?'

Briggs raised his eyebrows and smiled coyly. 'You never know.' He looked back at the screen. 'Although with this job, I sometimes wonder what the point is.'

'What do you mean?'

'Well, every detective I know with Major Crimes is either single or divorced. It's rare that any partner will put up with the hours we keep – we're here until the job is done. Full stop. As you discovered this weekend.'

'Munro's married,' Max said.

Briggs snorted. 'Barely. Bet you a tenner that marketing guy of hers breaks it off again before Christmas.'

'What's he like?' Max asked. He'd never considered Kate's husband as an actual person. He'd imagined him only as a blank face, a nameless avatar in her life.

'I've only met him once,' Briggs replied. 'Bland corporate type who watches *Line of Duty* and thinks he understands what we do all day.' He typed on his phone for a moment. 'Here.' He held up the screen showing the Facebook app. 'His privacy settings are shite.'

Max took the phone and looked at the face in front of him. Standard short haircut, reluctant smile. Sam Marshall was better looking than him, Max thought. More put together. Max ran a hand across his chin; he hadn't even shaved that morning. The thought that this man was his competition flitted briefly through his mind before he pushed it away again.

'Working hard?' Kate appeared behind them and Max quickly threw the phone back to Briggs.

'How's Yates?' Briggs asked.

'House full of screaming kids, mess everywhere, no one getting any sleep.' Kate slumped in the seat next to them. 'But she seemed blissfully happy.'

'Sickening, isn't it?' Briggs laughed.

'Vomit-inducing.' Kate scooted round on her chair and turned the computer on. 'Have you guys made any progress?'

Max pointed to the grey figure on his screen.

'That's Paul Sherwood?' Kate asked.

'Apparently,' Max replied. 'That's the best I could find. And the witness that made the statement to identify him on the ferry has died.'

The phone rang next to them and Briggs answered it. He signalled frantically, then thanked the other person on the end of the line, putting the phone down. 'Tyre tracks!' Briggs said. 'Results coming through now. And apparently the post-mortem on your John Doe last night has been done. Dr Adams is expecting you at the morgue.'

Kate clapped her hands together. 'Jamie, stay here and get started on those tyres. See if you can match them to anyone involved.' She looked at Max. 'You want to come with me?'

Next to him Briggs laughed. 'Take my advice,' he crowed. 'Save your lunch for later.'

52

Lucy was getting used to the routine; there was comfort to be found in doing the same thing day in, day out. Breakfast, clearing up, a lecture from Graham. Today they were in the sitting room in a big circle, the members of the Family who had been there the longest closer to Graham, newer members like her towards the back. Lucy had heard a few talks now. Sometimes they'd be more directed, and everyone would sit and listen. Other times, it was something practical – a how-to or a demonstration. Or, like today, there would be a topic for discussion and an opportunity to ask questions. Lucy didn't feel confident enough yet to ask anything herself.

This morning, Graham was talking about one of the most important steps for when the dissolution came: the grab bag. 'We are as prepared as we can be in here, but what if we have to leave the haven?' he said. 'What are the essentials to have ready?'

'Water filter,' said a man at the front of the room. Graham nodded and smiled at him.

'LED torch,' said another.

'Good,' Graham said.

'Emergency rations.'

'Wind-up radio.'

'Spare clothes.'

The list of possible items came thick and fast from around the room. Lucy couldn't keep track. There were ones she had heard before, but others that hadn't even crossed her mind. Did they really think iodine tablets were a necessity in England?

Graham carried on. 'This may seem a huge list of stuff, and the chances are we won't need half of it. We are at an advantage compared to most – we know something is coming and we are ready. This is why your donations are more important than ever. We need to keep our stocks high. We have skills we can use to barter with. We know how to live off the land and how to defend ourselves.'

'But how can we defend ourselves now the pigs have seized our guns?' the man said next to Lucy. 'Why did you let them take them? We should have stopped them.'

Graham smiled gently. 'The time will come when we'll need to use violence. But that time isn't with us yet. We still have some – stored away where they can't be found. We are not defenceless.' He leaned forward in his chair, resting on his stick for support. 'But you do bring us to a good point. What is the most important tool in a survival situation?'

A few answers were thrown around the room. Guns. Shelter. Food. Graham shook his head at every one.

'Your mind,' Lucy said. Graham smiled and pointed slowly at Lucy. She felt heads turn to look at her.

'Correct. What, er ...' Graham paused.

'Lucy.'

'What Lucy has said today is absolutely right. When the dissolution happens, it's vital to keep a cool head. To control that panic and fear, and use it to our advantage.'

As Graham continued to talk, Lucy's gaze wandered around the room. The others seemed transfixed by Graham – their eyes never wandering, their faces slack with awe. To the left of the room, Lucy saw Oliver, his chair a distance away from the others. He was watching Graham, his face stern. He knew, better than anyone, what they were all there for, Lucy thought. He'd had a lifetime of it. Then to the right, Lucy noticed Alex come in. He leaned against the wall, waiting. Lucy was glad to see him, but he didn't seem his usual self. His eyes were narrowed and his hands were fidgety. She tried to get his attention but his gaze was fixed on Graham at the front of the room.

Oliver stood up and joined him, Alex whispering in his ear. As Lucy watched, his face took on the same stern expression as Alex's. Oliver tried to encourage him out of the room, but Alex resisted.

Oliver watched his father for a second, chewing his lip, then walked to the front of the room and interrupted him. Graham paused, listening, then smiled, facing the group again.

'I'm sorry, my friends, but I'm going to have to end today's chat a little early,' he said, his voice light. 'Something's come up that needs my attention.'

'Anything we need to know about?' one of the men said.

'No, no,' Graham replied quickly, his hands held outwards in a calming gesture. 'Just a problem with one of our trees.'

He stood up and left the room, Oliver and Alex following behind. Lucy glanced at the other people in the room – unconcerned, starting to go about their normal day. But Lucy wasn't so sure. She'd known Alex for a while now and nothing got him worried. Especially not a few trees.

Lucy left the others, going into the corridor of the main house and looking up the stairs to the room Graham and Oliver used as an office. She could hear raised voices and followed the noise.

At the top of the stairs, Lucy paused. The voices were louder now: Alex's first, his tone short and barking, then

Graham's reply. She stopped by the door; it was open slightly where the catch hadn't quite found home and she gently pushed it open a few inches.

'What do you mean, they've found him?' Graham asked.

'They've found a body,' Alex barked. 'A body, Graham! You told me he'd left, that he'd gone to France. I knew you were lying, you son of a bitch, I knew it. You and Dougie. What else aren't you telling me?'

'Calm down, Alex,' Graham said, his voice slow. 'Stop jumping to conclusions. How do they even know it's Paul?'

'He was buried just down the road from here, Gray! Who else would it be?'

Lucy could see Alex's face through the gap in the door, Graham with his back to her. She couldn't see Oliver, but could hear his voice as he started to speak.

'We told you everything we knew back in January, Alex. Paul said he had a woman in France and he'd be in touch. That Saturday was the last time we saw him.'

Graham reached forward and went to take Alex's hand, but he pulled away. 'We don't know what happened to your father, Alex,' he said. 'But the last thing we need is you coming here now and upsetting everyone. We're on a knife-edge, the police are knocking at our door, and you come here accusing us of... What *are* you accusing us of, Alex?'

Lucy saw Alex shake his head, looking at the floor.

'We think you should leave, Alex,' Oliver said.

Alex turned to him quickly. 'You don't tell me what to do, kid,' he said, his voice bitter.

Graham nodded. 'But Oliver's right, Alex. You've always been a friend to our family. But you're asking questions nobody else wants answered.' Graham's face was stern. 'Do *you* know what happened to Dougie Brewer?'

Lucy's head started to spin. She knew that name; it was the body she'd found in the lake. What did Alex have to do with his death? And how did the Swifts know him?

Lucy saw Alex shake his head, staring at the ground.

Graham sighed. 'Alex, pull yourself together. Paul was our friend. If that body is him then we don't know anything about it. And unless you continue to prove your worth to the Family, you are no longer welcome here.'

Alex spun on his heel and moved quickly towards the door, his face like thunder. Lucy ducked quickly into the room to the right.

She saw Alex storm out, and then looked back to where Graham had collapsed into a chair. Oliver walked to his side and put an arm around him. She saw him whisper in his ear then pass him a pill and a glass of water.

Quickly, Lucy scuttled down the stairs and out into the courtyard. Alex was in the cab of his truck, the engine idling, and she ran to the driver's side window.

He jumped when he saw her.

'Alex, are you okay?' she asked. Up close, Lucy could see he looked terrible. His eyes were bloodshot, his face miserable.

He shook his head. 'Go inside, Lucy. Go back to your family.' He stopped and looked at her. 'Are you all right?'

Lucy smiled. 'I'm fine. Slowly settling in.'

He nodded. 'That's good. They'll look after you, they will,' he said. 'You'll be safe here, everything will be fine.'

Lucy stood back from the truck as he put the engine in gear and drove out of the compound. Alex's words echoed in her head. *You'll be safe here.*

But his voice had been hesitant. And in that moment, Lucy hadn't been sure who Alex was trying to convince: Lucy, or himself.

53

Another day, another dead body. But this cadaver in front of Kate looked very different to the last one: hard, dry skin clinging to muscle, the occasional white bone visible. Cleaned of mud, stripped of clothing, this corpse seemed more impersonal than Dougie Brewer's had been the week before.

Albie was in his office in the back room, holding up a hand to say hello as they arrived. Next to her, Max was hanging onto the contents of his stomach better than Briggs had. But then today, Kate had to admit, the smell was an improvement: a mixture of earth, formalin and freshly brewed coffee. Kate wasn't sure whether to feel hungry or revolted.

'I've finished with your guy,' Albie said, joining them by the table. 'Body was only buried about thirty centimetres from the surface, so relatively intact. Structural preservation of the muscles, soft tissues extensively present, no signs of insect activity or scavenging.'

'Cause of death?' Kate asked.

'It's what I thought yesterday. Massive blunt force trauma.' He moved them round to the back of the skull. 'There were two points of impact, as you can see here.' He drew their attention to the two straight holes in the bone next to each other with a slight gap in between. 'Each about two centimetres in width. Caused a significant intraparenchymal haemorrhage resulting in death, almost certainly within minutes.'

Kate squinted at the holes. 'And how hard would the impact have been to cause that sort of damage?'

'A huge amount of force. The blow went clean through the skull, straight into the parietal lobe. Have you found the crime scene yet?' he asked, and Kate shook her head. 'There would have been a lot of blood – you'll definitely find trace. My guess is the end of a crowbar or something similar. Find me your murder weapon and I can confirm.'

'Any other injuries?' Max asked.

'Not as far as I can see. Given the level of decomposition, I can't tell if there was any superficial damage. Chances are he didn't see it coming and went straight down.'

'And is this Paul Sherwood?' Kate asked.

'Given what we know, probably. Definitely male, age between fifty and sixty-five, height seems to stack up and hair colour's right. Blood type is a match. Clothes have been passed to the lab. You'll have to wait for DNA to confirm, but signs are looking likely.' Albie frowned. 'It's hard to be a hundred per cent accurate, but I would say he's been dead between six months and a year.'

'Fits the timeline,' Max muttered.

Albie nodded. 'Looks like your guy.'

Kate glanced up at the clock, then looked at Max. 'We'd better get back. Thank you, Albie,' Kate said, turning to leave, but he pointed towards his office. 'Do you think I'd drag you down here just for that?' he said, a smile on his face. 'I've had some results back on your friend Dougie Brewer.'

Kate followed him into the room. 'Tox results?' she asked.

Albie pushed a pile of papers off a chair and gestured for Kate to sit down next to him at the computer. Documents were piled high around them, photographs scattered among medical reports, files pushed into drawers, some of them seeming older than Albie himself. Max stood awkwardly behind them in the only space left in the room, next to the filing cabinet. Albie flicked the screen back into life.

'That was some list you sent me,' he said. He ran his finger down the text. 'Even with the cold water acting in your favour, most of them came back a big fat nothing. And some would metabolise too quickly to show up anyway. But we found two of the drugs you named. Trace elements, but they were definitely present.'

Kate moved closer to the screen. She felt Max behind her, peering over her shoulder. She looked where Albie's finger was pointing.

'Ketamine?' Max asked. 'Horse tranquilliser?'

Albie laughed. 'Norketamine, to be exact. And it's not just used on animals. It's a sedative, for anaesthesia. Do you know if Douglas Brewer had had an operation recently?'

'There was nothing in his medical records,' Kate replied. 'Why? Couldn't he have been taking it for recreational purposes?'

'Well, that's just it,' Albie said, leaning back in his seat. 'I would have said so, yes, if it wasn't for the second drug in his blood.'

He pointed to the screen again and Kate squinted at it.

'Rocuronium?' she asked. 'I've never heard of it.'

'It's a weird drug to be found in these circumstances, very niche,' Albie replied. 'Usually I'd see it in a post-mortem for a patient who died in theatre.' He regarded their blank faces before continuing. 'It's a muscle relaxant, bringing about paralysis, used in conjunction with sedatives like ketamine or propofol to anaesthetise during surgery.' He scratched his head. 'Usually it's given intravenously, but knowing there were puncture holes on the body, I can only assume someone injected him direct into the muscle. I can't think how else it would have got into his system.'

'So what does that mean for cause of death?' Kate asked.

Albie blew out a long breath. 'As we thought, you're looking at a murder, detective.' He shook his head. 'And I can only hope he was still under the influence of the ketamine when he went into the water.'

'Why's that?'

Albie frowned. 'Imagine being completely paralysed. You can't move your body, you can't even open your eyes for yourself. But your brain is fully awake. You can feel and hear and experience everything going on around you. Because that's what rocuronium does. But not only that, it paralyses your diaphragm, so you can't breathe without a ventilator. Now imagine someone drops you in a lake. You feel the cold water around you. Your heart starts beating faster, trying to get oxygen around your body when there isn't any. You can't move. There's nothing you can do to stop what's happening.' He paused, his face grim. 'It would be a terrifying way to die.'

The room fell silent, the three of them reflecting on Dougie Brewer's last few moments. Kate cleared her throat. 'So we're not only looking for a murderer, but a pretty sick fucker at that,' she said quietly, and Albie nodded.

Kate frowned. 'So who would use it, or know how to use it?'

'Anaesthetists mainly. Some other doctors, maybe some clued-up paramedics.'

Kate paused. 'Vets?' she asked slowly.

Albie nodded. 'Yes, a vet would probably know how to use it.'

Kate turned round and looked at Max. His face was grey.

'Graham Swift,' she said.

237

54

'All we have is circumstantial at the moment...'

Kate and Max were walking back up to the office from the car park, Max practically pulling on Kate's arm as they trudged up the stairs.

'You know it makes sense...'

'Max,' Kate warned. 'There's no way we'll get sign-off for you to go undercover. We need more than just suspicion. Plus, there's the risk of Alex Sherwood...'

As they walked into the office, Briggs grabbed them, interrupting their argument. 'I have news,' he said, a big smile on his face.

'So do we,' Max said excitedly.

Kate sighed. She didn't have the energy for this. It was like managing a pair of large, highly strung puppies. She directed them over to their desks and pointed to Briggs. 'You go first.'

'Lab came back on the fingerprints found in Dougie Brewer's flat – specifically on his stash tin.' He paused for effect and Kate looked at him impatiently. 'Alex Sherwood.'

'So he knew Dougie better than he says he did,' Kate said.

'Not only that,' Briggs said, 'but the tyre tracks you guys found at the lake come back to a Michelin Latitude Cross.'

'And?' Kate said.

'It's a tyre commonly used for SUVs or trucks. Like Alex Sherwood's Ford Ranger.'

Kate felt the familiar surge of anticipation. At last, they

had something. Evidence that pointed towards a suspect. 'So what's your theory, Jamie? Why did Sherwood kill Dougie Brewer?'

'We know Doug was friends with Paul Sherwood, right? Something happened that night they were out, Doug killed Paul Sherwood and buried him in the forest. Alex found out and killed Dougie.'

Kate looked to Max. His face was downcast. 'What do you think?' she asked.

'I still like Graham Swift for it,' Max said. 'Same theory could apply?'

'But you can't put Graham at Dougie's flat. Or a vehicle at the dump site,' Briggs responded, a smug grin on his face.

'But we do have a murder weapon,' Max replied.

Briggs looked at Kate. 'You do?'

'No,' Kate corrected. 'But we have an idea about cause of death, for both of them.' She told Briggs about the blunt force trauma to Paul Sherwood's skull, then explained the injection sites and the presence of the weird paralytic in Dougie Brewer's system, Briggs's eyes widening as she relayed what Dr Adams had said.

'But doesn't Sherwood have that job at the wildlife park?' Briggs replied. 'What if he had to anaesthetise the otters?' he added, one finger pointing at Max.

Kate held up her hands, stopping the banter before Max could retaliate. 'There are way too many "what ifs" here for my liking. We need more than theories.' She turned to Briggs decisively. 'Jamie – go back to Dougie Brewer's flat and get the landlord to formally identify Alex Sherwood as Brewer's dealer. And see if you can find a crime scene for Paul Sherwood's murder while you're at it.'

'You want me to luminol the whole of Portswood?'

Kate gave him a withering look. 'No. I want you to walk the route from the pub to Brewer's flat and see what you can find. Max? You and I are going to pay a visit to the otter sanctuary.'

Max looked grumpy. 'So we're going after Sherwood?' he said.

Kate looked at the whiteboard where Briggs had started writing up the latest evidence in thick black marker pen. *Tyre tracks, fingerprints, presence of drug in system.* 'It's the strongest evidence so far. Sorry, Max,' she added.

It was past four by the time Kate and Max made it to the sanctuary, and it looked like they were closing up for the night. But the sight of Max's uniform made the woman closing the front doors hesitate long enough for Kate to get out her ID. She let them inside, then bustled away to fetch the manager.

Kate and Max waited in the gift shop. Max picked up a cuddly otter and pointed it at her.

'Cute,' she said.

'When I have kids I want to go to places like this,' he said, placing the otter on his chest and smoothing down its fur. 'Got to be the plus side of having them, right?'

Kate opened her mouth then closed it again. Why was everyone around her talking about children? Even the most unlikely of people, like Max. And she could imagine him with kids. Crouching on all fours, mucking around. That's only because he's little more than a kid himself, she told herself sternly.

The manager came over and Max replaced the stuffed otter with its friends in the display. 'I hear you want to speak to me about Alex,' she said, and Kate nodded. 'He's not in any trouble, is he?'

'Why would you say that?' Kate asked.

'Well, we don't get the police here much,' the manager stuttered. 'So either he's in trouble or something's happened to him.'

'He's fine,' Kate said, avoiding answering the question directly. 'Was he at work today?'

'No, he works Tuesdays and Wednesdays.'

'And what's the nature of his job here?'

The manager pointed to one of the tables in the nearby coffee shop and the three of them sat down. Max got out his notepad and waited, pen poised.

'He looks after the otter den, and that includes the fifteen Asian short-clawed otters that live here. There's nothing that man doesn't know about otters,' she said, her cheeks flushing slightly.

'And how long has he worked at the sanctuary?' Max asked.

'Longer than I've been here, but I believe his whole life, pretty much. I know he used to help his father with the trees, then he got involved cleaning out the den. After a while he started giving the talks and doing feeding time. He's a big hit with the kids.'

And the mums, I bet, Kate thought to herself. She could imagine him in his shorts and boots, holding court over a gaggle of adoring mothers. 'Does he look after their health at all? Administer medicines, that sort of thing?'

'Most of that is done by the vet, but yes, he'd administer medicine if they ever needed it.' The manager stopped. 'What's this about? Is it about his father? I know he went missing in January.'

'What can you tell us about Paul Sherwood?' Kate asked. 'Was he often here?'

The manager thought back. 'When we needed trees tending to, we'd get Paul to do it. And we have a lot of trees.' She smiled. 'I heard they were a lovely family – Paul's wife would often come, too. People still gossip about it – they seemed so much in love, it was a real scandal when she left them.'

'His wife?' Kate looked across to Max. 'We weren't aware he was married.'

'Well, maybe not now. But certainly back then. Attractive woman. You can see a lot of her in Alex.' She stopped, her cheeks flushing again. Kate wondered how much of Alex this woman had actually seen. 'We have some photos, if you want to see them?' she said.

'Photos?'

'Yes, old ones. Wait here, I'll go and look.'

The woman bustled off and Kate turned to Max. 'There was a wife?' she asked.

Max shrugged. 'Guess we better find out who,' he said, as the woman returned and thrust an old photo into their hands.

It was a shot of Paul Sherwood, harness on, suspended at the bottom of one of the trees, smiling. Next to him, Kate recognised a young Alex, probably about ten, his arm round a woman, dressed in combat trousers and a white vest. She was tanned and pretty, with long brown curly hair and a full mouth. Kate looked closer at the photograph.

'Who does that remind you of?' she asked Max, pointing at the wife. 'Apart from Alex?'

Max squinted at the photo. 'Don't know what you mean,' he said as his phone rang and he stood up, walking away from the table to answer it.

Kate turned back to the manager. 'Do you know when she left them?'

She frowned. 'I don't, I'm sorry. But Alex was still young – it can't have been long after that photo was taken. I know his dad disappearing like that in January was hard on him. The two of them were a team, more like best friends than father and son.' From the other side of the room, Max was gesturing to Kate.

'I'm sorry,' Kate said, 'but it looks like we're being called away. Thank you for your help. Can we keep this?' she asked, referring to the photo, and the manager nodded.

Kate rushed to catch up with Max. He waved his phone at her as they climbed into the car.

'That was Jamie,' he said. 'The landlord positively ID'd Alex Sherwood as Dougie's friend. And not only that.' Max started the car, his face miserable. 'They've found the crime scene, SOCO are there now.'

'They found blood?' Kate asked, sitting up straight in her seat. 'Where?'

'Lots of it, in the alleyway behind Brewer's flat.'

Kate clapped her hands together. 'Briggs was right.' She poked Max's arm, mocking him. 'No undercover work for you, my boy.'

'Yeah, yeah. You don't have to sound so pleased about it,' he frowned, gunning the engine aggressively.

Kate settled back in her seat, smiling, as Max drove back towards the station. At last, they had made progress. At last, they could make an arrest.

Tuesday

55

The warrant came through first thing, and Briggs was unbearable. Max tried his hardest to ignore him, but he pushed the piece of paper into Max's face, doing a weird mocking dance in front of him.

'Told you it was Alex Sherwood,' he crowed, and Max snatched the warrant from him.

'You've got to prove it yet,' he said. 'Just because the landlord ID'd him and you have a few fingerprints doesn't mean he's guilty of murder. You have a warning for possession of a class B, at best.'

Max was pissed off, and not just because Briggs was being a wanker. Since his confession to Kate about contacting the Borderland Family he'd been emailing them, nurturing the relationship and trying to stir up some interest. Finally, the night before, they'd asked did he want to come and look around? Maybe stay a few nights? The opportunity was there, and Max was excited to get involved. But this Alex Sherwood arrest had derailed it. There was no way he was going undercover now.

It was before 6 a.m. and Kate was standing at the whiteboard, running through the evidence for the benefit of DCI Delaney. They had the tyre tracks at the lake, the fingerprints at the flat, the relationship with Dougie Brewer, and they were hoping the crime scene in Portswood would throw up something interesting. If they could find something that tied Doug Brewer to Paul Sherwood's murder, they had motive. And they had means – a quick injection to the thigh with the paralytic and Alex could have easily dumped him in the lake, he was certainly strong enough and with his work with the otters he knew how to administer medicines. Once they'd arrested him, they could search his car and house.

Delaney was nodding; it seemed she liked what she was hearing. So they were on the road, and half an hour later sat on the track outside Sherwood's house in a police van, ready to make the arrest.

'Are we sure this is a good idea?' Briggs asked, looking over at them both. 'It's a full moon tonight,' he added, referring to the police superstition that it brought out the worst in the general population.

'It'll be fine,' Kate replied. 'We can't hang around for the gun bunnies to be free, we'll be waiting for ever.'

Briggs had advocated going later, with backup and at least two vans full of armed cops. Max knew he was worried about the firearms and shotgun certificates Alex Sherwood owned.

'He's going to shoot us,' he muttered. 'It's going to be *Butch Cassidy and the Sundance Kid* in reverse.'

'Coop has his taser,' Kate replied, turning to Max. Max grinned and patted the bright yellow and black gun strapped across his chest.

'Great,' Briggs replied with a scowl. 'He can go first.'

'You can fill in the fourteen pages of paperwork then,' Max smiled.

'Better that than getting shot.'

Kate opened the door to the van. 'It'll be fine,' she

repeated, climbing out and pulling her stab vest back into place. 'Loner, with multiple guns, almost twice the size of any of us,' Max heard her mumble as she turned towards the house. 'What could possibly go wrong?'

Kate went first, walking up the path. She glanced back at Briggs and Max. Max put his hand on his taser, releasing it from its clasp.

Max saw her take a deep breath, then she banged on the door. The noise was loud amid the peace of the forest.

'Alex Sherwood, make yourself known,' she shouted. 'Police. Come to the front door, your hands where we can see them.'

Max held his breath. They saw a light come on, then the front door open. Alex Sherwood stood in the doorway in boxer shorts and a T-shirt. He saw Max's taser and slowly raised his hands in the air.

Briggs rushed forward, moving his hands behind him and cuffing him. He patted him down and nodded at Kate.

'Alex Sherwood,' she began. 'We are arresting you on suspicion of the murder of Douglas Brewer.' Alex looked at the ground, then slowly shook his head as Kate completed the warning. 'Do you understand?' she finished.

'Can I at least put some clothes on first?' he asked. His face was downcast, his shoulders slumped.

'Do you understand?' Kate repeated, and Alex looked at her.

'Yes,' he said bitterly.

Max walked with Briggs as he escorted Alex Sherwood to the van.

'Suspect secure,' Max called down his radio. 'Heading back to the station now.'

Kate climbed into the front of the van next to him. She sat in silence for a moment. He knew what she was thinking.

They'd joked around, but Briggs was right, things could have gone very differently. Alex Sherwood could have opened fire at any time, Max could have been shot, his colleagues could have been shot. But looking at Alex now, in a state of undress, confused from sleep, slumped dejectedly in handcuffs in the back of their van, Max wasn't so sure.

He looked over at Kate.

'What do you think?' he whispered to her. 'Have we got the right guy?'

'The evidence says it's him,' Kate replied, but Max noticed her previous confidence had dulled. She pointed to the keys in his hand and he reached forward and started the engine.

'Let's go and see,' she said.

56

At last, Lucy was out in the sunshine. It seemed her penance of washing-up duty was over, and she was free to get on with what she was good at – growing the fruit and veg.

When she'd initially met Graham, a large proportion of their conversation had been about her experience in her garden. She'd talked about her vegetable patch, about what she'd learnt, what thrived and the best plants for what type of soil. Everyone who lived with the Family had to contribute, she was told. And this was what she could do.

Lucy walked along the edge of the vegetable plot, pulling out dandelions and weeds as she went. Already she could see their problem: the soil was full of stones, the carrots overcrowded, and what was the point of planting seedlings in September? At this time of year, the best bet was to harvest what you could, then get ready for planting in the spring.

She crouched down and took a handful of soil in her palm. It was hard and claggy, and she let it fall through her fingers back into the bed. She'd need to do something to sort that out, too – did they have a composter around here?

Lucy brushed her hands off and looked around the garden. Some Family members were busy mowing the lawn, others seemed to be practising lighting fires. A vital survival skill, Lucy knew. She needed to get the hang of it herself.

On the far side she could see a large metal frame, and walked towards it. Sure enough, the remains of a greenhouse still stood; some panes were broken, but it was otherwise intact. She tentatively opened the door and stepped inside, treading on shards of glass, running her finger along the wooden tables that had been constructed down both sides. This would work just fine, Lucy thought to herself with a smile. Given time and a bit of attention, she could have this garden producing no end of food for them all.

It was good to have something to take her mind off things. After Isaac had left on Saturday she'd been convinced he would jump at the chance of coming to stay, but she'd heard nothing from him since. She'd asked Oliver if they'd had any calls but he'd shaken his head.

'I'd have to check with Dad, though,' he'd said. 'Maybe he's heard from him.'

Lucy had asked if she could phone, but Oliver had frowned.

'Give him some space.' He'd smiled. 'He'll come round.'

Lucy hoped he would.

She couldn't see any tools in the greenhouse, so she left, and looked across the garden for a shed. Perhaps there was one by the fence, behind some of the trees. Lucy headed towards the edge of the garden, pushing through the undergrowth to the tall wooden fence with barbed wire running along the top. But no shed. Lucy started following the boundary until she came to a gate. She hadn't noticed it before; she'd assumed the only way in or out of the compound was the main entrance, and she pulled at the handle. The padlock at the top rattled.

'What are you doing here?' a voice behind her shouted, and Lucy jumped.

She turned, coming face to face with Graham. She smiled.

'I'm sorry, Graham, I was looking for——' she started, but he interrupted her.

'Get away from there, why are you trying to leave?' he bellowed.

Lucy reeled. This wasn't the kind man she had come to know. His face was distorted with anger, and he brandished his stick at her.

'Go on! Get away from there!'

Lucy leapt away from the gate, narrowly avoiding getting Graham's stick in her face. She backed away, apologising, but he continued to shout, obscenities now, and she ran back to the house, her heart thumping.

She looked over her shoulder as she got to the kitchen door. Graham was still standing at the far side of the garden, watching her. The shouting had disturbed other members working outside, and they'd stopped, all eyes trained her way. She turned and ran straight into Oliver, nearly knocking herself over in the process.

'Woah!' he said. He held onto the tops of her arms, steadying her. He smiled, then saw her face. His expression turned to concern. 'What's the matter?'

Lucy looked behind her, but Graham had gone. 'Your dad, he ...' she started. 'I was down at the fence,' she said, pointing out into the garden. 'I was looking for some tools. I found the gate.'

'Was it locked?' Oliver asked quickly, his face serious. Lucy paused, frowning. 'Was it?' he asked again. He was still holding onto her arms and she felt his fingers dig into her skin.

'I ... I don't know,' she stuttered, and he let go of her arms. She rubbed them, feeling the sting where his fingers had been.

Oliver looked nervously in the direction Lucy had indicated. 'I better get down there,' he muttered. He turned back to Lucy, smiling again. 'We had a few break-ins before you arrived, and that's where they got in.' He thought for a moment. 'What did you need, anyway?'

'Gardening tools, trowel, spade, you know, that sort of stuff.'

'Make a list and we'll get it for you,' Oliver said, agitated. 'Now, if you'll excuse me, I'll check that gate. And go and find Dad.'

Lucy watched him go, striding off down the lawn. She frowned. Oliver had been smiling, but it hadn't made it to his eyes. It felt like he had something to hide.

Her previous good mood had evaporated. She waited until Oliver was out of sight, then turned to go back into the house, wrapping her arms around her. The sun was still shining, but Lucy suddenly felt very cold.

57

Alex Sherwood had been cautioned, all the recording equipment turned on and ready. Kate knew he'd been speaking with his solicitor. They all sat opposite each other in the interview room, Alex now wearing the standard-issue grey tracksuit, his clothes taken away as evidence. Kate placed two hands on the file in front of her.

It was time. He didn't look willing to talk, his eyes narrowed, slumped in his chair. At that moment Kate knew the SOCO team were picking apart his house and his truck. She was hoping for a syringe, for a vial of drugs, for mud on Alex's tyres to match samples taken from Dougie's dump site. Anything. But she also wanted to hear from him. She started the interview, Briggs by her side.

'How do you know Douglas Brewer?'

Alex didn't look up. 'No comment,' he said.

'Would you describe your relationship as friends, or just acquaintances?'

'No comment.'

Kate looked over to Briggs, who raised his eyebrows.

'Have you ever been to his flat in Portswood?'

A pause. Then: 'No comment.'

Kate chewed on her lip. 'Have you ever smoked cannabis with Douglas Brewer?'

'No comment.'

Kate nodded slowly. 'It's in your interest to speak to us,

Alex. We have a forensic link between you and Doug Brewer, but we're keen to hear your side of the story.'

'I've been talking to you guys for days, and where has that got me?' he muttered, receiving a warning look from his solicitor.

'We know you knew Dougie Brewer well. His landlord has confirmed you were a regular visitor, and your finger-prints on a tin containing cannabis would give some indica-tion why. When was the last time you saw him?'

'No comment.'

Kate tried a different tack. 'What do you do at the otter sanctuary?' Kate asked.

Alex's brow furrowed but he didn't reply. Kate waited a second.

'Do you ever administer drugs to the animals?'

He frowned. 'To the otters? No. The vet would do that,' he said.

'Have you heard of a drug called rocuronium?'

'No comment,' he said, but he looked interested in what Kate was saying, sitting up a bit more in his seat.

'Have you ever been to Ellingham lake?' Kate asked.

Alex shook his head again. 'No comment.'

'Have you ever taken your truck to Ellingham lake?'

'No comment.'

Kate pulled the photo of the tyre impressions at the scene out of the file. 'These were found down a track leading to the lake. They are a brand that would fit your Ford Ranger, and our forensics team are at this moment confirming that link for us.'

'Lots of people own trucks like mine,' Alex said.

'They do, that's true,' Kate replied. Alex didn't seem in the mood to talk. He had no incentive to, so Kate thought she'd give him a little motivation.

'We have the results from the post-mortem on your father, Alex.'

Alex looked up at her quickly. Kate held the silence for a moment.

'And?' Alex asked.

Kate softened her tone. 'I'm sorry, Alex, but the body we found has come back as a DNA match to your father. And we now know, in all probability, that he was murdered.'

Alex looked back to the table. Kate saw the corners of his mouth turn down and his chin wobble. She watched as he took a long breath in and let it out slowly.

'Who do you think killed him, Alex?'

Alex stared downwards. 'You tell me,' he said quietly.

It was time to put all their cards on the table.

'We think we know where, and we think we know when, Alex. We found a crime scene behind Dougie Brewer's flat, and the clothes your father's body was found in match the ones he was wearing that night when he went to the pub.' Alex looked up at her, meeting her eyes for the first time that day. 'Because of that, we believe Dougie Brewer may have been involved. And,' Kate continued, slowly, 'we think you knew that and killed him in retaliation for your father's death. Isn't that right, Alex?'

Alex looked at her. He opened his mouth as if to say something, then closed it again. 'I'd like to speak to my lawyer,' he said.

Kate sighed, closing the file in front of her and pausing the interview. Briggs showed Alex and his solicitor into another room, then came back and slumped next to Kate.

'Well, this is bloody annoying,' he said.

Kate nodded. 'We need to hope Forensics come back with something from the house or car. Did you see the look on his face?'

'He knows something, that's for sure,' Briggs said. He groaned. 'It's just so frustrating.'

There was a knock on the door and Alex and the solicitor came back into the room. Alex had a piece of paper in his hand.

Kate restarted the video.

'Interview recommenced at fifteen twenty,' she stated, and looked at the men in front of her.

'My client wishes to give a statement,' the solicitor said.

Alex cleared his throat. The room was silent except for the hum of the recording equipment. Kate almost held her breath.

'I have been friends with Douglas Brewer for many years. He was a friend of my father's, and I have been to his flat on many occasions, for social purposes.' He paused, looking up from the paper. He met Kate's eyes. 'I did not kill him. I do not know who did.' He looked down again. 'However, I do believe that whatever happened to my father had something to do with Doug Brewer and his friend Graham Swift. I would be happy to help police with their enquiries in this area, on the proviso that they do not use the information provided for this purpose to incriminate me.'

He laid the piece of paper on the table.

'Why do you think Dougie Brewer and Graham Swift had something to do with your father's murder?'

'That's all my client is willing to say today,' his solicitor said.

Kate glanced at Briggs. 'Interview concluded at fifteen thirty-six,' she said.

58

Alex Sherwood was shown back to his cell, and Kate and Briggs headed to the office, where Max was waiting.

'Well?' he asked.

'We need something definitive so we can charge him,' Kate said. 'All we have is a load of circumstantial evidence and theories. We have twenty-four hours.' Kate caught a glimpse of the clock on the wall and her body shrivelled up in despair. 'Oh fuck! Shit!' She picked up her keys and looked to Briggs and Max. 'Keep going, I'll be back soon.'

She raced out of the station, practically hitting two cars as she left the car park. As she drove she chastised herself. She had to remember one frigging appointment, the *only* frigging appointment, and she was already late. She jumped amber lights, pinching a car park space from under the nose of an old lady, who stuck her finger up at her and drove off with a screech of tyres.

The building was smart red brick, a gold nameplate on the outside. *Dr Marian Franklin*, it said. The best in the business: marriage counsellor.

And Kate was late.

She rushed into the reception area and was greeted by a woman with an arched eyebrow and a supercilious expression.

'What time was your appointment?' she asked.

'Half an hour ago,' Kate gasped. 'Is he still here?' She

looked at the phone in her hand: no messages, no missed calls.

'Your husband?' the woman said. 'No. Left fifteen minutes ago.'

Kate swore under her breath.

'Kate Munro?' Kate turned around. A tall, thin woman dressed in a severe black suit stood behind her.

'I'm Dr Franklin, would you like to come through?' she asked in a tone Kate didn't dare refuse.

Kate followed the woman into her office. Certificates lined every wall, along with thank you cards and snapshots of couples grinning. The marriage counsellor equivalent of baby photos in a fertility clinic, Kate assumed.

'Do you want to sit down?' Dr Franklin asked. Her voice was soft and low.

'No, not if Sam's gone,' Kate burbled. 'I should go and find him, I should—'

'You should have been here half an hour ago.'

Dr Franklin had settled herself into a brown leather chair, crossing one slim leg over the other. She had the sort of legs that nestled, a distribution of muscle and fat which meant she could curve one under the other effortlessly. She probably had a sodding thigh gap, too, Kate thought uncharitably.

'I know, but I was at work, something came up, the case—'

'That's what your husband said.'

Kate looked at her. 'What did he say?'

'That something would have come up at work.' The doctor paused and gestured towards the chair opposite her. Kate stayed standing. 'Is your husband used to making excuses for you?'

'He ... I ...' Kate stuttered. 'I can't always control what happens at work.'

'Can't, or won't?'

'I beg your pardon?' Kate said. I assumed you guys weren't supposed to be judgemental, she thought.

'Was it that something came up at work, Kate? Or was it that you didn't want to be here today, and work provided a convenient excuse?' The doctor said the words calmly, while Kate's face went puce. 'What was it about today which meant you didn't want to be here?'

'I didn't deliberately miss the appointment...' Kate started, but the doctor cut her off.

'Maybe not consciously, but I think on some level you did. Are you sure you want to save your marriage, Kate?'

Kate felt her teeth clench and she spun on her heel, pulling the door shut behind her with more force than was necessary.

'I don't have to listen to this shit. Bitch,' she muttered, as she stalked towards the car park. 'Who is she to judge me? What does she know about my life, my marriage?'

She climbed back into her car and slammed the door, hard. She picked up her phone and called Sam, but the phone went to voicemail. She tried again, then her phone pinged with the familiar tone of a text message. It was Sam.

I've gone back to work. We can talk this evening.

Fuck.

Not for the first time she wished for a large glass of Sauv Blanc, or a huge fuck-off bottle of vodka. She looked across the road and before she knew it she was outside the car and striding to the Tesco Express. The automatic doors slid open. Kate walked past the fruit and veg, straight to the alcohol aisle, then stopped.

The rows of wine called to her. She picked up a bottle of white and held it in her hands. It was room temperature, but it still had a pull. She could almost taste it. She could almost sense the moment when feeling this way, feeling this shitty, would stop, replaced by a blissful nothingness.

In the past, alcohol had been her go-to drug of choice. She could sink three or four glasses of wine without flinching and often had most evenings, frequently more.

And so, she'd promised Sam: no more drinking. So what? she thought. Where had that got her? But she knew, though, that she'd also promised herself.

No more drinking in the day. No more taking chances at work because she was too drunk or too hung-over to care. Her phone buzzed in her pocket and she looked at the message. It was Max.

Where are you?

What the hell was she doing? She was in charge of not one but two open murder investigations. She had a suspect in custody. She couldn't mess this up now.

Repulsed, she put the bottle of wine back on the shelf and walked out of the shop. She got into her car and put both her hands on the steering wheel. She had to leave. Now.

Kate started the engine and drove back to the station. She wouldn't think about her marriage. She would think about her team, about Briggs and Max, waiting for her. She would think about how to make the murder charge stick.

But as much as she tried to stop it, the doctor's words echoed in her head. Was Dr Franklin right? Had Kate, on some level, tried to sabotage her marriage? And more to the point, had that been her last chance to save it?

59

They had nothing.

Max watched Kate come back into the office, trying to gauge her mood. She didn't look good, throwing her phone across her desk and falling into her chair.

'Boss?' Briggs started tentatively.

'This better be good news,' Kate snapped, and Briggs looked nervously at Max.

'Well. No,' Max said quickly.

Kate glared at him.

'SOCO haven't finished yet, but they said signs don't look promising. The tyres on Sherwood's truck are Continental, completely different tread...'

'Could he have changed his tyres?' Kate interrupted.

'Unlikely. These look worn, and they didn't find any others at his property.' Max turned his screen around, showing a close-up photo of black muddy tyres. He paused, waiting for Kate's response.

She sighed. 'And let me guess, there's nothing at the house.'

Max shook his head. 'They've seized his firearms, but apart from that, nothing more than a bit of weed. And not enough to get him for intent to supply. No pharmaceuticals, no syringes or needles, only a few plasters and paracetamol.'

'And what about the truck?' Kate asked Briggs.

He shook his head. 'Nothing but mud and leaves.' He twirled the biro in his hand and Kate snatched it off him, slamming it down on the desk. Briggs looked at it, then continued uncertainly. 'They've taken samples, but no sign of blood, and no hair or skin that they can see.'

'In other words, no evidence that Alex Sherwood moved Doug Brewer's body in his truck. Fuck!' she shouted.

Max pressed his lips together and opened his eyes wide, giving a look to Briggs. He shrugged wordlessly in response.

'We did have something interesting back though,' Max added tentatively, and Kate stared at him. 'They've identified a second contributor to the blood found on Paul Sherwood's hat.'

'And do we have a hit for who it is?'

Max hesitated. 'Well, no.'

'Great,' Kate said sarcastically, then stood up and walked out of the office.

Briggs looked over at Max. 'What the hell was that all about?' he said.

Max shook his head. 'I have no idea.' He went to follow her, but Briggs put his leg out to stop him.

'Are you crazy?' he said. 'A woman that angry? You leave her alone.'

Max pushed his leg out of the way. 'It'll be fine.'

'Your funeral, mate, your funeral,' Briggs muttered.

Max hurried down the corridor the way he'd seen Kate go. He knew Briggs was right, but if he was going to convince Kate, he needed to grab her now. To give her some sort of way forward on the case. He saw her go into the women's toilets and, without thinking, followed her inside.

The toilets were empty except for a closed door to one of the cubicles. Max instantly regretted his decision; this was a foreign world that he was not welcome in. He went to leave, but before he could the cubicle door opened and Kate came out. She stopped in her tracks when she saw him.

'Really?' she said, an eyebrow raised. 'I don't even get one sodding moment away from you guys?'

'Sorry, I wanted to talk to you, and ...' Max tailed off. He hadn't felt more uncomfortable in his whole life.

Kate washed her hands. Then she leaned forward and looked closely at her face in the mirror, wiping a finger under her eyes. Max noticed that she'd been crying.

'Is everything okay?' he asked quietly.

Kate shook her head and sighed, her breath coming out in jagged bursts. 'Same old shit,' she said. She shook her head then ran her hands down her face. 'What did you want to talk about?' she said at last.

'Jamie told me about Sherwood's proposal,' Max started. 'About him working with us to get Graham Swift.'

'You're not going undercover, Max,' Kate said, anticipating his question.

'Just listen to me for a moment, boss,' Max pleaded, and Kate looked at him wearily. 'What if Graham Swift has got something to do with Paul Sherwood's death? What if he's responsible for both murders? We know he's a vet and can administer drugs, we know he was close to both men and was one of the last people to see Paul Sherwood alive. So all we need is evidence, right? And we're not going to get any of that waiting here.' He looked at Kate, gauging her reaction. She didn't look keen, but not as pissed off as before. 'We can hardly ask Alex Sherwood to get evidence – no jury's going to believe that continuity of exhibits – but send me in and I can collect everything we need. And it doesn't matter that Alex knows me, because he'll be helping us.'

Kate frowned. Max's stomach dropped: it was a no go again.

She looked at him, studying his face. 'Tell me, why is going undercover so important to you?' she asked.

Max took a deep breath in. 'Do you remember when we were talking at the weekend? In the car, by the lake?' Kate nodded. 'I haven't applied to take the NIE yet because ...' He paused. But he had to tell her. This was his last chance. 'I wasn't sure I could pass it. And then reality would be staring me in the face. Not good enough.'

'But you passed the undercover training?' Kate said softly.

'By some fluke.' Max laughed hollowly. 'I just want an opportunity to make up for sitting on my arse in Charlie's shadow for the past ten years. I want that chance to get something right, something big.' He reached forward and, in his excitement, grabbed her hands. 'And I know I can do this, Kate, I know I can.'

She looked down where he had her hands in his. Embarrassed, he quickly pulled them away and put them behind his back. 'Please, Kate?'

He could see her thinking, her face locked in a frown. Then, slowly, she nodded. 'Fine,' she said. 'Find me something that links Swift to these murders, and I'll do what I can to get sign-off. Something better than your speculation.'

Max smiled. At last!

'But leave Sherwood in custody for now. You have until we release him tomorrow morning. And you better hope your budding friendship with the Borderland Family has been good enough for them to let you in. Now bugger off out of the women's toilets before I put in a complaint about you.'

Max ran out of the toilets back to the office. This was the

break he needed. He'd been telling Kate the truth – he did want to prove what he could do to the people he worked with, but it was more than that.

He needed to prove it to himself.

60

Kate paused before she opened her front door. Sam's car was in the driveway; she knew he was home.

Inside, the house was silent. That was a bad sign. Her husband in a good mood filled the house with noise: music, singing, cooking, his general being had percussion. But this evening she shut the door and there was nothing.

She walked through the house, trying to find him. There was no point pretending something else was going on; her missing the appointment today had been a big fuck-up. But what she would do about it, she didn't know. And what Sam's response would be was even more unfathomable.

She found him on the sofa, his phone in his hand. He looked up when he saw her but said nothing. She rested on the edge of the chair next to him.

'I'm sorry I missed the appointment today, something—'

'Something came up at work,' he finished. 'Yes, I can guess.'

Kate held herself back from saying what. She knew to Sam it sounded like an excuse.

'I had stuff on at work, but I made it on time,' he said. Kate went to talk but he cut her off. 'And don't give me that "I'm taking bad guys off the street" bullshit. Every day doctors turn up to appointments, brain surgeons make an effort to save their marriages, and yet you can't. Why is that, Kate?'

She saw the disappointment on his face, an expression she had seen so many times before. She shook her head; she didn't know how to reply. She couldn't say why her marriage counselling appointment hadn't been in the forefront of her mind. It just wasn't. Even now, some part of her was at the office, thinking about Alex Sherwood in custody, knowing Max was still there, looking for evidence related to the homicides.

'If you invested even half the energy you put into work into our marriage, we wouldn't be in this situation,' Sam said, the bitterness creeping into his voice.

'What situation is that?' Kate asked slowly.

'This!' Sam shouted. 'This ... this nothingness! We barely see each other, and when we do, your mind is elsewhere. We don't talk, we don't laugh. We haven't had sex for months. Had you even realised that, Kate?' He shook his head. 'Nothing's changed, has it? It's all the same.'

Kate could feel her jaw clenching, not trusting herself to say the right thing.

Sam carried on. 'We split up last year, and we got back together, but for what? You said that things were different now, but they're not.'

'They are!' Kate said, suddenly annoyed. 'I've made such an effort for you. I have tried so hard, Sam. I ask nice questions about your day and try to keep my eyes open when you tell me about whatever report you're working on. I haven't said a word when you've talked about Felicity from the office – who, by the way, I'm convinced was the one you were screwing last year. But you don't give a shit about that. You just want me to be a good little wife, in some insignificant office job.'

'I don't, I just want you to ...' Sam stopped. 'I don't know.

Give as much of a shit about me as you do your work.' He looked at her. 'But that's impossible, isn't it?'

'It's different, Sam. You're my husband. My work is … I don't know. Something else.'

'It's nice you acknowledge that, because sometimes I wonder. Which would win, if push came to shove?'

As if answering that question, Kate's mobile started to ring, and Sam huffed in response. Kate didn't answer it, holding it out to him defiantly, the ringtone echoing around the room. It stopped, and the silence took over again.

'That proves nothing, Kate,' Sam said. 'Leaving one phone call doesn't mean you're committed to this marriage.' He paused. 'It's been the same from the beginning. It's always been the same.'

'What do you mean?' Kate asked.

'You wouldn't even take my surname.'

'Oh, for fuck's sake,' Kate cried out. 'This again? I told you at the time, I like my name. It was my name for twenty-something years before I married you. Why should I change it?'

'Because you *married* me. Because that's what people who love each other do!'

'Would you have wanted to change your name to Munro?' Kate asked. 'No, because in your mind, that's not what men do. Nice obedient women change their names. I bet *Felicity* would change her name,' Kate spat.

'Do you know what? Yes,' Sam shouted back. 'I bet she would. Because Fliss—'

He stopped abruptly.

'Because Fliss *what*, Sam?' Kate asked.

Sam stared at her. There was a long gap. 'Because if we were together, Fliss would be in love with me.'

The words hung in the room.

'I'm in love with you ...' Kate started, but Sam was shaking his head.

'No, you're not. Not in that way,' he said quietly. 'I want to be with someone who can't stop thinking about me. Who rushes home every night to spend time with me. Are you that person, Kate?'

Kate went to say something, then stopped herself. Words formed in her head. *I love you, Sam. Please give us one more chance. You're the most important thing in my life.* But she couldn't bring herself to say them. She knew he was right.

'And you think you can get that with Fliss?' was all she could mutter.

Sam paused. A shadow passed across his face; a slight hesitation to respond, a decision working through his mind. Then he spoke. 'I'd hope so. We haven't been having an affair,' he added quickly, pre-empting the thought in her head. 'But I'm not going to deny that there's something there ... And I want to give it a go. I'm sorry, Kate. I can't do this any more.'

She nodded slowly. There wasn't anything else to say. She turned and walked away from her husband, opening the front door and climbing into her car. Sam didn't follow her.

She looked back to the house, a tightness in her throat. She was desperate not to cry, not to let it break her, like it had last time. She pushed her nails into the palms of her hands, forcing back tears.

So this was how her marriage would end. With silence. With tacit agreement. Because Kate knew, when there was nothing left to fight for, what was the point in even trying?

Wednesday

61

Kate arrived at work early, and the office was practically empty. But Max was there, asleep, slumped on his desk. CCTV footage was paused on the screen in front of him, a mess of coffee cups and chocolate wrappers strewn around. She paused for a moment and watched him sleep: he looked peaceful, despite the unnatural position.

Briggs came in, throwing his bag on the desk. Max woke with a jolt, wiping his hand across his mouth and peering around, stunned. Kate looked away quickly, pretending to be engrossed in her emails.

'You been here all night, Sleeping Beauty?' Briggs said, scooting his chair over to Max's desk. 'Was it worth it?'

Max stretched in his seat and let out a big sigh. 'You get me coffee?' he asked, and Briggs handed him a cup.

Kate looked at him. 'None for me?'

Jamie rolled his eyes. 'Would I even dare?' he said, passing her one.

The three of them crowded round Max's computer. Max pointed at the screen then put his glasses on, blinking for a moment, waking himself up. 'So,' he said, 'I thought I'd focus on the CCTV we have. We know that if we want to pin Graham Swift to Sherwood's murder, then he must have had to transport his body from the crime scene to Ellingham lake, so I ran the ANPR again for the number plates for all of Swift's registered vehicles. And ...' He stopped, looking at the two of them. 'Nothing,' he finished to a disappointed grunt from Briggs. 'Footage doesn't go back that far. But, out of curiosity, I had a look at the back roads he could have taken – if you have a dead body in your truck, you're trying to avoid suspicion, right? – and found this camera on a Tesco Express in Linwood.' He pointed at the screen. 'They sent me the footage. See? In the background you can see the turning onto a single-track road. And look at the date.'

Sunday 14 January, 12.14 a.m. The evening Paul, Graham and Dougie went to the pub. And sure enough, Kate remembered the narrow road. It only led to one place – the Swift house, home of the Borderland Family.

'Go on,' Kate said slowly.

'Watch,' Max replied.

Kate and Briggs craned forward as a number of cars drove past the shop. Max slowed the video as a large black flatbed truck came into shot. He paused it, showing the grainy number plate.

'Toyota Hilux, registered to Graham Swift. And ...' Max said, seeing Kate about to ask a question, 'a brand compatible with a Michelin Latitude Cross tyre.'

'Okay, so you have his truck going down his road at the right time, but that doesn't link him to Paul Sherwood,' Briggs said, playing devil's advocate, watching as Max started the video again and the Toyota turned off down the track. 'He'd argue he was just heading home after the pub.'

'True.' Max sat back in his seat, clicking away from the CCTV and loading up another file. 'But then I thought, if the Swifts used that route to their house, perhaps Dougie

Brewer did, too. So I had a look for his car in footage from the week before he died.'

'But his car's parked in Portswood, covered in parking tickets. That's how we ID'd him in the first place,' Briggs said.

Max didn't say anything, but pointed to his screen.

'What am I looking at?' Briggs asked, straining forward.

'Just ... there ...' Max said, pausing the video and leaning back in his seat, his hands behind his head.

Kate and Briggs both looked at the footage. Like before, the video was black and white, and it was hard to make anything out. But sure enough, as they watched, Dougie's Vauxhall Astra drove into shot and then down towards the Swift house. Kate looked at the timestamp.

It was Friday 13 September, at 6.56 p.m. The day before his body was found.

'That's definitely his car?' Kate asked, and Max nodded. He took a long swig from his coffee.

Briggs frowned. 'But still, Coop. He could have been alive at that point.'

Max nodded, drinking from the cup. He put it down and changed videos. This time the screen was brighter: it was daytime, early morning. They watched the car go past, this time in the other direction.

Kate looked at the timestamp again, with a sharp intake of breath.

Saturday 14 September. Nine forty-three in the morning.

'We know Dougie was dead by then,' Kate said, mouth open. 'Lucy Barker found his body just past seven.'

'It's circumstantial, but it shows there's foul play,' Briggs added. 'Someone from that house knew Dougie was dead, and was trying to cover it up. Throwing us off by driving his car back to Portswood.'

Kate knew he was right. A car belonging to a dead man had been driven out of the Borderland Family residence. It was enough.

Max held his hands out in a bow, a smug smile on his face.

'Now can I go and have a nap?' he said. 'I'm bloody knackered.'

DCI Delaney's expression was inscrutable. She looked at Kate from under her perfect brows, then tilted her head to one side.

'And do you stand by your team's assessment?' she asked.

Kate nodded. 'I think they're right, yes. We know the car came from the Swift house. And we know Dougie was dead at the time it was driven. We've asked the tech team to work on the CCTV to try and get an image of the driver, but whoever it was was trying to hide the fact he'd been killed. SOCO have impounded it and are working on it now.'

DCI Delaney looked at her, thinking. 'So why not arrest Graham Swift? Or get a warrant and do a search of the property? Why do we need someone undercover?'

Kate had asked Max that very question. Why take the risk? 'We could do a search,' Kate replied to Delaney. 'But I would be worried about somebody in that place disposing of any evidence before we could find it. We know these guys are clever, we know they wouldn't just leave proof lying around.' She leaned forward in her chair and looked at her boss. 'And, despite our suspicions, we don't know it's definitely him yet. I want good solid intelligence that we can link back to both these murders and make it stick. I want to know exactly where that evidence is so when we go in we're fast and targeted. And aren't you the slightest bit curious about what they're doing in that compound? We know they were stockpiling guns. We believe they've been linked to a number of drug thefts around Southampton. So let's find out. Once and for all.'

DCI Delaney nodded slowly. 'Fine. Send me everything you have and I'll take it to the Chief Constable for authorisation. But I want to know something from you first, Kate.'

Kate raised her eyebrows. 'Anything.'

Delaney stood up from her desk and sat down on the chair next to Kate. She leaned forward towards her, resting her arms on her knees. Kate was surprised.

Delaney looked at her. 'If we're going to do this, put one of our officers in harm's way, then I'll need you to be a hundred per cent on the ball. We'll have a team from SO10, but you're going to be one of Cooper's main contacts in there – you'll be the one he'll trust. But I'll be honest, you don't look great today, so I have to ask. Is everything okay? Can you do this?'

Kate felt Delaney's gaze drilling into her. She was aware of the bags under her eyes, her hair tied back in a tight bun to hide the fact that she hadn't had the energy to wash it that morning.

After her argument with Sam last night, Kate had driven around for hours. She hadn't gone to the office, knowing that Max would be there and that seeing him wouldn't be a good idea in her emotional state. Eventually she'd gone home when she knew Sam would be in bed. She'd slept in the spare room again, leaving the house before he got up. She hadn't slept well, the failure of her marriage bouncing around in her head.

But she needed this. She needed work, this case, to keep her going.

'I've had some problems in my personal life, but it's all

sorted now.' Kate felt a lump in her throat, her eyes hot. 'I'll be fine, guv.'

Delaney thought for a moment, her fingertips tapping against her mouth.

'Can I give you some advice, DS Munro?' she asked quietly.

Kate nodded, the movement quick.

'I see what you do, Kate. You're determined, you're focused, you're everything I look for in a detective, and I know you could go far.' She stopped for a moment. Kate didn't dare reply. 'I heard what happened last year with the Patterson case. I know you made some mistakes, and I'm glad it hasn't tarnished your career.'

Kate felt Delaney's blue eyes on her. She stared at her hands, unsure how to respond.

'We need more women out in the world,' Delaney carried on. 'More women like you. Succeeding. Be that person. Set an example for the others coming through the ranks.' She smiled warmly. 'I'm here to talk any time you need me. Tell me if I can do anything to help.'

Kate cleared her throat, willing herself not to cry. 'I will, guv, thank you,' she muttered at last.

Delaney nodded, then took her seat back behind her desk. Kate stood, her legs slightly shaky, and Delaney looked up.

'I'll call you when I have the green light. Get your team ready.'

Kate shut the door behind her and stopped, her back against the wall, taking deep breaths in and out. Max appeared by her side, making her jump.

'Did she say yes?' he asked eagerly.

'Fuck, Max, you gave me a heart attack. Yes, she's going

to take it forward.' Max whooped, then grabbed her, picking her up and spinning her around, before putting her down again quickly, realising the inappropriateness of his actions. He took a step back and Kate laughed, surprised by his enthusiasm.

'It's not a done deal yet,' she said. 'Don't get your hopes up.'

Max nodded. 'Thank you, boss,' he said, trying to regain composure.

Kate shook her head. 'Calm down. And go home when you can, try and catch up on some sleep. If this does go ahead, it's going to be a long day.' She stopped. 'And take a shower, you don't smell so good.'

He laughed. 'I will,' he said, as he walked away down the corridor. He turned back and pointed a finger at her. 'You're not going to regret this.'

'I already do,' Kate replied, under her breath, watching him go.

62

The four of them sat in the interview room: Alex Sherwood and his solicitor on one side, Kate and Max on the other. Sherwood looked tired and pissed off. Not the best frame of mind to be asking for favours, Max thought.

'So here's the deal,' Kate began. 'You tell us everything you know about Graham Swift and the Borderland Family, and we'll release you today under investigation.'

Sherwood stared at them, his arms crossed.

'That wasn't the deal we discussed, DS Munro,' his solicitor said. 'We want your assurance that you're not going to charge Mr Sherwood with anything based on what he tells you.'

'Look, we're not interested in drugs charges, Alex,' Kate said. 'We couldn't care less if you've been dealing to Brewer, or smoking a bit of weed at his flat. Honestly, all we're concerned with are the murders – of Doug Brewer, and of your father. I thought that's what you wanted too?'

Alex sighed and looked at his solicitor. Max took in the man in front of him. It would be good to have a wall of muscle like Alex on his side, but was this the man he was going to trust? His survival inside that compound was going to depend on Alex getting him in, and keeping his mouth shut. It was a risk he was going to have to take.

'Fine,' Alex Sherwood said at last. 'What do you want to know?'

'Why do you think Graham Swift murdered your father?' Kate asked.

Alex relaxed back in his chair. 'I know the three of them had plans to go to the pub on the Saturday night, and I know things were tense between them, but Dad wouldn't tell me why. All he said was he going to have it out with Gray about something.'

'That doesn't mean he killed him,' Max said.

Alex gave him a patronising look. 'No, of course not. But when I asked them about that night they all said nothing had happened. But Dougie was always a terrible liar. I knew something was up. And after Dad—' he paused. 'Disappeared, I kept in touch with Dougie and Graham, sold Doug a bit of weed, visited occasionally to smoke. Then about a month ago I went round and he was off his face on coke, not his usual drug of choice, I don't know where he got it from. Dougie was talking about moving, about getting away. I remember he said, "I can't stop seeing Paul, lying there". I asked him what he meant but he clammed up and wouldn't say any more.'

'So why should we believe you when you say you didn't kill Dougie?' Kate asked. 'This sounds like motive to me.'

'Believe what you like, DS Munro,' Alex said. 'But I didn't. I'll be honest, I thought about roughing him up a bit, laying on a few punches to get him to talk, but it's not my style.' He stopped. 'Is that how he died?'

Kate shook her head. 'No. It's not. And when was the last time you saw him?'

'A few weeks ago. He was back to his usual sullen self. I left him in his flat with his weed. Alive,' he added. He crossed his arms again and leaned back in his seat. 'Can I ask how you intend to go about catching my father's killer?'

he asked. 'They're a tricky bunch. They're used to being secretive, hiding from the police.'

Kate looked at Max, her eyebrows raised. He recognised it as a final question: are you sure you want to go through with this? Max nodded slowly in return.

'We intend to put PC Cooper in undercover,' Kate said. 'And we're going to need your help to do it.'

'What? You?' Alex pointed a finger at Max and started laughing. 'You have to be kidding me.'

Max pressed his mouth closed, stopping himself saying precisely what he thought of Alex's hilarity. He was getting sick of this man's arrogance.

'You can't just wander up to the door and ask to be a member!' Alex continued. 'There's a vetting process, hoops you have to jump through.'

Kate sat forward in her seat. 'And that's where you come in, Mr Sherwood. You got Lucy Barker in, you can get Max in.'

'I've already been in contact with them on email,' Max interrupted. 'They're interested in getting me on board, I can tell.'

Alex Sherwood gave a loud sigh, then shook his head in resignation. 'I hope you're good at what you do ...' He paused.

'Max.'

'Max. Because you're going to need all your wits about you to survive in there. And if they find out who you are?' He shook his head again. 'Well. Let's just say it won't be pretty. It's like sending a lamb into the lion's den,' he muttered under his breath. 'They see you guys as their enemy, you know. Stooges for a complicit government.'

'All the more reason for us to get in there,' Max said.

'Fine, I'll make the introduction, I'll vouch for you. They'll be pleased to have a new injection of funds. I know they're starting to get desperate. Have they asked you for money yet?' Alex said to Max, who shook his head. Alex nodded. 'They will.'

'How much are we looking at?' Kate asked.

'It's normally a few thousand. I know they wanted six from Lucy. It might be more unless you can prove you have some skills they need.'

Max looked at Kate, questioning.

'We'll sort it,' she said. 'Now, what else do we need to know?'

63

They worked long into the evening. The money was authorised, ghost bank accounts set up and the team started their prep. Alex Sherwood had been released and had left to visit Graham Swift. Kate watched him go, wondering if they would ever see him again. He could disappear into the night, and this would all be for nothing.

She stood in the operations room and watched the Senior Responsible Officer from SO10, the undercover unit, brief Max next door. While Kate was still Max's supervisor, DI Jackson Nash had the experience necessary to be in charge of the entire undercover operation. Kate thought he looked like Idris Elba. He already had the salt-and-pepper hair and the hangdog expression; all he needed was the long grey coat and the Volvo. Kate had heard he was the best. He was gruff and direct and never smiled, but exuded an air of competence. Having Nash there gave her the reassurance she needed.

Alex's words echoed in her head. He'd told them the Family didn't allow mobile 'phones. They didn't allow calls home, and searched everyone's belongings on arrival. They rarely let their members leave the compound, and only then for vital trips such as shopping. Kate knew Max would need to find a way to get intelligence out and into their hands.

Briggs came and stood next to Kate, watching the conversation through the window.

'Are we sure he's up to it?' he asked. 'I mean, I know he's done the training, but it's a big undertaking.'

Kate shook her head. 'I don't know, Jamie. But if Nash has concerns, I'm sure he'll tell us.' She turned to him. 'Go home, we're going to need everyone operating at full capacity for the next few days, so go and get some rest.'

'Perhaps you should do the same, Sarge,' Briggs said as he went.

Through the window, Nash beckoned to her to join them inside. She went in and sat next to Max. As she did so he gave her a smile, but it wasn't his usual cocky grin – he was worried, and it showed.

'And do you smoke?' Nash asked Max, continuing the conversation.

Max shook his head. 'I gave up five years ago.'

'Time to start again.' He handed Max a packet of tobacco and some Rizlas. 'Get practising. Now go and speak to the IT crew, they'll set you up with the tech you need.'

Max stood, glancing at Kate before he left. Nash closed the door behind him.

'What are you thinking, guv?' Kate asked.

Nash shuffled the paperwork in his hand, his face grim.

'I don't like it, if I'm being honest, Munro,' he said. 'I don't like the control they'll have over our asset, the lack of comms, the fact the compound is built like a bloody fortress.' He sighed and looked at the plans in front of him. 'But Cooper seems psychologically robust, he's switched on and clever. He's tactical, I like the way he thinks.'

Kate nodded and waited for him to carry on.

'And I don't like these bastards. I've heard about them before, and like you, I'm curious to know what's going on behind those walls.'

'So are you happy to proceed?' Kate asked.

Nash frowned. 'Happy is the wrong word. But yes, I'll sign off on it.' He put the paperwork away in his bag and slung it over his shoulder. 'Go time is eight hundred hours tomorrow. I assume our source will take Cooper inside?'

Kate nodded. Their source. Otherwise known as Alex Sherwood.

'From that point on, we'll be waiting for Cooper to contact us. Comms will be on blackout. I'll be back tomorrow. We'll speak more then.'

Nash stood up and Kate shook his hand firmly. She hoped she was coming across more confident than she felt.

She walked back into the office, watching Nash leave. He was happy, and he'd been in charge of these undercover operations longer than she'd been in the force. So why was she still worried?

Kate wanted to crack the case; she wanted evidence on Swift so much it burned in the pit of her stomach. She should have been desperate to get Max in there to see what he could find. And if it had been anyone else, she wouldn't have hesitated.

'Well?' a voice asked from behind her, and Kate jumped.

'Are you done with the techies?' Kate asked and Max nodded, a big smile on his face.

'It's like James Bond in there,' he said. 'All those tiny gadgets to play with. But what did Nash say?'

'He said you seemed switched on and intelligent, so I don't know how he got that idea about you.' Kate smiled. 'But yes, we have the green light.'

Max punched the air, doing a twirl in celebration.

Such a fucking child, Kate thought, but she laughed despite herself.

'Now, will you buy me a pizza?' he asked, cheeky grin back on his face. 'Last dinner for a condemned man?'

Kate knocked his arm lightly. 'That's not even funny,' she replied.

64

Lucy opened her eyes. Her vision was blurry, the room distorted. She breathed out slowly through her nose, the bubbles rising up around her face, then pulled herself back to the surface of the bath.

The water was starting to go cold, and Lucy knew she'd overstayed her time limit in the bathroom. But she had no enthusiasm for rejoining the Family right now.

She poked her big toe into the opening of the tap, contemplating the corrosion around the edge. The rest of the bathroom was the same: curling lino, scratched enamel, a mottling of mould at the corners of the ceiling. Lucy thought that maybe the Swifts should spend some of that cash she'd given them on refurbishing the house, then chastised herself. Shiny bathroom suites wouldn't be essential when the dissolution came.

She took another deep breath in, holding it and lowering herself back under the water. Slowly she counted to sixty, then repeated it, without coming up for air. She felt her heart start to beat faster, her lungs strain, before she pulled herself back to the surface. She liked it under the water, where her hearing was muffled, her brain calm.

She still hadn't heard from Isaac. After much indecision earlier that day, she'd decided to contact him, but when she went to do so the phone in the hallway had gone. She'd crouched down, looking at the empty telephone point below, puzzled at its disappearance. Perhaps it was broken. Or ... Or what? Why would it have been taken away?

The disquiet in her mind was starting to come back. It had been good being with the Family initially, but now life was more familiar the worries were returning. Watching or listening to the news was forbidden, lest they get exposed to more government propaganda, but Lucy felt that isolation amplified her concern. If something happened, how would she know?

She missed the calm of her house with Scott. There was always someone in the room with her here, and even though they weren't talking to her, she felt their stares. The noises at night were unfamiliar – different people, their snores and mutterings keeping her awake. Even though now she had her gardening, she missed her old life. Going for a run by herself, the simple act of choosing what and when you ate.

And she missed Scott.

Her anger at discovering his affair had faded, replaced by a dull ache whenever she thought about him. She missed his arms around her when they watched TV, the warmth of his body next to her when she slept.

Lucy lifted her arm out of the water, looking at her wrinkly fingers, and her gaze moved down to the white jagged lines running the length of her forearm.

Being at university had felt liberating, to begin with. A first taste of freedom, away from the strict doctrine of her parents. She'd gone out with friends, danced until dawn, laughed, cried, been a normal teenager. And met Scott. But the guilt she felt when she slept with him had been immense. They were in love, true, but they weren't married. She would burn in hell.

The conflict had ripped her apart. She didn't believe in

God – unquestioned faith and obedience to a mythical being had never felt right – but eighteen years of teaching hadn't left her, and was burned into her core. Without the guidance of the church she felt empty inside, and the guilt had only compounded that.

She remembered how she'd felt. A merciful relief as she ran the razor blade into her skin, seeing the red bloom then multiply, merging with the bathwater. She'd felt nothing but peace as she'd slipped away, knowing she couldn't cope with the struggle between her upbringing and her new life. It was what she wanted.

But Scott found her, and pulled her back to the land of the living. Since then she'd sorted her head out – God and her parents were nothing to her now. And that was down to Scott: he'd never wavered, even in her darkest moments.

But what about her? The moment Scott had done something wrong, she'd abandoned him, when he had needed her most.

A loud banging on the door disturbed her from her thoughts.

'Okay, okay,' she shouted back, hoisting herself out of the bath and wrapping a scratchy towel around her body. She opened the door to the frown of one of her room-mates.

'It's twenty minutes, maximum,' the woman growled. 'You know that.'

'I'm sorry,' Lucy muttered, and scuttled down the corridor to the bedroom.

Their room was deserted for a change, and Lucy took advantage of the solitude. She got dressed into her pyjamas then perched on the bed, looking out into the darkness of the garden.

A figure came into view, walking slowly, his body bent,

relying on the stick in his hand to keep him upright. Graham. Lucy hadn't seen much of him since their run-in the day before. Oliver said he wasn't feeling well, and Lucy took some consolation in that: perhaps that was why he'd shouted at her. She hoped he was feeling better, but even so, what was he doing out there, by himself, at that time of night?

As she watched, he seemed to hesitate, then walk again in a different direction. Another figure came running up to join him – Oliver – and tried to guide him back to the house, but Graham seemed reluctant, pulling away. Poor kid, she thought. It wasn't a normal life for a twenty-something, but then, Lucy thought, what was? The world would be changing soon; there was no such thing as normal. *Everything will become clear.*

But even as she repeated the mantra to herself, for the first time she felt small seeds of doubt starting to grow. She felt that emptiness return. She wanted to believe in what Graham was saying, but everything was not clear.

Everything was more confusing now than it had ever been.

65

Hours later, Kate and Max sat at the table, empty dishes around them. Kate reached over and offered Max the last piece of garlic bread. He shook his head.

'I couldn't eat another thing, honestly,' he said, picking it up and putting it in his mouth.

Kate laughed.

'I need to go ...' he said, pointing backwards to the toilets. Kate watched him as he went: he'd got changed before leaving the station and she wondered how he made a simple navy shirt look so good. It reminded her of the night of the Christmas party – he was wearing something similar then, too. Jeans, shirt, something with buttons. She remembered her fingers stumbling over a belt. She remembered his breath on the back of her neck, her dress pushed up round her waist, his hands pulling her closer to him.

Fuck! Why had that popped back into her head? She could see him walking back over to their table now, and tried her hardest to think about something else.

Max sat back down in front of her. He looked at her strangely. 'Are you okay?' he asked. 'You've gone a bit pink.'

'Yes, fine,' Kate blustered. 'Have you heard what your code name is?' she said, quickly changing the subject with a smirk.

He looked at her, his eyebrows raised. 'No.' She stayed silent. 'Come on, tell me.'

'It's Jilly.'

'As in...?'

'Jilly Cooper,' Kate laughed. 'The romantic novelist.'

'*That's* what they went with?' Max was incredulous. 'They could have had Tommy, or Bradley or... or even Sheldon. But they went with Jilly?!'

'Briggs wanted Mini,' Kate said, practically unable to speak because she was laughing so much.

'Fuck him,' Max replied, then looked at her closely. 'You're joking,' he realised, and she nodded, still sniggering.

'Fuck you,' Max said, grinning.

'You know they're going to spend the whole time calling you "the asset", or something dull made up from your initials.'

The waiter came over to the table and put the bill in front of Max, but Kate pulled it towards her. Max put his hand on hers.

'I'll get it,' he said, but she shook her head.

'I'll claim it on expenses, we're not out on a date,' Kate replied.

'Aren't we?' Max said quietly. 'Because it feels like one.'

A silence fell between them. Kate felt the warmth of his hand on hers, then pulled it away quickly, knocking her glass of wine across the table. They scrabbled for napkins, clearing up the mess, then the waiter came over with the card machine and the moment was gone.

Kate looked at her watch, astonished to discover it was past eleven.

'You need to be getting to bed,' she said as they left the restaurant. Max held the door open for her, an eyebrow raised. 'Not with me,' she muttered.

The relaxed mood in the restaurant was gone, something

else in its place. Tension, yes, but not the type she would expect before an undercover op.

Her phone beeped in her pocket and she pulled it out, reading the message.

'That was Alex. He's expecting us at his place at eight so he can drive you to the commune.'

The mood turned. The enormity of what they were doing was clear. Alex would take Max there, but after that, he was on his own.

Kate looked at him – the messy hair, the ridiculous boyish dimples when he smiled. She wondered what it would be like to kiss him again.

Then before she could push the thought out of her mind, he put his hands gently on either side of her face, bent down and kissed her.

Last time it had been drunken, frantic, rushed. This time, standing by the side of the road, cars flying past them, Kate felt they had all the time in the world. His hands were in her hair. Hers had found their way under his coat, to the warmth of his back.

This was how a kiss should be. Not the perfunctory chaste greetings that she and Sam had been sharing, but something she wanted to go on for ever. A kiss she felt not just in her lips but all over her body.

Her phone went off in her pocket again, a sudden noise, waking Kate from her stupor. She pulled away from Max and looked at it, seeing a brief confirmatory note from Nash.

'We shouldn't be doing this,' she stuttered. 'I'm sorry.'

Max was looking at her, his lips pressed together, a stern expression on his face.

'This isn't the right time,' she finished.

'It felt right to me,' Max said softly, meeting her gaze.

'I ...' Kate started. 'I'm in no fit state to make decisions like this,' she said, words coming out in a rush. 'I made some mistakes last year. I did things I shouldn't have ...' She stopped herself, but Max had already taken a step back.

'I'm sorry you thought of it like that,' he said. He pushed his hands in his pockets and turned away.

'I didn't mean ...' Kate said. 'I didn't mean us, I meant ...'

But Max had gone, striding away from her. He raised one hand up as he walked. 'I'll see you tomorrow, DS Munro,' he shouted without turning.

'Shit! Shit!' Kate hissed under her breath. She looked up to the darkened sky, cursing again. She hadn't meant it to come out like that. Their little tryst in the cupboard had been awkward, yes, embarrassing at the time, yes. But nothing in comparison with some of the other mistakes she'd made last year. And now she'd got to know Max Cooper better, she'd looked back on it with an amused sort of pride.

She watched Max stride up the hill and disappear round the corner. At the time when she needed him to trust her the most, she'd wrecked it.

But it wasn't just the professional loss she was cursing herself for. It was the personal one, too.

66

Since Isaac had left Scott's house at the weekend, Scott had buried himself in paper. He'd phoned in his excuses to work, then done what he did best – research, analyse, dissect. And come to decisions.

Everything he'd read about cults and brainwashing told him that extracting Lucy from the clutches of the Family wasn't going to be easy. Getting her out against her will seemed unreliable, not to mention potentially illegal, so gentle persuasion was going to have to be their plan.

The websites all made their recommendations. Keep in contact, express love, write notes of everything they say for your records. Don't act angry or hostile, don't give them money, don't be judgemental. He'd failed at a few of those already, Scott realised with a sting.

But he was still baffled. These recommendations were all well and good written down on paper, but putting them into action was going to be much harder. Especially when he had no way of contacting her first.

Isaac had persisted with the main house number he'd used before but had got nothing except a continuous tone. He'd given up for the time being, waiting for Scott to go back to him with a plan.

Scott remembered the guy he'd met that day here at the house. The infamous 'Alex'. Scott knew he was connected to the cult, he'd got Lucy in there – so he was hardly going to help him get her out again. But it was worth a try.

He googled Alex's number using the few details he remembered from the side of the truck, then dialled it. After a while, the tone switched to voicemail and Scott heard a male voice talk about tree surgery, asking the caller to leave a number. Scott ended the call, then tried again. This time someone answered.

'Is that Alex?'

'Yes. Who's this?' The voice at the other end was suspicious.

'It's Scott, Lucy Barker's husband.' There was a long pause. 'Please don't hang up, please, I want to get Lucy out of the Borderland Family.' Scott spoke quickly, aware he wouldn't have long to persuade Alex. 'I know I made some mistakes, and I'm so sorry, but I love her.'

Scott waited. Please, please, he thought to himself. Please give me a way in.

'Stay away from there, Scott. You have no business going near that house.' Alex's voice was gruff, his tone stern. 'I'm warning you, just stay away.'

And that was it. Scott looked at the redundant phone in his hand. Alex's response had been as he'd expected, but there was no way he was giving up now.

He had one last idea. And he really didn't like it.

Taking a deep breath, he dialled the number. It rang out. He tried again.

'Fuck off, Scott.'

Jen's voice came through, loud and clear and undoubtedly pissed off.

'Jen, please. I need to talk to you.'

There was a long pause, then a sigh.

'What?'

Scott steeled himself. 'I'm sorry, but I need your help. Lucy needs your help,' he added quickly. He knew that Jen didn't care much about Lucy – her actions with him over the last year told him that – but he hoped some part of her would feel guilty. He hoped Jen had some sort of conscience for what she had done behind her friend's back.

Another gap. Scott imagined the expression on her face. Mouth pursed disapprovingly, eyes glaring.

'Why?' she said. 'I thought Lucy was happy at that ... that commune place.'

'Isaac went to see her and he's – we're – worried.' Scott explained about the plan to get her out, and the fact that they couldn't contact her. 'I thought,' he finished quickly, 'I thought you could do a search on your system and see if there's another phone number for them.'

Scott had remembered something Jen had said, pillow talk, after one of their 'sessions'. She told him a story about an ex-boyfriend she'd contacted out of the blue, after searching for his number on the NHS database.

'Completely forbidden, of course,' she'd laughed. 'But there's all sorts of information on there if you look.'

'Why should I do a favour for you?' Jen said, at last. 'It could get me fired, Scott.'

He took a deep breath. 'I know, and I'm sorry, Jen, for everything that happened. I shouldn't have ... I don't know. I was a dick.' Scott paused for a moment and he noticed his hands were shaking. 'But don't do it for me. Do it for Lucy, please. You used to be friends. She thought so. At least.'

'You're an arsehole,' she said in response. But then Scott heard Jen sigh. 'Fine,' she growled. 'Give me their names and I'll call you back.'

Scott relayed Graham and Oliver Swift's details and hung up. This had to work.

Even if it took everything he had, Scott would get himself into that house. He would see her again.

He would get Lucy back.

Thursday

67

'Are you ready?'

The extraction team had been briefed, the observation post was in place. The covert team had done what they could with cameras, but security in the house was tight, Nash had said, with people everywhere. So they had a few on the perimeter, and Max would have to do the rest.

Only Max could find out what was going on; get the detailed intelligence required on the targets for the raid.

DI Nash stood in front of Max, looking him up and down. 'You've had your training, you know what to do. From the moment you step inside that compound, you're no longer a cop. Forget every instinct you know.' Max nodded. 'You've got a grade one gob on you, mate, so use it. Blag all you can, especially if you get into a tight spot. But remember one thing: you get blown out, get out of there as quickly as you can. Clear?'

Max nodded again. 'Yes, guv,' he replied.

'Good. Let's go,' Nash said. And the four of them filed out.

As they drove Kate looked out of the window. Snippets of the M27, grey concrete, fast cars, lorries. Almost as if sensing the mood in the car, Briggs had left the radio silent. Max moved in the seat next to her, and she turned, realising he'd been looking at her. He smiled thinly.

All she wanted to do in that moment was reach over and hold his hand. To reassure him it was going to be okay.

The road had changed into the dual carriageway of the A31. Greener now that they had edged into the New Forest.

Kate looked away from Max, but at the same time moved her hand to the middle seat between them. She heard him shift, then the slightest touch as his finger met hers.

Her stomach jumped. Staring out of the window, she moved her hand closer to Max's, her little finger over the top of his. No more than the tiniest bit of contact, but enough to make her breath catch in her throat. An interaction more charged than anything she'd had with her husband in over a year.

Briggs turned off towards Burley, then down the track that led to Alex's house. They still didn't know if they could trust him. She had confidence in Nash's team, but Alex Sherwood was relatively unknown. But there was nothing they could do about it now.

As they edged towards the house, they saw Alex waiting outside. Max moved his hand away from Kate's and she saw him close his eyes for a second, then pick up his rucksack.

They stopped and climbed out of the car. The day was cool but clear, sunshine casting a glow across the trees and heathland of the New Forest.

Nash approached Alex, holding out his hand.

'DI Nash,' he said. 'Nice place you have here.'

Alex nodded in response. 'Thank you.' He looked at Max. 'What's in there?' he asked, referring to Max's bag.

'Clothes, toiletries, books, nothing much,' Max said.

Alex pointed to the mobile in Max's hand. 'Get rid of that. They'll only take it off you and sell it.'

Max held it out towards Kate, showing her the unlock code quickly, and she took it, slipping it in her pocket.

Alex gestured towards his truck. 'Shall we go? They're expecting us.'

Briggs walked forward and shook Max's hand. 'Good luck, mate,' he said. Kate kept her distance for a moment, then gave him a hug. She felt his arms pull her closer to him, her cheek against the soft cotton of his shirt. Then she pulled away, only too aware of Nash and Briggs watching.

'Look after yourself,' she said, gruffly.

One last wordless shake of Nash's hand, and Alex led Max to his truck, Max climbing in alongside him in the cab. Alex started the engine and they moved out of the driveway.

Nash looked at Kate and Briggs. 'Come on,' he said. 'I'll take you to the OP.'

The observation post was a white van marked with the logo of Southern Electric, parked in a lay-by next to a large telegraph pole. A few cones had been scattered around the van, but otherwise there was nobody in sight.

Nash pulled up alongside, and the three of them got out. He banged on the truck and the door was opened by someone Kate assumed was a cop, wearing a yellow high-vis jacket and hard hat.

'Boss,' the man said, moving aside to let Kate, Briggs and Nash into the tiny space.

The inside of the van had been kitted out with wall-to-wall screens. Black and white images played out, views Kate guessed were the grounds of the compound. In front of them, another man sat wearing headphones.

'All set?' Nash asked the cop and he nodded.

'Alpha Sierra has driven inside,' he said, quoting Alex

Sherwood's code name and pointing to one of the cameras. It showed the courtyard where Kate had been stood just days before. Kate joined them, watching Alex and Max climb out of the truck. Two men were approaching them, and Kate recognised Graham and Oliver Swift. Alex embraced them both, then pointed towards Max. Both men shook Max's hand, a warm smile on Graham's face. They spoke for a moment, then started to walk towards the main house.

'That's it then,' Nash said to Kate. 'Your man's inside.'

Kate nodded, not trusting herself to speak. A mantra thrummed in her head. *Please be safe. Please be safe. Please be safe.*

But as much as she tried to reassure herself, as much as she looked at the cameras, at the trained cops watching in the OP, knowing the extraction team were waiting just out of sight, she couldn't help the feeling of dread washing over her.

Because for the first time, Kate let herself accept the simple fact that Max Cooper meant more than just a colleague. She wanted him, she wanted to be with him, and the moment she realised that, he was walking away.

Walking away to play the riskiest game of his life.

Part 3

68

Max had been told what to expect. He knew what to do, how to act – but nothing had prepared him for the reality.

The man that greeted him in the courtyard was frail, but his handshake was firm. Graham Swift smiled as he welcomed Max into the Family, embracing Alex like they were old friends. Graham's son, Oliver, seemed more wary.

'It was me you were talking to on email,' he said, shaking Max's hand. 'I liked how you said the desire to survive at all costs should eclipse all other needs.'

'Do you agree?' Max asked.

'I do,' Oliver nodded. 'Survival of the fittest.'

'Come on.' Graham smiled. 'Let's get you settled in. We can talk shop later.'

Graham escorted Max up the large stone steps into the main house. Out of the sunshine, the air was cool and Max's eyes took a moment to adjust to the darkness. He could smell the tempting aroma of toast and bacon, and people bustled all around him.

'We've finished breakfast,' Graham said. 'Although we could rustle something up if you're hungry?'

Max shook his head. 'No, thank you. Just keen to get started.'

'Of course.' Graham pointed up the staircase. 'Oliver can take you to your bedroom, and then I'll get one of our

newest members to show you round. Alex,' Graham continued, 'let's leave them to it.'

Alex nodded to Max, then left. That was it. Max was on
his own.

Oliver had started walking up the stairs and Max followed
him.

There was a row of doors off the dim corridor, and Oliver
opened one. Inside there were two single beds: one neatly
made up, the other bare, with a stack of sheets and a duvet
resting on top.

'You'll need to do your own laundry, make your own bed
every day, look after yourself,' Oliver said. 'We'll assign you
to the rota shortly.'

'Rota?' Max asked.

'Cooking, cleaning, washing-up, that sort of thing. We're
a co-operative here, we all take our turn. And you said you
were good with engines.' Max nodded. 'Then we'll put you
with Pete in the garage. He could do with a bit more help.'
Oliver gestured towards Max's rucksack. 'Can I take a look?'
he asked, and Max handed it to him.

Oliver placed it on the bed, taking out the contents. He
examined Max's clothes, checking the pockets carefully. 'I'm
sorry to do this,' he said, 'but you wouldn't believe what
some people try to bring in. Drugs, mainly. We can't be too
careful.'

'No, of course.' Max watched Oliver silently. He picked
up the two books Max had brought with him. 'Interesting
choices,' he said. 'Why these?'

They were two battered hardbacks: *1984* and *Brave New
World*. 'They help me remember what we're fighting against,'
Max replied.

Oliver looked at him for a moment, then shook his head.

'I'm afraid we can't let you keep them,' he said, putting them to one side. 'Distractions from the here and now.'

They were disturbed by a knock behind them. A pretty blonde stuck her head round the door. 'Graham said I could find you here,' she said. 'I'm your tour guide.'

Max recognised her at once. He'd never actually met Lucy Barker, but after the week he'd spent looking for her, her picture was etched into his brain. She was more attractive than her police photo had made out, with a friendly smile that lit up her whole face.

Oliver caught him staring and laughed. 'I thought you two might get on.' He picked up the books. 'I'll leave you to it,' he said. 'Lecture is at ten.'

They watched Oliver leave, and Lucy turned to him.

'Shall we?' she asked, and Max nodded, still speechless in front of his infamous misper.

Max followed behind her as they trailed round the house. They paused in each room, Lucy explaining what it was used for. The bedrooms, Oliver and Graham's accommodation, the office. There were people everywhere they went, but Lucy ignored them, mentioning no names. Max smiled at a few, but got nothing in return.

She stopped in what seemed to be the dining room. A row of long tables had been pushed aside and chairs arranged in a semicircle. It was empty, and their shoes echoed on the hardwood floor.

'This is where we have our meals – eight a.m., one p.m. and six p.m. every day. And it's cleared to make way for our lecture at ten.'

'Well, as long as we have flexibility,' Max joked.

Lucy looked at him, stony-faced. 'Routine is the

centrepiece of any civilisation. We eat together, we learn together,' she said as she walked away.

Max nodded sternly, inwardly chastising himself for his flippancy. This was no time for his usual act.

He followed her through to the kitchen, then into a small room. Inside there was a single bed with a curtain to the side, and a bedside table on wheels.

'Medical room,' she said.

'Do you have a doctor here?' Max asked, surprised.

Lucy shook her head. 'At the moment we go to our regular GPs.' She frowned. 'Supervised visits. But when the dissolution comes we'll need to be self-sufficient.'

Max looked at the cupboard on the wall. It was basic, the door secured by a padlock.

'What's in there?' he said.

'Drugs,' Lucy replied.

'Antibiotics, painkillers? That sort of stuff?' Max asked. 'Where did it all come from?'

'People bring it with them. Packs from when they've had medical treatment and prescriptions. Pills they didn't need, leftovers from relatives. You'd be amazed what people have at home,' she said, and turned to leave.

And you'd be amazed what you can steal from a pharmacy, Max thought. He took one last look and allowed himself to be showed out. He needed to get into that cupboard. Find something in there that linked the Family to one of the violent thefts across the city.

Lucy opened the back door and they walked out into the garden. The good weather had finally broken, making way for autumn, and Max noticed a chill in the air. All around them, the trees were turning dark green and golden, leaves starting to fall.

Lucy walked quickly across the grass and Max followed her. People looked up from their chores as they passed, men raking the garden, a few pruning bushes.

'You'll get involved in this soon,' Lucy said. 'No doubt Oliver will put you on the bigger stuff.'

'He said everyone took their turn on everything,' Max replied.

Lucy snorted. 'They say that, but in reality all the women do the cooking and cleaning, and the men do the stuff outdoors. Mowing the lawn, sorting the trees, that kind of thing. They talk about this feminist utopia, but old habits are ingrained.'

Max sensed an undercurrent of resentment in her voice. 'Does that bother you?'

She shrugged. 'It's just how it has to be.' She stopped in front of a large vegetable patch. 'This is my domain,' she said, proudly.

Max looked at the neat beds, soil turned over and ready for planting. He remembered her garden from her home, watching her as she bent down and pulled a weed from the soil. Maybe she wasn't so different from the person Scott had known and loved. Maybe it took more than the threat of an apocalypse to truly change someone.

A loud bell sounded. They both looked towards the house; people around them had downed tools and were heading inside.

'Lecture time,' Lucy said, and started walking back.

Max followed her, checking out his surroundings as he went. The garden was ringed by a high wooden fence, tall trees towering up behind. He knew the team were out there, watching, but it didn't bring him any reassurance. There were more people in here than they'd guessed. And more walls.

Max's tiredness was starting to catch up with him. Feigning the confidence needed to keep his head up was exhausting, and he hadn't slept well the night before. Worry about what he was walking into, but also about what had happened with Kate. Everything between them last night had seemed so natural, so easy, and he'd kissed her without thinking. But then her reaction? And this morning she'd seemed different again. The mere touch of her hand had been enough to calm his fractured nerves.

But he couldn't think about that now. He couldn't let himself be distracted by Kate. Not when so much was on the line.

By the time the two of them got to the dining room, most of the chairs were taken, and Max could see how many people lived at the house. He counted along the rows: twenty-three in all. Fourteen women, two children and seven men, not including him. He wondered about the gender split. Did Graham Swift deliberately look for women – easier to subdue? – or was it a symptom of the world he was selling? Despite the fact that nobody was seated in the chair at the front, the room was silent. Nobody looked at each other, nobody seemed to be friends.

Oliver came into the room, and everyone looked up. He stood in front of the group, his hands clenched awkwardly in front of him.

'Unfortunately, my father is unwell, so you'll have me this morning.' He smiled and sat down, looking at his hands. He seemed to be composing himself, and Max felt sorry for the nervous kid.

'I want to talk specifics today,' Oliver began. 'I want to talk about urban survival.'

He looked up, facing the group.

'Now, I know my dad has his own views,' Oliver said, to a ripple of amusement from the room, 'but when the dissolution comes, the reality is we're going to have to leave our home at some point. We're going to need food and provisions, and the places we're going to go to get these will be our towns and cities.'

Oliver shifted in his seat, looking more confident now. He continued: 'But they won't be the places we recognise. Crime will be widespread. People will be desperate. Buildings and other structures will make observation difficult and you'll need to trust your instincts. More so than in any other environment.' Oliver looked serious. 'So what should you do to survive?'

Max glanced around the room. There was no doubt, Oliver Swift was engaging, all eyes locked on him. But nobody seemed to want to answer the question, waiting for Oliver's wisdom.

Oliver changed his position, his feet on the seat of the chair, perching up against the back. Everyone in the room was now looking up at him.

'Avoid drawing attention to yourself,' Oliver continued. 'No running. No bright colours. Nothing valuable. No torches. And I know this won't be hard for some of you, but look as grubby and messy as possible.' Another scattering of laughter. 'And finally,' Oliver said, 'no violence.'

'But won't we need to defend ourselves?' a woman asked. Her face went red as heads swivelled to glare at her, angry at the person who had dared to challenge their leader. But Oliver seemed unperturbed.

'There's a time for self-defence, but for all you know, the person in front of you might be an experienced fighter,'

Oliver said. 'And the last thing you want in the dissolution is to be wounded. If you're injured, you can't look after yourself. And if you're injured badly, you're a liability to the group.'

The room fell silent. Even Max knew what he meant. Survival of the fittest. He'd written it in the email to Oliver flippantly, a pretend mindset to get him here, but now he was inside he felt the meaning of those words more keenly than before.

Max felt completely isolated. Any wrong move could expose him, and he was surrounded by people who would do anything to protect their way of life.

Even kill.

69

Kate had a headache. She'd spent the day in the OP with the team, watching the tiny cameras, listening to the crackling voices over the microphones. She had barely eaten all day. Briggs had gone back to the station to continue raking over evidence, but Nash remained and was now signalling for her attention. She pulled the headphones off.

'Go home, detective,' he said. She hesitated, and he added: 'We'll call you if anything happens.'

'How's he getting on?' Kate asked.

Nash shook his head. 'So far so good. Let our boy settle in, DS Munro,' he said. 'These things take time.'

She nodded and, after making Nash promise again to call her, left the van, walking the hundred metres down the road to her car.

She'd watched Max all day. She'd watched him smile, talk to Lucy Barker in the garden, take in his surroundings. And she'd seen the nervousness: the slight wrinkling of his forehead, the tapping of his fingers against his thigh. But she knew Nash was right – it would take time for Max to relax and get what they needed.

Watching him with Lucy Barker had been a surreal feeling. She had wondered how Lucy had been getting on, and now here was her answer: she seemed relaxed, showing Max around with a smile. Kate thought about Scott Barker, in that big house. Alone.

Marriages were such a private undertaking. Nobody, not even your closest family, could ever know what was going on behind closed doors. Not even Lucy's husband had known she was going to leave, and Lucy herself had been unaware for over a year that her husband was cheating on her with her best friend.

And now, Kate's marriage was over too. As she pulled into her road, she automatically looked for Sam's car outside their house. It wasn't there. And for the first time she felt a sense of relief. She didn't have the energy for an argument tonight. She didn't know what else there was to say.

The house was in darkness, and she gradually turned on the lights as she walked through. She hadn't seen Sam that morning and she could see he'd emptied the dishwasher, finished the washing-up and put it away. Passive-aggressive tidying to the last.

Kate didn't call out. She switched the lights off again, picking up the two mobile phones from her bag and taking them up the stairs to her bedroom. Body weary, eyes tired, she went through the motions of getting ready for bed. Taking off her clothes, putting on an oversized T-shirt and cleaning her teeth. Coming back into the bedroom, she paused in front of the wardrobe, opening the doors to Sam's side.

It was empty. Hangers swung on the empty rail. She pulled open the drawers. Everything had gone.

She took a deep breath and let it out slowly. So that was it then. Over.

She climbed into bed and put the two phones in front of her. One was hers, and she plugged it in to charge, checking the ringer was set to maximum volume. She didn't want to miss Nash if he called.

The other phone belonged to Max.

Kate pressed it into life.

She looked at the passcode screen, then typed in the six digits he had given her at Alex's house that morning. She liked that he had trusted her without hesitation, knowing she might have needed to get into his contacts should anything happen while he was in the compound. Not that anything would, she told herself sternly.

The phone opened to an array of brightly coloured apps. Kate pulled the duvet over her and turned the light off, her face lit only by the glow of the screen. She scrolled through, eventually coming to the photos icon, opening it up.

Kate knew she was snooping. She was doing the exact same thing she had got in trouble for with Sam, but this was different. Max wouldn't mind. She wasn't looking to find out something to split them apart, like with Sam. This time she was looking for something to bring them closer.

Max felt far away from her, cut off from the team. She flicked through his photos, seeing faces of people she didn't know, a blurry stage from an unknown concert, people sitting in a pub garden in the sunshine, then one of him, a selfie, taken on a beach. There were a few, Max trying out different expressions, and she smiled, pausing on the last one. A big grin, his eyes squinting against the sun, his hair blowing in the breeze.

She looked at it one last time, then closed her eyes. She knew she was being a wuss but she let it go, indulging her pathetic daydreams for a moment. She wished she was with him. But no, not there. Not where he was now. Instead she wished he was here, in bed, tonight, with her.

Kate fell asleep, the phone still clutched in her hand, her thoughts full of Max.

Friday

70

Max hadn't slept well. His room-mate, an overweight middle-aged man named Jim, slept on his back, and consequently filled the room with resonating snores the whole night. At 3 a.m., Max rather uncharitably thought that if the apocalypse came, Jim would be the first person Max would kill. And then eat.

The bell went off at seven, and after a dribbly shower, Max headed down to the dining room. If Lucy had seen him, she ignored him, and he took an empty seat at the far end of the table, receiving a bowl of porridge from the woman serving. Whatever the other failings of the commune were, food was not one of them. The porridge was creamy and rich, sprinkled with plump sultanas. Max realised that Graham's recruitment strategy had a certain amount of genius to it. Well-fed campers were happy campers, and he'd obviously found a few people that could cook.

A grey-haired man wearing steel-capped boots and a work belt slung round his waist appeared next to him.

'You're with me,' he growled. He pushed Max's empty bowl aside and handed him a large overcoat, gesturing for Max to follow him.

The weather had turned, and rain was coming down in sheets. Max put the coat on, doing it up to his nose, ignoring the smell of stale sweat and sawdust. The man walked quickly ahead of him to the outhouses, striding with purpose, pausing only to unlock the large garage doors and swing them open.

Inside the garage the man turned to Max and held out his hand. He smiled.

'Pete,' he said. 'Oliver says you're a mechanic.'

Out of sight of the main building, Pete chatted away amiably. His demeanour had completely changed. Max had nodded slowly, then hoped that the few skills he had learnt over the years came to some use. But whatever Pete's misgivings at Max's abilities, he didn't seem to care. He seemed happy just to have company.

The two of them spent hours tapping away in the engine of an old tractor. Pete shared that it had been gifted to the commune but had broken down on the first day. (Max wondered whether that was a euphemism for 'stolen', and memorised the number plate.) They heard the bell for the ten o'clock lecture. Max looked up but Pete ignored it.

'You're with me,' he said, his head buried in the depths of the tractor. 'Pass me the socket wrench.'

Max handed him the tool and watched as Pete worked.

'How long have you been here?' Max asked.

'Seven years,' Pete replied from the engine. 'I was one of the first to join. Just out of a messy divorce, living on the streets, and Graham offered me a roof for my services. Half-inch driver?' he finished, and Max passed it across. 'It's changed a bit since then, though.'

'What do you mean?'

He paused for a moment, then went back to the tractor. 'More people like you. Seeking salvation.' He stood up, straightening his back out. 'In the early days we were a disorganised bunch. Since Oliver came home, things seem a little more ...' He stopped, searching for the right word. 'Purposeful. Give that a try?'

Max turned the key in the ignition. The tractor roared into life, filling the garage with diesel smoke. Pete raised his hand and Max gave him a high five. They turned the engine off again and Pete stood back, leaning on the tractor, pulling a box of Marlboro Reds down from a high shelf next to them.

'Contraband,' he said with a smile. 'Proper fags are considered too expensive when the dissolution comes.'

He offered one to Max, who shook his head, taking the pouch of tobacco out of his pocket. Luckily it seemed that despite the lack of practice over the years, his fingers could remember how to make a decent cigarette. He put the finished roll-up in his mouth.

'Don't you believe in the dissolution?' Max asked.

Pete took a long drag on his cigarette, then handed Max the lighter. He squinted at him through the dim light of the garage. 'Listen, you seem like a good bloke. But you shouldn't go around asking questions like that.' He blew out a long plume of smoke. 'They don't like questions here, full stop.'

'Who doesn't?'

Pete tilted his head to one side. 'Just keep yourself to yourself. Don't seem too cheerful, don't stick your head above the parapet. Because I'm telling you now, you won't like what happens if you do.' He finished his cigarette and dropped it on the concrete floor, grinding it underfoot. 'You stay here, I'm going back to the house. Get the keys to next door.'

Pete ran outside, back into the rain, leaving Max alone in the garage. This was his chance.

He walked quickly along the line of vehicles. The garage

was large, with the tractor, an old Ford Fiesta, a quad bike and a truck. Max hurried to the far end, gently pulling the tiny camera out of the custom-built seam in his waistband. He switched it on, then crouched next to the tyres of the truck, taking a quick succession of photographs. But he knew, even without looking closely, that this wasn't the vehicle they'd seen on the CCTV. This was a Nissan Navara, and they were looking for a Toyota Hilux.

Max hid the camera again as he heard Pete's footsteps crunching on the gravel.

He appeared in the doorway and gestured Max to follow him out into the rain, into the building next door.

And there was the black Toyota Hilux. Max felt his heart jump, but forced himself to stay calm, following Pete inside. His eyes adjusted to the dark in the garage and he looked around, taking in the rows of tools hung up across the wall that Pete was now perusing. Possible murder weapons, he thought.

'What are we doing in here?' Max asked.

Pete held out a large adjustable spanner. 'Need this. But here's a job for us later, when the rain stops.' He pointed to the Toyota. 'Graham mentioned it needs a good clean, something about selling it, so we'll have to take it out into the courtyard and give it a hose down.' Pete gestured outside, where the rain was still pouring. 'Maybe tomorrow.' He walked out of the garage and Max followed him, wistfully looking back as the doors closed. 'No shortage of stuff to be done in the house,' Pete added as he refastened the padlocks.

The truck was locked away again for now, and Max had his target. But it sounded like he would need to be quick. Because before long all evidence would be washed away in seconds with a swish of water from the hose.

71

Max spent the rest of the day in Pete's shadow, keeping busy. They fixed the headboard of a bed, stopped for lunch, then tackled the broken light in the kitchen. Max kept an eye out for anything untoward, but as yet, apart from the dirty Hilux and the row of tools, he hadn't seen anything of note.

As Pete struggled mending a window in one of the front bedrooms, Max saw Alex's truck pull up in the courtyard outside.

'Can I pop out for a ciggy?' Max asked as Pete twiddled with the catch, and Pete grunted in response. Max didn't waste any time, going down the stairs, passing Alex as he stood talking to Graham in the corridor. Alex ignored him as he went by.

The rain had stopped – bad news for the fate of the truck – and Max sat on the stone steps rolling a cigarette. He felt twitchy. This place gave him the creeps, and Pete's warnings that morning hadn't helped.

Max heard footsteps, then Alex stood in front of him, blocking out the rest of the afternoon light.

'Want one?' Max asked, and Alex nodded.

Max handed him the cigarette he'd just rolled, and Alex put it behind his ear. 'I'll save it for later,' he smiled, then left, climbing into his truck and driving out of the compound.

Max felt claustrophobic, locked in this place. With shaking fingers he put the second rollie to his lips and lit it, savouring the harsh taste at the back of his throat. The nicotine woke him up, focusing his attention.

'There you are,' Pete said, coming up behind him. 'Finish that. We have work to do upstairs.'

Max stubbed the cigarette out and followed Pete back into the house. A bed in pieces awaited their arrival in one of the bedrooms, and Max noted the proximity to Graham and Oliver's accommodation. So when Pete asked him to fetch a bigger screwdriver, it was the only opportunity he needed.

Closing the door behind him, he looked down the corridor. Nobody in sight. He casually walked two doors down and pushed the handle. Silently, he rehearsed the excuses in his head. *I'm sorry, I'm new, I got lost. I thought it was the bathroom. This house is so big, you never know where you are.* But the room was empty.

Graham and Oliver's quarters were modest – no more than two bedrooms and a bathroom in the middle. He went first into what he assumed was Graham's room, the older man's clothes draped over the chair, an assortment of drugs on his bedside table. Max took photos of everything, looking for a hairbrush or anything he could steal for DNA. But there was nothing. He moved into Oliver's bedroom, smiling as he saw the two books taken from him on Oliver's bedside table.

For a young man, the room was strangely sparse. There were a few survivalist textbooks on the shelves, next to a photograph of a younger woman. He squinted at it – a girlfriend, perhaps? But the photo looked old, colours fading, clothes out of date. Max thought he recognised her, but then shook his head, taking a quick photo of it anyway. Into the bathroom next, and Max saw two toothbrushes in a mug next to the sink.

'What are you doing in here?' Max heard a female voice behind him, and turned quickly. It was Lucy. 'This is the Swifts' bathroom,' she said, frowning.

Max laughed, forcing a grin and thrusting his hands quickly into his pockets.

'I know, but I was desperate,' Max smiled. 'I think the different food must be having an effect on me, I didn't think I could make it any further.'

Lucy studied his face closely, then glanced round the room.

'Just get out of here.'

He moved past her. 'What are you doing here, anyway?' Max asked.

'Oliver ...' She hesitated. 'Oliver asked me to fetch something.'

She seemed anxious to get away, and almost pushed him into the corridor.

Max walked away from her quickly, picking up the screw-driver for Pete along the way. But one hand stayed in his pocket, his fingers pushing the toothbrushes further down, firmly wrapped in the plastic bag he had hidden there.

72

Lucy didn't know what to make of the new guy. He was friendly, charming – but he seemed wrong for this place. The rest of the men were either older and rootless, or younger but nerdy. The sort you would expect to be beaten up at school. But this guy? He seemed normal.

And now she'd caught him snooping around in Oliver and Graham's rooms. She'd got him out of there quick, not just in case he was caught but before he asked any awkward questions.

Her missing leaving note still niggled at her. She remembered the day she left. Flustered, she'd walked out of her house with the blue envelope clutched in her hand. It had been Oliver who had gone back with it. Oliver she'd told to put it on the hallway table. But it hadn't been found. So where was it?

She watched Max walk off down the corridor, then gasped as someone caught her arm. Graham.

She turned to face him, ready for the worst after the verbal onslaught the day before. But his smile was warm, his body language open.

'There's a phone call for you in the office. It's your husband. Be quick,' he said. But he was still holding onto her arm, his grip firm. 'He's been calling you since yesterday on our private number. God knows how he got it. Get rid of him, Lucy.'

Lucy recognised the warning tone in his voice as he let go of her arm. She hurried across to the office. The old-style phone receiver had been left on the desk and she picked it up.

'Scott?' she said, tentatively.

'Lucy? Oh, thank god. I've been trying to get hold of you.'

'Have you? Why?' Lucy was suddenly worried. Had something happened to Isaac?

'I just wanted to talk to you, I'm sorry,' Scott said. He was speaking slowly, and Lucy could tell he was measuring his words carefully. She glanced behind her out of the door, watching Graham in the corridor. She turned back round, feeling his eyes on the back of her neck.

'What do you want, Scott?'

'I'm sorry, but I need to see you. To apologise properly. I know I've been a shitty husband, and I can't bear to think of us parting ways like this. Please let me come to the house.' He paused. 'And then I'll leave you alone,' he finished, quietly.

'If this is another trick, Scott—' Lucy started, but he cut her off.

'It isn't, I promise.'

Lucy turned, and Graham was still watching her.

'Fine,' she said, and she could hear Scott breathe a sigh of relief on the other end of the line. 'Come by tomorrow at half nine.'

She put the phone down quickly before Scott could say any more.

'Is there a problem?'

Graham was behind her, blocking her exit from the office.

Lucy shook her head. 'No, no problem.' She pointed to the phone. 'He wants to visit, to apologise. I said he could come tomorrow.' She could feel her body tense. 'Just this once, Graham, I promise. I need to keep him on side. The Family are going to need the proceeds from the sale of the house, and there's no point causing trouble with him now.'

Graham frowned for a moment, thinking. Then he took her hands in his, the same way he had when she'd moved into the haven. Then, she'd felt reassured by him. Today, it was different. She'd seen a side to Graham she was unsure about. Something she didn't trust.

'Fine. Let him come,' Graham said, and Lucy gave a sigh of relief. 'But this has to be the last time. I don't see you with him. You need someone more committed to our beliefs.' He smiled. 'And I must admit, I did have some hopes for you and our new gentleman.'

'Max?' she said, surprised.

He nodded. 'You look good together. Creating the next generation of our family.'

Graham let go of her, leaving Lucy alone. The thought of someone thinking about her – and her and Max – in that way made her feel odd. Like she wasn't a person, but breeding stock, like a sow in a factory farm.

She pushed the thought out of her head, and walked quickly down the stairs and out of the house to her vegetable patch. A few hours in the peace and quiet would make her feel better, she told herself. A bit of fresh air would silence those concerns.

73

Kate and Briggs had the same idea. Both were in the office early, desperate to get the case landed.

DCI Delaney had even been down to visit, keen to hear of any progress.

'Lab have matched blood samples found in the alleyway behind Dougie Brewer's flat to the DNA of Paul Sherwood, so it looks like that was where he was murdered,' Kate confirmed. She pointed to Briggs, next to her. He was back on the CCTV, scrolling through hours of footage from January, trying to place Graham's truck near to the crime scene.

'And the car?' Delaney asked.

'SOCO are processing the evidence and so far they've pulled fingerprints and hair samples, neither of which are a match to Brewer.'

'But we don't know who they're from?'

Kate shook her head. 'Nothing in the system.'

Delaney frowned and stood in front of the whiteboard, staring at the photos of Oliver and Graham Swift. 'Let's hope Cooper gives us something soon,' she muttered.

Kate hoped so too. The sooner he delivered, the sooner they could get him out of there. She'd already called the OP that morning and they'd confirmed that Max was up, fed and apparently helping some guy fix a tractor.

Kate smiled at the image. She liked the idea of Max slightly grubby, a spanner in hand.

Kate's phone rang, and she jumped, hastily answering it.

'We have some photos,' Nash said without a greeting. 'Looks like tyres, sending them to you now.'

He hung up, and Kate clicked refresh on her email.

The photos loaded and Briggs scooted his chair over to her side, laptop open.

'We'll get Forensics to do a proper comparison, but what do you think?' Kate asked.

Briggs pulled up the shot of the tyre imprint and looked at the photo on the screen. He shook his head.

'He's way off,' Briggs said, and Kate could see his disappointment.

'I'm sure he knows that.' Kate leaned back in her seat. 'Give him time,' she said, echoing Nash's words.

The day dragged. Kate didn't like this sort of shit – sitting around, doing nothing. She took some of the CCTV footage from Briggs but she couldn't concentrate. She fidgeted, wanting to be out there. Her phone pinged, more photos coming through from the OP.

She opened them up.

They were shots of a bedroom this time. Books, and small boxes by the side of an unmade bed. They looked like prescription drugs. A photo frame. Two toothbrushes by the side of a sink. Photos aren't any bloody good, Kate thought. You can't get DNA from a photograph.

She could have screamed with the insignificance of it all. What was he thinking?

She leaned in closer, moving the images back and forth in front of her eyes. Briggs glanced over.

'He took the photographs for a reason,' he said.

'Really, Jamie?' Kate shook her head. 'I can't see it.'

Briggs took the mouse out of her hand and she sat back in her chair, watching as he went through the shots again on the screen.

'Wait, wait there,' she said, and he paused on the one of the photo frame. 'Blow that up.'

Briggs zoomed into the photo. It was a woman – long brown hair, tanned skin, pretty – with her arm round a boy Kate recognised as Oliver Swift. She squinted at the screen, then took a sharp breath in.

It was the same woman from the photo of Paul Sherwood and Alex as a young boy.

Next to them the phone rang and Briggs picked it up. She watched him talk for a second, then gestured to him to hang up.

He put the receiver down. 'What?' he asked her.

'Put a call out, I want Alex Sherwood back in here.'

Briggs shook his head. 'We don't have to, Sarge. That was the front desk. He's already downstairs.'

74

So far, so good.

The thing about being the new guy in a place that didn't seem to encourage friendships was that Max could mooch around without being asked any questions. But he always felt eyes watching him, silent stares on his back.

He wanted to get into the medical room, so Max knew he needed an excuse to be in the kitchen. After dinner he saw his opening and wandered through, carrying a load of dirty plates.

One woman was next to the sink, and frowned when she saw Max. He placed the plates alongside an already teetering stack.

'Do you need some help?' he asked. She looked at him, disbelief in her eyes.

'Do you have your allocation yet?' she asked. 'Of chores?' she continued when he looked blank.

'With Pete, I think. But no, nothing like this.'

'Then, here.'

She handed him the dishcloth and walked out of the room.

He surveyed the kitchen. The woman had made a start, but dirty crockery and saucepans covered every surface. The people who cooked were obviously not the same as the people who cleared up, and they made no effort to assist the shift coming after them.

Max started opening the cupboards in turn, looking for anything that might be helpful. Suddenly he was aware of someone watching him.

Oliver was standing in the doorway. He was holding a notebook and passed it between his hands. Max had seen it before: in front of Graham at dinner. He'd been writing in between mouthfuls, his gaze fixed downwards. Max had wondered what was so important on those pages.

'What are you doing?' Oliver asked.

'Looking for a dishwasher,' Max replied, and Oliver laughed.

'We don't have one. When the dissolution comes and electricity fails, we're going to need our power for more important things, rather than saving time with our dirty dishes. It's good to get used to it now.'

Max nodded. 'Fair enough.' He held out the dishcloth. 'Want to help?'

Oliver smiled and shook his head. 'I wouldn't want to deny you your learning opportunity.'

'I've done washing-up before,' Max said, trying to make light of the situation.

Oliver smirked. 'I meant about actions and consequences. You offer to help someone, they take advantage. You learn not to offer again.'

'And that's a good thing?'

'In the world we're heading towards, Max, it's the only thing.'

Oliver turned and shut the door firmly behind him. Max shook his head, then ran the washing-up water. It was a strange place. He had assumed from everything they had said that living here taught you the benefits of communal living, but it seemed it was every man for himself. Unless it meant serving the Swifts. The veneration towards the two men in charge seemed ingrained, almost automatic. Apart from providing the place to stay, Max wondered how they'd managed to foster such obedience.

The hubbub outside the kitchen died down, and Max paused, listening. It sounded like the dining room had been cleared and he poked his head round the door to check. Sure enough, the room was empty, all chairs carefully back in place, table wiped down and clean.

Max shut it behind him again. He looked at the door to the medical room. It was as good a time as any.

Inside, Max switched the light on and walked quickly up to the cupboard. He peered at the padlock securing it shut. He was in luck – it was cheap and basic, so he went back into the kitchen to see what he could find to help.

He opened drawer after drawer, eventually coming across one full of assorted crap. Old receipts, broken pieces from who knew what, pens, random cables, but also a few paper-clips and a small hairpin, which he bent into an L shape. Max hurried back into the medical room and went to work.

It was a frustrating thing to do. Max had never been good at it in the first place, but in the desperate need to be quick it felt almost impossible. He made a few botched attempts at pushing up the pins, to no avail, and felt a bead of sweat roll down his back. Standing up, he took a deep breath.

Remember your training, he told himself. Envisage the pins, hold the picture in your mind as you push each one in turn. He felt the almost imperceptible pressure, applying the force he needed. At last, feeling like he'd got somewhere, he put the end of the hairpin inside.

Slowly he turned the piece of metal and he felt the lock

move. It was new and well oiled, the metal clicking into place. He held his breath, and the padlock sprang open.

Max closed his eyes with relief, then looked inside the cupboard. Lining the shelves neatly was an array of drugs, filling it to the brim. He quickly took his camera out and started snapping. As he worked his way methodically along, he recognised names from the list he'd sent to Dr Adams. Loperamide, ranitidine, ketamine, oxycodone, diamorphine, amoxicillin. An assortment of dressings, syringes and needles. Ethyl alcohol, superglue, silver nitrate and EpiPens. Max didn't even know what some of this stuff was used for.

At the bottom of the cupboard was a small fridge. Max bent down and pulled it open. It contained one small cardboard box: the word Esmiron was written on the side, and then, in small letters underneath, rocuronium.

Max picked up the box. This was what he was looking for. This was what had been found in Dougie's system. The lid was open, and he peered inside at the small glass ampoules. But where he'd expected to see a space where one was missing, what he saw surprised him. Not one, but two of the vials were absent.

He knew it didn't have to mean anything. Maybe the box was already short when it was stolen, or it was used a long time ago. But that little void gave Max a sense of unease. Knowing how Dougie had died, he'd be a lot happier if he knew where the second vial had gone.

Because Max had a horrible feeling in his bones. Something more was to come.

75

Kate glared at Alex Sherwood across the table. They were back in the interview room, the uncomfortable one with the hard chairs and the recording equipment. Kate had cautioned him while Alex watched her, his face expressionless.

'Could you explain this, please?'

Briggs turned the laptop around to face him. On the screen was the photograph Max had taken of Oliver and the woman from Oliver's bedroom.

'What do you want to know?' Alex said coolly.

His attitude only served to piss Kate off more. 'Can you explain why Oliver Swift has a photograph of your mother in his room?'

Alex looked at it, then up at Kate.

'Oliver and I have the same mother,' he said.

Kate was furious. 'And you didn't think it would be helpful to mention this sooner?' she shouted.

'I didn't think it was relevant.'

'You didn't think ...' Kate's voice tapered off, rendered speechless in her fury. She shook her head at Briggs, then tried again. 'I think it's pretty sodding relevant that your half-brother is part of the family that you think murdered your father.' She glared at him across the table. 'Start talking,' she said.

Alex scowled. 'My father met my mother at university. Same place he met Graham Swift. They got married. They had me. Then Graham decided he wanted her for himself and they had an affair. She left us and moved in with Graham. She had Oliver. She died.' He stopped and stared at Kate. 'End of story.'

'And yet Graham and Paul were still friends?' Kate asked.

'I wouldn't describe them as friends. They didn't speak for years. But when Mum died they found consolation in each other. They'd both lost the woman they loved. Graham had a small boy to bring up. They put it behind them.'

'And how old were you and Oliver when your mum died?'

'I was twenty, Oliver was seven.'

'And are you and Oliver close?'

'What do you think?' Kate glared at him again and he sighed. 'No, we're not. I find him a strange kid. Hard to get along with. I've got nothing against him, but do I consider him my brother? No,' he said, firmly.

'Don't you think it could be motive?' Kate asked.

Alex shook his head. 'Graham stole my mother from my father. It would make more sense the other way around, if Graham was dead and Dad was still alive. So, no. Besides, it was over twenty years ago. Why would you do it now?' He looked from Kate to Briggs then back again. 'A long time to hold a grudge, don't you think? Now, have you finished shouting at me?'

Kate frowned. She didn't like being lied to, but the man had a point. Not that she was going to admit it out loud. Her initial anger was fading, replaced by the same frustration and worry from before.

'Fine,' Kate muttered. 'You can go.'

'Don't you want to know why I came here in the first place?' Alex said, leaning back, relaxed, in the chair. 'I've seen Max,' he finished, and Kate sprang up in her seat.

'When? How?' she asked. 'How is he?'

Alex raised his eyebrows. 'Shouldn't your guys be telling you that?' he paused, then reached down into his bag, pulling out a pouch of tobacco.

'You can't smoke in here,' Briggs said, and Alex gave him a withering look.

'Here,' he said, handing Kate a rolled cigarette.

Kate took it, then slowly unravelled the ends. She tore gently down the length of the paper, letting the tobacco fall, then carefully opened it out on the table.

Written inside were the words *SAT 0800*.

'Max gave this to you?' Kate asked, and Alex nodded.

'You're welcome,' he said, standing up. 'Now can I go?'

Kate agreed, and Alex opened the door. In the doorway, he paused, looking back.

'Listen, if you want to know more about what Graham and my dad were like at uni, go and speak to one of my dad's exes. He dumped her to go out with my mother, but they all stayed friends for years, too. Her name's Susannah Carpenter.'

'There must be thousands of people by that name. Anything else to go on?' Briggs asked.

'Yeah,' Alex said. 'She's still at Southampton University. Did her PhD there, then went on to lecture.'

Kate smoothed the note against the tabletop. She looked up at Alex.

'Alex?' she said, and he looked back. 'Thank you.'

He nodded and was gone.

Briggs looked at the note. 'You're going to pass this to Nash?' he asked. When Kate didn't reply, he stared at her. 'You're not trained to go in for a meet, you know that, right?' he added.

She nodded. 'Of course I'll pass it to Nash,' she replied.

But she knew she would do nothing of the sort.

76

It took Max two hours to finish the washing-up.

It had been therapeutic, the monotony of clearing away. And it wasn't like he had anything else to do.

When he emerged from the kitchen, the house was in darkness. It was almost ten o'clock and he assumed the other residents were in bed. He was about to climb the stairs when he realised the front door was open slightly, and he heard a sniff coming from the other side.

Lucy Barker was sat on the top step, looking out into the darkness.

He coughed gently behind her and she turned.

'Oh, it's you,' she said.

'You okay?'

She nodded, then sniffed again. He joined her on the step.

'I'm a bit ... I don't know.' She wiped her nose with a tissue. The rain had stopped and Max wondered how long it would be until the truck had its fateful deep clean. 'Just a bit homesick.'

Max nodded. 'I can understand that.'

'You can?'

'Of course. You're in here, away from the people you know and love. Of course you're going to miss them.'

'I'm not saying I miss them. I just ... I don't know,' she said again. 'I know why you're here,' she added.

Max felt his stomach drop. He paused for a second, trying to control the jitters. 'You do?' he asked slowly.

'Yeah.' She looked over and the dim light caught her eyes. 'They thought you would make a good match for me.'

Max stopped. 'Sorry?'

Lucy laughed quietly. 'When the dissolution arrives they're going to need to repopulate.' She paused. 'They need good breeding stock. Healthy young people.'

'Good...' Max raised his eyebrows. 'You mean, like race-horses?'

Lucy smiled. 'If you like.' She gestured back to the house. 'Look at the people living here. Too many old men. They need guys like you.'

Max paused. 'Isn't that a bit clinical?'

Lucy nodded slowly. 'But that's what survival is all about, isn't it? Calculated actions designed to get the best results.'

'Do you think that's what Graham's doing?'

'Don't you? I've been here two weeks now. Nothing they do is by accident. It's all...' Lucy stopped, her hands going over her mouth. 'It's nothing, forget I said it.' She glanced back to the house, up at the darkened windows. 'We should go to bed.' Then she stopped and looked at him. 'Not together, I didn't mean...' she added quickly.

Max touched her arm. 'Don't worry. I know what you meant. Good night, Lucy.'

She turned and went back into the house. Max stayed outside, resting his elbows on his knees and his face in his hands. He sighed. He knew how Lucy felt. The homesickness was real for him, too. He longed to sleep in his own bed. Even sharing a joke with Briggs would seem like a luxury right now.

But the desire to catch these bastards burned in the pit of

his stomach. He could feel there was something more sinister going on than they'd suspected from the outside. And Lucy knew it, too.

He took one last cooling breath of fresh air, then stood up to go into the house. But before he went in, he peered up at the windows.

Oliver Swift was standing there, watching him.

Saturday

77

I'll tell him later, Kate muttered to herself as she pushed through the undergrowth. Ask for forgiveness, not permission, she thought, knowing full well she was breaching protocol. But she couldn't risk Nash saying no.

She'd parked her car at the far side of the lake and walked to the spot they'd assigned as the drop point. It had been scouted by Nash as the easiest place for Max to reach from the back gate of the compound, concealed by high trees, but with access from the road for the team.

She looked at her watch for the hundredth time: 8.23. Max was late.

'What are you doing here?'

She turned towards the whisper behind her. 'You sent a message,' Kate said.

'I was expecting Nash.'

'Oh. Right.' She looked at Max. He was dressed in a checked shirt and jeans; he was unshaven and looked tired. 'Did you get out okay?'

'I'm getting better with padlocks.' Max ran a hand down his face and frowned. 'Are you going to take these, or what?'

Kate was taken aback by his gruffness and held out the evidence bag. He placed two toothbrushes inside in their own plastic bag and she sealed it shut.

'Do you know which is which?' she asked.

'I didn't think to ask,' he snapped back.

'Fine, I'll go.'

Kate started to walk away, until a hand on her arm stopped her. She turned, angry.

'Kate, please,' Max said. He pulled her round to face him, gently holding the tops of her arms. 'It's just ... you surprised me. I can't think about you in there. I can't ... I'll go mad.' Max looked back over his shoulder. 'I need to go, someone will notice.'

'Jesus Christ!' The loud whisper made both of them jump and Nash pushed his way out of the undergrowth. He looked at Kate, his face thunderous. He opened his mouth, then closed it again, before turning to Max.

Nash pointed at the evidence in Kate's hand. 'Is that it?' he asked, and Max nodded. 'Then go, quickly. Now.'

Max disappeared back into the trees without another word. Nash glared at Kate from underneath lowered brows, then pointed an angry finger towards the road. She started walking, hearing his heavy footsteps behind her.

Back on the track, he gestured towards her car and they both climbed inside. She drove out to the road, Nash still silent next to her. After about a mile, he pointed towards a lay-by and she pulled in.

The onslaught started immediately.

'What were you *thinking*?' he shouted, his voice echoing round the inside of the car. 'You go to a meet without telling me? You don't notify the OP, you don't take any precautions? You know you could have blown his cover? You know you were putting his life at risk?'

He stopped and Kate went to explain before he

interrupted her again, his voice low and cool this time. 'Is there something I should know about, DS Munro?'

'What do you mean?'

'That little ... meeting ... out there,' he growled. 'Was that an evidence drop, or something else?'

Kate shook her head quickly. 'No, guv. Nothing else. I'm sorry, I was just worried. No more than concern for a member of my team,' she added quickly.

Nash took a long look at her. 'Fine.' He picked up the phone and made a call. 'Is the asset back in place?' he asked. 'Good.'

He hung up and turned back to Kate. 'Looks like your little stunt hasn't caused any problems.' Kate felt the relief flood her body. 'Now take what you have there and get it processed. And don't you dare even look in the vicinity of this house from now on without my say-so.'

Kate dropped Nash back near the OP, chastened. Not only had she nearly screwed up the operation, but her detective inspector now thought there was something going on between her and an officer in her command.

And there wasn't, obviously. Nothing. But Kate couldn't deny how she'd felt when she'd seen him. A mixture of relief and excitement, but something else, too. Something she didn't want to put a name to right now.

Her phone rang, Briggs's voice coming over loud and clear on the overhead speaker.

'Sarge? You got it?'

'Yep, two toothbrushes, hopefully one with the DNA of Graham Swift. Heading to drop it off at the lab now.' Kate felt a flush of guilt, knowing that her actions had probably got Briggs an earbashing from Nash too, despite the fact that she hadn't told him what she was going to do. 'You okay?' she added, tentatively.

There was a pause.

'You owe me one, boss,' Briggs muttered.

'Sorry, Jamie.'

'Par for the course, working for you.' He sighed. 'Come and pick me up from the station on the way through,' he continued, back to business as usual. 'We're off to Southampton University.'

'You found Susannah Carpenter?' Kate asked.

'Professor Susannah Carpenter now,' Briggs replied. 'And she can't wait to talk to us.'

78

Lucy hovered in the doorway, waiting for Scott to arrive. She was jittery and nervous, like she was going on a first date. With her husband? Her estranged husband, at that. How could she be feeling like this, when today was supposed to be their final goodbye?

It had to be this way. Graham had caught her after breakfast and reinforced that non-believers had no place at the haven. He was right, logically she knew that, and she reminded herself of how she'd felt being at home. Constantly scared, watching the news on repeat, searching for evidence of the coming dissolution. And Scott had never listened, ignoring her efforts to talk to him, and then having an affair with her best friend. This was not a man who could protect her.

But she'd done terrible things, too. Because of her actions he'd been arrested for her murder. She'd put him through hell, believing she was dead. Hadn't he suffered enough? After all, a marriage went two ways, and wasn't marriage for life? In sickness and in health?

She heard the buzz of the intercom and a voice answering it from the office upstairs. There was a pause, and Lucy looked over her shoulder. Had Graham changed his mind? But then the gates slowly started to open, and Lucy saw Scott's Audi drive in.

He parked up and, after a pause, climbed out.

Her stomach jumped as he walked towards her, and he smiled. She felt herself smiling back.

They stood in front of each other. He was tense, Lucy could see it on his face, and in the way he clasped his hands together in front of him. Lucy moved forward to peck him on the cheek and in their nervousness her lips caught the edge of his mouth. She remembered what it had been like to kiss him.

'I thought you might change your mind,' Lucy said.

'I wanted to see you.'

'Do you want to come in?' she asked, and Scott nodded.

She led the way up the stone steps into the massive hallway where Graham and Oliver were waiting. Lucy introduced them and the three men shook hands.

'Thank you for having me today,' Scott said.

Graham smiled. He seemed warm, back to his usual self. 'You are more than welcome to visit,' he replied. 'As long as your motives are as innocent as you claim they are.'

There was silence in the hallway as Graham's words sank in.

'One thing I've learnt,' Scott said slowly, 'is that I need to listen more to my wife. And take responsibility for my failings in the past.'

'She's no longer your wife. Hasn't Lucy been clear about that?' Oliver said bluntly, stepping forward into the light from the doorway.

'Excuse my son,' Graham said. 'His passion sometimes overtakes his manners.'

Oliver looked sharply towards his father, and Lucy saw a flash of something behind his eyes. Then the smile reappeared, and his body language changed. 'My apologies,'

Oliver said. 'But the question remains: why do you still think you and Lucy are together?'

'Because I love her, and I always will,' Scott said, and Lucy looked up at him quickly, feeling her face blushing. 'I do, Lucy, and I'm sorry I didn't say that enough before.'

Lucy nodded, her sudden emotions rendering her speechless.

She felt Graham's hand on the small of her back. 'Let's leave you two to have your conversation, shall we?' he said. Then he turned to face Lucy. 'Remember what we discussed,' he added quietly.

But before Lucy could reply, another figure rushed in through the front door. Max stopped abruptly, blinking in the darkness of the hallway. Lucy saw his surprise as he took in the group of people in front of him.

Graham held his arm out towards Max, ushering him towards Scott. 'This is Max,' Graham said. 'One of our newest members.'

Scott laughed nervously. 'This is so weird,' he said, leaning forward and shaking Max's hand. 'But we've already met, haven't we?'

79

Susannah Carpenter, Professor of Pharmacology, wasn't what Kate had expected. Tall and slender, she was wearing clothes more suited to a corporate lawyer – fitted dress, high, impractical heels, hair tied up tightly in a bun. She met them in the hallway of a slightly shabby building on campus, then showed them up the stairs to her office.

Kate thanked her for meeting them and Professor Carpenter pulled two chairs forward and gestured for them both to sit down.

'I was working anyway,' she said. 'And I'm very sorry to hear about Paul. How can I help?'

The office was small but tidy, files and bookshelves lining the walls. A gentle perfume filled the air, something soft and flowery. A laptop idled on the desk, surrounded by piles of what seemed to be lecture notes.

'As my colleague mentioned on the phone, we're investigating Paul's possible murder,' Kate began, 'and we hoped you could provide some insight into the relationship between him and Graham Swift.'

'And Jane Gaunt, I assume?' she said. 'Or Jane Sherwood, then Jane Swift, as you'd know her.'

Kate nodded. 'Did you know them well at university?'

Professor Carpenter smiled. 'I must admit, I never thought I'd need to talk about this ever again. It was a funny time. We were young, you know, so hormones and emotions were always running high. In hindsight, it was a lot of fuss over nothing.'

'What sort of fuss?'

She leaned forward and picked up the bottle of water on her desk, holding it in her hand. 'It must have been our final year at uni, and I'd been going out with Paul for a few months. Nothing serious, but he was a nice bloke. And then on a night out, I met his housemate, Graham, and his girlfriend, Jane.'

'I thought Jane left Paul for Graham?' Briggs interjected.

The professor shook her head. 'No, no, she was with Gray first. I could never work out why she then chose Paul over Gray, but there it was, on that night out, Paul snogging Jane in the doorway of a nightclub. I saw them, we had a fight, and that was it. But not for Gray.'

'How so?'

'Graham was furious. I'd known him for a while, and he was one of those slightly entitled guys, you know? What he wanted, he got, and he really wanted Jane. He and Paul got into a proper fight, Paul punched him, the police were called. No one pressed charges, but Gray was angry, no doubt about that. Of course, a few years later I heard from a friend that Jane had left Paul and her little kid and had gone back to Graham. That didn't surprise me either.'

'That she'd leave her child?'

'You'd have to have known Gray. He was single-minded – and charming. He could persuade you black was white, and years later you'd still believe it.'

Kate nodded. She had seen him in action; she could well believe the persuasive powers of Graham Swift.

'Was he one to hold a grudge?' Kate asked.

But Susannah shook her head. 'Are you asking me whether

I think Graham killed Paul? No,' she answered before Kate could confirm. 'He won, didn't he? He had his girl, and they had Oliver.'

'You know about Oliver?' Kate said, surprised.

'I used to teach Oliver,' the professor said. 'Actually, when you first mentioned you wanted to talk about the Swifts I assumed it was Oliver you wanted to discuss.' She put the water bottle down, then picked it up again, seemingly more for something to hold in her hands than because she actually wanted a drink. Kate waited for her to carry on. 'He was always a little ...' She thought for a moment, considering her words. 'Off,' she said at last.

Kate tilted her head to one side. 'Really?'

'Yeah, just one of those students you had your doubts about, you know? I thought about mentioning it to the Dean, but then he left and it wasn't relevant any more.'

'Mentioning him to the Dean?' Kate looked at Briggs, who seemed as puzzled as she was. 'What was he doing? Messing around with women, that sort of thing?'

'Oh no, nothing like that,' the professor said. 'Just ...' She stopped. 'Let me give you an example. We do a few practicals in class. One involves having a tube put through the nose to test stomach contents for gastric acid. It's not pleasant, as you can imagine.' Kate looked at Briggs; his face was green. 'But there's always a few people who volunteer because they like being the centre of attention, or even because they like experiencing uncomfortable things being done to them. Not only did Oliver volunteer, but he always wanted to do it to the others. In fact, he seemed to enjoy it.'

'He was a bit of a sadist?'

'Yes, I'd say so. We also did some tests on the effect of alcohol or nitrous oxide on things like reaction times and visual acuity, but also electric shocks and applying painful stimuli to the Achilles tendon. He was always keen to get involved in those, too.' Briggs went to ask but the professor guessed what was coming. 'And yes, both as the person receiving the shocks, and the one giving them.'

Kate and Briggs nodded slowly, taking in the professor's words.

'Professor Carpenter,' Kate asked, digesting the information. Something wasn't sitting right against the background research they'd done on Oliver Swift. 'If you don't mind me asking, those seem particularly strange practicals to be doing on a psychology course.'

Professor Carpenter frowned. 'Psychology? Oliver Swift wasn't taking psychology.'

Kate's mouth dropped, a bad feeling coming over her. 'What course was Oliver taking?'

'Oliver was a med student,' she said. 'He was training to be a doctor.'

80

Max didn't dare breathe. All eyes were on him. He forced
out a laugh.

'Nice to see you again, Scott,' he said, the smile heavy on
his face.

'Where do you know each other from?' Oliver asked.

Max had been thinking about Kate since the moment
he saw her in the forest. He'd been so absorbed, so blinded
he hadn't even looked as he swung through the front door
into the hallway. And there was Scott bloody Barker, standing
right in front of him.

Don't say it, don't say it, he thought over and over again.
If he does, run, run like the bloody wind and get the hell
out of there.

'Work, isn't it, mate?' Max said. 'But it's been a while.'

Scott Barker paused, studying Max's face. 'Yeah, absolutely.'
He smiled. 'How long has it been? Two years?'

Max nodded.

'Where did you work?' Oliver asked.

Max turned to him. 'That big headquarters on Chestnut
Avenue.'

'I used to work there,' Oliver said. 'What department?'

Shit shit shit. 'Finance,' Max said. 'But not for long.'

Oliver nodded slowly. 'I was a temp in finance. Where
did you sit?'

'Third floor, Green Street,' Max replied, remembering the

brief trip to visit Scott. It had been less than a week ago but it felt like years. 'Penned in like battery hens,' he laughed. 'It wasn't for me.'

'I thought you seemed familiar,' Oliver said slowly. 'That would be why.'

Max smiled. 'Small world, eh?' He reached over and shook Scott's hand again. 'Nice to see you, mate.'

He nodded at Lucy, then turned and forced himself to walk casually up the stairs to the bedroom. He shut the door behind him, then slumped heavily on the bed, burying his head in his hands. Shit. That had been close. Had Oliver and Graham believed him? What were the chances of the one person from the investigation walking into the house? Fairly fucking high, Max thought, cursing his lack of foresight. But Scott hated the Borderland Family. What was he doing here?

The door opened and Max's room-mate came in. 'Pete's looking for you,' he said. 'He's in the kitchen.'

Max stood up. He was more careful this time, checking for Scott and Lucy before he went back down the stairs. His legs felt weak, his stomach still turning somersaults. There was something thrilling about being undercover – the rush of deceiving and getting away with it – but this was something else. This was terrifying. But the house was quiet, the few people he passed barely giving him a second glance. He went into the empty dining room, casting his eye over the arrangement of chairs. As usual, they'd been cleared back into a semicircle, one lone chair at the front of the group. And left on it was the notebook. Graham's notebook.

Checking around him, he went over, picking it up. Graham rarely went anywhere without it, always tucked under one arm, or writing, pen in hand. Max had wondered what was on those pages, what plans Graham Swift had been concocting.

But when he opened it up, he was confused. Each page was covered in scribbles, filling every line. But they weren't grand schemes, they were mundane activities. He flicked through – it was all the same.

I have to be ready for the doctor at 10 a.m. tomorrow, Max read. *I am making a cup of a tea and a sandwich. I have had a shower.*

Then next to the statements, there were dates and small ticks. Max frowned. What the hell? Was it some sort of code?

He heard a rattle in the kitchen and quickly put the notebook back down on the chair. A head poked round the doorway.

'There you are,' Pete said. 'We have work to do. Come and help me with this bloody sink.'

Max rushed to join him. Pete was right, he did have work to do.

He needed to find out what was going on in this weird place. And he needed to get it done quickly, before something else went wrong.

81

Lucy showed Scott silently through the house to the living room where they could talk. Graham and Oliver had left them alone, trusting Lucy to be obedient. To convince him this was where she was staying and that their marriage was over.

Scott had taken a seat on one of the sofas, and Lucy joined him. He was mute; Lucy couldn't tell what he was thinking.

'Is this what you want, Lucy?' he asked quietly.

She stayed silent. She didn't know what to say.

Scott turned to her, gently taking both her hands in his. 'Because I'm sorry. I'm sorry for what I did, with Jen. I'm sorry for not taking your concerns seriously. For not listening when you needed me the most.' He stopped. 'If this is what you want, if this is where you'll be happy, then I'll leave you alone. But I need to know, Lucy, is it this or nothing?'

'What do you mean?' Lucy asked.

'I mean, is this the only solution? We have a big house of our own. Isaac could live with us. I know that's important to you. He's waiting to hear back from me today. He's worried about you, Lucy.' She could see Scott was serious. And knowing he'd been speaking to her brother was a massive weight off her mind. 'Could we carry on with preparations at home, and live a life where you could be happy? Together?' he finished.

Lucy stopped. Originally she'd thought it was an option, but it had seemed so hard, doing it alone. But if she had Scott to help her?

She'd been living at the compound for a fortnight now. She'd seen the cracks show. Harsh words exchanged between residents, unequal distribution of work. She'd seen the huddles in corners. She knew things were being planned – illegal things – that made her feel uneasy. It was the same feeling she'd had when she was outside – the anxious buzz was back, but for a different reason.

She looked at Scott. 'I don't know,' was all she could honestly say.

He looked away from her, out of the window. He seemed to be thinking. Then he turned back.

'Listen, Lucy, I don't know whether I should tell you this, but I've resolved never to lie to you again, so I must. Whatever the consequences.'

Lucy felt her stomach drop. 'Is it about Jen?'

'Jen? No.' Scott shook his head emphatically. 'No, that's over, I promise you. It's about that guy we met in the entrance hall.'

'Max?' Lucy said, puzzled.

'Yes. He's a cop.'

Lucy looked at Scott as if he was crazy. 'Don't be ridiculous. He's not.'

'He is. He was the policeman investigating your disappearance. That's how I know him.'

'So what's he doing here?'

'I don't know. He must be working undercover or something. But I don't think I realised it in time. I don't think our bullshit conversation was good enough to keep them fooled.'

Lucy stopped. That would make sense. The constant questions, the way he seemed to be taking every little detail in, the fact that she had caught him in Oliver and Graham's room. And the feeling that he was the only one in here she truly trusted, despite the short time she'd known him.

'We need to warn him, we need to tell the police,' Lucy said, quickly. 'Have you got your phone?'

'No, they took it off me when I arrived.'

Lucy grabbed his hand and opened the door, looking out into the corridor.

'You go and see if you can find Max. I'm going to make a call.'

'Be careful,' Scott said, and headed off one way, while Lucy rushed towards the office.

It was nearly lunchtime and the majority of people were starting to crowd towards the dining room. Lucy crept up the stairs to the office and shut the door behind her. She picked up the receiver and dialled 999.

'Police,' she said when it was answered. 'I need to speak to Detective Sergeant Kate Munro.'

82

'Lucy, it's DS Munro. How can I help?'

The moment Kate and Briggs had got back from the university, they'd started digging. Oliver Swift had initially enrolled at Southampton University to study psychology but had switched to medicine in the middle of his first semester. He'd quit by the end of his fourth year, but it was clear: Oliver Swift had medical training. Had Max realised that? Kate started wading again through the photos Max had taken, pausing when she came to the shots of the drug boxes in what Kate assumed to be the Swifts' bedroom.

Donepezil. Memantine. Risperidone. Kate typed the names carefully into Google, reading the information that came up on the screen. Used to treat dementia. For short-term medication of persistent aggression in patients with moderate to severe Alzheimer's.

'Briggs,' Kate called. 'Graham Swift is receiving treatment for dementia.'

He looked her way and frowned. 'How bad?' he asked.

And then the call came in from Lucy Barker.

'Lucy? Are you there?' Kate asked again. But nobody replied. 'Lucy?'

She could hear a faint hubbub in the background, then some rustling. 'Lucy?' she called again.

Briggs frowned at Kate. 'What's going on?' he mimed.

'DS Munro.' A voice came on the phone. But it wasn't Lucy. It was a man. 'I forgot you and Lucy were acquainted.'

'Who's this? Where's Lucy?' Kate shouted down the line.

The man laughed. 'She's fine, don't worry. Having a bit of a lie-down.'

'Oliver, is that you?' Kate tried hard to control her anger. 'Put Lucy back on the phone.'

'It was quite something, that appeal when Lucy went missing,' Oliver continued. He didn't seem to be in any rush, his voice amused. 'I enjoyed watching your press conference knowing Lucy was downstairs with us.' He laughed and Kate gritted her teeth. 'It's frustrating, isn't it, DS Munro, when you've missed something that's been in plain sight all along?'

Kate went to speak but the line had gone dead.

'Who was that?' Briggs asked.

Kate felt a wave of panic wash over her. 'Get on the radio to Nash, check they have eyes on Max.'

Briggs picked up the radio quickly and started talking. Oliver's words echoed in Kate's head. She turned back to her computer, pulling up the footage from the press conference.

There was DCI Delaney, and Kate's own sweaty face next to her. The camera zoomed in on Scott Barker – calm, measured, coming across like he'd buried Lucy in his base- ment. Then the perspective changed as the journalists started asking questions. The camera scanned the crowd. There was Jen Lewis. Then the journalist who clearly thought Scott had killed Lucy. It panned out again, catching faces sitting in the audience.

Kate caught her breath. She scrolled back as Briggs ap- peared behind her, the radio in his hand. She paused the video. There, on the screen, was Briggs. And next to him, in full police uniform, was Max.

She turned quickly to Briggs. 'Get him out,' she shouted. 'They know he's a cop. Get him out.'

83

It was now or never. Max watched Pete struggle under the sink for a moment, then made his move.

'Weather's cleared,' he said, as casually as he could. 'Shall I have a go at cleaning that truck?'

'Fine, yes. Go and sort it. Keys are on the table.' Pete poked his head out from the cupboard, his hands full of plumbing. 'Just do a good job.'

Max grabbed the keys and rushed from the kitchen, taking the back door out to avoid bumping into anyone, then round to the front of the house. He noticed Scott's Audi parked in the driveway, and hurried past to the garages.

After a few fumbled attempts with the keys, he pushed the door open. It was dark inside, and Max clicked the light. A bare fluorescent tube flickered on, showing the truck in all its glory. Max breathed a sigh of relief. It was still dirty, the tyres caked with mud, a large green tarpaulin draped over the back.

Tools dominated the wall behind it. The organisation was haphazard, some hanging two on a hook, others littering the floor.

But Max's first priority was the truck. He walked round to the back and bent down to look at the tyres. His memory was vague but these seemed more like the ones he'd been expecting – a diagonal criss-cross pattern. He took photo after photo, then stood up to look inside the flatbed.

He removed an edge of the green tarpaulin. He knew this could hold the key to what had happened to Doug Brewer two weeks ago. This could be the truck that had driven him round to the lake, where he'd been dumped alive in the water, to die a terrifying death.

Not to mention the method of transport for Paul Sherwood's bloody body from Portswood, way back in January.

He pulled a large torch from the wall and clicked it on, lighting up the bottom of the flatbed. Slowly, he moved across, trying to touch as little as possible, seeing nothing but mud and stones and dirt. But then, there it was. Two single hairs, caught in a clump of mud. Max quickly took a photo, then stood up, thinking.

Perhaps he should call it in now, he wondered. Get the SOCOs to do their job. There would be more in the back of that truck, that was for sure. The extent of the crime scene behind Dougie's flat meant Paul Sherwood's blood must have been left behind, even if someone had tried to clean it up.

But he wouldn't contact the extraction team just yet. He needed ten minutes more, maximum. That evidence wouldn't disappear in those ten minutes.

He had a murder weapon to find.

Dr Adams had told them that Paul Sherwood had been hit by something with a double flat end with a gap in between – like a crowbar. As much as Max thought it unlikely that it would have been brought back here from the crime scene in Portswood, he walked over to the wall of tools and started working his way along it, scanning every item for the possibility.

Then he saw it. A claw hammer. Blunt head on one side but double prongs on the other. Without picking it up, he looked more closely. It was covered in dust and looked clean, but Max knew blood could be hiding in the crevices. And it had a porous wooden handle – perfect for retaining biological matter.

This was enough now. It was time to go home.

He started to turn, but as he did so he noticed the light from the doorway dim. Someone was behind him. He felt a sharp prick on the back of his arm.

And everything went black.

84

Briggs had radioed the extraction team. Kate knew it was only a matter of minutes before Max would be out of the compound.

At the same time, Kate called for a patrol car. She wanted to get down there and quick, and a Response and Patrol vehicle was the best way to do it.

But even at full speed, blues and twos screeching down the M27, Southampton to Ringwood was a long way. Too long. Desperately, she waited for confirmation that Max was safe, but the radio was silent. She messaged Nash.

No response. Then a crackle over the radio. 'Perimeter breached, suspect in custody.'

Briggs replied: 'Is the asset secure?'

Kate waited, her hand tapping anxiously. Silence. Then a voice: 'Asset is in the wind, repeat, we have no eyes on the asset.'

'*Fuck!*' Kate shouted. A wave of guilt washed over her. She should have made the call to pull him out the moment she put the phone down on Oliver. She shouldn't have waited to look at the press conference footage.

But at least they had Oliver. Or did they?

She snatched the radio from Briggs. 'Please confirm, what suspect do you have in custody?'

'Graham Swift.'

'Where is Oliver Swift?'

Another pause. 'We don't have a location on Oliver Swift.'

Briggs looked at her, his eyes wide. She knew what he was thinking. Max was with Oliver. And if that was the case, they didn't have long to find him.

85

Black.

Dizzy.

Max felt hard metal underneath his back. He could hear the rumble of an engine and his body was jostled to and fro. He opened his eyes, head spinning. His vision was blurry.

The movement came to a halt. Max realised he was on the back of a truck. His body felt heavy. He could make out dappled sunlight – he was looking upwards, through a canopy of trees. But he couldn't think straight; images came at him in a confused, jumbled mess.

There was a faint aroma of mud and wet leaves. Something near him smelt like diesel.

He didn't know how long he'd been out. He couldn't remember how he'd got there, what he was doing, but he knew none of this was good.

It was suddenly quiet. He heard footsteps and moved his arm to rub his eyes. A face swam into view.

'You're awake. That won't do.'

Oliver Swift.

With a jolt he knew where he was, what was going on, and he moved his arm behind him to push himself up, to try to get away. But his movements were slow, his body still drowsy.

A hand roughly pushed him down and he fell backwards,

his head hitting the metal with a bump. He tried again to move but everything was sluggish and weak.

Max saw a bag placed next to him and heard a zip being opened. Ripping – plastic against paper. The clink of glass. Then a sharp prick in his thigh.

'There's something strangely beautiful about these drugs,' Oliver said. His voice was steady and even. 'How you can perceive everything that's going on around you, but not be able to do anything about it.'

Max felt like he couldn't breathe. He tried to move his arm up to his throat but nothing would respond. He felt a mask go around his nose and mouth, and his chest move.

'I'm breathing for you now,' Oliver said. Max saw his face loom in front of his eyes. He was smiling. The fucker was smiling. He continued: 'Rocuronium doesn't affect the muscles of the heart, but it does paralyse the diaphragm, so without me doing this...' Max heard the whistling noise of the bag stop. 'Your brain won't get any oxygen.'

Max felt dizziness overwhelm him. Then the wheezing of the bag started up again. 'If I stopped for long enough, you'd get brain damage and die. I'm all that's keeping you alive right now, Max.'

Max felt like someone was sitting on his chest, holding him down. He couldn't move. The helplessness took over and he screamed in his head. But no sound came out. He could see, his eyes were open, but he couldn't blink, he couldn't look to the left or right. Just upwards, to the sunshine above.

Max felt the panic build and his heart rate start to increase, pounding in his chest. Oliver moved back into his line of sight.

'Easy now,' he said. Oliver leaned forward and Max saw a hand over his face, then felt his eyelids close. All he had now was a vague awareness of light and dark. He could only imagine what Oliver was doing. 'If you get too excited there won't be enough oxygen to go round. And you know what that means?'

Brain damage. Death. Dr Adams's words echoed in his head. *It would be a terrifying way to die.*

He needed to calm down. He thought about Kate. He imagined her face, her smile. He remembered kissing her. He held that image in his head as the repetitive wheeze of the bag continued. In and out. In and out.

Max listened for police sirens, for anything that could indicate someone was on their way. But nothing, except the bag forcing air into his lungs.

While that was happening, he would be okay. While that was happening, he would hold onto the hope that he would see her again. Because he had to. Because what else was there?

'I feel stupid, you know. For letting you get inside the Family.' Oliver carried on. He was talking faster now, the excitement of his position of power getting the better of him. 'But it wasn't until that horrible charade with Scott Barker in the hallway that I realised something was up. So I checked the press conference on Facebook, and there you were.'

You fucking crazy nutter, Max raged inside his head. But nothing, still nothing came out.

'You're here for Dougie, I assume? Stupid sod had to get a sense of conscience.' Oliver laughed, high-pitched and shrill. 'He was going to go to the police. It would have ruined everything. Everything me and Dad have worked towards. It was rash of me to dump him so close to the house, so close to Paul, but I was in a hurry. And I was curious to see what this stuff would be like. Did the same to him as I have to you today.'

Max felt the panic rising again. One by one he tried to move different parts of his body: his toes, his fingers, open his eyes, but still nothing. Only the repetitive in and out of the bag.

'Do you know how long it takes for the brain to die?' Oliver asked. The bag stopped moving. Max felt his concentration dip, his heart rate rising as he realised he wasn't breathing. His brain felt muddled. His lungs were on fire, desperate for air.

'No more than a few minutes, Max,' Oliver said. Then: in and out, in and out. 'But that's a boring way to go, don't you think?' He paused the bag again for a moment, and Max felt the fear take hold, claustrophobia building in his body. He was aware he'd started to cry, tears running down his face.

Oliver laughed, then started up again. 'I almost wish I'd taken a bit longer with Dougie. But he was my first, so I was nervous. I rushed a bit.' Max could feel Oliver's breath on his face now, warm and sour. 'I could do anything with you right now, and you couldn't stop me.'

Max felt something cold and metal scratch slowly down his cheek. His heart jumped as he realised what Oliver must have in his hand.

'I've always been surprised how easily a scalpel can slice into the body,' Oliver whispered in his ear. 'You'd think it would resist, but once you puncture the skin, all you need is the pressure from a single finger.' Max heard Oliver laugh again. 'You could be my own personal anatomy class. Chop you up into little bits, right here in the forest.'

Max felt his hope fade. He was powerless, in the middle of nowhere. No one would know where he was before this psycho finished him off. He would never see Kate again. He summoned every bit of will in his body, but still nothing. He was trapped.

It felt like every part of him had been removed. Everything but his soul.

He realised Oliver had changed position, but the bag continued going in and out. He felt his shirt being lifted up, cool air on his skin. Then the chilling, slow scratch of the scalpel running across his stomach, still not breaking the surface.

'Shall we start here?' Oliver said, softly. 'Or maybe here.'

The blade moved round to his side and suddenly Max felt a sharp pain as the scalpel entered his skin. The shock tore through him, increasing as Oliver moved the knife, fraction by fraction, a hot, searing cut.

Max felt his heart pound as the torture increased and he screamed out, to no avail. His consciousness began to fail; he couldn't hold on any more. The agony was all-encompassing now, taking over his entire body.

As he slipped away, he heard the sirens.

He felt the bag stop, and the wind on his face, drying his tears.

The mask had gone.

There was nothing keeping him alive.

86

The police car was going full speed as it bumped down the drive into the compound. It screeched to a halt in the courtyard, and Kate dived out, Briggs right behind her.

Nash was standing in front of a black SUV, shouting down the radio. Officers in black swarmed the house; people were being led out in handcuffs, loaded into the waiting police van.

'Check the cameras, they must have got out of here somehow,' Nash bellowed, then turned to Kate. 'He's not here. We've searched the whole estate.'

'And Oliver Swift?' Kate asked.

Nash shook his head and turned his attention back to his radio. He listened for a moment, then climbed into the SUV, Kate and Briggs jumping in with him without waiting for confirmation. Nash started the car and put his foot down, sending a plume of gravel into the air.

'Just before your call, a truck went out, then around to the back of the house,' Nash shouted over the din of the engine as he reversed at full speed out of the gate. 'Towards the lake.' He changed gear, then gunned the SUV down the tiny dirt track.

None of them said a word as they were jostled roughly across the potholes. They all knew what was at stake. And they knew now what Oliver Swift was capable of.

Kate hated herself for getting it wrong. All along they'd

assumed it had been Graham, that Oliver was no more than a victim himself, held at the whim of his father. But now Kate was sure.

And Max was missing. What if they were already too late? What if...? She choked back her emotions. They had to be in time. They had to be.

The car began to slow.

'Why are you stopping?' she shouted, but Nash pointed to the path.

'Which way?'

The dirt track had tapered off to a T-junction. Pick the wrong route and the consequences could be disastrous.

'Fuck!' she shouted, and opened the car door, starting to run down the left-hand path, Briggs close behind her. Nash took the hint and turned down the right fork, the engine revving as it disappeared into the trees.

Kate sprinted down the track, her arms pumping, negotiating the puddles at full tilt. The trees cleared, and in the distance, Kate could see a black truck. Behind her she could hear Briggs calling Max's name, but she couldn't see him. She still couldn't fucking see him.

But then she reached the truck, and there he was.

Her breath caught in her throat. He was motionless, lying on his back, his eyes closed. His shirt was drenched with blood, a lake of red expanding next to him. Kate jumped onto the truck to his side, her knees painfully hitting the metal of the flatbed.

Albie's words ripped into her consciousness. *You can't breathe without a ventilator.*

He couldn't breathe! She needed to move, and fast. Kate tried to remember her training.

Tip the neck back, pinch the nose, open the mouth.

Kate put her lips against his and blew. She turned her face away and watched his chest fall, then did it again. She was aware of Briggs by her side, his fingers searching for a pulse on Max's neck. She felt blood on her hands, sticky and warm. But she didn't stop. Breath after breath, she watched his chest rise and fall, Briggs counting a rhythm next to her.

Don't die, Max, she repeated in her head with each breath. *Please, be okay. Please.*

She heard footsteps in the distance, Briggs shouting instructions, the name of the drug, then Nash pulling her away as medics rushed towards them from the green and yellow fast response car, crowding his body, equipment and supplies in their hands.

'Let them work,' Nash said quietly, as he lifted her away from the truck.

Kate stood watching, stunned, her hand over her mouth.

'Heart rate 134, BP 180 over 105,' Kate heard them shout. 'Airway secured, endotracheal tube in place.'

She saw a bag being attached to a tube coming out of his mouth, people attending to the source of the blood at his side, then a loud electronic voice as an ambulance reversed down the tiny track.

Nash walked away from her, relaying messages down the radio. Kate knew she should be helping the manhunt to find Oliver, but she couldn't move. She couldn't leave Max, not again.

More paramedics arrived with a stretcher. She saw them roll him one way then the other onto it, then carry him swiftly into the ambulance. The doors slammed and it pulled away, quickly disappearing into the trees. She heard the siren start up then fade into the distance.

Kate felt dazed. The panic had left her shaking. They'd found Max, but had they been too late?

She felt Briggs by her side, and looked up at him. He was staring down the empty track, his jaw tight.

'He'll be okay,' he said, his voice breaking. 'He's in good hands. Our boy will be okay.'

Kate nodded slowly, feeling a lump in her throat. She pushed back the tears. Now is not the time to cry, she told herself.

A helicopter swooped overhead, disturbing the silence. A voice crackled over the radio.

'We have eyes on the suspect. Repeat, eyes on the suspect.'

Kate turned towards the location given. The determination and fear that had driven Kate to that point was still there, but she felt something else now.

Pure bloody fucking anger.

87

Lucy woke on the floor of the office. She sat up slowly, her head dizzy, her hand exploring the back of her skull. She winced as her fingers came into contact with the bump.

Slowly she remembered what had happened. What Scott had told her about Max. She remembered picking up the phone, but after that, nothing. Someone must have hit her and knocked her down.

She stood up, holding onto the desk for support, and picked up the phone. She held it to her ear: there was no dialling tone, no way she could make a call. But as she replaced the receiver, she saw the edge of a light blue envelope sticking out from under some paperwork. With two fingers, she pulled it out.

She saw her handwriting on the front. It was her letter. The one she'd asked Oliver to go back and leave for Scott. It had been Oliver who caused the police search, and Scott's frantic worry. Why would Oliver have done such a thing?

But she shook her head. She had other things to worry about now.

Max.

She opened the door of the office and made her way down the stairs. She heard sirens in the distance, saw people rushing around, and looked out the front window of the house.

The courtyard was a mass of yellow and blue cars,

policemen in black starting to advance towards the front door.

Lucy made a decision. She still needed to warn Max. If he was in the house, now the police were here he would be safe. But what if he was out in the woods? Lucy knew better than anyone about the network of tracks leading to the lake. There wasn't time to explain to the cops. If Max was out there, she would find him.

Quickly, Lucy ran through the dining room and out the kitchen door. Ignoring the ache in her head, she sprinted across the lawn to the back gate. It was open, the padlock hanging ajar.

She was responsible for this. Max had been the police officer looking for her when she'd gone missing, and for some reason, he'd ended up in the commune. She still didn't know what was going on, but she knew nothing about this place was good.

She rounded the corner of the path and saw a truck in front of her, then watched Oliver jump down from the back of it and run towards the lake. She followed him at a distance, curiosity overtaking any hesitation she may have had.

The track came to an end, and Lucy saw the lake. On the sunniest days, the water would shine a bright blue. Warm and welcoming. But today it was grey, the surface choppy in the wind.

She looked across it and saw Oliver pacing the long wooden walkway leading out to the water. He had his hands on his head and he seemed to be talking to himself. Lucy moved closer, starting down the boardwalk.

Oliver heard her footsteps and turned. Lucy could see he was crying.

'Oliver?' she called tentatively. 'Are you okay?'

He stared at her, pulling at his hair again. 'Nothing's okay! How could it possibly be okay?' He resumed pacing across the deck. 'Why can't you people leave me alone?'

Lucy walked towards him slowly. 'Let me help you,' she pleaded. The poor kid. Who knew what his father had put him through? 'I know your dad has done some terrible things, but it's over now. He's not in charge any more.'

Oliver laughed loudly, mocking her. 'In charge? That old man? He's not in charge of his own shoes and socks, let alone anything that happens at that house.' He turned on his heel, walking to the end of the jetty. 'For a year all I've done is look after that old bugger. Make sure he gets dressed, make sure he takes his pills. Drag him in at night when he goes for a wander. All that lost sleep, all that worry that someone would find out, and for what?' He'd started crying again. 'To watch him die slowly? A walking corpse, that's all he is.'

Lucy was stunned. 'Graham's ill?' she said quietly.

'And it was an accident, you know.' Oliver continued talking, ignoring Lucy's question. 'It wasn't Dad's fault. Some days he's completely normal, you'd never guess, but on others he thinks he's at university again. Goes completely bonkers, and if I can't get the drugs in him in time, it's a nightmare.' The talking seemed to be helping; Oliver was calming down. His pacing had stopped and he looked out across the water. 'Of course, he'd had a few drinks with Paul, and the stupid old bastard went back to university in his mind, back to when Paul stole Mum from him. Snatched a hammer out of the back of my truck and hit him with it before Doug and I could pull him off. But Dad couldn't go to prison. So we drove Paul's body here and buried him in the woods. Sent Pete off to France with his passport. Job done.'

Lucy gasped. What was Oliver telling her? That Graham

had murdered someone? Suddenly things started to add up. The body in the lake. But Oliver was talking about a guy called Paul, when the police had said the body in the lake was Douglas. What was going on? How could so many people be dead?

'Oliver,' she asked slowly, trying to contain her horror. 'Who did Graham kill?'

'Paul,' Oliver said. 'But Dougie couldn't go to the police. It would have risked everything. The haven, the Family. Everything we'd tried so hard to build over the years. All those people, looking up to me.'

Lucy backed away from Oliver.

It had been his fault. The dead body in the lake – Dougie Brewer. That had been Oliver.

She glanced around them. They were still isolated; nobody knew where she was. She was completely alone with a murderer. She felt the danger, a shivering dread taking over her body.

She needed to keep him talking. She knew the police were nearby.

'But what about the dissolution?' she asked, desperately trying to keep her voice calm.

Oliver turned towards Lucy. 'That was Dad's thing, it had always been his soapbox. But why not? It's as plausible as any other theory about the future right now.'

'So why, Oliver? Why protect the Family, when you didn't believe?'

He looked at her, his lip curled. 'You'd never understand. Not some prom queen like you,' he mocked, scornful and patronising. 'I felt at home with these people. All my life, nobody's appreciated me. I was bottom of the class at uni. Bullied at school.' As he said it, his hand gently touched the scar on his chin, and Lucy wondered what Oliver had been through growing up. He carried on: 'But here, with the Family, I was respected. I was in charge, for the first time in my life. I was in command.'

Lucy shook her head; she couldn't believe what she was hearing. She'd trusted them. When she'd found the body in lake, it had been the start – she'd known then the dissolution was coming, a feeling reinforced when she found the photos on Scott's phone. But that hadn't been fate, or the beginning of the end of the world. The Borderland Family weren't her saviours. She'd wrecked her whole life because of it, and that sign had been no more than the actions of one fucked-up kid.

But Lucy realised she didn't feel helpless any more. She was furious.

Oliver looked away from her, to the track. They could hear voices by the edge of the lake, loud sirens and shouting. A helicopter swung into view above the trees.

Oliver tensed, then started running towards her down the pier, back to the forest. Lucy was relieved: she was safe now – the police were close. But she knew he was trying to get away. He went to push past her, but she grabbed him, hanging onto his shirt with all her strength. He tried to pull away, and they struggled together, Lucy getting a better grip, wrapping her arms around his body.

Even though he was bigger and stronger than her, she clung on. But the jetty was narrow and the decking slippery. Oliver lost his balance and fell.

With a cry, they both tumbled into the water.

88

Kate and Briggs sprinted down the track towards the lake. But when they got there, the water was calm. Kate glanced at Briggs, questioning. He shook his head, resting his hands on his knees to catch his breath.

Kate put a call out on the radio: negative. Oliver Swift still hadn't been found.

Then they heard the shouting. Briggs looked at Kate.

'Is that a woman?'

They stopped and listened, then Kate started running again, towards the jetty. Her feet hit the wooden decking and she heard it again. A female voice calling out, frantic splashing next to her.

At first Kate didn't recognise the woman in the water. Her blonde hair was wet and plastered to her head, her skin grey and cold.

'Lucy?' Kate quickly knelt down on the pier and held out her hand. Lucy grabbed it, panting, pulling herself up and flopping face first onto the wood. She rolled onto her back, looking up at the sky.

'I couldn't save him,' she said, gasping for oxygen. 'I couldn't get to him in time.'

'Who?' Kate asked, looking down into the water. 'Oliver?'

Lucy nodded, still breathless.

Kate called into her radio. 'Search and rescue teams

required at the northern edge of Ellingham lake. One person in the water.'

Lucy started shivering, her wet clothes dripping. Kate crouched next to her while Briggs continued to stare into the depths, looking for any sign of Oliver.

'I followed him here, I don't know what happened. He grabbed me and we fell in.' Lucy shook her head, her teeth chattering. Behind them the team had arrived, a paramedic rushing over and putting a blanket round Lucy. Kate helped her to her feet.

'I assumed he could swim but he was flailing around, then he went under. By the time I got to him, he'd disappeared.' The paramedic started to lead Lucy away, Briggs with them, but Lucy looked back at Kate. 'I'm not a good swimmer,' she said. 'I'm sorry.'

Kate stayed on the edge of the pier, looking down into the black water. She heard footsteps behind her.

'Rescue teams are five minutes out,' Nash said.

'It'll be too late by then,' Kate replied. She looked at Nash and asked the question she barely dared to say out loud. 'How much did we screw up, guv?'

He pressed his lips together for a moment. 'We had no indication our perp was Oliver Swift. All signs pointed to the father.' He looked into the inky depths. 'We're sure he's down there?'

'That's what Lucy Barker said,' Kate replied.

'We'll maintain the perimeter and keep the search going just in case.' He turned, then looked at Kate. 'What happened with Cooper wasn't your fault.' He touched her arm and the simple gesture made a lump form in Kate's throat. 'It was my operation, my responsibility.'

Kate's head dropped as Nash walked away. She thought

about Max on his way to the hospital, with who knew what horrific damage to his brain. She knew he might not survive. She knew that even if he did, there was a chance he wouldn't be the same person any more.

She thought about how terrified he must have been, unable to move, unable to breathe. Now she was alone, she let herself start to cry. She sobbed quietly, all the emotions from the day coming to the surface. It had been her fault. She should have put an end to Max's idea of going under-cover before it even took hold.

She sat down on the wooden pier and looked out across the lake. It was calm here now. Nothing but the trees moving softly, the birds singing.

Oliver Swift was down there somewhere. He must have struggled in the same way, desperate for oxygen, feeling the air ebb from his lungs. Now floating in the water as Dougie Brewer had all those weeks ago.

Life had a funny way of catching up with you, she thought, as she wiped away her tears. Karma really was a bitch.

Sunday

89

Kate glared at the man opposite her. He looked old and tired. He stared at the table, barely confident enough to meet her eyes. This wasn't the Graham Swift she had first met: this was a shell of a man, destroyed by the actions of his son.

DI Nash was next to her; a lawyer next to Swift. Nash had already warned Kate he didn't know how far this interview was going to go. Doctors had assessed Graham as lucid, but without any notes about the progression of Graham's dementia, they didn't know how long it would last.

For now, he had been cautioned and the video was rolling.

'Please tell us about the events of Saturday the thirteenth of January when we believe you murdered Paul Sherwood,' Kate began.

'I don't remember that day,' Graham mumbled.

'Tell us what you've been told happened.'

He looked at Kate. His eyes were red and rheumy. 'Oliver said I killed him.'

'Go on.'

He looked back at the table. 'He said I was confused, and thought it was forty years ago. I thought Paul had stolen my girlfriend and I was angry.'

'So you attacked him with a hammer.'

Graham didn't move.

379

'Did you?'

'I don't remember.'

Kate clenched her jaw. 'So here's what I know.' She pulled the file over to her and looked at the pages. 'We found a bloodied hat in Doug Brewer's flat which contained a large amount of blood and brain matter from Paul Sherwood, and traces of your DNA.' She looked up at Graham. He was still staring at the table.

She continued. 'We have a claw hammer, found in your garage, with your DNA on the handle, and Paul Sherwood's blood on the top. We have a large patch of blood outside Doug Brewer's residence. And blood on the wheels of a Toyota Hilux, registered to your name, not to mention all sorts of trace evidence in the back. And we have one of your residents, Pete Gibson, happy to testify that on Monday the twenty-second of January he was given Paul Sherwood's passport to go on the ferry to France, then come back using his own ID. And he was given that passport by you. I'd say that was pretty compelling evidence that you murdered Paul Sherwood, wouldn't you?'

Graham started to cry, large tears dropping onto the table. His hands were constantly moving, his fingers shaking.

'Wouldn't you, Mr Swift?' Kate pushed.

She felt a hand on her arm and looked over at Nash. He was shaking his head. The lawyer was glaring at her.

'Move on, DS Munro,' the lawyer said. 'My client has no more to add on this matter.'

She sighed. 'Fine.' Kate looked at Graham again. He was hunched over the table, thin shoulders obvious through his shirt.

'What can you tell us about the murder of Douglas Brewer?'

Graham looked up sharply. 'I don't know what you're talking about.'

Kate leaned down and picked up the laptop next to her. She pressed play on the audio file, turning it around so Graham could hear. The lawyer leaned forward, interested.

'This recording was taken from your bedroom on Thursday evening, using a covert listening device in a hardback book, planted by our undercover policeman,' Kate said. She tried hard not to think about Max, concentrating instead on the voices on the tape.

'...and I'm sure nobody saw me,' the voice said. It was Oliver.

Another man answered: 'Are you certain? You're saying you drugged him, drove him round to the east side of the lake, and nobody noticed? And the truck must be full of all sorts of...' The voice paused. 'We need to get it cleaned up.'

The second voice was nervous and frantic. The recording hissed and the voices were muffled, but it was still possible to make out who was talking. It was Graham Swift, no doubt about it.

The first voice spoke again. 'Fine, you get Pete to do it tomorrow.'

'Oliver...'

'Enough, Dad.' The voice was stern. 'It's done. You started this. Ask Pete to wash it in the morning. Clean up your mess, and mine.'

Kate paused the recording and looked at Graham. 'You knew what your son had done, and you covered it up. I'm confident to say that with this, you're facing additional charges of perverting the course of justice, assisting an offender and obstruction of a police investigation.' The lawyer sat up straight in his seat. 'And,' Kate continued, her anger growing, 'I'd be tempted to add conspiracy to commit murder to the collection.'

The lawyer scrabbled to attention. 'You have no evidence that my client was behind his son's actions,' he babbled.

'Your client,' Kate shouted, losing her temper and jumping up from her chair, 'was the figurehead of the organisation. It was on his property that a number of unlicensed guns were seized. Not to mention pharmaceuticals found, stolen in a series of violent thefts carried out across the city. As far as those people in there were concerned, he was in charge. Your client was responsible for everything that went on behind those walls, and I'll be damned if you try to claim otherwise.'

Kate felt Nash pulling her back into her seat.

'Interview concluded at fifteen twenty-five,' Nash said, and he escorted Kate out of the room.

DCI Delaney was waiting for them in the corridor.

'He's going to get away with it,' Kate hissed at Nash when the door was closed. She turned to Delaney. 'They're going to pull the diminished responsibility card, guv, and he'll get away with it.'

'Kate,' Nash said, pointing her towards the small window in the interview room door. 'Look at him.'

Swift was sobbing, his head on his arms on the table. The lawyer looked uncomfortable next to him, making a phone call.

'That's not a man getting away with anything. Whatever the outcome, he's never going home again. That compound's been taken apart, all the residents have either been arrested or gone home. And Oliver Swift is dead. His son was fished out of Ellingham lake this morning, Kate. He's dead.'

Kate stopped, chewing on her lip. Nash was right. The old man in that interview room was ill. He'd been broken by everything he and his son had done, and life as he knew it was over.

Even if Oliver had survived, lab results had come back confirming a match between Oliver and the DNA and fingerprints found in the driver's seat of Dougie's car. It wasn't definitive proof, but Kate knew they would have kept going, gathering enough evidence to convict in the end. Graham would have been alone, either way.

Delaney pulled her round to face her. 'Kate, Jamie said you hadn't been to the hospital.'

Kate shook her head, tears threatening behind her eyes.

'Go and see Max,' she said softly. When Kate didn't reply, she added, 'It can't possibly make you feel any worse, can it?'

'No, it can't,' Kate whispered.

Kate had never driven slower through the streets of Southampton. She wished for an accident, a broken-down bus, anything to put more delay between her and Max in hospital. She couldn't bear to face him, to see the consequences of her decisions.

She parked in the multistorey car park and walked at a snail's pace towards the main entrance of the hospital. Down wide echoing corridors, and up the slow clunky lift to the ICU. She saw pale faces, beeping equipment, patients hooked up to monitors. She knew things could have been much worse.

Kate loitered in the doorway, nervous about seeing him. Then he looked up, and she smiled.

She walked towards him. Despite the way she was feeling – the guilt, the worry – she found herself with a big grin on her face and sat down on the chair next to the bed.

'No chocolates?' he asked. His voice was hoarse, no doubt

from the breathing tube that had now been removed. 'Not even a bunch of grapes?'

She shook her head. 'You look like shit.'

Max ran his hand through his hair, and it stuck up on end. 'Yeah, well. Doctor says I'll be out soon.'

He grinned and they looked at each other for a moment.

'And you'll be okay?' she asked.

'I still feel a bit groggy and sick. But yeah,' he replied. 'No brain cells in here to kill. Although I'm going to need some sympathy for the knife wound.'

'The doctor said the cut was superficial!'

'You try having a scalpel shoved in your side by a deranged killer and see how good you feel after it,' he replied. 'On the plus side, the drugs are great here. I can't feel a thing.'

'Max, I'm so sorry,' Kate blurted out.

He looked at her. 'What for?' he asked softly.

'For not putting the call out quickly enough. For not realising you were visible in the press conference footage. For not thinking Scott Barker could visit.' Kate realised to her horror that she was crying. Big, fat, snotty tears running down her face. She looked down and wiped her nose with the back of her sleeve.

She felt his hand on hers and he squeezed it tightly.

'Kate, you saved my life,' Max said. She still couldn't look at him. 'It wasn't your fault. I knew Scott had noticed me. I could have decided to leave at any time, but I didn't. At the end of the day, it was up to Nash to make the call.'

Kate laughed with a sudden release. 'Let's blame Nash,' she said, and Max handed her a tissue. She blew her nose loudly.

'Although I don't want to work for you any more,' he said tentatively.

Kate looked up quickly. 'I said I'm sorry, I said...'

'No, Kate.' Max stopped her. 'I don't want to work for you, because if I do, then we can't do this...'

And he leaned towards her and kissed her, very softly. The world stopped. Everything she had worried about disappeared with the feel of his lips on hers. Kate placed her hands on either side of his face and kissed him back, then touched his hair, winding her fingers in the tufts at the back.

She stopped, her face still close to his.

'Consider yourself reassigned,' she whispered.

And she kissed him again.

Epilogue

Lucy looked around the hallway. Her coats were on their hooks, her shoes next to the front door. It was clean and tidy. On the surface it seemed nothing had changed in the weeks since she had left. But she had. She was a different person now.

She could feel Scott watching her, so she put her bag down and opened the back door.

'Do you want tea?' Scott called.

'Please,' she replied, and stepped into the garden.

Lucy had always loved being outside. Even before the vegetables were planted and the air-raid shelter had been converted, she'd spent time out here, looking at the trees, breathing in the air, listening to the birds.

She walked further down, through the vegetable garden, badly neglected in her absence, out among the wild flowers behind. The grass had grown tall, and she was surrounded by thistles and stinging nettles, mixed in with the blooms. But she didn't care.

She lowered herself to the ground, feeling the wet seeping into her jeans as she lay on the grass. She looked up at the white clouds.

She remembered the day before, doing the same. Lying on the wooden pier, her clothes freezing, looking up at the sky.

*

As they hit the lake, the cold water had been shocking, causing her to gasp. Oliver had been underneath her as they fell and she could feel him kicking and thrashing, his foot coming painfully into contact with her shin.

They both surfaced, winded in the cold. Next to her she could see Oliver frantic in the water, gulping in air. Lucy knew about cold water shock. She knew how the surprise of the bitter water caused your heart rate to spike and forced you to take an involuntary breath. She knew how it could drown even the most skilful of swimmers, unaccustomed to such an experience.

But Lucy was used to the lake. She knew about acclimatisation and forcing yourself to stay calm. She knew the feeling of breathlessness would pass.

It was clear Oliver didn't. He was floundering next to her, barely breaking the surface. Panicking, inhaling water directly into his lungs.

He reached for her, again and again. On the first pass he missed her, but on the second he grabbed her upper arm, pulling her under. She pushed him away, taking a deep breath, but then he was on her again and they were both going down.

She opened her eyes, but she couldn't see anything in the green. Water in her ears, everything on mute. She could feel him next to her, constantly flailing, hanging onto her arm. She knew that people had drowned in situations like this, the panicking victim taking their saviour with them.

But Lucy wouldn't let that happen. She felt his hand on her arm and she prised him away, finding the top of his shoulder, then pushing him down. Her lungs were straining but she knew his body was already under stress. She knew he would use up his oxygen quicker.

Then, at last, he stopped moving. His arms let go and she pushed up to the surface, gasping for breath.

She blinked and looked towards the pier, where someone was standing. She shouted and swam towards the woman, allowing her to pull her out of the water, where she lay face up on the wood, catching her breath.

'I couldn't save him,' Lucy had lied. 'I couldn't get to him in time.'

A figure stood above her, silhouetted against the light. Scott held out his hand and pulled her to a sitting position. He passed her a mug of tea.

'Everything okay?' he asked.

'Yes, fine,' she said.

He knelt down in the grass next to her. 'I'm glad you're home,' he said with a smile.

Lucy looked around her.

'So am I,' she replied.

Acknowledgements

To Ed Wilson. You, sir, make dreams come true. To you, Hélène Butler, and everybody else at J&A, thank you.

Thank you to the amazing team at Orion Fiction: particularly to Harriet Bourton, Lucy Frederick, Ben Willis, Alainna Hadjigeorgiou, Lucy Cameron and Jenny Page. It is such a joy to work with you all.

To Dr Matt Evans. I always knew this book was going to be about Lucy's disappearance and the involvement of a group of apocalypse preppers, but I had no idea how it was going to end. It wasn't until a chance comment from Matt that the whole conclusion became very clear. It seems that anaesthetics is a field just right for a bonkers psychopath, and I am forever indebted to Matt for bringing Oliver Swift to life. Thank you, Matt.

To PC Dan Roberts, you make writing these books possible. School run conversations have never been so inappropriate, and thus even more enjoyable as a result. Thank you.

To the brilliant experts I bother relentlessly with my bizarre queries – namely Susan Scarr, Sarah Thorne, Laura Stevenson, Stephanie Fox, and Charlie Roberts – thank you. All mistakes made and liberties taken with the truth are down to me, and me alone.

Thank you to Janet de Lange, Richard de Lange, Chris

Scarr and Teresa Andrews for taking the time to read and feedback on the early draft.

As per my usual habit, I have stolen a few names. So, to Pete Swift, Karen and Glyn Barker, Gemma Coleman (née Sherwood), Tor Riley (née Lewis), Mike and Rachael Cooper, Albie Gaunt, and Scott Munro, sorry, and thank you. As I hope you know, the characters are like you in name only. Please consider it a compliment.

To Chris and Ben. As always, thank you, from the bottom of my heart.

Finally, thank you to Flo, Matt, and the lifeguards for keeping everyone safe at Ellingham lake. It is a gorgeous tranquil place to swim, that I cannot recommend enough. (And nobody has ever found a dead body. At least, not as far as I know ...)

Credits

Louisa de Lange and Orion Fiction would like to thank everyone at Orion who worked on the publication of *Nowhere To Be Found* in the UK.

Editorial
Lucy Frederick
Harriet Bourton
Ben Willis

Copy editor
Jenny Page

Proof reader
Kate Shearman

Audio
Paul Stark
Amber Bates

Contracts
Anne Goddard
Paul Bulos
Jake Alderson

Design
Debbie Holmes

Joanna Ridley
Nick May

Editorial Management
Charlie Panayiotou
Jane Hughes
Alice Davis

Finance
Jasdip Nandra
Afeera Ahmed
Elizabeth Beaumont
Sue Baker

Production
Ruth Sharvell

Marketing
Lucy Cameron

Publicity
Alainna Hadjigeorgiou

Sales
Laura Fletcher
Esther Waters
Victoria Laws
Rachael Hum
Ellie Kyrke-Smith
Frances Doyle
Georgina Cutler

Operations
Jo Jacobs
Sharon Willis
Lisa Pryde
Lucy Brem

Don't miss DS Kate Munro's gripping first case in...

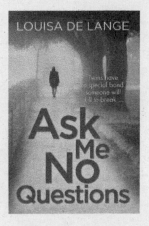

TWINS HAVE A SPECIAL BOND SOMEONE WILL KILL TO BREAK...

As children, Gabi and Thea were like most identical twin sisters: inseparable.

Now adults, Gabi is in a coma following a vicious attack and Thea claims that, until last week, the twins hadn't spoken in fifteen years. But what caused such a significant separation? And what brought them back together so suddenly?

Digging into the case, DS Kate Munro is convinced the crime was personal. Now she must separate the truth from the lies and find the dangerous assailant – before any more blood is spilled...

'Will keep you guessing till the last page'
CARA HUNTER

Or Louisa de Lange's psychological thriller debut...

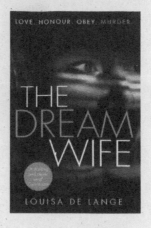

Annie is the dream wife.

Mother to two-year-old Johnny and wife to David, she
is everything her husband expects her to be — supportive,
respectful and mild — but what he expects of her isn't who
she truly is.

Annie is a prisoner in her home.

Her finances, her routine, her social life are all controlled by
him. It's the love for her boy that she lives for, and at night
she dreams of a world where she is free.

But Annie is going to fight back.

And you won't believe how she is going to do it...

'So clever and twisted and disturbing'
ELLE CROFT